DEADLY TRADITIONS
A COZY MYSTERY CHRISTMAS ANTHOLOGY

JUSTINE MAXWELL   MOLLIE COX BRYAN

ERIN SCOGGINS   ESTELLE RICHARDS   ELLIE BALLARD

SAM CHEEVER   GAYLE LEESON   SHEENA MACLEOD

DIANNE ASCROFT   MELICITY POPE   WENDY H. JONES

SAGE SO

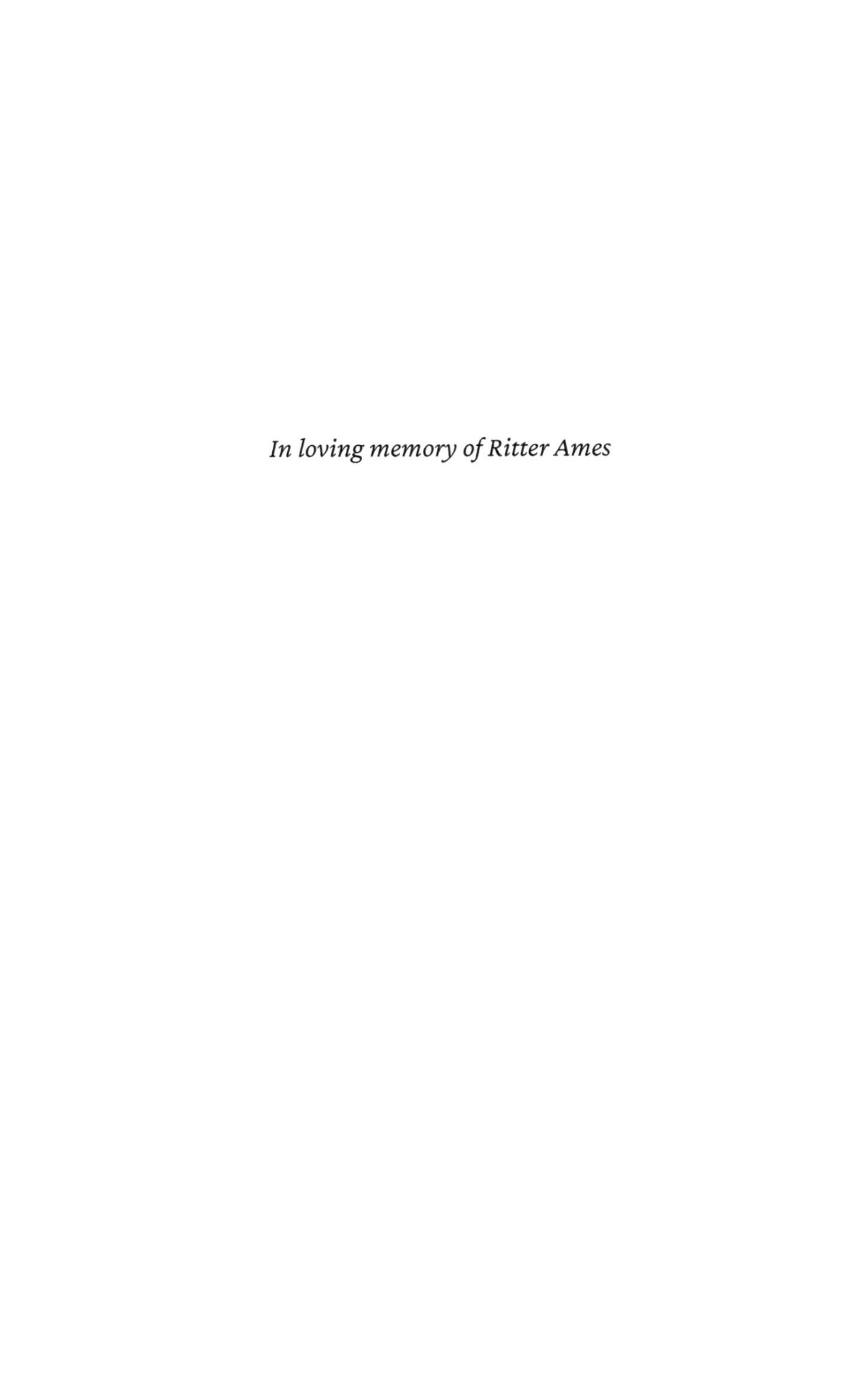

In loving memory of Ritter Ames

LARCENY AND GINGERBREAD LATTES

JUSTINE MAXWELL

When her town's annual gingerbread house competition erupts into chaos, coffee truck barista and amateur sleuth Hazel Hewitt can't help but stick her nose in. Who is responsible for this Christmas calamity? And is there a bigger mystery afoot?

CHAPTER 1

"ONE *LARGE* HOT cocoa and one small gingerbread latte for me, please. Decaf, of course," Eleanor ordered, grinning up at me from the sidewalk outside the Pine Lakes Community Center. Puffs of white floated from her wrinkled lips as the chilly mountain air meshed with her breath as she spoke.

I started the latte and then began pouring cocoa from one of two massive vats on the counter of my coffee truck, peering down at her wryly. "And who is the large for?"

"Mr. Branson is with me tonight," she replied. "He deserves a large. He's so skinny, that man."

I chuckled and traded her the drinks for cash, thanking her when she told me to keep the change. As the next customer stepped up, I caught Eleanor handing her beau-of-the-week his drink. His eyes widened like he wasn't sure how he'd ever drink so much hot cocoa. Maybe he was so skinny because he wasn't used to eating or drinking anything in a large container of any kind. Though, what did Eleanor expect? Pine Lakes Retirement Home wasn't exactly known for serving massive portions to its residents, as Eleanor should know since it's where they both resided.

I made quick work of the next order and tendered the sale, then thanked the woman profusely for the rather large tip she deposited in my Frosty the Snowman tip jar on my coffee bus's ledge. Decorating my converted VW Bus for Christmas was what made this my favorite time of year. I'd hung colorful Christmas lights all around the roof and large serving window. There were wreaths, gingerbread houses, bows, and even fake snow on the windows and windshield. Something that Nico, my brother's grouchy partner on the Pine Lakes police force, had given me a stern talking to about since he feared it would interfere with my ability to drive. Eye roll.

That man, I swear.

Nico and I had gotten along like oil and water when he'd first rolled into town and thought me a murderer when my high school ex-boyfriend had been poisoned after visiting my mobile coffee bar. It wasn't me in the end—obviously, since I'm standing here serving cocoa outside the community center and not rotting away in prison—and I'd even helped him find out who'd *actually* committed the murder.

I'd almost thought we'd moved from enemies to friends during that whole ordeal, but in the months since, he'd dialed back his smiles quite a bit. Sure, he still gave them, but not nearly as willingly as I'd thought I was going to receive them. Especially considering how worried he'd been about me when catching the killer got a little hairy. But that's a story for another day.

"Are you excited to see what people come up with this

year for their houses?" my mom asked as she entered the bus through the side door with another sleeve of paper cups and plastic lids.

We'd had quite the turnout tonight. Everyone was here for the Pine Lakes Annual Gingerbread House Competition, and since this was the first year Bean Around Town was operational during the holiday season, we'd had no idea what to expect as far as sales. Next year, we'll have a lot more cups at the ready and order a few extra containers for cocoa. But with my mom running back and forth between here and our brick-and-mortar store, the Busy Bean, for supplies, we were doing all right.

"I'm very excited to see something new," I said sardonically as I handed off another round of cocoa and lattes. "But I have a feeling we're in for the same old same old as far as the winning house."

My mom chuckled as she set out the fresh cups. "We'll see. You never know. Maybe someone else will win this year."

I snorted and continued helping customers. The same batty old woman, Betty Nichols, had won first place in the gingerbread house competition for the last nine years, and she had her sights set on a decade straight of grand prizes. I wasn't even sure why anyone else would enter considering her streak and the fact that no one had even come close. But here we were.

Just as I was about to ask the next customer if they wanted whipped cream on their cocoa, a flash of a pale white hand reaching into my Frosty the Snowman tip jar caught my eye. I scowled at Ronald Draper, a teen at Pine Lakes High known for having fingers so sticky you'd think he'd been dipping his grubby mitts in my backstock of caramel sauce.

"Ronald," I hissed, eyes wide. "Dropping in a tip before you've ordered?"

He snatched his hand back with a chuckle and tucked it into the pocket of his coat. "Yeah, I'm big on tipping ahead of service."

"I'm sure you are. Get out of here before I call Ryan," I ordered, jerking my chin. He knew my brother was a detective—and not just because Pine Lakes was a small town and everyone knew everyone, but because he had *experience* with him.

Ronald's face contorted into a mixture of chagrin and annoyance before he stalked away to join Clarence Draper— one of his slimy uncles—in the shadows near the door.

With a shake of my head, I looked down at Mr. Sampson, another resident of the jam-packed retirement home. "Would you like some whipped cream, sir?"

"Yes," he replied gruffly, watching Ronald's retreating form. "I always knew that kid was trouble. His dad was trouble before him, and his granddaddy was the most trouble of all. Don't even get me started on those uncles of his. That side of his family is full of bad apples that don't fall far from their rotten tree."

I handed over his drink and accepted his card, running it through my machine and handing it back with a grin. "No worries, Mr. Sampson. Maybe he can still turn himself around. He's only fifteen."

Mr. Sampson eyed me dubiously over the rim of his cocoa. "Fat chance, sweetheart. People don't change."

I shook my head as he walked away and kept my smile in place for the next round of Bean Around Town lovers to place their orders. It was almost time for the competition to start, so I'd better hurry up with this line unless I wanted them to give up so they could go inside for the big event. But that was the trouble with running a mobile coffee cart in a town like this. Stopping for conversation was part of the charm in running this business, and not doing that would remove a bit of the soul behind it. If that meant fewer sales or tips for me, so be it.

CHAPTER 2

As was tradition, the annual gingerbread house competition began with an extensive speech from Mayor Kingston while we all sat in folding chairs in the center of the room or stood packed in like sardines along the back wall. Long tables surrounded us on three sides, each one holding a masterpiece created by someone in the town.

There were no requirements to enter the competition. They could be a child of only five who did the whole thing themselves and therefore never won because the judges weren't the sentimental types. They could be professional bakers and decorators from our local bakeries or restaurants, like my best friend, Lexi, who owned Mountain Sugar, a bakery on Main Street below the apartment we shared. Or they could be any old amateur gingerbread house enthusiast, which was the category our nine-years-in-a-row winner fell into. A fact that she *loved* to boast about. Being a self-taught champion had always been a point of pride for her.

After the speech, we were released to wander around the

room and check out the numbered houses. We'd picked up a small notecard and a pen at the door to record our favorites and would vote by dropping it into a gingerbread house-shaped box with a slit at the top on our way out. Then we'd mingle outside, and I'd serve more cocoa and coffee while the judges deliberated.

Usually, the city set up tables of black coffee and cocoa from a store-bought mix, and it was a self-serve situation. But allowing Bean Around Town to set up shop this year had definitely elevated this event, and it was fun to hear people say so as I moved through the room and assessed the houses to find my favorite.

"Have you picked one yet?" a smooth-as-butter voice with its telltale New York accent asked from behind me.

I didn't need to turn to know it was Nico, my brother's partner. I kept my eyes trained on the absolute horror show of a kid's creation as I answered dryly. "I think I'm going for this one."

"You should. No one says you can't vote for your own house, right?"

Now, I did turn to face him. "Very funny, Baretti."

"So, you're saying you didn't make it, then?"

"No. I don't enter these contests. My thing is coffee, and my artistic skill begins and ends with being able to draw something that kinda looks like a heart in the foam of a latte."

"I've seen you try that," he said with a tilt of his head, "and I don't think it looks much like a heart at all. Maybe a diamond, though, so good job there."

"Thanks."

"You're welcome."

Realizing this was a strange place for him, considering he was relatively new to our town—having moved here from New York earlier this year for reasons I still didn't know—I quirked a brow at him. "Why are you here? Pine Lakes Annual Gingerbread House Competition doesn't really strike me as your thing."

He scoffed. "Are you kidding? Who wouldn't want to analyze the creative talents of our townspeople in a way that doesn't matter at all, only for them to be awarded prizes that are likely not even worth as much as they spent on the ingredients to build these things? Not to mention the time investment."

We meandered along the row of houses on the left side of the room, and I chuckled darkly. "Like I said. Not your thing. So why are you here?"

"Your grandma made me come."

I shot him a look. "No, she didn't."

"She did. She said she would die if I didn't come, and I didn't want to risk that. What if she really croaked, and somehow you wound up looking like the murderer? We'd find ourselves squaring off in an interrogation room again, and we wouldn't want that, now would we?"

Memories flooded my brain of the last time he'd had me in that monochromatic box, questioning me about a crime I hadn't committed. It'd been horrible and unjust at first— well, all around—but there had also been some surprising moments of warmth that had stabbed into my gut and an attraction to him that was probably the worst idea on a planet full of bad ideas. No, I wouldn't want to find myself in that room being questioned for murder again; but being in there with him *in general* didn't sound as bad as it should. Not by a long shot.

"This one is actually pretty impressive," he commented as we made it to the old biddy's prized entry.

"Ah, yes. I'm glad even *you* can appreciate its beauty. It'll probably win actually."

"You think so? We're only a third of the way through them."

I shrugged. "She always wins."

"How do you know who made it? None of them are labeled."

"A couple of reasons. First of all, I know this one was made by Betty Nichols because it looks like the last nine she's done—and they've all won first place. She's hoping this year will be number ten."

His brows shot up. "Wow. Even more impressive."

"If you like a monopoly kinda vibe about the whole thing," I returned under my breath, teasingly wrinkling my nose at one of Betty's friends when she scowled at me from the other side of the table.

"What about the others? Can you tell who made them too?"

I scanned the houses on the next table. "Yeah, some. When you've been to enough of these, you can start to tell people's styles. This one here was made by old Mr. Jenkins. He buys every single package of Rolos at the grocery store during the month of November because he uses so many of them."

Nico looked down at the house with its Rolo walkways,

driveway, roof, and edging around the entire base. There was even a back patio made of the circular chocolate candies. "Nice. What about this one?"

"Ah, this one is Lexi's. Obviously, I'd know that since we live together, but come on."

He chuckled. "I take it there are no rules about the gingerbread house being a residence as opposed to a mini bakery?"

"Nope."

"Are you going to vote for Lexi's?"

I blinked up at him, intending to make a sarcastic remark, but then accidentally got mesmerized by the deep-chocolate brown of his eyes that reminded me a little of the Rolos we'd been looking at. Except they were so dark right now, you could hardly see his pupils. Nico was Italian, like my family and me, so his olive skin and dark-brown hair and eyes were striking and warm. Despite the often chilly quips we exchanged, he exuded warmth.

"Did I lose you?" he asked, stepping closer so I could smell the clean scent of his cologne that also held a note of clove.

I shook my head to clear it. "Um, yes, I'm gonna vote for Lexi's. I always do, but again, Betty will probably win."

"You never know," he replied as we came upon a massive house that caused both of our steps to falter as we approached. "See? Look at this beast."

CHAPTER 3

"*Beast?*" Mrs. Daniels asked, her chin raised while thin red lips pursed into an annoyed oblong shape that should have made them look fuller but instead had the opposite effect. "It's not a beast. It's a masterpiece."

We stared at the house as she held her arms out with pride. It was two stories high—a first for this show—and was an exact replica of the house my friend Cory had lived in since he was a kid. Even though we were almost in our thirties now, he still lived in the basement of his parents' magnificent home. Long story short, he'd had a rough go of it thanks to that slimy ex of mine who'd been murdered recently. But now that he had a girlfriend he loved and a new job, I was sure he'd move out soon.

"Hi, Mrs. Daniels," I said cheerfully. "You're right. It's great. I had no idea you were such a gingerbread artist."

She waved a hand with a mocking laugh. "As if, dear. I hired it out. Everybody knows that."

Nico and I exchanged a look. Then I turned back to her

with my face pinched in confusion. How had I not heard about this? "You can do that?"

"There's nothing in the rules that says you can't," she replied high-handedly.

I thought about all the times I'd heard the rules repeated for the guests before the show. I'd been coming to this event since I was a kid, so I'd heard the spiel countless times. But I'd never read the handout with the official rules for the contestants because I hadn't wanted to enter once I realized kids *never* won, and my skills hadn't advanced beyond what a child could do. Maybe she was right. Who cared if it was hired out as long as it was yours to enter? Eh, no. I didn't like it. But since this wasn't my circus or my monkeys, I didn't comment.

"That doesn't seem fair," Nico observed, crossing his arms over his chest.

I patted his shoulder. "What, you can't hop off those justice scales even for a gingerbread house contest, detective?"

He gave me an annoyed look, but before he could comment, Mrs. Daniels broke in. "Look at this. Bet you've never seen an entry like this before."

Nico and I watched as Mrs. Daniels reached for the lip of the roof, pulling it toward her to reveal several golden hinges allowing it to open and close. Curious, we peered into the house, and I gasped when I saw the interior was decorated just like her real home a few streets over.

There were tiny chocolate and pretzel and candy-created items that were intended to be small replicas of her decor and furniture. The rug they'd gotten from Turkey seemed to be made from a facedown chocolate bar with golden piped icing in swirling patterns. There was the mirror they'd brought home from Spain—more golden icing had been piped delicately around the edges, and something shiny mimicked the glass that surely couldn't be edible. That was one rule I remembered—everything used must be edible.

Nico noticed at the same time. "What'd you use for the glass of the mirror? Or the windows, for that matter?"

"It's made of sugar," she confided with a rueful smile. "They use sugar glass in the movies when someone falls through a window, you know."

Something else shiny caught my eye, and I was startled, not knowing how I'd missed it before. "Is the chandelier sugar glass too?"

"Yes, totally made of sugar. It's an exact replica of the one in our foyer. Isn't it grand?"

Mrs. Daniels's boasting had drawn a crowd of people so close that Nico and I found ourselves with no choice but to scoot nearer to the table—and each other. I didn't know if it was the fact that people were crowding around me in a way that suggested they had no idea what a personal space bubble was or if it was my proximity to the tall, dark, and handsome detective, but suddenly I felt flushed, and my breathing grew too fast to hide. I had to get out of there.

Ever observant, Nico took one look at me and parted the sea of onlookers with his large, lean form, allowing me an exit as he followed after me. "That was intense," he said after we made it into the center of the room. "You okay?"

"I'm fine. I just didn't want one of them to push me into the table and be responsible for ruining Mrs. Daniels's house.

I bet it cost her a fortune, and now I have a feeling she'll probably win over Betty."

He looked down at me with narrowed eyes. "Do you think that's fair though? Seems to me she's flirting with cheating by hiring it out."

I agreed with him, but I liked to *disagree* with him more. Even if only to watch his nostrils flare with annoyance. Call me crazy, but I found it pretty cute. Shrugging, I played with one of the silly white puffs on my ugly Christmas sweater that was supposed to represent snow. "Eh, it's not Mrs. Daniels's fault nobody thought to add it to the rules. If someone has an issue with it, I bet it'll be a new rule next year."

Nico harrumphed but didn't comment further. Then his whole posture changed as my brother walked up with my best friend in tow. Nico nodded at them and took a deliberate step away from me, tucking his hands into the pockets of his slacks. Why he wore slacks and a button-down under his crisp New York fashion coat to a small-town gingerbread house competition was beyond me. But then again, he also wore a full *Men in Black*-ish suit as one of the few detectives in Pine Lakes instead of the simple polo and slacks the rest of them wore, so I shouldn't really be that surprised.

"Haze," Lexi said, grabbing my arm with wide eyes. "Have you seen Cory's mom's house? It looks just like the one they live in! I can't even!"

I nodded and tossed a look over my shoulder where the crowd was still gathered around it. As I swung back to look at Lexi again, my attention was snagged by Betty, who looked as bitter as a coffee bean. Well, as bitter as a coffee bean *before* we got ahold of them at the Busy Bean, of course. Because once we roasted and ground and brewed them, they were smooth and full-bodied.

"Betty does *not* look happy," I said in a low tone.

"She looks like she wants to take a sledgehammer to the thing," Ryan added, then slid his gaze over Nico. "Didn't think this would be your scene."

"Your grandma invited me," Nico replied with a shrug.

Ryan's eyes flared as he looked at me, and I held my hands up. "I know. Shocked me too."

"She's so weird. Where is she anyway? I haven't seen her or Mom all night."

I scanned the faces of the crowd, coming up empty. "Mom said Joe had an emergency job on the other side of town, and they were going to wait for him and head over together. They should be here soon."

My mom's fiancé, Joe, was an electrician. He worked decent hours most days because his clients were commercial property owners, but when the odd emergency popped up, he'd been known to pull an all-nighter to get the job done.

Some people would probably find that kind of thing exhausting, but as someone who'd grown up watching her mom and grandparents run their own business in the form of our town's only coffeehouse, it was the only life I knew. And now that we'd opened Bean Around Town as an extension of the Busy Bean's offerings—and it was my brainchild and totally under my charge—I worked even more than I had before. It was why I didn't date if I was being honest. Who had time for romance when there were lattes to serve and beans to grind and to-go cups to order? Not me.

"Well, I hope they get here soon so they can get a good look at all of the entries before it's time to vote," Lexi said with a pout.

She knew her gingerbread bakery was good, but there were some competitors who'd campaigned for votes for months before this event, and she wasn't one of them. Sure, in the end, the panel of judges had the final say on the winners, but the public votes factored into their results and almost always resulted in an honorable mention prize if some house they didn't deem worthy of getting first, second, or third place was highly popular with the voters. No doubt, Lexi was hoping she could at least snag that spot, if nothing else.

"Let's go finish looking," I said, nodding toward the side of the room I hadn't yet made it to. "We've only seen the first half."

Lexi frowned. "You started on that side? We started on the opposite."

"It's fine. You go that way, and we'll go this way, and we'll meet you by the door when we're done?" I suggested, hooking a thumb over my shoulder.

Lexi nodded and pranced off, but Ryan lingered for a minute, looking between the two of us with an odd expression on his face. Then he shook his head slightly and followed Lexi when she called out to him. Poor guy. He had no idea my best friend had been pining over him since we were all practically kids, and she didn't seem to care to let him in on the secret that only I knew.

Hmm. Maybe I should push them into it?

"What are you thinking so hard about?" Nico asked, one

perfectly manscaped brow arched. Such a typical New York Italian. I bet he got his hair cut every Friday without fail too.

"Nothing. Let's go."

About fifteen minutes later, Nico and I made it to the door right as Lexi and Ryan finished their perusal of the entries. And not a moment too soon, either, because right then, the mayor picked up his mic and cleared his throat before raising it to his ruddy, round face.

"All right, everyone," Mayor Kingston said into the mic, causing a shriek of feedback to bloody our ears. He winced and glared at his assistant, who'd been helping with the sound system, then waited for her to give him a thumbs up before continuing. "We hope you've had time to check out all the entries in this year's competition. And if you haven't, well, you should have gotten here sooner because there's been plenty of time."

The four of us exchanged looks as a few people chuckled, but clearly, no one thought Mayor Kingston was as amusing as he thought he was.

Where were Gram and Mom? They should have been here by now.

"Now," he went on, gesturing to the door, "if you'll please step outside and enjoy some refreshments from Bean Around Town so we can give our wonderful judges time to deliberate, we'll call you back inside when it's time to reveal the winners."

Bodies started moving toward the door in a sea of either excited murmurs or frustrated sighs—depending on how far they'd made it around the room. As the four of us went outside and I started to dash over to the bus so I could start my refreshment dispensing, I jolted when I saw my mom and grandma were already serving the customers who were standing in line. Joe stood chatting with locals with my trusty canine companion, Latte, on her leash beside him.

"What are you guys doing?" I asked as I jumped through the door of Bean Around Town and threw on my apron. "Didn't you want to go inside and vote?"

Gram scoffed and waved a hand. "I'm not participating in that hogwash this year. We all know who's gonna win."

I sent her a wry smile as I squeezed in to help. I loved it when they came in here and we had three generations of Italian women serving coffee and not scrimping on the smiles. This was my happy place, no doubt about it.

"Well," I said as I picked up a freshly Sharpie'd cup that my mom had just placed on the counter for me to pour hot cocoa into, "you might be surprised this year."

CHAPTER 4

AFTER THE THIRTY-MINUTE deliberation from the judges, Mom, Gram, and I closed up the coffee truck and made our way to the seats our friends and family had held for us. The room had been rearranged slightly with the tables scooted back toward the walls so there was more space in the center for chairs. Long partitions had been erected in front of the displays so we couldn't see whose creations were still sitting in the same place and which ones had been moved to a new table front and center.

They'd used four banners from the mayor's campaign office to block the sight of the houses that sat behind them. And judging by the fact that there were four of them, I guessed this year's winning lineup would include an honorable mention after all.

I squeezed Lexi's hand as she sat—or squirmed really—in the chair next to mine. "This is it. I hope you win!"

"Me too," she replied, glaring at the four large banners with the mayor's face prominently displayed on each of them. "You'd think they'd make banners specifically for this event since it's an annual affair instead of using his campaign signage. I get that they want to reveal the winners one at a time, but ugh, his actual face is annoying enough to look at in 3D. Do we really have to sit here and stare at four more versions of his smug smile?"

Snorting, then coughing in an attempt to cover it, I leaned over to whisper, "Normally, they use those white boxes to cover the winning houses until they're ready to pull them off one by one. Remember?"

"Oh, right."

"How much you wanna bet Mrs. Daniels's house was too big to fit under the box, so they had to improvise in order to avoid a dead giveaway?"

She nodded, and her lips pulled down like she was impressed. "True. But since our town super sleuth is in the audience, it was a dead giveaway anyway, wasn't it?"

I chuckled. "Guess so, yeah. But I'm special."

Nico leaned across Ryan, who sat on my other side, keeping his voice low as he said, "Guys, how much you wanna bet they only used those stupid signs so it wouldn't be obvious the big house won? If they'd used anything else, it'd give it away, right?"

"Good call, man," Ryan replied, patting his fellow detective on the shoulder before turning to us with a smile that said, "That's my partner, right there."

I glared at him—and Nico too—before turning back to Lexi. "I thought of it first."

"Of course you did, Miss Marple."

"Let's kick things off with our honorable mention,"

Mayor Kingston said, wrapping his hand around the pole of the banner. "Congratulations to Lexi Cunningham," he yelled, sliding the banner away with a flourish. "Your bakery in real life is one of our town's most treasured eateries, and your replica was definitely a favorite with the people tonight."

Lexi screamed and bounded from her seat, bowing and grinning as the crowd cheered for her. Of course I was the loudest and on my feet, too, even though normally the honorable mention didn't get a standing ovation. When she returned to her seat holding a hand-painted gingerbread house ornament with the year on it as her prize, I pulled her into my arms and squeezed her tightly.

"Great job," I said against her neck. "I knew you'd win!"

She let go of me and sat down, cradling the ornament in her hands. "Well, I won something anyway."

"The most important prize, if you ask me," I said proudly, slapping my brother's leg. "Right, Ryan?"

My brother gave Lexi a huge smile. "She's right. Better to win the vote of the people than to have a bunch of crotchety old folks deciding if it's good enough."

"Hey," Gram said, reaching across Nico to whack him on the back of the head, "I resemble that remark."

We all laughed and turned back to the mayor as he announced the winner for third place. It was a cute house, I'd give the art teacher from Pine Lakes High that—so if anyone would have an issue with Mrs. Daniels hiring hers out, surely people with artistic talent should be excluded too, right? Well, no, because my bestie was a whiz with icing decorations so that would push her out just the same.

Brushing it off, I joined the rest of the town in clapping for Miss Gormley as she went up to retrieve her twenty-five-dollar cash prize and ten-dollar gift card to the local hardware store. What that had to do with Christmas or gingerbread houses, I didn't know. But this event's sponsors rarely fit the theme.

"Maybe you should sponsor the event next year," Lexi whispered to me. "You can do ten-dollar Busy Bean gift cards. I bet you make enough cash having the truck outside to more than make up for it, and it'll bring you more business."

Since Lexi owned and operated her own small business with the bakery, I never doubted her sound mind on the topic. But this was a great idea and would surely be more exciting to the winners than a gift card to the hardware store.

"Good idea," I replied with an air kiss. "I'll tell the mayor later before he books someone else."

"And now for our first- and second-place winners," Mayor Kingston said, suddenly looking a little ill. "This was a hotly debated situation, as I'm sure you can imagine once you get a look at the winners. But in the end, we had to go with the best house, regardless of how ... *complicated* it made our judges' deliberations."

The mayor paused as he looked pointedly at one judge in particular. Mr. Smythe—the elementary school teacher who appeared to have had a stick up his rear since about 1973, if you asked me. The resentful scowl on his pudgy face couldn't have been more obvious if he'd held up a sign that read *I didn't win this argument, and I'm highly offended by it.*

"Ah, I bet we all already know what's up," Lexi muttered.

I nodded. "I thought it took them longer than usual to choose the winners. They normally don't need so long to sort it out."

"Right, because Betty gets their commitment to vote for her before the leaves have even fallen around here."

I giggled as Mayor Kingston moved to the banner in front of second place, shooting Lexi a look as Betty's very cute gingerbread house came into view. It was a one-story ranch style home with a large courtyard in the center. She'd cleverly used candies shaped like LEGO bricks to create a colorful fountain in the center with strings of sour candy cascading from the top to represent the water.

The crowd's reaction to Betty winning second place instead of first was a mixed bag. Some cheered and yelled things like *'bout time*, which was rude even if we were all thinking it. Others grumbled that it wasn't fair for someone to hire out their build and dethrone a woman with real talent. And even though I agreed that it was about time someone else won the title of Gingerbread House Champion this year, I kind of understood the unrest over it too.

It was a tough subject to figure out, but fine. In the last year, my family's historical coffee shop, the Busy Bean, had been engulfed in flames thanks to the work of an arsonist with a bone to pick. And then not long after that, my ex-boyfriend had been murdered, and I'd been the prime suspect for a time. It's been quite the year, so if my only emotionally disturbing situation this holiday season surrounded the ethics of hiring out the building of a gingerbread house to dethrone the queen of builds, I'd take it.

I must have been lost in thought when the mayor moved

his giant face—the one on the banner—away from the winning gingerbread house, because the horrified cries from the people of Pine Lakes was my only hint that something was amiss.

My eyes snapped forward, but people had already jumped to their feet in front of me, and I couldn't see what the problem was. Bless my Italian roots, but we were generally small people. My mom was five two, and Gram was five feet tall only in stilettos, which to my knowledge hadn't happened in this century. I didn't know how tall my dad was because everyone looks tall when you're a child, and that was the last time I'd seen him. But judging from the fact that my short little self couldn't see over the rows of people blocking my view of the winning house, clearly he hadn't done me any favors.

I stood on my toes and tried to see as people talked over each other with outraged exclamations of unfairness. Had Mrs. Daniels lost after all and that was what they thought was unfair? Or were they simply saying it was unfair that she *did* win, even though they couldn't possibly be shocked by it?

Oh! Maybe it was something else entirely. Had they finally picked a kid as the winner? GOOD. I'd be happy to see that, not shocked and sickened like the rest of these loony tunes.

But no ... wait. That couldn't be it. They looked much too distressed for their reactions to be about who won. Unable to stand it any longer, I put a hand on my brother's shoulder for balance and climbed onto my chair so I could see. And then I gasped, my hands flying up to clap over my mouth.

Mrs. Daniels had won, but the beautiful house she'd hired someone to create? It was completely ruined.

Ryan, who'd jumped onto his chair, too, even though he was at least a little taller than me but apparently wanted my view as well, looked down at me with a grim expression. "Well. That kinda looks like someone took a sledgehammer to it."

CHAPTER 5

PEOPLE CROWDED around the table so they could see, but the chaos quickly grew out of hand. Ryan leaned over to Nico and yelled, "Do you think we should clear the room before everyone starts trampling each other?"

"Not if they want to find out who did this. No one should leave," came Nico's stiff reply. His eyes raked around the room, and he sighed heavily. "I'll go call in some uniforms to help us with crowd control. You go talk to the contestant."

Nico headed for the door, and Ryan started to move through the crowd. I took one look at Lexi and knew we were on the same page. We charged after my brother, just as eager to talk to Mrs. Daniels about who she thought might have done this to her house as Ryan was.

"You'd better catch the vandal who ruined my creation," Mrs. Daniels yelled the second she saw the three of us approach her.

The woman practically radiated with fury, her limbs shook and her otherwise perfectly styled hair looked a touch like she'd grabbed her scalp with enraged fingers and pulled when she'd first seen the big reveal. It made her appear as unhinged as her gingerbread roof at the moment.

Ryan held out his hands in a placating gesture, and right as the mayor approached to speak with them, Cory Daniels appeared next to Lexi and me with his brows nearly reaching his hairline. "I told her not to hire it out, you know."

I chuckled and crossed my arms. "That's very unsupportive, Cory. I'm shocked by you."

"Whoa, hey. I don't think someone should have smashed the thing, but I had a feeling it would cause drama in one way or another. We all know how seriously the town takes this competition."

"We sure do," I said through a sigh.

Nico had moved to the door and now stood in front of it, asking people not to leave. Most were too curious about who might have done this to care that they had to stay. Where else would they rather be if they wanted to know what happened firsthand? The people of Pine Lakes may love to gossip, but witnessing firsthand drama? Nico wouldn't need to work hard to make them want to stick around for that.

"Who do you think did it?" I asked Cory.

He shrugged. "I'd put my money on Betty. She planned to take home her tenth first-place prize."

Lexi snorted. "Maybe she put the order in, but those eighty-year-old hands are for placing Skittles onto a row of white icing, not for whatever kind of weapon was used on your mom's house."

"You have a point there," I conceded.

Ryan walked up to us then, scratching his head. "Obviously Betty is denying any involvement, and there was a solid ten minutes when the judges left the room after they'd set up the banners around the winning houses. It really could have been anyone. There are like five entrances to this room and people everywhere. It would be easy to slip in and out without anyone noticing."

I tilted my head. "If there are tons of people here, why would it be easy to slip in without being noticed? Surely somebody had to have seen them."

"Not if they were distracted with their gingerbread lattes and gossip. Plenty of crimes are committed with tons of people around. There's too much going on for them to stick out."

"Hang on. You sound pretty negative, Ryan Hewitt," Lexi said. "It's like you don't think we'll figure out who did this."

He smirked and tucked his hands into his front pockets. "If we do, I hope it doesn't take too long. No one wants to spend all night questioning a hundred witnesses over a smashed gingerbread house."

"So, what, you'd rather they just get away with it?" I asked.

"Look, obviously it stinks. But it wasn't like they smashed it before the voting. Mrs. Daniels already won, and now she'll take home her winnings and not have to display this thing in her house until it goes stale. You know she was going to have to throw it away eventually, right?"

"Ryan, you have to at least look into it," I insisted.

My brother sighed. "Of course we're going to look into it. But don't get your hopes up. We're not gonna keep these people here all night if the quicker solution would be for Mrs.

Daniels to forget about pressing charges, pick up her prize, and go home a winner."

Without another word, Ryan walked up to a group of people whispering together. No doubt he wanted to hurry up and question people so he could be done with it. Was he right? Was it pointless to enter into a hard-core criminal investigation when Mrs. Daniels had already won and the only thing hurt in this whole mess was her pride?

"Haze," Cory said, nudging me with his arm. "My mom's waving us over."

Taking a deep breath, I followed him to face his mother, wincing when she blew her nose with a surprising amount of force into a silk handkerchief. One that probably cost more than my jeans, and these were the good ones too. You know, like clearance-section-of-Nordstrom-Rack-as-opposed-to-Ross good.

"How are you holding up, Mrs. Daniels?" I asked, fixing a sympathetic smile on my face. "I'm sorry someone did this to the house, but congratulations on winning before it happened! It would have been so much worse if someone had done it right when we got here."

"Hazel's right," Lexi added helpfully. "We were all able to enjoy how much hard work went into it before it was ruined, so that's good, isn't it?"

"Yes," she sniffed, looking down at the house like she'd actually spent months laboring over it with her bare hands instead of writing a check. Er—sending a Venmo? Either way. "It's such a shame that someone's jealousy got the better of them in this way."

I peered over at Betty, standing off to the side with a

concerned expression on her lined face. She wrung her hands in front of her and bounced from foot to foot like she was scared. Did that mean she was guilty? Or just nervous we'd think she was?

"I'll be right back," I said to Lexi, Cory, and his mom. Without waiting for their reply, I headed for Betty. "Hi. I'm sorry about the second-place thing. You doing okay?"

"Me? It's Mrs. Daniels you should be asking."

"I already did."

"Is she?"

I looked from side to side. "Um, sort of. Not really. She's upset."

"Ugh, understandably. Imagine, you put all this effort into being a sneaky, conniving, rule-breaking-if-the-rule-had-been-there cheat, and then boom—you don't even get to bring it home to enjoy for the rest of the holiday season."

Momentarily speechless, I just stared at the older woman and watched her watch Mrs. Daniels with what definitely looked like sympathy in her light-blue eyes.

"So, you feel bad for her that someone smashed it, but you still hate her for having hired someone to make it?"

"Exactly. She took my number-one spot because she was smart enough to find a loophole in the rules and run with it. Lemme tell you, little girl, if I'd thought of it first, I would have done it, too, and I would have hired a much better architect than she did. I would have had the Taj Mahal of gingerbread houses, and I would have kept up my winning streak. But *no,* she thought of it first, and I hate her for that. But I wouldn't want someone to smash up her house. She won not-so-fair and not-so-square, but I'm okay with that."

Head spinning from the twisted logic that I was sure made perfect sense in her brain, I turned around to survey the room. Mom, Joe, and Gram were chatting with friends from Gram's book club. Lexi was still with Cory and his mom, and she was rubbing Mrs. Daniels's back while looking up at her son with a *why am I the one comforting her?* look. A few uniformed officers were interviewing witnesses, Nico and Ryan among them. But their faces were all very distant, like they'd been sucked into a vortex of small-town gossip, and they weren't being told anything of value whatsoever.

The urge to act snaked up my spine. I'd taken a liking to sticking my nose into investigations when they involved me, and even though this one didn't, what else was I supposed to do? They wouldn't let anyone leave, and I couldn't very well drive my coffee truck through the front door and serve more gingerbread lattes.

"Betty," I hedged, scooting close enough to smell a hint of that fabric softener with the fluffy teddy bear on the bottle. "If you didn't smash her house, do you have any idea who did?"

She made a little humming sound as she thought about it. "Well, I'll tell you one thing. Mr. Smythe was more than a little miffed by the whole thing. He said she'd spat on the entire spirit of the competition."

"By hiring it out?"

"Well, sure." She waved a hand and lifted her chin. "Mr. Smythe feels this event is about celebrating amateur craftsmanship. Anyone could hire an outside source to create their entry, but what would be the point if everyone started doing it? Between you and me, he was a little more than miffed. It was more like ... outraged."

"*Outraged*, huh?" I turned to find Mr. Smythe, raising a brow as he stood in a huddle with the other judges. Whatever they were discussing caused them to continuously look over their shoulders to make sure no one was listening, and if that didn't smell like guilt, I didn't know what would.

"Thanks for chatting, Betty. Congrats on your second-place win, though. I know it wasn't what you wanted, but ..."

She shrugged, looking resigned to it. "It is what it is, dear. I know I've still won first place out of those who constructed their own houses, and so does everyone else in this room. That's all that matters to me."

Nodding, I turned and made a beeline for Mr. Smythe. One suspect down, *him* to go.

CHAPTER 6

"Mr. Smythe," I said as I approached, offering a smile to the other judges, "sorry to interrupt, but can I steal you away for a sec?"

A slow smile spread over his round face. "Of course, Ms. Hewitt. I'd be honored."

"Er, thanks." I led him away from the group, then when we were far enough away from listening ears, I spun around and adopted what I hoped looked like a casual stance. Inside, though, I pulled on my interrogator hat and was ready to rumble. "So, Mr. Smythe. I heard you were pretty mad about the fact that Mrs. Daniels hired someone to make her ginger-bread house."

He straightened to his full height—which wasn't much taller than mine, to be honest—and stuck out his chest and bowling-ball-shaped belly in indignation. "Well, clearly. Nowhere in the rules does it say contestants can hire a professional to create their house."

"Nowhere in the rules does it say they can't," I quipped, playing the devil's advocate in the hopes it would get him flustered enough to say things without thinking.

"It shouldn't have to!" he roared, causing more than a few heads to turn in our direction.

Getting back to the subject at hand, I cleared my throat and showed Mr. Smythe I had no intentions of cowering at his show of temper. The dummy. I'm Italian. I'd be a pretty mopey person if I got upset or offended every time someone raised their voice in an argument—or even at a friendly family dinner.

"Maybe you're right," I allowed, spreading my hands in a placating gesture. "Maybe there shouldn't have to be anything in the rules about hiring out the work. But in this case, it wasn't there, so you can't really fault Mrs. Daniels for doing so."

Again, my attempt at goading him worked, and he blew out a stinky breath through his nose. Man, his nostrils needed a Tic Tac. Was that a thing?

"Ms. Hewitt, since you obviously don't possess even an ounce of morality when it comes to fair competition, why don't you get to the point? Why did you ask to *steal me away*? It's been longer than a 'sec,' and I'd rather speak to people who share my same values in the spirit of friendly competition."

"Fine. I wanna know if you smashed the house."

He rolled his eyes. "Oh, I see. Did I miss your graduation from the police academy? My apologies."

"No. I'm not asking *officially*. But the cops don't seem too eager to stay here all night and figure out who did it, so I'm helping out."

"Well, you're barking up the wrong tree with me, young lady. Need I remind you I'm standing on much higher moral ground than you are? Why would someone who was offended by the blatant disrespect of the spirit of this event retaliate with a petulant act like that?"

His oddly old-fashioned way of speaking caused me to suddenly feel like I'd been dropped into an episode of *Sherlock Holmes*. It was on the tip of my tongue to say, "Right you are, good chap," but I held it in. Though, that didn't take away the truth of the mocking sentiment. He really did have a point, as much as I hated to admit it. Sure, Mr. Smythe was a temperamental son-of-a-gun, but he was coming from a place of righteous bluster. It wouldn't make sense for him to have smashed the house out of spite. No. A more suitable reaction would have been for him to try to get the vote over-turned or call for an appeal or something like that.

Realizing that might have been what he was discussing with his fellow judges, I narrowed my eyes at him. "When I walked up, what were you talking to the other judges about? Because if I had to guess, I bet you were trying to convince them to rethink the winner now that the house is a mess."

Again, another eye roll. "That wouldn't be in keeping with the spirit of things either, would it?"

"No." Frustrated by my own lack of experience in questioning suspects without making myself look like an idiot, I looked at the ceiling. "Fine, so I guess I believe that you didn't smash the house."

"Oh, well, now I'll sleep much more soundly when my head meets my pillow tonight."

This guy should be wearing a cravat and waistcoat for all this high-handed language, I swear. "Great. But while I have you, can you think of anyone else who was as outraged as you are but maybe doesn't share your ... abundant sense of morality?" That last part was said with a little smile, hoping he didn't take it as mocking as much as acknowledging his viewpoint.

Tucking his hands behind his wide back, he lifted his chin as he thought about it. "Not off the top of my head. Much to my dismay, my compatriots on the judging panel were neither bothered nor offended by Mrs. Daniels's blatant lack of respect for the parameters of this competition."

Wrinkling my nose to keep from laughing, I nodded. "Sorry to hear that. Well, thanks for your time, and I'm sorry if I added to the drama by asking if you did it."

"Not at all, Ms. Hewitt. I'm glad I was able to sufficiently convince you that I am not the man—or *woman*—you seek. Good luck with your amateur investigation."

"Thanks," I said with a wry smile, turning away from him to find my next victim.

But before I could take another step, Nico moved into my path with his head tilted to one side. "Your brother thinks you're sticking your nose where it doesn't belong again. Is that true?"

"He calls it 'playing cop,'" I told him, pursing my lips with a few innocent blinks.

"So do I."

"Well, that's fine. Everyone has hobbies, right? What do you play when you're not actually *being* a cop?"

"What would you say if I told you I *played* barista and served up some knockoffs of your espresso drinks?"

I patted his bicep in what was meant to be a friendly gesture and ignored the shot of fire that ran up my arm. "I'd say good for you, and I'd offer to teach you everything I know."

"No you wouldn't."

I shrugged. "Why don't you take up the craft of coffee, and we'll find out?"

"Because that would be like encouraging you to take up the craft of policing, and I'm not gonna do that."

"Why not?" I asked, crossing my arms over my chest.

Something flashed in his eyes then. Something like anger, but not quite as negative as all that. Protectiveness, maybe? "Because, Hazel," he said, stepping close enough so I could smell the clove in his cologne again, "you almost died the last time you got wrapped up in police matters. No, the last *two* times, if the stories I've heard are true. It's not safe for you to parade around like you have the skills and training of a detective when you don't. I won't have it."

My brows went up automatically. "You won't? Nico, you sound like my brother. And I'll tell you the same thing I tell him. I appreciate the big brother protectiveness, but I promise, I'm a smart woman. I can take care of myself."

He stared at me for a long moment, seeming to choose his words carefully. Then he looked at the ceiling before saying, "It's not big brother protectiveness, and I never said you weren't a smart woman. Just … be careful."

Without waiting for me to reply, or to properly digest everything he'd just said, Nico turned on his expensive loafers and sauntered away. Swaggered, even. I stared at his retreating form until he was lost in the sea of townspeople, then let out the breath I hadn't realized I'd been holding.

What the heck was that?

CHAPTER 7

"How's the sleuthing going?" Lexi asked, eyeing the ruined house like a kid being tormented by a pile of treats they were told not to eat.

I watched her carefully. She wouldn't really pluck a licorice string off the house and eat it, would she? I mean, I knew the girl could decimate a bag of Twizzlers like nobody's business, but *ugh*. I wasn't one for violence, but I'd totally slap her hand out of the air if she even tried it. What were besties for if not to save them from snacking on candy that'd been handled by the rando who was hired to build this thing?

"Well, I'm convinced that Betty and Mr. Smythe are innocent," I replied, giving Mrs. Daniels a pitying smile as she joined us right in time to hear that. "Sorry I don't have better news."

"Me too. Thank you for trying," Mrs. Daniels said. She looped her arm through Cory's as he meandered up to what was once a magnificent gingerbread house. "Cory, you should go home. They're letting people leave now since the police department is apparently coming up as empty as Hazel here."

"What about you?"

She sighed. "I'm going to stay until they make me leave. I'm determined to find answers. *Someone* needs to be held accountable."

Cory, Lexi, and I all looked at each other with subtle notes of *oh, brother.*

"I'll stay with her," I offered, then winced. If they were letting people leave, I needed to get back to Bean Around Town so I could hopefully squeeze a little more business out of this whirlwind of a night as people hung around to continue chatting about the excitement of it all. Even with everything that had gone wrong, this town loved nothing more than an annual event taking an unexpected turn for the dramatic.

Shaking my head, I bit my lip in apology. "Actually, wait. I should get to my truck. I'm sure people will want a gingerbread latte or cocoa to pair with their ... *mingling.*" I hadn't wanted to point out they'd stick around to keep gossiping. Not to the subject of the gossip, anyway.

"We'll do that," Gram said, making me jump as she spoke from behind me. "Your mother is already out there. I'll join her so you can keep up the good work."

Unlike my brother and Nico, Gram encouraged my interest in some of the crimes we'd seen in Pine Lakes lately. Not that she'd ever want me to hang up my Busy Bean apron and join the force, but still. She praised my cleverness and enjoyed watching me *play cop*.

"Thanks, Grams. I won't be long, and I'll help you guys close up when everyone leaves."

"Sounds great. Good luck."

I thanked her again and watched her walk away, catching Nico's eye as he looked up from whomever he was speaking to. Narrowing my eyes at him in challenge, I turned back to the mess that looked like something a reindeer had thrown up after a long night of binge eating decorations.

With a frown, I leaned closer to the wreckage and inspected what was once the foyer. "Mrs. Daniels," I said, moving a section of the roof so I could get a better look, "where's the chandelier?"

Mrs. Daniels leaned closer, then reached in and dug through the rubble. "It's not here."

"That's weird. There should at least be pieces of it somewhere if it was smashed up with the rest of the house, right?"

"You'd think so," Lexi agreed as she looked around the debris. Then she gasped. "What if someone took it? What if that was the motive for smashing the house and not something related to Mrs. Daniels winning the grand prize?"

Mrs. Daniels frowned. "Why would someone want to steal a mini chandelier made of sugar glass? It's worthless."

"Right. *We* know that," I said, "but I bet whoever took it didn't. Maybe they thought it was made of real diamonds or something."

"Oh, don't be absurd. Who would think I'd put real diamonds into a house that's supposed to be made only of edible items?"

I bit back a snort. Those golden hinges from the roof looked even less edible now than they had when I'd first seen them. If those things weren't from the hardware store that'd sponsored this year's event, then I was a monkey's uncle.

"Maybe the thief thought he could pawn them and pass them off as real even if he did figure they were fake?" Lexi asked, the perfect Watson to my Sherlock.

"I think you might be right about pawning them, whether he knew they were real or not. And if we're right, I think I know exactly who our culprit is."

"You do?" the other two women asked in unison.

"Yep. Ronald Draper."

Even though I wanted to run off to find the teenage klepto, I forced myself to take a chill pill and told Mrs. Daniels and Lexi all about Ronald's attempt to steal the money from my Frosty the Snowman tip jar earlier tonight. They were shocked, but only mildly. Everyone knew Ronald couldn't resist the urge to take something that didn't belong to him. How he wasn't in juvie by now for his petty crimes was a bigger mystery than I'd come across yet.

When I finally broke free from my conversation with my friend and the ... well, victim, I guessed ... I headed for the door and shot into the chilly December night. If there were still people hanging out and socializing in this covered courtyard of the community center, surely Ronald would be lurking nearby in search of more spoils. Unless he was smarter than I gave him credit for and had gotten out of Dodge with the stolen chandelier before he got caught.

But then I spied him leaning casually against a lamppost

with a to-go cup with my company logo on it, and I grinned. *Gotcha.*

"Hey, Ronald," I said cheerily as I walked up with way too much pep in my step. "How's the coffee?"

"Delicious. Worth every penny."

I swallowed, sincerely hoping he hadn't used *my* pennies from my tip jar. Not that many people tipped me in pennies. Okay, yeah, most of Gram's book club friends were known to drop random change in there like it was a piggy bank instead of a tip jar, but still.

"Glad to hear it," I replied, still smiling. "Hey, you didn't happen to find a crystal chandelier on the ground in there, did you? Not a big one." I held up my hands about four inches apart. "About yay big, made of sugar glass?"

His eyes widened fractionally before he cleared his throat and shook his head. "Nope. But I'll let you know if I find one."

"Great. Thanks." I hesitated, wishing there was some way I could frisk the teen and see if the stolen goods were in the pockets of his worn winter coat. But that was wrong on several levels, and I knew it. Even without *actual* police training.

I wondered idly if the people of Pine Lakes cut this kid some slack because they knew he lived in a ramshackle single-wide with his surly uncles, one of whom had recently been released from prison. I couldn't possibly be the only person who took pity on him despite his sticky fingers.

Just as I was about to attempt casual conversation with Ronald in an effort to trick him into admitting what he'd done, Nico ambled up with his hands tucked casually into his own winter coat. His much nicer, just-stepped-off-the-cover-of-*GQ-Magazine*, winter coat. He even smelled like those thick, folded pages that advertised men's cologne. Rich and spicy and— *Totally* not the point.

Ronald pushed off from the light post and stood ramrod straight as he stared at our town's newest detective with wide eyes.

Hmm. Guilty, much?

"What's up, Nico?" I asked cheerily, wrapping my arms around myself and rubbing my hands over the thin fabric of my long-sleeved shirt.

Even with all the thinking about winter coats, I hadn't been reminded that I'd forgotten mine inside the building until Nico walked up and made me wish I could tuck myself into the open front of his for warmth. *Dang it, Hazel. Get a grip.* It was his fault though, what with all that talk about him not having brotherly feelings for me and thinking I was smart. Not to mention wanting me to be careful. He was messing with my mind.

Wordlessly, Nico's gaze tracked over my shivering form, and he removed the coat and draped it over my shoulders without even asking if I wanted to wear it. The obnoxiously argumentative side of me that I was forever keeping in check wanted to object to the gesture, but I held it back. I wasn't *that* petty, and I could accept his kindness without needing to remind him I was an independent woman who was perfectly capable of retrieving my own coat if I was really that cold.

And *fine*, maybe being wrapped in the coat that was still

warm from his body heat and smelled so good I wanted to drown in it helped take the wind out of my sassy little sails.

"What are you guys chatting about over here?" Nico asked in his thick New York accent, smiling at Ronald like he hadn't even considered him as a suspect.

Ha. Point for me.

"She wanted to know if I'd seen the missing chandelier anywhere," Ronald stammered.

Man, he was definitely guilty. Maybe my presence hadn't caused this kind of reaction in him because I wasn't a cop, but Nico was totally capable of hauling him off to jail and throwing away the key. Or, you know, giving him a fine. That was the more likely punishment for vicious acts of gingerbread house destruction, right?

Nico gave Ronald a bland smile. "Did she?" Then he turned his dark eyes to me and flared them slightly before turning back to the kid. "Well, let us know if you find it, will ya?"

"Sure," he replied, looking uneasily between us before scampering away.

"What was that all about?" I hissed, looking over my shoulder and sighing as Ronald's scrawny form disappeared into the night. "I was getting around to questioning him about where he was when the house wasn't being watched."

"No need. He didn't do it."

"How do you know?"

"Because I was with him during that short window of time. I'd seen him trying to steal from your tip jar, and I was giving him a not-too-subtle warning that if I ever saw his hands anywhere near you or your tip jar again, I'd cut them off."

I balked. "You did *not.*"

"You're right," he said with a chuckle. "A detective would never do that. But I *did* let him know I'd seen him and told him he'd better be careful because I'd be keeping an eye on him from now on. There's no way he would have had time to do all that damage. Although our conversation hadn't lasted the full ten minutes that the room was empty, I kept my promise and didn't let him out of my sight until you closed up the truck and went inside."

Despite the cold, my body warmed at his concern for me. Nico Baretti came into my life like a wrecking ball, bent on putting me away for a crime I hadn't committed, and we'd butted heads at every turn throughout that process. This new development from bickering to banter would take some getting used to, no doubt about it.

But again, my shifting feelings for Nico had nothing to do with the reason I'd rushed outside without my coat and was now bundled up in his, so I shook my head to clear it and got back on task. "Okay, so. I've already ruled out Betty and Mr. Smythe, and now you're saying Ronald didn't do it. Who are your suspects?"

"Uh, did I miss something? When did I trade one Hewitt for another as my partner?"

"Since now, obvi. He's nowhere to be found."

"He gave up for tonight and walked Lexi back to the bakery."

I blinked, sure I hadn't heard him right. "*My* Lexi?"

"Is there another Lexi in Pine Lakes?"

"Well, there's Alexa Goldman, but she doesn't go by Lexi anymore because Dickie Willis called her Sexy Lexi in eighth grade, and it annoyed her so much she tried to get her parents to officially change her name. In the end, she decided not to let people shorten her name, so she's just Alexa now."

His lips pulled into a straight line in response to my long-winded way of saying that no, there wasn't another Lexi in Pine Lakes. Nico wasn't used to small-town peopling, poor guy.

"Why did Ryan walk Lexi home? It's not far."

He shrugged. "Don't know. I didn't ask. Either way, he's gone, and so are most of the uniforms. And my only suspects were the two you've already dismissed—though, to be clear, I'd come to the same conclusion on my own."

"Of course you did."

His lips twitched. "Anyway, I think that means we can call it a night."

I wanted to argue, but he was right. With no more suspects and most of the town having already left, what more could we do?

"Do you think we'll ever figure out who smashed the house?" I asked, glancing back at the community center, feeling a little like I'd been playing my Solitaire app and had no more moves left and no ability to tap the undo button a hundred times so I could keep playing.

"Probably not. But they don't call them cold cases for no reason." Nico sighed and shivered slightly, looking a little like a cold case himself since I was still wearing his coat.

I pulled it off my shoulders and handed it back to him.

"Thanks for the coat. And for ... well, thanks in general. I'm gonna go grab my stuff from inside before they lock up."

"You're welcome," he replied, slipping his arms into the sleeves and pulling it over his broad shoulders. "Have a good rest of your night."

"You too, detective."

CHAPTER 8

Feeling more than a little sullen that I hadn't solved the mystery surrounding the winner of tonight's competition, I trudged home from the community center with my eyes glued to the sidewalk. Mom and Gram had cleaned up the truck and driven it to the parking lot of our brick-and-mortar store before heading home to the bungalow they shared, so without the high of having solved the puzzle, all I felt was guilty that I'd shirked my responsibilities to the family business while I was running around trying to catch a criminal.

It wasn't like this was a murder investigation—a good thing, obviously—so it wasn't super important. The fact was, Mrs. Daniels had won the grand prize whether or not anyone thought she should have, so catching the person who crushed her house wasn't a matter of life-and-death. But I hated giving up on a problem, no matter how insignificant. And even though no one else seemed to think it was a big deal, I could tell Mrs. Daniels felt violated by the assault on her masterpiece.

Maybe I could stop by their house and see how she was holding up. I wasn't sure what good it would do as far as solving the mystery, but misery loves company, and I was pretty sure she was the only person other than myself who hated that we still didn't know who did it.

I rang the doorbell when I arrived on their front porch, checking my watch to make sure it wasn't too late. Something I probably should have already done, but oops.

Cory answered the door and gave me a smile and a nod. "Hey, Haze. Did you figure it out?"

"No," I said with a childish pout. "But I wanted to stop by and see how your mom was doing."

"She's not home yet."

"She's not?"

He shook his head. "Nah. She's at the police station, probably trying to bribe them into taking this seriously. I don't think she'll get far though."

I snorted. Mr. and Mrs. Daniels used their wealth to get their way whenever possible. Their huge and too-regal-for-this-tiny-mountain-town home was perfect for them, even though it stuck out like a sore thumb with all its imported artifacts and decor.

Cory stepped back and opened the door wider. "Wanna come in and wait for her? You must be freezing."

"Sure," I replied, not having anything better to do but go home and sulk about my lack of super-cop skills.

But when I stepped into the toasty warm house and glanced toward the high ceiling of the foyer, my jaw hit the floor with a deafening thud. "Cory Daniels, are you freaking kidding me right now?"

He followed my gaze, his face twisted in confusion. But then his jaw joined mine at our feet, and he blinked a few times as if he couldn't believe what he was seeing. And I didn't blame him. Neither could I.

"Are you seriously telling me you've been home for an hour and haven't noticed this?"

He gulped as his eyes flicked between my face and the ceiling above our heads. Or more specifically, the *empty spot* on the ceiling where the family's prized antique chandelier —reportedly once housed in the foyer of some British aristocrat or another—should have been.

"I guess I don't really look up when I come in?" He sounded more than a little embarrassed.

Giving him a small smile with one half of my mouth, I nodded. "I mean, why would you, right?"

"Right."

"So ... clearly the whole thing at the gingerbread competition was just a distraction for ... this." I gestured to the ceiling with both hands, still totally shocked.

How had whoever done this even managed to break into the house, use a ladder to remove the chandelier, and get out without being seen? Yes, most of the town had been at the community center, and it was way too cold for any neighbors to be taking an evening stroll, but man. They were crafty, I'd give them that.

"I'm gonna call Ryan," I said, pulling out my phone. He answered after the third ring. "Hey, breaking news."

"Lemme guess, you solved the crime."

I rolled my eyes and paced the foyer, my fingers pressed into my temple. "Actually, I *found* the crime."

"Uh, more words, Haze. I'm lost."

"While everyone was wrapped up in the gingerbread house calamity, someone was at the Daniels' house stealing their chandelier."

There was silence on the other end of the line for so long that it caused me to pull the phone away from my ear so I could make sure I hadn't dropped the call.

Finally, he cleared his throat. "You're there now?"

"Yep."

"Okay. Don't move—and don't touch anything. We'll be right over."

I thanked him and got off the phone, turning to Cory with a shrug. "They're on the way."

"This is wild. But ... I can't figure out the endgame. Even if they wanted to sell that monstrosity, wouldn't they be caught as soon as they tried?"

I bit my lip, thinking it over. "Well, I'm no black-market expert or anything, but I'm sure whoever did this had a plan for that."

"Probably."

"Where did your parents get it? I know it's some fancy British artifact, but did they order it online?"

He snorted, shaking his head. "That's just what they like to tell people. The real story isn't that interesting."

"No?"

"Nope. They got it at an estate sale here in town. Who knows where it really came from originally."

That had my ears perked. Maybe it wasn't that the thieves wanted to steal it so they could sell it. Maybe it had sentimental value for the previous family. "Whose estate sale was it?"

My old friend lowered his chin. "How should I know?"

Chuckling, I nodded toward his pocket, assuming he kept his phone there. "Text your mom and ask her."

"She's gonna freak."

"You don't have to say anything about *why* you're asking, just ask her where she got it."

He didn't look too sure, but he pulled his phone out and texted her. She replied right away, and he turned the phone around so I could see her text on the screen.

Marion Kemper.

And that name hit me like a bolt of lightning. Marion Kemper was the great-grandmother of none other than our teenage klepto—Ronald Draper. And I knew this because everyone thought it was weird that such a fancy family had spawned a brood of lowlife criminals.

But how the heck had Ronald pulled this off? Nico had already ruled him out as a suspect. But ... had anyone been watching his uncle? Or ... ah. Maybe even his other uncle. The one who'd gotten out of prison recently for *you guessed it*— grand larceny.

"I have to go," I said suddenly, making Cory's eyes grow wide as I moved for the door. "Tell Ryan and Nico what you told me when they get here. They'll want to do their police work or whatever, but I don't have time for all that procedural stuff."

"Where are you going? What are you talking about?"

"Tell my brother I'll be at Ronald Draper's trailer."

Cory balked. *"Ronald Draper?* There's no way that kid broke in here and stole this thing. He's like fifteen, and it probably weighs more than he does."

Not wanting to waste a second, I waved him off as I slipped out the front door. "Just tell them!"

CHAPTER 9

When I pulled into the trailer park where Ronald lived with his uncles, the place was dark and quiet. I didn't know how many of his neighbors had been to the community center with the rest of the town tonight, but if they were home, they were all settled in for the night by the looks of things. It was eerily still on the cold December night as I let my car door click shut instead of slamming it like I'd almost done in my haste to get up to the door.

Knocking softly, my mouth parted slightly as I realized how stupid it was for me to come here alone and not wait for my brother and his partner. But I wasn't known for being very patient, and clearly, I hadn't started playing it safe like Ryan and Nico wanted after the last debacle I'd been wrapped up in. *Oops.*

"Who is it?" came the gruff reply from the other side of the door.

"Um, Girl Scout Cookies." I winced. *Really?* That was all I could think of to say? Girl Scout Cookies sold by an adult in the dead of winter after nine o'clock at night? Right.

"Go away. Can't you read the sign? No soliciting."

I looked to my right and found a battered old metal sign hanging near the door. The letters were worn and the *n* in *no* was practically nonexistent. He should probably replace it, since the *no* was the key word in the sentiment.

But then ... *wait. He believes me. Weird.*

"Oh, this sign? No one ever means that when it's cookies," I replied brightly.

The door whipped open, and I found myself staring into the hardened eyes of Clarence Draper. He wore a white undershirt that had yellow stains under his pits and what looked like a drop of spaghetti sauce on the mound of his stomach. And I'd know. Being Italian meant I'd dripped my fair share of red sauce on my clothes, no matter how many times my mom and grandma warned me against wearing lightly colored outfits to dinner.

"Aren't you the coffee girl?" Clarence asked with the thick strips of dark hair over his eyes pulled so tightly together they almost formed a unibrow. "Why don't you just sell your cookies out of your coffee cart instead of buggin' people at home?"

"Um, well, good idea." Was he seriously still believing the cookie story? Whatever. If the biggest part of this lie for him to get over was believing I'd go door-to-door instead of selling them out of my coffee bus and not the fact that I wasn't an adolescent girl, I'd run with it. "I'll do that next time. But for now, can you let me in so I can show you this year's lineup of cookie flavors?"

I'd bought enough cookies from our local troop to know the lineup didn't change much year to year. And I also knew it wouldn't be cookie season for another couple of months. But since Clarence didn't, I pulled out my phone and Googled, quickly bringing up a photo of the cookies and descriptions for him to browse while I checked out his trailer. Surely, a massive chandelier wouldn't be easy to hide in such a tiny space, would it?

Clarence yanked the door closer to his body so I couldn't see inside. "It's not a good time. Sell them out of your coffee cart, and I'll buy some later."

Out of ideas—since this one had been ridiculously stupid anyway—I tucked my phone back in my pocket with a resigned sigh. "Okay, look. I'm not really here to sell cookies. I'm here to ask you a couple of questions about something that happened tonight."

"What, the gingerbread house nonsense? I had nothing to do with that. I left before it even happened."

I fought the urge to smile at his admission. Clarence wasn't the sharpest tool in the shed, and he obviously didn't think I knew the *real* chandelier was missing. Maybe he thought no one had noticed it yet. If it weren't for me, no one would have until whenever Mrs. Daniels made it home, and maybe by then he'd have stashed it somewhere.

Well, sorry not sorry, buddy. "Oh, you left early?"

"Yeah. I wasn't even there during all that. I dropped off my nephew so he could have some good, wholesome fun. That's not a crime, is it?"

No, it wasn't. But dropping off his nephew so he could pull off an elaborate scheme to steal a valuable item from an unoccupied house was *definitely* a crime. Larceny, in fact.

"What time did you leave? Just so I can make sure I understand."

He tilted his head, eyes narrowing into slits. "Okay, hang on. Are you a coffee girl or a cookie seller or a cop?"

"Um, coffee girl who feels bad for her overworked and underpaid brother who *is* a cop," I ventured, deciding not to touch the cookie thing with a ten-foot pole and hoping to appeal to his blue-collar worker vibes. This guy was in construction if my memory served me, so he was no stranger to long hours and hard work and could sympathize. I hoped. Then again, I was accusing him and his brother of theft. So maybe not. "I just want to help out however I can, and everyone was pretty upset after that house got smashed."

"Well, like I said. I didn't do it. I left the community center before the voting even started. Don't know exactly what time it was because I don't wear a watch, but there ya go. Is that all?"

I heard a sound that was almost like a wind chime—if it were made of crystals—from inside the trailer. Clarence coughed loudly into his fist as if he could belatedly cover the sound, so I played it off like I hadn't heard it. Was that Ronald in there messing with the chandelier? Or was it the thieving uncle?

Either way, there was no doubt in my mind the missing monstrosity was hiding inside, and I'd bet my bottom dollar that the other uncle had been the one to smash the ginger-bread house, with Ronald conveniently outside where he could be seen during the smashing, and Clarence at the house stealing the chandelier!

In my mind, a tiny version of myself did cartwheels. But on the outside, I continued to pretend I wasn't putting pieces of this mystery together like a prize-winning puzzler. Sure, maybe my brother and Nico would have reached this conclusion on their own eventually, but by then, who knew where this thieving trio would have stashed the loot?

"Actually," I said, smiling cheerily as the sound of gravel crunching under tires as Ryan's unmarked cruiser pulled up next to my car, "I do have one more question."

Clarence stood straight as a board at the sight of Ryan and Nico getting out of their car, then flicked his gaze back to me. "What?"

"Where the heck did you guys plan to hang your grandmother's old chandelier? Did you think it'd make a good front porch light?"

Fury surged through the man as Ryan and Nico approached. "That old lady never should have let her stuff go to that dumb estate sale instead of giving it to us. We deserve it."

"Sure, you do," I said with an eye roll. Then I turned to my brother and his partner. "Guys, I'm pretty sure the chandelier is in there, along with Clarence's brother and probably Ronald. Though, maybe you can take it easy on him. He's just a kid."

Ryan chuckled, and Nico blinked at me. "Oh sure, now you're playing cop, lawyer, judge, *and* criminal advocate?"

"And Girl Scout, apparently," I teased. "Anyway, I'm cold. Can you bust in there and wrap this whole thing up?"

"Not without a warrant," Nico said in a clipped tone.

"Does it help if I said I heard it clinking around? That's like, reasonable doubt … er, probable cause. Right? You know, that thing where it's like, 'I heard something so I can go in.' Boom, Sparta-kick to the door."

"You watch way too many crime dramas," Nico said under his breath.

Clarence wedged himself even tighter between the doorframe and the door itself. "No way. You need a warrant."

"The jig is up, Mr. Draper," Ryan said in an easy tone. "Considering the fact that the chandelier once belonged to your grandmother and your brother recently got out of prison for grand larceny, I'd say my sister hearing the clinking sounds gives us plenty of cause to ask you to step aside. It's over."

With one last furious look in my direction, Clarence moved back and pushed open the particle board door. That thing definitely wouldn't have survived a Sparta-kick. I gasped in delight as I took in the giant crystal chandelier taking up the majority of the living room area, looking a little worse for wear, but would otherwise be returned to Mrs. Daniels in one piece.

But then my eyes caught movement on the wall behind the chandelier, and I gripped the sleeve of Nico's coat as I stared at an ugly floral curtain dancing from the winter wind. "Look. The window."

There was no sign of the other Draper uncle in the cramped trailer. And since, unlike Clarence, he was skinny as a twig like Ronald was, that clinking I'd heard was probably from when he'd dashed by the chandelier so he could shimmy out the window.

"He's long gone by now," Clarence said with a sigh.

"Don't worry," Nico told him as he pulled a set of cuffs out of the leather pouch on his belt, "we'll find him. But for now, we'll make-do with you. Clarence Draper, you're under arrest."

CHAPTER 10

"Hazel, I can't tell you how happy I am that you figured out this mess. Thank you, thank you, thank you," Mrs. Daniels said the next day, grabbing me into a hug that nearly broke a rib. She was normally so prim and proper that the move surprised the heck out of me.

"You're welcome," I managed to croak into her shoulder.

She pulled back and squeezed my shoulders. "My husband thought I was crazy for how much I loved that chandelier, but just look at it. It's beautiful, isn't it?"

I peered over at the mass of crystals on the floor of her foyer. Right now, it looked like a mess, but with her money and connections, she'd have it repaired and hanging back where it belonged in no time. "It's definitely beautiful. I'm glad to have helped."

"Not that we needed it," Ryan said with a playful eye roll. He and Nico had begrudgingly brought me with them to return the chandelier to its rightful owner because Mrs.

Daniels had insisted on thanking me. "We would have figured it out."

Mrs. Daniels and I looked at my brother and his partner as if we were both calculating how long that would have taken them, considering their blatant lack of interest in the gingerbread crisis. If I hadn't come over here to tell Mrs. Daniels how sorry I was that her big night had taken such a dramatic turn, Clarence and his brother might have been long gone with their spoils. Once Ryan and Nico had gotten Clarence to the station, he'd admitted they were arguing over what to do with it when I'd shown up, but in any scenario, they knew they all needed to get out of there—and fast.

They just hadn't gone fast enough. Well, not all of them, anyway. Poor Ronald had apparently snuck out with his skinny uncle, and they were both in the wind.

"Hazel," Mrs. Daniels said, turning back to me without acknowledging my brother's comment, "I'm having a Christmas dinner party next week when my husband gets back from his business trip. We would be honored if you would cater it."

"Cater it?" I asked, not understanding my place at a fancy dinner party.

"Yes, hot cocoa and Lexi's baked goods. She can make a variety of Christmas selections for us, right?"

I nodded enthusiastically. "She'd love to and so would I. Thank you!"

"It's the least I can do. Dinner will be served around seven, so I expect we'll be ready for you around nine. But get here a little early so you can set up, and I'll make sure to leave you space in the driveway for your truck."

After a final bout of thanks, Ryan, Nico, and I said our goodbyes to Mrs. Daniels and headed into the bitingly cold morning air.

"I think we're gonna get some more snow today," I said, inhaling through my nose and then wincing from the icy burn. "I can smell it."

"You can *smell* it?" Nico asked with a sardonic smile as we reached the car.

"You're from New York. You're telling me you can't smell the change in the air right before it snows?"

He scoffed. "Trust me, smelling the air in New York City is nothing like what you're doing now. In fact, it's a health hazard."

"What are you even doing here?" I asked. My curiosity over that particular mystery still bugged me every time I saw the man. "Why did you leave New York and move to Pine Lakes?"

Nico's eyes darkened a little before he looked away. "Have you ever heard the expression curiosity killed the cat?"

Without bothering to reply, I reached for the car door to get out of the frigid breeze that'd just picked up. But Nico reached for it at the same time, and my cold hand collided with his, shooting a contrasting blast of heat up my arm when I jerked back. He didn't seem to notice, though, and wrapped his fingers around the handle and opened the door for me.

I eyed him dubiously. "I don't think I like the optics of

you opening the door for me when I'm getting into the back seat of a cruiser."

"Good. Remember the image," he shot back with a wink. "And Hazel?" he asked, causing me to stop with one leg in and one out.

"Yeah?"

"Great job on this whole gingerbread thing. I wanted to throttle you for rushing over to that trailer without waiting for us, but I'm glad you were able to keep Clarence from making off with it before we got there."

"Throttle me, huh?" My lips pull up into a teasing smile. "Careful, detective. You're starting to make me think you care a lot more about my well-being than you do about me sticking my nose where it doesn't belong."

Nico's face was so unreadable I found myself wishing for a translator, so I huffed and slid into the car.

"Want us to drop you at the Busy Bean?" my brother asked over his shoulder as Nico got in next to him.

"No, I need to go get Latte from Lexi and take her for a walk. The dog, not Lexi."

"Figured," Ryan replied. Then he cleared his throat as he pulled away from the curb. "Maybe I'll grab a box of donuts for the guys while we're there."

Leaning forward so I could stick my face between Ryan and Nico, I grinned wickedly. "Looking for an excuse to talk to Lexi, brother?"

"Sit back and put on your seat belt," Nico ordered.

But even as I did as I was so snarkily told, I didn't miss the look that passed between the two men in the front of the car. *Interesting.*

I HOPE *you enjoyed this mini mystery! Stay tuned for the next installment of the Coffee Truck Cozy Mystery series, where Mrs. Daniels's dinner party turns into a deadly night to remember!*

Click here to check it out!

For updates on that release and other cozy news and reviews, join Justine's newsletter at www.justinemaxwell.com.

About Justine Maxwell

Justine Maxwell writes cozy mysteries with brave heroines, strong family bonds, and a touch of romance. She has degrees in psychology from Northern Arizona University and Grand Canyon University. She hopes to one day become a reclusive author in a mountain cabin near Flagstaff, AZ. Until then, she'll be a busy mom of four small children and one (allegedly) hypoallergenic pup, writing in the midst of chaos.

KILLING THE CAROL
SAM CHEEVER

FaLaLaLaLaLa the songbird's dead.

It seems like a bad joke. I mean, Carol Ling? What cruelty of parental whim would make people name a kid Carol when her last name was Ling? But that's not really the point, is it? The point is her death. Or really murder. Somebody must have decided that killing Carol was the best way to…er…kill caroling. If anything would induce me to murder it's hearing myself caterwauling Christmas songs in front of an endless array of unfortunate victims. The term, "mating cats" comes to mind. Though, I'm pretty sure mating cats are more in tune than I am.

CHAPTER 1

"I'm pretty sure I don't need the corset," I told the flashily clad octogenarian clomping around my bedroom in a pair of hot-pink kitten-heeled slippers. Pinella Gerrard was an eighty-year-old spinster who thought she was a sexpot. And, since she'd decided to adopt me, I was currently suffering under her questionable expertise regarding the period costume I was being forced to wear for the evening's caroling event in the town square.

Humming along with the Christmas carols playing on TV, Pinella tugged the top of her leopard-spotted bra up above the too-low neckline of her pink angora sweater and pulled on the waistline of her yoga pants. "Of course you do, dolly. You want to look your best for that handsome Mr. Dietz, don't you?" She straightened the neckline of my dark blue velvet dress. "This color really makes your pretty blue eyes pop."

"Thanks." I'd opted to leave my long, dark-gold hair loose and curling over my shoulders. When I pulled it back into the bun I'd initially planned on, my rounded cheeks gave me a "chipmunk with a mouth full of acorns" look that wasn't flattering. Unfortunately, I'd gained a few pounds recently, as I always did around the holidays.

I sighed, tugging on the slightly too tight waistline of the gown. "I'll be wearing my cloak the whole time anyway. He won't even see me in the dress."

"He's not coming here after?" Pinella asked in her trademark New York City accent. She waggled tattooed eyebrows and winked at me. "Remember dolly, if you don't want him, I'll take him off your hands."

I nearly grinned at that. Dietz would not thank me if I told Pinella she could take a run at him. Not that I ever would. I was pretty much crazy for the guy. And I thought it was safe to assume he felt the same.

"You can't have him," I said, grinning at her. "Get your own guy."

"I been tryin', dolly. Your sexy neighbor won't give me the time of day." She sighed. "I've borrowed about fifteen pounds of sugar from him so far, wearin' my sexiest clothes. And he hasn't once taken the bait." She patted her rounded belly. "I'm pretty sure I'm wearin' those fifteen pounds of sugar in my middle."

My sugar-begging neighbor was referring to Doug, my mostly monosyllabic next-door neighbor whose medical use of marijuana made him jovial and laid back. But didn't do anything to make him amenable to the oversexed octogenarian's wiles.

Pinella eyed the corset. "Are you sure you don't want to wear the girdle?"

I didn't bother explaining to her…again…that it wasn't a girdle. "I'm not going to wear it. You can borrow it tonight if you want."

Pinella clapped her hands, giddy with excitement. Snatching up the corset, she headed for the door. "What time do you need me there?" she asked over her shoulder.

"Five o'clock. Don't be late." Technically, my neighbor hadn't been invited to carol with us. The event was only supposed to be for my community theatre group. But Pinella had all but begged me to let her come. And I'd heard her sing. She had a loud, beautiful voice. I was planning on standing next to her and mouthing the lyrics in the hopes that everybody would think it was me singing.

From the next room came a high-pitched warbling howl. I smiled at the sound. My dog Shakespeare, an adorable gray Pomeranian with bright button eyes, loved to sing when Jingle Bells came on. He had a very unique howling technique that I was hoping would drown out my own off-key wailing should Mrs. Gerrard somehow escape from my sphere.

As it turned out, Pinella beat me to the town square. She'd made an early entrance, giving one and all a thorough look at her get-up. I had to admit, it was memorable. Rather than the Dickens-esque, Christmas Carol theme we'd been aiming for, Pinella provided a stark injection of the seedier side of an 1843 Christmas. Dressed like a woman of ill-repute in a boob-lifting bodice that showed more wrinkly flesh than anyone ever wanted to see, Pinella was breathing a bit shallowly and her face was the color of beef sausage before it was cooked.

I stopped in front of the older woman and stared into her bulging eyes. "Are you okay?"

She offered me a badly-painted cherry-red smile. "I'm perfect. Don't I look pretty?"

Pretty was a stretch. Pretty, actually, was a terrible contortion of reality. But the desperate glint in her overly made-up eyes made me pull her into a hug. "You're gorgeous."

I left her beaming and went in search of the woman in charge. The square was filled with singers and holiday shoppers. Happy voices drifted over me in the brisk, afternoon air. A real pine Christmas tree consumed the center of the square, its multi-hued lights twinkling happily as piped Christmas tunes filled the air.

I spotted the woman I was looking for a dozen feet away and braced myself for the conversation ahead.

I wasn't at all sure that Carol Ling hadn't been selected as the committee head for the caroling event solely on the power of her unfortunate name. However she'd gotten the job, she'd taken it very seriously.

Carol gave me an angry, pinched look as I approached. The two actors who'd been chatting with her nodded at me and fled, clearly happy to get out from under Carol's judgmental regard. "I can't believe you invited people to join us," she bit out before I'd even had a chance to say hello. "That woman looks like a street walker from the eighteen hundreds." Given that Carol was a severely buttoned up version of the characters we were portraying, I could under-stand why Pinella's formidable fashion-busting style would offend her.

"There was really no stopping her, I'm afraid." I gave Carol what I hoped was an apologetic smile. "Everybody wants in on such a fun event. You've outdone yourself," I said, tugging on my velvet cloak, which was a deep blue like the too-tight dress.

Carol flushed, her pale green eyes narrowing slightly with suspicion. "You know the rules, MayBell. If she causes any trouble, you're responsible."

In direct opposition to her sour personality, her brooch of white, red, and green bells burst into a tinny rendition of Shakes' favorite song. He perked up as Jingle Bells played, lifting his head to howl his delight.

"Pinella is in her eighties," I said, avoiding Carol's point like the plague. "What trouble could she possibly cause?" I swallowed hard on the heels of that obvious obfuscation. My elderly neighbor was capable of getting into no end of trou-ble. And the idea that I had to babysit her nearly made me run for home.

Down by my boots, Shakes continued howling as Carol's Jingle Bells brooch burst into another Christmas tune. He danced happily as he sang along, his bright button eyes sparkling with pleasure.

"I can't believe you brought that beast," Carol growled out.

Fortunately for the health of his psyche, Shakes wasn't paying her any attention. His tail had begun wagging as the theatre group started to warm up their voices for the upcoming song-fest. I decided it was time to get out of Dodge before Carol spotted the other two people I'd invited. "That's my cue," I told her with a forced smile. "Time to get ready."

Carol flapped a bony hand dismissively. "Don't let that creature poop on the sidewalk."

I assumed she was referring to Shakes and not Pinella. Short of stuffing the offending orifice with cotton balls, I couldn't stop my dog from doing his business. But I did have a pocket full of plastic bags to clean up any messes he made, so I figured I had it covered.

"Yo, ho, ho!" called a familiar voice.

I looked up with a grin and searched the crowd for the owner of the voice. My brother Argh, nicknamed for the eye patch he'd had to wear as a kid because of rampant eye infections, strode toward me with the aforementioned patch adorning his handsome face. Since he no longer had to wear the patch to protect his eye, I assumed it was part of his costume.

Shakes barked happily, straining at the leash to reach his favorite uncle.

I watched nearly every woman in the square turn and stare as my handsome brother, dressed as a wealthy rogue from the eighteen hundreds, strode confidently through the crowd, leaving panting women in his wake. "Hey, Miss May."

I stood on tiptoe and kissed his cheek. "I'm glad you came. Where's Dani?" Dani Kraft was Argh's girlfriend. A kick-butt security professional, Dani gave my difficult brother a run for his money and I loved her for it.

"She has to work tonight. She told me to apologize for

her. She's really disappointed." He leaned closer and whispered, "Between you and me, it's a blessing. Her voice is even worse than yours and I didn't think that was possible."

I smacked him on the arm. "You're a horse's backside."

He grinned rakishly. Glancing around, Argh frowned. "Where's the other half of the dynamic duo?"

He was referring to my boyfriend and current partner in crime investigations. "Eddie's stuck on a case. He just texted me."

"He's going to miss the big moment," Argh said. "Wherein everyone in town learns just what a horrible singer you are."

"Nobody's going to learn that," I argued. "Because I'm going to hide in Pinella's shadow with Shakes as a buffer."

Argh bent to scoop up my dog, earning himself a plethora of doggy kisses on his nose and cheeks. "So, we're starting the program with Jingle Bells?"

I nodded happily. "With a follow up of Grandma Got Run Over by a Reindeer."

"A personal favorite of mine," Argh said approvingly.

"Shakes likes it too. By the time we get through those two, nobody will even know I exist. I plan to melt quietly into the crowd, mouthing the words as my two beards cover for me."

Argh chuckled.

"Attention, everyone!" Carol Ling bellowed. "We're behind schedule. We need to take our places and get started."

Bodies shifted and collided, apologies flying as we fought to take our assigned spots. Argh took a spot near my right shoulder and I glanced around, hoping Eddie would arrive soon. Somebody hummed a note and we all followed suit, synchronizing our voices.

A woman on the far side of our group cued us with the bells and we were off. Next to me, Pinella let loose, her voice rich and deep. Along with Shakes' clear, strident howl, my neighbor's beautiful voice was the perfect entertainment to draw all eyes to them.

Judging by the crowd's reaction, they were a big hit, leaving me in wonderful, relaxing obscurity behind them.

Then, the group swayed around me and people yelped in surprise as a tall figure with a head full of dirty-blond dreads pushed through the crowd. When the man spotted me, he grinned widely, waving and calling out my name as if the choir of voices around him didn't exist.

I sighed, trying to hide under the hood of my cloak. Unfortunately, the intruder stopped directly in front of me, lifting his voice to be heard over a rousing chorus of I Wish You a Merry Christmas. "Dude!" he all but shouted.

I put a finger over my mouth, frowning. "Shh! Sing."

An hour later, the ordeal was over. The group broke up amid happy banter, splitting off into groups to head toward nearby restaurants or bars. I stood in stunned silence, trying to decide if my right ear had been permanently ruined.

"Dude," the cause of my hearing loss said. He infused the single word with an ocean of meaning.

I turned to him, grimacing as he grinned and waved at my fellow thespians, who would probably spend their evening discussing his ear-shattering high notes and despair-inducing forays into the bass range. "How'd you find us?" I asked my medically-euphoric neighbor.

"That lady with the funny name told me where you were."

"Carol Ling?" I asked.

"That's her." He frowned. "Is that name a joke?"

"Unfortunately not." I stood on tiptoe and looked around. "Where was she when you talked to her? I need to ask her something about our next caroling event." I was going to try my best to get out of it.

Doug frowned. "She was over there." He pointed toward an alley across the street. "But she wasn't very happy."

"That's pretty much business as usual for Carol," I assured him.

"It's probably the name thing," Argh said, joining us. "I'd be cranky if my parents named me Carol Ling too."

"Dude," Doug said laughing. His voice was rich with irony.

"What?" Argh asked.

"Your name is Argh," I told him.

"That's not my name," my brother argued. "It's my brand."

"Whatever," Doug and I said in unison.

A shrill scream interrupted our conversation. Argh's head snapped toward the sound and he took off running across the street, his hand reaching into the back of his velvet breeches for what I suspected was his gun. I took off after him, tripped over my skirt and nearly went to the ground. A strong hand on my arm kept me upright. I looked up into the concerned and sexy gaze of Eddie Dietz, private investigator and my boyfriend. "I just got here," he explained. "What's going on?"

"Somebody screamed," I answered. "It came from over there."

He nodded and didn't ask any more questions, just fell in beside me as we hurried across the street. Eddie pushed gently but firmly through the crowd, towing me behind him. We jolted to a stop as we finally cleared the small group of people clogging the alley and saw Argh. He had his cell phone out and was calling for an ambulance.

I tried to see past him to the body draped across the filthy alley floor. Judging by the skirt I could see fanned out around a pair of skinny legs, it was a woman. A moment later, the tinny sound of Jingle Bells sifted our way. And Shakes started to sing.

I knew who the victim was. And judging by the stillness of the prostrate form, Carol Ling would never sing again.

CHAPTER 2

"Dude!"

I nudged Doug with an elbow. "Shh!" Pulling him to the side, I spoke in low tones. "You said Carol was upset when you talked to her. Do you know why? Was there anybody else in the alley?"

His shaggy blond brows lowered in thought. Given his predilection for medically-approved marijuana, my neighbor's thought processes were often painful to observe. "Nope nobody."

My shoulders sagged. It had been too much to hope for. "Okay. I need to find out how she was killed." I turned away, determined to find Argh and try to trick him out of the information.

"After those three people left, she was alone," Doug said, his brain apparently on a three second delay.

"What three people?" I asked, biting back frustration.

He shrugged. "They didn't introduce themselves, May. Even though I told them who I was." He shook his head.

"Such unhappy looking people. They needed to chillax. Life is too short."

I waved my hands in an attempt to get him to stop babbling. "Hold up. They were upset?"

"Dude! I just told you that."

"Describe them to me."

When he frowned again at my tone of voice, I apologized. "I'm sorry. I'm just trying to find out what happened to Carol."

"The woman was crying. Her body language was all closed up, you know? She was turning in on herself for sure."

"And the others?"

"Two men. One of them had a red face. He looked mad. He kept glaring back over his shoulder."

"At Carol?"

Doug shrugged. "Maybe. I guess he could have been upset about the overflowing dumpster. It's pretty nasty in there. I think I saw a rat. Though, it might have been a small cat with no hair on its tail. I only got a quick look at the thing."

Sighing, I rubbed my face. Most times, Doug could go whole weeks saying nothing other than "Dude," with different inflections to indicate his meaning. I suddenly missed those times. "And the third person?"

"He was upset too. It was probably because of the scratches on his cheek. Somebody really tore into that guy."

I grabbed Doug's arm. "Stay right here. I need to get Argh."

"Dude?"

"It's important. She might have DNA under her fingernails."

"Dude!"

"I'll be right back."

"We found the woman Doug saw," my brother the police detective told me. "I'm going to interview her later."

"Do you need help?" I asked, giving him my best "helpful sister" look.

Unfortunately, if there was anyone my acting expertise didn't work on, it was Argh, who saw the best and the worst liars and actors in his line of work. "Nice try, MayNot. Dad would have my head if I brought you along on a suspect interview."

"Dad" was Lieutenant George Ferth, Argh's boss and the uber-controlling patriarch of the Ferth clan. Argh was right. Dad would birth kittens if he found out I was sticking my nose into another murder. Unfortunately for him, Carol's death hit way too close to home for me to ignore it. "Come on, Argh. You wouldn't even know about the three suspects in the alley if it wasn't for me."

"Actually, it was your pot-head neighbor who gave us the information, but nice try MayBee."

I glared at him. He stared back at me with neutral cop face.

I sighed. "You know Eddie and I will just investigate behind your back if you don't let me help."

Our glares clashed for a long moment and then he nodded, his expression fierce.

Oh, oh.

I was already turning away, preparing to run when he called to one of the uniformed cops. "Baker, I need you to take my sister in."

I started to run. Behind me, I heard a bass voice ask, "What's the charge, Detective?"

I didn't wait around for Argh's response. Spotting Eddie chatting up an attractive female cop near the barrier, I shoved a rush of jealousy away and hurried over to them. Giving the attractive uniformed cop an insincere smile, I looked at Eddie. "We need to leave."

He nodded, recognizing the urgency in my expression, and waved goodbye to the cop. "Thanks for the info, Sarah."

I was already hightailing it toward Eddie's truck, which was parked across the street. Shakes yipped his disapproval of our too-fast gate. "Sorry, buddy. I've got the PoPo on my tail."

Eddie chuckled. "Argh?"

"He threatened to arrest me for trying to help with the investigation."

I scooped Shakes up and placed him on the seat and then climbed in after him.

"You know he can't really do that, right?"

"Maybe not. But he'd put me in an interview room for a couple of hours just to stop me from going behind his back on this."

Eddie started his truck and pulled away from the curb. Watching in the rearview mirror, I spotted Baker's oversized form as he ducked under the barrier tape and stared after us. He wore a smile that told me he'd slow walked after me, giving me a chance to escape my older brother's overprotective ways. I made a mental note to buy the big cop a muffin the next time I went to the station.

"So, I got some useful information," Eddie told me. He slid me a look when I didn't respond and correctly read my mood. "I was just trying to get the scoop on our suspects, May."

"And you couldn't get it from an ugly guy?" I turned to him, giving him the full force of my frown. "You headed straight for the attractive woman cop to pump for info."

Eddie gave me an unapologetic shrug. "My powers of persuasion don't work on guys."

He wasn't wrong. So, I relaxed slightly. "What did the beautiful Sarah tell you?"

"I wouldn't call her beautiful," Dietz said. "She doesn't hold a candle to you."

When I threw him dual raised eyebrows, he smiled. "Good save, right?"

I tried to hold the frown, but found it impossible. If my boyfriend was anything, he was charming. And he was right, women had trouble resisting his charm. Including me. I shook my head. "What did you learn?"

"I know who the woman suspect is. Would you like to go talk to her?" His grin told me he already knew the answer to that.

JENNIFER PLOTZ LIVED in a small ranch on an untidy patch of land that bordered a neighborhood park. It was a festive neighborhood, filled with blow-up elves and snowmen, with twinkling lights hanging from nearly every house and tree. Our quarry had a wreath on her front door, but no other decorations. I realized as we stepped onto the front porch, that the wreath wasn't even a Christmas one. Frozen red leaves and a couple of withered gourds hung limply from what had likely been a fall decoration.

Dietz rang the bell.

A voice burst from the silence and I jumped. Eddie pointed to the camera doorbell.

"I'm sorry," a woman's voice said. "I'm not interested in being sung to."

I looked down at myself and realized she thought we were carolers. "This isn't what it looks like."

"Ms. Plotz?" Eddie held his PI credentials up in front of the camera. "We'd like to ask you some questions about Carol Ling."

A deadbolt slid open and the door followed, revealing the slightly plump form of a pretty strawberry blonde with rosy cheeks and worried hazel eyes. She came out onto the porch in her stocking feet and closed the door behind her. "What about Carol? Did something happen to her?"

Eddie held out his hand and she took it. "I'm Eddie Dietz, Dietz Investigations. This is my associate, May. Can you tell me the last time you spoke to Carol Ling?"

Jennifer crossed her arms over her chest. I admired her long-sleeved tee shirt, which declared that she was easily distracted by dogs, coffee, and yoga. I suddenly wished I'd brought Shakes to the door to soften up our witness. "A week or so ago, I guess. She and I have been writing a song together."

Eddie nodded. "You're a song writer?"

"I am. In fact, I was the one who got Carol into it. She's written some lyrics that showed promise. I encouraged her to keep writing. In a year or so, she'll probably be pretty good." Jennifer shrugged.

"How did you two end up writing together?" I asked.

"She asked me to help her write a song to submit to songsub.com."

"Songsub.com?" Eddie asked.

Jennifer nodded. "It's a place where you can submit lyrics and music and hopefully have a known artist pick them up. I figured it would be fun, so I agreed to work with her." She frowned. "But I only did it with the understanding that I'd have top billing."

"Was that an issue?" I asked, sensing that there was anger behind that statement.

"I found out that Carol had submitted it under her name."

"That must have made you mad," Eddie prompted.

"Of course it did!" she said angrily. She made a visible effort to calm herself. "Sorry. It's still a touchy subject for me."

"When you last spoke to Carol," Eddie said. "Did you have it out with her?"

"I did. I told her if she sells that song, I'm going to sue her for everything she has."

"How did she react?" I asked. Knowing Carol, I could imagine how she would have reacted to the threat.

"She was belligerent. She claimed she'd written ninety percent of the lyrics."

"Did she?"

"Maybe fifty-five percent. But she didn't write any of the music. That was me and Jerald."

"Jerald?" Eddie typed notes on his phone as she talked.

"Another song writer. I introduced them. Jerald agreed to help me with the music on the project."

"Did Carol leave him off the submission too?" I asked.

"She did. He wasn't happy."

"How unhappy was he?" I asked.

"To be honest, I thought he was going to kill her. I've never seen him so mad."

"Do you think he could have? Killed her?"

Jennifer's gaze jerked to Eddie's. She looked genuinely surprised. "Carol's dead?"

Eddie nodded.

"How..." Jennifer sagged against the door. "What happened to her?"

"Somebody strangled her with the ties on her velvet cape," Eddie said. "It seemed very personal. As if the killer had suffered a personal injury at Carol's hands."

Jennifer stared at him another moment and then reached behind her for the door handle. "I've said all I'm going to say."

"Did you kill her?" I asked before Carol could disappear into the house.

For a moment our eyes met and I saw the cold calculation in hers. Then it was gone and I wondered if I'd only seen what I wanted to see. Without another word, Jennifer Plotz closed the door in our faces.

Eddie turned to me. "There can't be too many Jeralds in the music world."

"Let's go find him."

We passed Argh on the road as we drove away. I ducked below the window as soon as I spotted him and Eddie waved. I could picture my brother's rage when he realized we'd beaten him to the interview. "Do you think he saw me?" I asked Eddie, sliding back up on the seat and glancing through the rear window as Argh pulled into Jennifer Plotz's drive.

"He didn't see you," Eddie said, his voice filled with amusement. "But Shakes was peering out at him as we passed, so I'm pretty sure the gig is up."

CHAPTER 3

My phone rang and I answered without looking at the screen. "Hello?"

"Punkin, you're coming to dinner tomorrow night," the Lieutenant said in his no-nonsense way. "I'll see you at seven."

I glanced at Eddie, grimacing. "I'm actually busy tomorrow," I told my forceful parent. "Can we do it Thursday?"

"Tomorrow," he said. Then his tone softened. "I haven't seen you or the rodent for over a week. It's important to make time for family."

The softening of his voice reminded me of something I should have never forgotten. The anniversary of my mother's death. We'd lost her to cancer a few years previous, and the Lieutenant always grew sad and needed to be with his family in the weeks around that sad date. "I'll be there," I told him. "But I may be late..."

"Precisely at seven," he said. "I'll see you then."

I sighed. "All right."

"Your sister and brothers will be here too," he said, then hung up before I could say goodbye.

I slumped in my seat, earning a soothing kiss on the hand from my best furry friend. Hugging Shakes close, I buried my face in his sweet-smelling fur.

"Problem?" Eddie asked.

I didn't speak for a moment. Then, pulling my face from Shakes' wriggling body, I blinked away tears. "Dad's insisting that I come to dinner tomorrow night. The whole family's going to be there. I'm sure I'll get double barrels from them about this murder and my supposed interference."

He was silent for a moment. "But that's not why you're crying. Is it?"

He was too perceptive for his own good. "No. Mom died four years ago next month."

Dietz reached over and wrapped his warm fingers around my hand, holding it in a firm, supportive grip. "Way too many people die this time of year."

"I think it just feels that way," I told him. "Because there's so much pressure to make memories and have happy times during the holidays. It seems more tragic to lose someone during that time." I pulled air into my lungs and released it slowly, scrubbing tears from my cheeks. Then I pushed the sad thoughts to the back of my mind, determined to lose myself in the investigation. "So, how are we going to find this Jerald guy?"

"If he writes music, his name will have popped up somewhere."

"Do you have any connections in the music industry we can ask?"

"I don't," he admitted. "But I know someone who does."

DANI KRAFT HAD WORKED as a security professional for Eddie's old college buddy James Thomas. When James had to leave the business because of legal issues, Dani had been promoted to CEO of his successful security company. But it wasn't her experience in management that we were hoping would help us in our current investigation. It was her time on the street, working personal protection for the rich and famous.

"Hey," Dietz said as Dani answered the phone. "You're on speaker with May and me."

"Hey, girlfriend," Dani trilled happily. "You owe me a shopping trip. I'm coming up blank on a Christmas gift for your brother."

"I know. How about Friday evening after you get off work?"

"I think I can do that. I'll call you Friday morning after I see my schedule for the day and we'll set a time."

"Perfect."

"Now, what can I help you two with?"

Eddie and I quickly filled Dani in on the Carol Ling murder and what we'd learned so far. She interjected a few times with questions, but otherwise remained silent. "And that," Eddie finally said, "...brings us to the reason for our call."

"You want to know if I've ever performed PP duties for any music big wigs?"

"Have you?" Dietz asked hopefully.

"Actually, I protected Vonda Williams a few times. She's much nicer in person than she appears professionally."

"That's good to hear," I said, grimacing. "She seems pretty tough."

That was putting it mildly. Vonda was a regular in the music news due to a reputedly sizzling-hot temper and a serious lack of personal boundaries.

"That's all theater, May," Dani scolded. "You should know all about that."

"Touché," I said, ceding the point. "Will she talk to us?"

"I can give her your numbers," she said, her tone firm. "It's the best I can do."

"We'd appreciate it," Eddie said. We said our goodbyes and Eddie disconnected, glancing at me. "Are you hungry? It's dinnertime."

"I am a little. But it needs to be something fast, I want to beat Argh to the punch on the Jerald interview."

As luck would have it, Dani called back as we pulled into my favorite burger spot. She gave us Vonda's number. "She says it's okay for you to call her."

"Great. Thanks for your help," Dietz said.

"My pleasure. I'll talk to you Friday morning, May."

"Yes, ma'am."

Eddie wasted no time calling Vonda Williams as I nibbled some fries. The person who answered the phone sounded too young to be the singer. Eddie introduced himself and asked to speak to Vonda.

The voice on the other end rose in an angry shout, which it took me a beat to realize wasn't directed at us. "Sorry," the woman said. "These idiots don't know anything about laying tile."

Eddie gave a confused laugh. "Vonda?"

"That's me! You're Dani's friends?"

"Yes," Eddie said, glancing my way. "Eddie Dietz and May Ferth. It's a pleasure to speak to you."

"Not that way," she barked, which I was pretty sure was also directed at the tile guys.

I dove into the brief silence that followed. "We really appreciate your help. Do you know a guy named Jerald by any chance? We don't know his last name, but it's our understanding he writes music."

"Jerald Troka. The man's kind of weird. But I'm pretty sure he could lay tile better than this crew!" She shouted the last part of her statement, followed by the sound of footsteps, and then a door closing. "Ah, that's better," Vonda said. "It's good if I don't watch." She sighed, followed by the sound of furniture screeching across concrete. "Jerald wrote good music. Even great music, occasionally. But he just wasn't consistent."

"What do you mean?" Eddie asked.

"I've performed a few of his songs." More furniture screeching. "They were really good. Most of his stuff is trash. But he really nailed it on the latest one. He sent it to me to test my interest and I was ready to buy it from him. But then I got a visit from someone else who said she was working with the songwriters, following up on the submission. She said she was the artists' representative and wanted to know if I was going to buy the music or not. To tell you the truth, I wasn't wild about her attitude."

"Was her name Carol by any chance?"

"Hm. Carol, Callie, Kristine. I'm not sure. I don't remember names unless the person is important to me. My business manager would know. My instincts were to throw her out on her ear. I hate drama of any kind. It kills creativity. But that song spoke to me in a way nothing has in a while. I ended up writing a contract with her for it."

"Whose name was on the contract?" I asked.

"Just hers. She claimed the group wrote it under her leadership. I didn't care who I wrote the check to. I just wanted that song." Vonda made a disgusted sound. "Francis is always yelling at me for my careless business practices. I guess this mess proved him right. I should have demanded she show me her contract with the artists, but I didn't care enough to do it. Jerald is small potatoes in the music business. I'd be surprised if he even had a formal contract with the woman."

"Did she give you any proof at all that she was affiliated with the group?" Eddie asked.

"Of course. She had a recording of the song, which I did listen to. It was even better than I'd hoped after reading the music and lyrics."

"How did Jerald react to finding out you'd signed the contract with someone else?" I asked, sharing a meaningful look with Eddie. If the payoff was large enough, we were looking at motive for murder.

"Not well. My business manager, Francis, had to threaten to send the police to Jerald's home for harassing us. I tried to tell Jerald the woman had represented herself as their agent, but he wasn't hearing anything I said."

"If you don't mind my asking," Eddie said, "How much money are we talking about?"

"Just a couple hundred thousand dollars. Not that much because Jerald doesn't have a reputation to sell. But with me singing it, this song might have climbed the charts. For him, it could have meant the difference between Raman noodles for dinner every night, and steak and lobster."

Definitely a motive.

"Did you ever hear from Carol again?" I asked.

"Nah. She slithered away." Vonda laughed. "She's probably hiding from Jerald. I've never seen him that mad. I wouldn't have wanted to be in her shoes."

"Do you think he might have hurt her?" Eddie asked.

"Jerald? Not a chance. He's all bark and no bite."

"Can you share contact info on Jerald Troka?" Eddie asked. "Even a phone number would help."

"I can do better than that. My business manager should have the man's address on file. Hold on, I'll get Francis on the phone."

JERALD TROKA LIVED ONLY twelve minutes away from Vonda, in a mobile home park in the scenic hills rimming Asheville. The Mountain View Mobile Home Park was well maintained and sat on a pleasant lot with a white picket fence and an abundance of flowers.

"Looks like Jerald's creative streak runs to gardening as well as music," I noted as Eddie parked the truck.

"Off the top of my head, I wouldn't peg this as the home of a murderer," Eddie said quietly as he opened the pristine white gate and allowed me to precede him up a pretty flagstone walkway.

I climbed a set of curved concrete steps and knocked on the door. "What do you want?" a gruff voice asked. I jumped in surprise as a big guy with messy dark hair and a heavily pockmarked face came through the gate behind us. He was holding a pair of hedge trimmers and wore a scowl. "This is kind of a remote location for carolers, isn't it?"

"Ha," I said loud enough for the man to hear. Then I murmured to Dietz, "I should have changed clothes before we came."

The man with the trimmers wore khakis and a navy wool coat with a burgundy sweater under it. He seemed a bit over-dressed to be trimming bushes, and a few months past the time to do it. I noted the scratches on the man's pocked cheek and knew we'd found one of the people Doug had spoken to in the alley.

Eddie pulled out his credentials. "Jerald Troka? Eddie Dietz. I'm a private investigator, working alongside HPD. This is my associate, May."

I glanced away guiltily. Dietz hadn't said he was working *with* the Hillside Police Department. He'd said he was working alongside them. Technically true, if slightly deceiving.

"What exactly are you investigating?" Troka asked.

"Carol Ling's murder. We understand you knew Carol."

Jerald lowered the trimmers, a frown blossoming on his unattractive face. "Murder? Somebody killed Carol?"

"I'm afraid so." I said. "Have you spoken to her lately?"

Jerald stiffened, his dark brown gaze turning hostile. "You think I killed her." It wasn't a question. "Why would I kill a woman I barely knew?"

Eddie slipped the laminated card bearing his credentials back into his pants pocket. "We understand you had a motive."

When the other man bristled, the trimmers rising a few inches between them, Dietz held up a hand. "Mr. Troka, please put the trimmers down."

"I don't think so."

Dietz and Troka stared at each other for a long, tense minute. Finally, Troka complied, his gaze swimming away. He lowered the trimmers to the ground and stepped back. "I've never hurt a woman in my life. Yeah, Carol Ling made me really angry." He reached up to rub the pink scratch lines on his cheek. "But, *she* attacked *me*. I didn't attack her."

Dietz nodded. "Tell us what happened."

"We were working together. There are four of us. The idea was to write and produce a song we could sell to Vonda Williams. I'd heard she was looking for a new song for her spring album, and approached her about giving ours a look." He shook his head. "Then I get a call from Marty..."

"Who's that?" Eddie asked.

"Marty Sanders. He was going to perform the song for us. Marty sometimes does Broadway. He's got a great voice."

Eddie nodded.

"Anyway, Marty heard Vonda Williams had already

acquired a song so he asked some of his connections to get the details. Carol's name came up and I realized what she'd done."

"Jennifer told us you were planning to submit the song to songsub.com," I said. "She didn't mention Vonda."

Jerald nodded. "We were going to submit to both. Vonda was a distant hope. She only takes about one out of every five-thousand songs submitted to her."

"What happened when you learned what Carol had done?" Eddie asked.

"As a group, we decided to go talk to her." He nodded toward me...or rather my costume. "She wasn't answering our calls or texts, but we knew she'd be caroling tonight."

Motive and opportunity, I thought. Looking at Jerald's beefy hands, I knew he also had the means. "You found her," I said. "You argued and she scratched your face. Did you retaliate?"

Jerald's gaze snapped to me. He shook his head. "I couldn't have done it," he said, his tone impassioned. "I experienced childhood trauma. My best friend fell out of a fishing boat and drowned. It had been my idea to go out in the boat, even though I knew we weren't supposed to be out there because Scott couldn't swim. I've lived with the guilt of that day my whole life."

He apparently didn't think we looked convinced because he added. "I can't even kill a mouse. I've got one in my house right now. I went as far as to buy traps, but in the end I just couldn't kill it."

Tears ran from his dark eyes. "I'm not a killer."

"Could any of your friends have done it?" Dietz asked.

Jerald frowned. "I don't know. I doubt it. Jennifer's a victim of domestic abuse. She's scared of her own shadow. Marty just didn't seem that mad about what Carol did. He's a fatalist. He told us we could write another song. I don't think he understood how important that song was to us. It represented a ticket out of obscurity. For Jennifer, it was a way to stand on her own." He shook his head. "It was going to change our lives."

Instead, I couldn't help thinking, it had ended Carol's life.

CHAPTER 4

"Well, Jennifer obviously lied to us about when she last saw Carol," I told Dietz. Shakes was curled up in my lap, his tiny body a riot of gray fur the texture of dandelion fuzz. His brown button eyes were closed and his tiny chest rose and fell in sleep. It had been a long day for him.

"But I don't think she killed her," I added as we drove across town toward Marty Sander's home. "None of our current suspects seem plausible."

Eddie slid me a look. "I disagree," he replied. "I could make a case on any of them."

My phone rang and I looked at the ID. "It's Dani." I frowned, hitting Accept. "Hey, I didn't think we'd hear from you again tonight..."

"Stop talking and listen."

I blinked in surprise. I'd never heard Dani speak that way. Especially to me.

"I can't get there in time. I need Eddie to go inside and

see if she's still alive. You stay out of there or Argh will kill me. Stay in the car and call 9-1-1."

I opened my mouth to ask questions but there was screaming on her end.

"Dangit!" Dani was breathing hard into the phone, her voice wobbly like she was running. "Vonda's house," she screamed. "Hurry!"

"But...?"

Dani was gone. My throat closed up and I suddenly felt sick. "Dani's in trouble. I heard screaming."

Eddie accelerated. "Where?"

It took me a beat to realize what he was asking me. My mind was roiling. Then it clicked what she'd asked us to do. "No. She wanted us to rush to Vonda's house. She needs you to check if she's alive and for me to call 9-1-1."

He slowed enough to make a quick U-turn and roared off again. "Why not call your brother?"

"I don't know. But Dani was in the middle of something intense. I'm guessing she figured we might still be in the area and we could get there faster."

"Well, we aren't too far from the address Vonda gave us. We'll be a little early for our appointment, though."

I nodded. Vonda had agreed to speak to us in person the following morning. My heart started to pound. "What could have happened to her? Dani doesn't know if she's alive."

Eddie took a turn on two wheels and roared forward, the big tires eating up the curvy road. "Vonda must have called Dani in a panic. Dani's first instinct would be to call HPD, but it would take them a good forty-five minutes to get here this time of day. I'm not even sure this is their jurisdiction. It could belong to the Asheville PD."

The last thing Vonda needed was to be neglected in the name of a turf war.

Dietz whipped the truck around another turn, the tires squealing and then gripping, shooting us forward. The road where Vonda lived was beautiful. A forest of trees hugged the road on either side and arched overhead as Eddie's big truck flew through its curves and over its hills.

Vonda's driveway was gated but the gate was open. One side hung at an odd angle, as if something had crashed through it. Two giant wreaths sagged off center from the halves of the gate, their red-velvet bows mashed and ornaments broken.

The house was built into the trees, enormous windows looking out over the stunning vistas. A pond shone in the dying sunlight off to our right, a fountain sending the pleasant sound of falling water through the space.

Eddie braked hard and threw the truck into Park. Vonda's front door stood open. "Stay in the car!" Eddie barked as he climbed out. I promptly ignored him.

Following him to the house, I noted an array of blood specks dotting the curving concrete walkway leading to the door.

Eddie slipped quickly up the steps and tucked himself off to the side, his gun in a two-handed grip in front of him. He looked at me and frowned, shaking his head. "Stay down," he whispered, and I nodded.

He edged toward the opening. "Hello? Vonda?"

Silence met his call. He looked at me again. "Stay. There."

I scowled at him.

In a blink, he'd ducked inside the house and disappeared from view. I remembered Dani's instructions and dialed 9-1-1.

A gravelly voice answered after a couple of rings. "9-1-1 What is your emergency?"

"We're at Vonda Williams' home and there's blood. It looks like somebody broke into her house."

"Are you in a safe place?" the man asked.

"Yes, but my boyfriend is a private investigator. He went inside."

"Ma'am, please call him back. You should both wait for the officers to arrive."

"I'll stay outside. Just please hurry." I disconnected the call and shoved the phone into a handy pocket in my velvet cloak. Besides being warm and comfortable, the cloak was practical too. I was quickly reevaluating my hatred of period clothing.

Though I'd still rather eat nails than wear that corset.

There was a shout from inside and the pounding of footsteps over something crunchy. "Eddie!" I screamed, forgetting my musings as I dove through the door. I didn't get far before a large dark blur flew past, a fist slamming into my shoulder and sending me flying. I hit the ground, skidding across broken tile and slamming into an upholstered chair that was shaped like a hand.

In the distance, shrill barking told me Shakes' canine senses were working. He knew something bad was going down.

More footsteps thundered toward me and I shoved

myself off the ground, biting back a groan. If there was more trouble coming my way, I wanted to be on my feet to meet it.

Eddie ran into the room, his worried face softening with relief when he saw me. "Are you all right?" He grabbed hold of me and pulled me into a hug.

"I'm fine. But I predict I'll have a bruised tushy and a sore shoulder tomorrow."

He tightened his grip until I squeaked.

"Sorry." Releasing me, he kissed me gently on the lips. "When you called out to me, and he took off running in your direction..." Shaking his head, he hugged me again.

"Did you see who it was?" I asked hopefully.

"No. It happened too fast. He came up behind me and shoved me. By the time I picked myself up from the floor, he was running in your direction."

"The police are on their way," I said, my voice muffled by his coat.

"Good."

"How is Vonda? Is she badly hurt?"

"She was hit on the head with a crowbar. There's a lot of blood."

Right on cue, sirens blared in the distance. It sounded as if they were coming fast.

Eddie led me to where Vonda lay draped over a pile of tile boxes. Her face was too pale and she was twisted where she'd landed, one side of her face bloody. A crowbar lay on the ground beside her.

"I didn't move her, just in case she has a spinal injury," he said.

"I guess we can count Jerald out of this," I said. "He

couldn't have made it here ahead of us. At least not long enough ahead to have done this before we arrived."

Eddie frowned, glancing at his watch.

"Marty?" I asked.

"I'll be interested in finding out whether old Marty has an alibi."

"If that *was* Marty who ran past me, he's a big guy. He could have strangled Carol."

The sirens I'd been hearing were close, emergency lights flashing urgently through the window of the room where we were standing.

Eddie took my hand. "Let's go tell them what we found when we got here. As soon as they release us, we need to go talk to Marty."

In the end, it took a phone call from Dani to get us released. The uniforms who responded to my call seemed inclined to think we'd had something to do with the attack on Vonda. No amount of reasoning convinced them otherwise. Fortunately for us, Dani knew one of the cops and she vouched for us.

As we climbed into Dietz's truck, his phone rang. He put it on speaker. "Dani. Thanks for running interference. You're on speaker with May and me."

"Hey," she said. "Are you both okay?"

"A little bruised," I said, gently working my shoulder. "But otherwise good."

"I'm really sorry I sent you guys into that mess. Vonda called me in a panic. Somebody was going after her and all I heard at the end of the call was screaming. I panicked."

"I take it you're running PPD for someone?" Eddie asked.

I knew from hanging around with cops that PPD meant personal protection detail.

"A local politician. Someone tried to shoot her. I won't say I understand the sentiment, but let's just say the arrogance runs deep with this one. If you know what I mean."

"Got it," Eddie said, grinning. "EMTs said Vonda should be okay. She's lucky we got there so fast. Though the guy was still there when we got to her place."

"Seriously? What an idiot."

"I know, right?" I agreed. "We think we might know who attacked her. We're going to check on that next."

"Okay. Keep me posted. I'm going to the hospital. I'll see if I can speak to Vonda. If I learn anything useful, I'll let you know."

"Thanks, Dani."

CHAPTER 5

SHAKES SNIFFED the corners of the front stoop, his feather duster of a tail happily whipping the air as he investigated. The front door of Marty Sanders' house opened on the first knock. The man who stood in the doorway was tall and broad-shouldered, with dark hair cut business style, dark eyes and a square jaw. "Marty Sanders? We'd like to ask you a few questions."

"Are you cops?" His gaze found Shakes and he smiled. "I guess not. Unless canine cops have shrunk considerably since I last saw one."

"I wouldn't count him out," I told the man. "Shakes is a lot fiercer than he looks." Putting the lie to my words, my dog smiled at Sanders, tail still wagging.

Dietz showed his credentials to the man. "We aren't with the police, but we work alongside HPD occasionally."

Sanders settled a cool gaze on Eddie. "What can I help you with?"

I studied his demeanor. Sanders was a cool customer. He

fit Jerald's description of a laid-back guy pretty well. Though he was dressed in black slacks and a black turtleneck, his feet were bare and his dark hair was neatly combed away from an unlined forehead. He didn't look like he'd just committed a crime of passion.

"We've been investigating Carol Ling's murder."

Sanders' shoulders softened as if he'd been tensing them. "Carol's dead? That's terrible."

"We heard you had a disagreement with her tonight. You, Jerald Troka, and Jennifer Plotz."

Sanders frowned. "Where did you hear that?"

"Jerald told us the three of you confronted Carol in an alley at the caroling event," Eddie said. "We also happened to be there."

Sanders skimmed a look over my velvet cloak. "Ah, that explains the weird costume."

I gave him a smile I hoped would disarm. "To tell you the truth, I'm turning into a fan of the cloak. It's warm and comfortable."

He nodded. "I can imagine."

"Mr. Sanders?" Eddie urged.

The man sighed. "Jerald was telling the truth. We did confront Carol in the alley. She stole from us. But I can assure you that we left her alive."

"Where did you go after that?" Eddie asked.

"I came home. I'm not sure where the others went."

"Is there someone who can verify that?"

Sanders looked at Eddie, his dark brows lowering. "You think I killed Carol?"

"It seems like a strong possibility," Eddie agreed.

"I wouldn't have killed her," he said, looking at me as if I were the key to us believing him. "I didn't really care about that stupid song. We can always write another one."

His words were almost verbatim what Jerald had told us he'd said. "If you didn't kill her," I asked. "Who do you think did?"

He seemed hesitant to answer my question. Eddie and I stayed quiet, forcing him to be the first to speak. "Jennifer was really mad," he finally said. "I've never seen her so angry. She screamed at Carol for a full fifteen minutes before she stormed out of there."

His portrayal of Jennifer Plotz didn't match Jerald's. Troka had described Jennifer as "scared of her own shadow". The woman we'd spoken to hadn't seemed all that fearful.

"And Jerald?" Eddie asked.

Sanders frowned. "Jerald has emotional baggage. He's spent decades trying to deal with his friend's accidental death. I can't imagine how he'd suffer if he'd actually killed someone."

I nearly sighed. Everything in their stories seemed to line up.

"But Carol scratched Jerald's face," Eddie said. "We have an eye-witness that said he had scratches on his face after the altercation."

Sanders laughed. "She did slap him, but she didn't scratch his face. Were you aware that Jerald has a cat? Mean little thing. But he loves her to death."

I watched Sanders for a moment as he and Eddie talked, only half listening. Something about him seemed so familiar.

Then it hit me. "What were you doing at Vonda Williams' home tonight?" I asked.

He winced, the first real sign of emotion he'd shown since we'd arrived. "Why do you..."

I interrupted him, suddenly certain I was right about him. "I was the one you shoved down on the way out of the house."

Sanders closed his eyes, his entire body drooping. "Okay. You're right. I was there. But I didn't kill her."

Eddie and I shared a look. The man didn't realize Vonda was alive. "Let's go inside, Mr. Sanders," Eddie said. "I think you need to start from the beginning."

Sanders inclined his head, looking like a beaten man. He stepped back and we followed him into a small but elegant room, furnished with what looked like expensive antiques. When he caught me ogling the furniture, he gave me a wistful smile. "My grandmother left this stuff to me when she died. She and I used to haunt antique stores when I was a kid. It was our favorite thing to do together."

His sorrow lived in the lines of his face.

"You and your grandmother were close?" I asked.

He nodded. "She sang in the Italian opera. She had a beautiful voice."

And he sang on Broadway. It seemed he and his grandmother had more than antiques in common. "The pieces are beautiful," I told him, meaning it.

Sanders indicated a divan that was covered in forest-green velvet, and took a seat in an elegant chair upholstered in cream colored fabric with tiny pink and green flowers on it. Eddie sat down on the divan, but Shakes and I wandered over to the built-in bookshelves on either side of a crackling fireplace. It seemed Marty Sanders enjoyed more than just antique furniture. He also owned a full array of classic literature, the books were hardbound and covered in leather with gold embossing. I smiled at the Jane Austen section, skimmed my fingers over Ayn Rand and Edgar Alan Poe, and sighed at the sight of War and Peace and Anna Karenina.

As my mind returned to the conversation behind me, I turned back to the men, deciding I'd better sit down and pay attention. But a piece of paper on the floor beside an intricately carved wood desk caught my eye.

Shakes dove on the paper, no doubt intending to eat it if I didn't get to it first. Everything was food to Shakes. Dirt, rocks, grass, paper. He was discriminating in some things, but not his eating habits.

"No," I scolded him softly, tugging him gently away from the paper. I bent to pick it up, intending to drop it into a nearby wastebasket, and hesitated, my pulse picking up as I saw the words across the top of the printed sheet. *Purchase Agreement.* Below the title was the usual legal jargon with a place for the contractees' names. Carol Ling and Vonda Williams.

The rest of it was torn away. But I didn't need to see the whole document to know that I was looking at motive and opportunity for the attack against Vonda Williams.

Eddie's gaze swung my way and sharpened when he saw my face.

I walked over and handed him the damning scrap of paper. He scanned it quickly and nodded at me. Pulling out my cell phone, I dialed a familiar number. It rang three times and an annoyed voice answered. "Where are you, MayBell? You'd better not be elbows deep in my murder investigation."

I was very happy to deny the charge. "I'm not. But I need you to come to the home of Marty Sanders. We have reason to believe he was involved in an attack on Vonda Williams tonight."

Sanders jumped up from the couch, but Eddie was already standing between the other man and me. He had a hand on his gun, but didn't remove it from its waistband holster. "Please sit down, Mr. Sanders. I believe you've already created enough problems for yourself."

"You don't understand," Marty Sanders told Argh on the other side of the one-way mirror glass. "I only wanted to talk to Ms. Williams. I certainly didn't hit her. I could never hurt such an incredible talent."

Eddie and I shared a look and I barely kept from rolling my eyes. "Nobody could *ever* do anything bad in this case," I told him. "If I had a nickel for every time I've heard that today."

"You'd have three nickels," Dietz said.

Argh held up the torn paper. "Yet you claim you found her badly injured and didn't call for help. Then you ransacked her office before you left, and stole the contract between Carol Ling and Ms. Williams, destroying it. What part of that behavior screams innocence, Mr. Sanders?"

"I know it looks bad," Sanders started to say.

"It looks very bad," Argh agreed. "It looks like you fought with Vonda Williams about that contract, hit her in a fit of temper, and then searched for the contract and destroyed it. There doesn't appear to be a digital copy of the contract on Ms. Williams' computer either. I'm sure our computer forensics folks will find the shadow of that document still sitting on the hard drive. Did you know that nothing is ever really deleted from a computer?"

Sanders shook his head, running long fingers through his shiny black hair. "I only wanted to talk to her."

Twenty minutes later, Argh met us in the hallway outside the interview room. "It's clear he's guilty," he told us. "We're dusting for prints and processing the scene now. As soon as Vonda Williams wakes up and verifies that it was Sanders, we'll be able to close the case." He looked at me, his hostile gray gaze dark with anger. "Don't think this absolves you from interfering in my investigation," he told me.

"Vonda Williams wasn't an active part of your investigation," I told him. "Eddie and I just happened to be there at the wrong time."

"Right," he said. "Go home, May. Stay out of police work. Surely you have a funeral to crash or something?"

"I don't crash funerals," I told him, my teeth gritted. "I'm a paid participant."

"Mm hm."

I watched my arrogant excuse for a brother saunter away

and fought the impulse to box his ears like I had when we were kids.

"Let's go home," Eddie told me, flinging an arm over my shoulders. "I know a certain little dog who's probably frantic for a potty break about now."

CHAPTER 6

I was so tired I nearly fell asleep on the way home. Only Shakes' mania kept me awake. He was jumping from my lap to Eddie's as if he really had to go.

"I'm hurrying, buddy," Eddie told my little drama king. "We're two minutes away."

Settling the little pom to the ground in the parking lot of my apartment complex, I nearly had to run to keep up with him as he led me to his favorite patch of grass and I waited as he looked for just the right spot.

Eddie's phone rang. He glanced at the screen, throwing me a surprised expression as he answered. "Hey, Jerald. Is something wrong?" He listened for a minute, frowning. "Oh? Okay. Sure. Can you come here?" He rattled off my address as I gave him a curious look. When he disconnected, he said, "Jerald heard Sanders was arrested for attacking Vonda. He says there's something we need to know about Marty Sanders."

"How'd he get your number?" I asked.

"He claims Vonda gave it to him after we showed up at his house."

"That would have been about the time Sanders was at her house. Maybe he heard something," I said, feeling excited.

My doorbell rang twenty minutes later. I opened the door to find Jerald standing in the middle of the hall, staring at the force of nature that was Doug.

My neighbor glanced at me. "Dude?"

"It's okay, Doug. He just needs to talk to us about a case."

Doug frowned, eyeing Jerald from head to toe. "Dude?"

Jerald lifted his hands. "I'm harmless, I promise."

Eddie came out into the hall and Doug inclined his head. "Dude."

"Hey, Doug. Thanks for keeping an eye on things."

Doug skimmed Jerald one final look and returned to his apartment.

"Sorry about that," I told our visitor. "He's a little over-protective."

Jerald laughed. "One of the benefits and curses of living in an apartment."

"So true. Come inside. Would you like a beer?"

Shakes charged Jerald, barking unhappily. "Hey," I scolded. "It's okay." I gave Jerald an apologetic smile. "You surprised him."

Shakes quieted in my arms, his brown button eyes keeping a close eye on our visitor.

"I won't keep you," Jerald said as he stepped into the

living room. "I just wanted to let you know that ever since I heard Marty was picked up for attacking Vonda Williams, I can't stop thinking about something he said tonight in the alley."

"What was that?" Eddie asked.

My cell rang and I pulled it out, looking at the screen. "I need to take this. I'll be right back." I hit answer and ducked into my room. "You're not sending Baker over to arrest me are you?"

Shakes padded in behind me and dove into his kennel, a.k.a. the Pom Hilton. He circled three times and then settled down with a sigh.

"I would, but he's already told me he likes you better than me and won't do it."

I grinned. There were two muffins in Detective Baker's future.

"I wanted to let you know that Marty Sanders finally admitted to attacking Vonda. But he couldn't have been the one to strangle your friend Carol. May, the killer's still out there somewhere. So, keep your eyes open and your head up."

"Why couldn't he have done it?"

The bedroom door creaked as Eddie joined me in the room.

"He has a condition that makes his hands and wrists really weak. There's no way he could have strangled Carol."

"What kind of condition?" I asked.

"Peripheral neuropathy. He's under treatment, but he's physically unable to perform the type of gripping he'd have had to do."

The bed dipped as Eddie sat down next to me. I turned to tell him who I was talking to and blinked in surprise. The man sitting on my bed wasn't Eddie. I opened my mouth but Jerald shook his head, the gun in his hand mere inches from my face. "Hang up, May," he said so softly I wouldn't have heard him if he hadn't been sitting so close.

"I've got to go," I told my brother. My mind raced. If I let Argh go without telling him we were in trouble, Eddie and I would be on our own. Also, Dietz's absence was more than concerning.

Shakes stirred in the Pom Hilton but lay back down again, seemingly oblivious to the man with the gun. But he gave me an idea.

"No," I told Argh when he started to say goodbye. "I'll be late getting to dinner tomorrow. I'm taking Shakes to that new dog park and then I'll have to drop him off at home. You know how Dad hates my poor dog. I don't dare bring him along."

"May? What are you trying...?"

Jerald shoved the gun against my cheek, pressing hard enough to bruise.

"I have to go. Night, Mark."

I disconnected, but not before I heard the shocked silence on the other end of the line. I rarely called my brother by his real name. In fact, I could probably count on three fingers the number of times I did so in a year. Between that and the lie about the Lieutenant and Shakes, Argh would have to know something was up. I just prayed he took action. "What did you do to Eddie?" I asked Jerald.

"He's going to have a headache for a while." Jerald's lips

curved in a mean smile. "It probably won't be for long, though. I can't really leave witnesses behind."

Shakes whined in his kennel and I tensed, hoping he didn't draw Jerald's attention to him.

I spoke quickly as the man's gaze started to turn toward my dog. "What do you want? Nobody's even looking at you for Carol's death. I'm not sure why you're here right now."

He clucked his tongue. "Such a liar. I was surprised when you and your boyfriend showed up at my door. But imagine my surprise when I found out you're a cop's daughter. I know what you're doing. You're looking into Scott's death aren't you? Dang cops will never let that go."

"Scott?" In the Pom Hilton, Shakes suddenly jerked upright, his tail wagging fast and high, which told me he was on the alert. He bounced out of the kennel and through the bedroom door.

Hopefully, he'd heard Dietz stirring. I just needed to keep Jerald talking until Argh got there to help. "Who's Scott?"

When Jerald smiled, ice crawled down my spine.

"Oh, wait. Was that your childhood friend? The one who drowned?"

"Don't play dumb. I know you and your PI boyfriend are digging into my past. I can't let you pin Carol's death on me, MayBell Ferth. I can't let you drag up ancient history to hang me with."

"But you did kill Carol," I said, sick of his lies. "You doubled back when your friends went home and strangled her."

He shrugged.

"Why?"

"Why did I kill Carol?" He shrugged. "She annoyed me." He reached up and rubbed his fingers over the scratches on his cheek. They looked angrier than the last time I'd seen them. "It was easy enough to go back to the alley. Nobody saw me. Carol thought I was there to apologize for getting so mad. She never even saw it coming." His grin was terrifying. His eyes were cold and dead. I realized I was looking at a true sociopath.

"Why did you kill your friend Scott?"

"He kept whining about how he wasn't supposed to be in the boat. I told him he needed to learn to break some rules. But Scott wasn't a rule-breaker. He just didn't have it in him." Jerald shrugged as if he were discussing the fact that his friend hadn't liked mushrooms on his pizza. "One less whiner in the world."

"My family will come after you if you kill me."

"It's okay. I'm tired of this place, anyway. It's time to move on."

In the next room, Shakes was whining and scratching at the front door. Jerald frowned, looking in that direction. "And speaking of whiners." He stood up, waving toward the bedroom door with the gun. "Come on. That dog's annoying me. It's time to put it out of its misery."

Over my dead body!

I needed some kind of weapon. Scanning the room as he shoved me toward the door, I saw nothing but beauty products and discarded clothes. If only I still had that stupid corset, I could compress him to death with it.

Jerald gave me another shove and I stumbled forward. On a whim, I let myself hit the ground. I lay there for three beats, stalling. He kicked me on the leg and I bit back a cry. The last thing I wanted was to draw Shakes to me.

My dog was still scratching at the door. He started to bark and I called out for him to stop. Climbing as slowly as I could to my feet, I swung my gaze around the room but didn't see Eddie. I finally spotted his boots sticking out from in front of the couch. They weren't moving.

Anger spearing through me, I grabbed the first thing I could find and swung it at Jerald. The small but heavy metal lamp hit him on the nose. His head jerked back from the impact and blood ran from his nose. Unfortunately, he recovered quickly, punching me in the temple.

I hit the ground and the world spun. A furry missile shot past and Shakes launched himself at Jerald.

No! I tried to sit up, to stop him, but I was so dizzy.

My dog was a dervish, snarling and growling, flinging himself at Jerald and dancing away when the man tried to kick him. A gun went off mere inches from my head, and I screamed. The gun went flying, clattering against the tile floor of the adjacent kitchen. Shoving myself into a seated position, I fought to stay conscious, only to nearly be taken down when a wave of dizziness swamped me.

My eyes kept trying to close. I wrenched them open. My hand found the metal lamp again and I swung it as hard as I could, clipping Jerald on one thigh. It wasn't much of a hit, but it distracted him from my dog for a minute.

Then I realized there was another person battling Jerald. A person who wasn't wearing his boots.

Eddie punched Jerald in the jaw and the other man stiffened, wobbled in place, and slowly crumpled to the ground.

Pounding shook my front door. "May! What's happening? Let me in!"

Argh!

The cavalry had arrived.

CHAPTER 7

"Why was Shakes scratching at the door?" I asked my boyfriend as Argh led Jerald Troka out in handcuffs.

"Doug was out there."

"But why?" I asked, frowning over at my neighbor, who was holding Shakes and speaking to him in gibberish. Not for the first time I wondered whether Doug could be an alien from another planet. I smiled at the thought.

"May?"

"What? Oh, sorry. My mind wandered."

"It's no wonder. You probably have a nice headache. I'm sorry I didn't get to you before that neanderthal hit you."

"I'm fine. Tell me what happened here. Why was Doug in the hall? And what happened to you?"

Eddie grimaced. "Unfortunately, Troka caught me off guard. He pistol-whipped me. But he didn't hit me as hard as he thought he had. I managed to duck away at the last minute. When I shook it off, I heard Doug skulking around outside the door. You know how he does that scratching thing rather than knocking sometimes?"

I nodded. *Alien.*

"He wanted to come in but I wouldn't let him. I asked him to call 9-1-1 and wait for them."

"And you?"

"I was dazed for a few minutes, but when I shook it off I heard him talking to you in your room. I was trying to figure out how to get to him without putting you in even more danger when I realized you were coming out here. Then I jumped him. Unfortunately, I couldn't manage to do it before he hit you." Eddie rubbed the bruised spot on my temple. I grabbed his hand and eyed the red spot on his head. "I'm okay, Eddie."

"Well, MayBell," said a judgmental voice behind me. "This is another fine mess you've gotten yourself into."

I swung around to scowl at my brother. "Zip it, Super-patch. We've had a rough day."

Eddie's lips twitched, but he shook his head. "Your sister was no more responsible for what happened than you were, Ferth."

Argh's face flushed. Eddie's intimation was clear. If Argh and the police had done their due diligence with Sanders sooner, we would have been on our guard about Troka. "Anyway," my brother said, scooping up my dog and allowing himself to be kissed on the nose. "I'll see you and the rodent at dinner tomorrow. I think Dad misses this little guy more than he misses us."

Smiling, I said, "See you tomorrow."

He handed Shakes to me and left. Doug hovered in my doorway, looking worried. "Dude!"

"Yeah," I agreed. "Tough night. But we're all good," I told him. "Thanks for your help."

He cocked his head. "Duuude." His smile was gentle and sweet as he left, closing my door behind him.

Unexpected tears burned my eyes.

"Hey," Eddie said, pulling me into a hug. "I think I'll sleep on your couch tonight. If you don't mind. I don't feel like leaving you alone after what just happened."

Nodding, I said, "I'm good with that." Toeing off my shoes, I stretched out on the couch, pulling him down with me. "I think there's room for two." I closed my eyes as an indignant yip ripped through the quiet.

"I'm sure you meant to say three," Eddie said, a grin in his voice.

I murmured sleepy agreement. A soft bundle of fur snuggled up to my front, and I fell asleep as Eddie settled into place behind Shakes and me.

It had definitely been a rough day. But snuggled up with my two favorite men, life was just about as perfect as it could be.

Would you like to go on more adventures with May, Eddie, and Shakespeare? Visit the book page for the Grave Theatrics mystery series here: https://samcheever.com/books/#grave

ABOUT SAM CHEEVER

USA Today and *Wall Street Journal* Bestselling Author Sam Cheever writes mystery and suspense, creating stories that draw you in and keep you eagerly turning pages. Known for writing great characters, snappy dialogue, and unique and exhilarating stories, Sam is the award-winning author of 100+ books.

To learn more about Sam and her work, visit her website: https://samcheever.com

Sign up for Sam's newsletter and get a free cozy mystery novella: https://samcheever.com/newsletter/

O DEADLY NIGHT

ESTELLE RICHARDS

Gwen Russo, a retired opera singer, runs into trouble while caroling in the snow at her new retirement community.

O DEADLY NIGHT

Gwen Russo pulled the Swiss dotted curtain aside to peek out the front window. Snow, falling thicker than ever, thicker than the fuzzy little dots on the sheer fabric in her hand.

She picked up her mug of hot water with lemon and took a sip. Just the right temperature, hot but not quite scalding. It wouldn't do to burn her tongue before her solo.

But would she even get to sing if this snow continued?

She inhaled more of the sharp lemon scent, letting it soothe her nerves. Years of memories of drinking lemon water before performances bubbled up in her mind, crowding around like an appreciative audience after a perfect aria.

But snow.

She dropped the curtain and paced back across her tiny living-dining-kitchen space and stopped in front of the little white refrigerator. The apartment size fridge fit snugly in its two feet of space, and was short enough that Gwen could dust the top of it without a ladder. Nothing like the stainless steel monstrosity that had ruled the kitchen in Phillip's San Diego house.

She took another sip of lemon water. It was not the time to think about Phillip, nor about her feelings of anger or betrayal. The past was the past. She still had songs in her future.

Tonight even, unless the snow ruined things. Gwen set her mug on the itty-bitty kitchen counter and paced back to the front window to look out again. The flakes fell as heavily as ever.

She took her phone out of her pocket and scrolled to the entry for Marcia, the volunteer leader of the Christmas caroling group. Finger over the call button, Gwen hesitated.

Marcia Whitcomb, with her stick-straight chin length silver bob and sense of constant motion, was the mobilizing force of the Piney Grove Retirement Village. Head of more committees and organizer of more groups than Gwen could imagine even joining, Marcia could be a tiny bit intimidating.

She didn't mean to be, of course. Marcia was just one of those people born with more energy and drive than most. She made things happen. Bullied people into volunteering for tasks she deemed necessary. Energized the tired and prodded the lazy.

Gwen didn't want Marcia to get the impression that she was lazy. Tired, maybe. Gwen was alarmed sometimes at how tired she was. The cold she'd been so accustomed to as a child took on a sinister new character as a retiree. Many a night she'd gone to bed as soon as the sun went down, even if the northern prairie sunset came before five pm.

Tonight was supposed to be different. It was her first Christmas at the retirement community, and when Marcia asked which groups she was joining, she said the choir.

Now they were supposed to go Christmas caroling from door to door all around Piney Grove. That would be easy enough in the building where the memory care unit was and the more elderly and frail residents who needed full-time care.

But the independent living units opened to the outdoors, facing each other around a commons. In June, when Gwen first arrived, the commons was full of flowers, an idyllic setting for residents to meet at the picnic tables and benches scattered here and there. Now the commons was a solid white, lumpy with snow drifted over the benches and tables.

Singing in the freezing cold would be a challenge, but Gwen hadn't even imagined it would be snowing like this. She turned away from the window and told herself to get a grip. Marcia would have a plan.

She paced back to the kitchen to drink more hot lemon water and keep her vocal chords clear and limber. The telephone on the kitchen wall rang, its harsh jangle making her start. Had they all once used these old-fashioned things instead of the modern smart phones? They were part of the standard package at Piney Grove, and most residents used them for communication locally, saving the smart phones for grandchildren and the outside world.

The second loud ring brought her across the floor and she picked up the receiver.

"Russo residence, Gwen speaking." Old training died hard.

"Have you heard from Marcia? I've been calling and calling and she's not answering. I just don't know where she could be," a nervous alto voice said. "Oh, this is Patty by the way."

Patty was also in the choir, and had a nice voice, though untrained, and a tendency to rush ahead a measure if the director didn't keep an eye on her.

"No, I haven't."

"Oh well, I guess I'll just have to see her at the cafeteria. Can you believe how much it's snowed? Talk about a white Christmas. Oh someone's on the other line. Maybe that's her. I better go now. Bye."

Patty hung up before Gwen could speak again. The woman reminded her of Phillip's assistant Blake, a young man who had followed the director around like a puppy, always seeming nervous and eager to impress.

She frowned at the thought of Blake. His job as assistant to the opera company director gave him access to everything. Under his helpful exterior he kept a sharp eye out, secretly gathering every bit of gossip and dirt he could find. And look at how that had turned out.

She heated some more water and pulled out a fresh lemon wedge and a book. She would sip, read, and calm down before it was time to leave. She set the timer on the stove for an hour, so she would have time to bundle up in winter wear and walk down to the meeting hall for vocal warmups before caroling.

The timer beeped almost before she knew it. The well-loved pages of Hercule Poirot had made the hour fly by like a minute.

Gwen crossed to the coat closet by the front door. One thing that Piney Grove didn't skimp on was spacious coat closets. She took out her long heavy tan wool coat and bright blue cashmere scarf.

The coat, something she would never have needed in San Diego, had been a gift from Phillip's son. A going away present – or more properly a pointed send-off message – in place of the expected inheritance. They hadn't married, but he'd always assured her he would take care of her. His will, leaving everything to the grown son he hadn't seen in more than a decade, was an added shock on top of the shock of his heart attack.

She wound the scarf around her neck, pulled on a matching knitted hat, and dug the fur-lined gloves from her coat pocket. She let her long red hair, threaded with silver and tamed into its habitual braid, fall down the length of her back, under the coat.

Ready at last, she took a deep breath and opened the door. A swirl of snowflakes danced into the entryway before she could close the door behind her. She took out her key to lock the door, and wrinkled her brow at the slick sheet of paper she found on the doorknob. Who would leave a flier advertising a pizza parlor in this weather?

Not wanting to be late, she stuffed the flier in her pocket and left.

At nearly seven o'clock, the sun had been down for hours. But the carpet of snow and the blanket of clouds reflected the sodium orange light of the streetlamps, bouncing it back and forth, giving the world an eerie orange glow. Fat snowflakes floated through the tangerine gloom, lowering visibility even more.

Gwen followed the path to the meeting hall as it wound around the snow-filled commons. The fast-falling snow had already deposited a layer over the path, defying the rock salt the maintenance crew had spread on the cement. At least it kept it from immediately going icy. She shuddered, imagining herself slipping on ice, helpless and alone, slowly being buried in snow.

Reaching the double doors of the meeting hall, Gwen glanced back over her shoulder. Her footsteps were already disappearing under the onslaught of fat snowflakes, turning into shallow dimples in the glittering snow.

Once through the second set of doors, a cackle of voices surrounded her. The smell of coffee competed with the smell of wet wool. The meeting room's dropped ceiling kept all smells effectively bottled up.

A pile of hats and gloves lay on the long folding table just past the foyer, too near the coffee urn for her taste. An empty creamer cup trailed dribbles of liquid, straining to soak into all the nearby knitwear. She scooped it up and deposited it and some of its brethren into the trash can.

The tidier surface let Gwen relax enough to pour herself a cup of coffee. Black of course. The idea that any member of the choir would drink dairy before singing baffled her. Didn't anyone else have any training?

She took a sip of coffee – it tasted almost as weak as drinking hot water that had merely looked at coffee grounds – and looked around the room. The dozen members of the choir had assembled into their usual groups.

The three men stood together near the plastic Christmas tree. In San Diego, everyone was so afraid to offend anyone that they wouldn't have dared put up an actual Christmas tree. But in Minnesota they shrugged off such qualms.

A pair of women with dyed hair and careful makeup stood a few yards from the men, pretending not to study them. In a retirement community, the skew of male to female population was such that if a woman wanted to replace a dead husband with a live one, she couldn't afford to miss any opportunity.

The foursome nearest Gwen and the coffee urn all had their phones out and were showing off photos of grandchildren. Gwen knew from experience that she was welcome to join them, at the price of oohing and ahhing at their photos. But since she didn't have grandchildren, there would be no reciprocity. The grannies were not interested in other types of conversation or photos. At least, not with a relative newcomer. Not with Gwen.

She sighed in relief when Patty and Marcia stepped out of the ladies' room. Patty was in the middle of talking, as she typically was, but Marcia quelled her with a movement of her hand.

Marcia cleared her throat, and the room grew quiet as the choir members turned to their director. Patty sidled across the nubbly gray industrial carpet to stand beside Gwen.

"Thank you all for being here on time. We have a tight schedule this evening. We have agreed to sing one carol outside each individual living apartment, as well as four songs per hallway in the assisted living and memory care buildings, and finally our full lineup in the cafeteria."

Marcia looked around the room, making sure every eye was on her. "Management agreed to pay the staff for their time if they choose to stay late enough to hear us sing in the cafeteria, but the offer is time limited. So we can't dawdle our way through the rest of the village if we don't want to play to an empty room."

Patty leaned in to Gwen's shoulder and whispered, "Can you believe Marcia got them to pay overtime so the staff can listen to us sing? I wish I knew how she did it. Why, I can hardly get my son's dog to sit when I—"

Marcia's glare made Patty cut off the rest of her story. Gwen privately thought that Patty might be more persuasive if she could bring herself to use the power of silence once in a while, the way Marcia did.

"The lineup will be just as we rehearsed. Carol of the Bells, then Hark the Herald Angels, and so on." Marcia gave the members of her choir a long look. "Are we ready?"

There was a general muttering and murmuring of assent, punctuated by one of the men's bass rumble of, "You bet."

Gwen gulped down the last of her coffee and dabbed at her lips with a napkin, mingling the scents of coffee and lipstick. She threw away her trash and got her scarf, hat, and gloves back on. All around her the rest of the choir rushed to sort out their own hats, scarves, and dripping mittens.

The snow was still falling in a thick stream of fat white flakes when the group finally stepped outside. Gwen wondered if Marcia might call off the outdoor portion of their caroling, but she marched right through the snow and led the choir down the path to the first door.

Marcia rapped on the door and it was quickly opened by a short haired woman in a heavy sweater and corduroys. She stood in the open door, an eager smile on her face. Warm lamplight spilled out around her.

Marcia raised her hands to begin the song, and Gwen's heart skipped as the old joy of singing welled up inside her. She opened her mouth and let rise the lovely voice she'd been blessed with, and that she'd spent so many years training.

When the song ended, their audience of one clapped her hands like she was trying to get every speck of flour off them after rolling out cookies.

Marcia kept the choir on schedule, moving them on to the next door, ignoring the woman's call for an encore. Pinpricks of cold burst on Gwen's face as the snowflakes continued to fall.

They walked two by two, keeping to the path. Marcia and the three men led the group, followed closely by the two women on the prowl. The grannies came next, while Gwen and Patty brought up the rear. Gwen was glad to be last in line, as all those tromping boots ahead of her made the path easier for her stylish caramel brown leather boots with their smooth soles. They kept her feet dry, but lacked the practical rubberized treads of northern style boots.

A smooth flowing cloud of condensation left her mouth as she continued to control her breathing. Over the years of singing, the practice had become second nature. Beside her, Patty's breaths came out in little puffs with each step.

"I'm so glad Marcia let me join the caroling group," Patty said. "I sang in church choir as a girl, but I know I don't have

the best voice. It's so much fun going and singing for everyone, don't you think?"

Gwen nodded, her mind only partly tracking Patty's
chatter. Her tongue had found a tiny bud of lemon pulp
between molars, and prodded at it, releasing tiny bursts of
tartness.

The nod was enough to keep Patty going. "It's one of the
more prestigious groups in Piney Grove. Anyone can join the
knitting circle or sit in at bingo, but not everyone can be a
singer. And people love to hear us. I got so many questions
this past week about tonight's schedule. Nobody would miss
it, not even for a special episode of Jeopardy."

With a low whoosh, a small blue spruce beside the path
shed its coat of snow, leaving a ring of snowy lumps around
it almost like a frozen circle of toadstools. Gwen shivered a
little, glad the lumps of snow had missed the path.

Soon they reached the last unit on this side of the path. A
pair of blue spruce in the yard matched the older grove of
trees behind the building, giving it the illusion of being a
secluded cabin in the woods. When Gwen had seen Carla
Amundson, the woman who lived in the end unit, that
impression was strengthened. Carla wore her salt and
pepper hair in a long tangle, like a witch out of a fairy tale,
and favored long tie-dyed broom skirts paired with looping
strands of beads. The smell of patchouli clung to the woman,
and her low voice bore the husky reminder of years of
smoking.

Marcia rapped on the door. She pulled up the puffy red
sleeve of her coat to look at her rubberized black digital
watch. She rapped again, starting to frown. The choir,

waiting to perform, stamped their feet and rubbed their hands together.

Marcia knocked a third time, then shook her head. "You snooze, you lose. Moving on."

Patty clutched at Gwen's arm. "This isn't right. Carla was so excited about tonight. There's no way she would miss it."

The rest of the choir was already rounding the turn to bring them to the doors on the other side of the commons. Patty's eyes darted back and forth between the departing choir and the closed door in front of them.

"Maybe she went to the cafeteria," Gwen offered, hoping to catch up to the rest of the choir before Marcia noticed their tardiness.

Patty's lips twitched into a frown. With a last look at the door, she joined Gwen and followed the choir down the path.

The holiday decorating committee, no doubt led by Marcia, had done their best to transform the Piney Grove cafeteria. Artificial pine garland, wound with red and gold ribbon and twinkle lights, looped across the walls about seven feet off the ground, or as high as a person on a single step stool could reach. With the overhead lights off, Gwen had to admit the large, normally impersonal room looked festive.

The round industrial eight-person tables were covered with red tablecloths. Each table had a scattering of paper snowflakes and a candle in the center. Like the garland, the candles were artificial, or electric in their case, as the real thing would be a fire hazard. Consequently, the cafeteria kept its usual smell of lemon cleaner and overcooked peas.

The choir was set up at one end of the room, in front of the food service windows. The windows had their metal shutters pulled down. A green velvet cloth hanging across the wall obscured the shutters and dampened the sound reverberation off the metal. A rectangle of masking tape on the green speckled tile floor marked off the designated stage area.

Marcia had somehow found a real spotlight for the show. The heat of the spotlight on her face brought Gwen back to her days singing in San Diego, where the insular world of local opera fans all knew her name. A bead of sweat formed above her lip and she swiped at the saltiness with her tongue.

The seats were filled with residents and staff. Every eye focused on Gwen as she began her solo. Her pure soprano voice rose into the first verse of "O Holy Night." On the next verse, the rest of the choir joined in harmony.

By the end of the song, the show's closer, all the staff were on their feet applauding. Many of the residents pushed themselves out of their seats as well. A wolf whistle from the back of the room brought Gwen back down to earth. She was singing in a cafeteria in a retirement home, not on stage at the opera. It still felt good.

As they filed out of the designated stage area, Patty's fingers pinched at Gwen's arm, tugging her sweater.

"I didn't see her. She's not here," Patty hissed in Gwen's ear. The scent of mentholated cherry cough drops accompanied her harsh whisper.

Gwen ran a hand over her arm, smoothing down the sleeve of her sweater. "Who's not here?"

"Carla!"

Several people looked up at Patty's exclamation. When they saw that it was just Patty, most turned back to their conversations.

Gwen wanted to turn away too, wanted to bask in the admiration of the audience. She wanted to go back to her warm cozy living room, drink the single glass of wine she allowed herself in the evenings, and read a chapter of her Hercule Poirot book before bed.

But a glance at Patty's insistent face told her that she would have no peace until Patty was satisfied. Patty would pluck at her sleeve, call her phone, knock on her door. It was easier to just deal with her now.

"She's probably asleep in bed, forgot what day it is." Gwen knew her half-hearted protest would go nowhere.

"We have to check on her. What if she fell?" Patty invoked the horror that drove single seniors to live in places like Piney Grove. To fall, alone, and lie there unheard and unhelped. To end that way. Gwen shuddered.

"Fine. We can go knock on her door again." Gwen let herself be led to the coats and out the door.

The snow had dwindled to a few sparse flakes here and there, but the temperature had dropped. Biting cold seared every inch of unprotected skin. The night wasn't fit for man or beast, and Gwen wished once again that she was still in San Diego.

The snow on the ground had crusted over in the chill. Every footstep crunched and crackled. It was slippery, and

Gwen hoped those years of martial arts courses Phillip had insisted she take would help her fall well if she had to fall.

She remembered the concern on Phillip's smooth, handsome face after a series of break-ins in the parking lot of the opera's rehearsal space had turned into muggings. She could still taste the piquancy of the bite of pecorino romano cheese she'd popped in her mouth a moment before he announced that she would be taking martial arts. She hadn't needed the martial arts to protect herself from any muggers, and it had done nothing to protect her from Phillip's own son stealing her expected future. There wasn't a martial art for that.

Patty held Gwen's arm as they picked their way back down the path to the far secluded corner of Piney Grove. For once the little woman was quiet, when Gwen wouldn't have minded a little distracting chatter.

When they reached the door, Patty stepped forward and rapped on it, her rhythm an unconscious imitation of Marcia. She waited a few seconds before knocking again.

An icy wind rushed through the branches of the spruce in the yard, scattering snow and pelting Gwen's face with stinging ice crystals. The temperature had dropped so low that she couldn't smell pine any more, just cold.

She stomped her feet, trying to regain sensation. The smooth sole of her boot slid on the slick pavement, sending a shock of fear up her spine. A long-buried instinct made her bend her knees, which saved her from falling.

Patty turned to her with a defeated expression on her round face. "She's not answering."

The fear in Gwen's gut heated into anger, and she pushed

forward, brushing past Patty. Gwen banged on the door with the flats of both fists, pounding out a demanding crescendo.

A clanging noise inside made her stop. She leaned in and listened.

"Carla? Are you ok?" she called in her ringing voice.

No reply.

"Carla? Did you fall?"

Still no reply.

"Hang on, we'll go get help. The manager has a key."

A muffled voice from inside yelled, "No! I'm fine. Go away."

A gust of wind howled down the commons and shushed through the spruce trees, forcing clumps of snow out of the branches. Nature's snowballs hit the ground in a drumbeat accompaniment to the singing wind.

Patty hunched her shoulders and gave Gwen a helpless look. "I guess she didn't want to hear the choir. We should go."

She turned to leave but Gwen put a hand on her shoulder. "Something is wrong. I can hear it."

Snow pelted her face as Patty turned watery blue eyes up to her. "How can you hear anything over this storm?"

"Training. I didn't spend an entire career training my ear for nothing. We need the manager."

"Why?"

"That wasn't Carla."

All the color drained out of Patty's face, making her look like an under-baked sugar cookie. "It wasn't?" she whispered.

Gwen shook her head. "Someone else is in there, and they don't want us to know. We have to help her."

"Should we go for the manager?"

"You go, and try to hurry. I'll keep watch here."

Patty gave a doubtful look to the snowy common, then nodded her head twice. "Wish me luck."

As soon as Patty had gone, Gwen crouched down by the front door and felt around on the ground. The pavement was gritty with salt, but she soon found what she was looking for.

The welcome mat was frozen to the cement. Gwen pushed and pulled at it. It didn't move. She took off a glove so she could use her nails to try to pry up a corner. She managed to tear a fingernail to the quick, but the rug didn't budge. She stood up and kicked at the rug in frustration.

Her finger throbbed where the nailbed was exposed. She put it in her mouth for a second. The taste of blood only fueled her determination. She put her glove back on.

The wind howled some more, and she thought she heard voices inside Carla's place. One voice sounded angry. One scared.

Gwen closed her eyes, filled her lungs, and focused on her breath. There had to be something she could do. After a moment she opened her eyes again. Of course. Carla wouldn't put a spare key under the mat, not when the mat would freeze to the ground all winter. She probably had one of those fake rocks to hide her key inside.

Gwen crouched down again and started feeling around in the dormant flower bed next to the door. She prodded each mound of snow. The first two were a dead plant and a garden gnome, but the third surprised her.

A pile of slick paper rectangles with pictures of pizza and a hole on one end had been dropped in the garden. The blizzard had covered it like it covered everything else in its cold implacable embrace.

She pulled the doorhanger she'd found on her own door out of her pocket. It was the same.

She prodded at another pile of snow and found the fake rock she'd hoped for. A house key, the same brand and style as her own, lay cradled in the little plastic contraption.

Clutching in the key in her hand, Gwen stood. She took a long look over her shoulder, checking the commons for help. No one was there yet.

She drew herself up to her full height and repeated the breathing exercise that had steeled her for her stage entrance on many an opening night. In, hold, count, out. It was now or never.

Gwen slid the key into the lock and slowly turned it. The bolt slid back. She waited for a reaction from inside. Nothing.

It was time for her entrance. She pressed the handle down, swung the door open, and slipped inside. A flurry of snow gusted in behind her like confetti.

The layout of the room was the same as Gwen's, with the living room in front, flowing into a dining area and kitchen. Gwen would have expected tie-dye and psychedelic décor, but the couch was an ordinary green and brown plaid and the coffee table dark brown with built-in shelves underneath. A faint sweetness in the air, reminiscent of fresh baked brownies, wrestled with the stink of sweat and fear.

Two shocked faces whipped around and stared at her from the dining area. Carla was tied to a chair. A pile of salt and pepper hair was puddled on the floor by her feet. The younger man sitting across from her held a pair of kitchen shears in one hand and a skein of Carla's hair in the other.

The man looked to be about 50, too old for the acne that nested on his cheeks and forehead. He had dark circles under his eyes, and the lines around his mouth suggested a habitual bitter frown. He wore heavy boots, dark pants with fraying cuffs, and a faded sweatshirt.

Carla had a bright red streak of blood on her ear. The hair on one side of her head had been shorn off in choppy patches. In one spot there was a two-inch tuft of hair while in another the shears had been so close to the scalp they'd nicked the skin. She wore her usual tunic and broom skirt. Her feet were bare, and she clenched and unclenched the toes in a continuous rhythm.

For one long moment, everyone stared at each other. A fresh blast of arctic wind on her back shook Gwen out of her silence.

"Let her go!"

"Chris, it's over," Carla said, her low voice the whiskey rumble Gwen remembered.

Chris's lip curled into a sneer. "Over? Just because some old lady arrived? It's not over until I say it's over."

"Chris, be reasonable."

Gwen scanned the room, looking for anything she might use to take Chris by surprise, get the shears away from him.

"Reasonable? You stole my inheritance, and I want it back!"

"I didn't steal anything. Keith was my husband."

"He was my father! And he left me nothing. All those years, working for him, waiting for him to get out of the way so I could turn the business into something real. And for what?"

"We thought you liked working with your father. And I know he enjoyed working with you. Didn't you enjoy it?"

"Don't pretend you know anything about my feelings. You're not my mother," Chris snapped.

The only thing in reach was a light green throw pillow with a purple peace sign embroidered on it. Gwen put a hand on it, taking a slow step forward. Chris didn't seem to notice her movement. She would have to choose her moment. She took another step forward.

Carla tried again to talk sense to her stepson. Instead of calming down, his face reddened and he yanked on her hair and cut another hank off with the shears.

Carla was running out of hair. Gwen worried about what Chris would do when that happened.

He raised the shears again, a furious glint in his eye.

Gwen sprang forward and swatted at the shears with her pillow. The shears clattered to the floor. Chris moved to retrieve them.

Carla kicked out and grabbed the shears with her toes. She yanked them under the chair. Gwen hit him in the face with the pillow.

The distraction worked and he forgot about the shears, turning on Gwen instead. He rushed at her, arms out. She ducked to one side, put a leg out, and used his own momentum to flip him onto the floor.

Momentarily stunned, Chris gaped up at her. Then he growled and rolled over to get up to his feet.

Gwen couldn't let him have another shot at her. She sat on his back, hard, and yanked one of his arms backward.

He cussed at her and squirmed around trying to throw her off. If she could only remember the exact hold that would keep him down.

Chris bucked, pulling his arm out of her grasp. He was going to get up. Cold panic clawed at her.

She surged forward, trying to get any kind of hold on him at all, but he was too strong. She was in trouble. The self-defense classes hadn't been enough.

There was nothing for it. Only one other thing she knew how to do.

Gwen sang.

She let out a high C, mere inches from his head. Chris scrambled to cover his ears. Gwen filled her lungs again and sang like it was opening night, a shattering high note that reverberated around the room.

On the floor under her, Chris covered his ears and tried to pull into himself like a turtle into its shell.

When she let off her high note, applause sounded from the open front door. Patty was back. She clapped while the manager and a uniformed police officer rushed into the room to take charge.

❄

Patty, Gwen, and Carla sat around Carla's kitchen table. Carla had made a pot of watery Minnesota style coffee and insisted they stay and eat a brownie with her. The heater was working overtime to dispel the cold that Gwen had brought in when she left the front door open.

Carla had swept up her shorn hair and dumped it unceremoniously into the kitchen trash can. Gwen wasn't sure she could have done the same thing, at least not so calmly, if it had been her own long red tresses that were lost.

"I can't thank you enough," Carla said again.

"Please, it was nothing." Gwen took a sip of coffee to hide her face.

"And when you hit that high note? I thought you'd break every glass in the place." Carla chuckled.

Patty leaned forward, face inquisitive. "Is that really possible? Breaking glass just by singing a high note?"

Gwen shrugged one shoulder. "That's more of a sideshow trick, not really the kind of thing they encourage at the opera."

She took another sip of coffee. She hadn't understood why everyone up north made their coffee so weak. But maybe it was so they could drink it in the evening without worrying about getting to sleep. It was barely more than lightly flavored hot water.

"Do you think he would have killed you?" Patty asked.

Gwen rolled her eyes internally at Patty's nosy question.

"Honestly, I don't know. If you would've asked me last week, I'd say of course not. But I've never seen him so desperate before."

"So that's a maybe."

"I just feel lucky you arrived when you did," Carla said. "But I have to ask. How did you know to come?"

"Last week you said you wouldn't miss the caroling for the world," Patty said. "We were in the cafeteria waiting for them to refill the salad bar. I remembered thinking it was kind of funny, because I never think of hippie types as being religious, but caroling is definitely religious. Or at least it is to me. So many songs about the Savior's birth."

"I'm glad you remembered. Most people hardly listen, but you do."

Gwen blinked. Carla was right. Patty was gossipy because she listened and cared. Maybe she had misjudged the round little woman.

Carla put her hand over Gwen's, clasping it warmly. "I'm so lucky to have friends like you. I really can't thank you enough."

Gwen looked in her eyes. Carla had lost half her hair and been threatened by her own stepson, but was overflowing with gratitude. Maybe the old hippie was on to something.

Gwen smiled at her and clasped her hand, then took Patty's hand as well. "I feel like the real lucky one tonight."

"Me too," Patty said. "Now who wants to sing some carols?"

About Estelle Richards

Estelle Richards writes the Lisa Chance Cozy Mysteries and the March Street Cozy Mysteries. Find her online at www. EstelleRichards.com.

SILENT SNICKERDOODLE

ELLIE BALLARD

When restaurateur and reluctant sleuth Marnie Tipton enters the Clear Springs Holiday Cookie Exchange, she expects more fierce competition than friendly exchange. But when the contest judge suddenly collapses, Marnie suspects a Grinch has come to town. Can she find the saboteur before it's too late?

CHAPTER 1

THE PITIFUL SLICE-AND-BAKE discs stared up at me from their aluminum resting place while my boots printed tracks in the fresh blanket of snow. Thanks to an on-the-fritz coffee maker during breakfast service, I was, as usual, running late. The treats from Price Barn's refrigerated section emerged from my oven only twenty minutes earlier, crisp around the edges with still-gooey centers which didn't set in time for my departure. Despite my best attempts to ease into the turns, the inked-on designs shifted on the slippery ride over. Still, if I squinted, I could kinda sorta make out the shape of a Christmas tree or snowman.

It's for the less fortunate, Marnie Tipton.

The reminder looped on repeat in my brain, willing me to take each step forward. In Clear Springs, sitting out the annual cookie competition — and forgoing the entry fee to be donated to the local food bank — was the pinnacle of poor manners. Every local business and wannabe *Great*

British Bake Off champ was expected to submit something or risk being the subject of a Santa-sized scandal.

Even if that something was nothing more than a pile of goopy dough.

The food bank was Old Reliable for us Tiptons during the leaner moments of my childhood. Mom was either between jobs or making an emergency exit from an ill-fated relationship when I'd spied her flipping over couch cushions, hunting for loose change. Having a guaranteed next meal made the scary times seem a little less frightening.

So, entering was the least I could do. Plus, I'd already skipped last year's competition to grieve Stu's death. My one time exemption was all used up.

Strands of garland decorated Coyne Pavilion's Doric columns with a cheery red ribbon tied around each. A banner hailing the *CommUNITY Holiday Cookie Exchange!* provided a threshold between your run-of-the-mill small town holiday charm into an all-out seasonal spectacle.

You would never know that the Pavilion was the same place I spent my fifteenth summer shoveling horse dung from the stalls to make some extra cash. Today it was a full-blown winter wonderland, complete with fake snow and a live nativity manned by Bill Jenkins and his two boys. But an air of competition filtered through the atmosphere that even Blake Shelton's honky-tonk rendition of "Jingle Bell Rock" couldn't drown out.

I glided past the Rotary Club's Giving Tree. Cutout paper tags in the shape of presents hung from the branches. Each tag contained the name and wishlist of a patient at the regional Children's Hospital who wouldn't be spending the holidays at home this year. I paused and plucked a few at random for The Pumphouse to sponsor and shoved them in my pocket.

Candlelight flickered from the life-sized menorah and kinara that flanked each side of the tree, and a rotund Kris Kringle, who looked an awful lot like Bert Phelps, roamed the interior, handing out candy canes and *Ho-Ho-Hos!* to children as they scurried past.

Dina spotted me from her perch at the far end. She and her husband Grizzy were trying — and failing — to referee a contentious game of dreidel between a gang of miniature Santa's elves who had descended into full-on sugar highs. Through the chaos, I spied their own kids Bear and Olivia behind the disguises' cartoonish costumes. My best friend gave me a sad, helpless wave.

I pushed toward the enormous crowd amassed in front of the judging table. The contest's sole judge and my most loyal customer, Orville Johnson, sat upon his throne, holding court while we peasants awaited his final vote on the year's *best* cookie.

"Best" didn't exactly come with a clear-cut matrix of criteria, though. That designation was subject to Orville's whims from one year to the next. Three years ago, he catapulted anything containing mint to the top slots. Two years back, it was cloves. Rumor had it that a legendary spreadsheet circulated around town, documenting the top three cookies each year since 1971. It didn't seem to help anyone, though.

"Marnie has an unfair advantage," Amber Easton pouted aloud as I made my way through the sea of people. Pairs of suspicious eyes trained on me. "Orville eats at her restaurant every day. She knows exactly what he likes!"

I contemplated whether to respond to my least grateful customer when a shock of gray cropped hair atop a white coat scurried by me.

"I'm coming, I'm coming!" Prudence Harrington called out to nobody in particular, her short legs making a mad dash toward the entry table. She waved a large Tupperware in one hand and a fistful of dollars in the other.

At least I wasn't the *very* last person to arrive.

The tidy pharmacist pushed her way to the front of the line and dropped one inviting sugary creation on the judging platter and shoved the money and container into the arms of volunteer Celeste Edwards. Then, without grabbing a Baker's Choice slip, Pru turned and sped away just as quick as she'd arrived.

"One day, the pharmacy will give me time to eat a real lunch!" The older woman threw her hands up in the air as she ran.

"Marnie!" Celeste leaned over the entry table and wrapped me in a hug. Her greenhouse, Fine Vines, had graciously donated a sleigh-full — okay, a Subaru-full — of red and white poinsettias for the event. "I was wondering when you'd arrive with your—"

My distant cousin took the aluminum carrier from my hands and examined the contents. Her lips twitched with the hint of a frown.

"The nostalgia!" She forced the corners of her mouth upwards. "I used to beg my mama to get these whenever they started showing up at the supermarket."

"Thanks." I couldn't bear to look at her.

"Y'know, everyone's been talking about the salted caramel linzers an anonymous baker left in the Methodist Church's Little Free Pantry. One of the Rotary ladies tried one and can't stop raving about them."

An unseasonable heat crept up my neck and spread across my cheeks as I recalled the perfectly cut treats I left in the pantry before an early morning shift last week. "Oh?"

"We've all been waiting to see if the baker would show up and submit them." She tilted her head low to find my eyes. "Y'know, I kinda suspected *you*."

A boisterous, nervous laughter erupted from me. "Oh, don't be ridiculous. I do food, Celeste, not baked goods." My baking proficiency wasn't something I felt prepared to debut. Not now. Maybe not ever. A bit of shame over a pathetic entry was a heck of a lot better than pressure to perform.

"Well, get to tastin' then." She handed me a ballot then waved me on down the line.

The Baker's Choice competition emerged five years earlier as a grassroots rebellion against Orville's dictatorial tendencies. Expanding the court of judges was out of the question; nobody wanted to risk Orville blowing a gasket at the suggestion. So a secondary competition was born to put some power back into the hands of the people.

I stepped into line and started loading the plate with one of each cookie.

"Competition gets steeper every year." I turned to greet the sweet voice behind me, only to come face-to-face with a crazed-looking reindeer with googly eyes staring back at me from its spot-on Maggie McHugh's ugly Christmas sweater.

The reclusive librarian's presence was a testament to the contest's rich tradition in this town. *Nobody* missed it.

"Where do people even get the ideas for these things?" I plucked a particularly impressive homemade Mallomar concoction and examined it from all angles. Every cookie on the table was more impressive than the last.

"Netflix." She winked at me as we loaded up side-by-side.

"We ought to be gettin' back, Maggie." A deep voice drawled behind us.

Out of the corner of my eye, I identified Greg Johnson's lean silhouette. One part inventor, one part sleazeball odd jobber. A few years back, a rumor went around town implicating him in the disappearance of the pit boss at the casino. He was also my mother's ex-*something*. I mean, did he really get to qualify as an ex-boyfriend if he'd been secretly married while they lived together?

"Don't be ridiculous." Maggie swatted a hand in his direction. "We haven't tried a single cookie yet! Plus, don't you wanna see your uncle pick his winner?" Maggie jerked her head in Orville's direction.

"That old bag hates peppermint." The irritation in his voice matched his squirmy body language. A blizzard of sadness came over me. Most of Orville's loved ones were dead, and clearly he wasn't close to his living family, either. "He ain't picking your white-chocolate-whatever."

"White chocolate peppermint cookies are a holiday classic." Maggie smoothed a fuzzy antler on her sweater.

"You two got somewhere better than this to be?" My words came out with more of an edge than I'd intended.

"Greg's been helping me out with all those dang computers we bought for the library. He needs the money and I need the help. But we're taking a paid lunch to enjoy the festivities."

With full plates, we watched Celeste make the final adjustments to Orville's clip-on mic before he dug into his first taste.

"Ugh, gingerbread." He forced a single bite down and discarded the headless body. "Next."

A worried murmur filtered through the crowd. The judge was going to be tougher than usual to please today.

The old man lifted the pillowy concoction Prudence dropped off and chomped in. Everyone waited with bated breath.

"Hmmm." He chewed and considered the flavor profile. "*Licorice*. Interesting. It's like a licorice sugar cookie, but fluffier. Subtle, sweet, and just a touch salty. A perfectly balanced, but bold cookie." Orville settled his spectacled gaze on the audience as he took a second, rather large bite. "And I like a bold baker."

A buzz circulated. A few onlookers tossed their hands up in defeat. If this was any indication, the old man favored strong, unique flavors this year. He lifted a spiral notebook close to his face to scribble a thought.

"Yeeeeow!" He screamed into his microphone, shaking his hand like it was a Yule log on fire. "Celeste, grab my clottin' powder from my coat pocket!"

As the townsfolk scurried into action, I spotted a trail of blood rolling across his palm. Maggie ran to his side with her phone's keypad lit up.

"Aw, calm down." Orville snapped. "It's just a dang paper cut."

Celeste sprinkled a few drops of powder onto the cut and delicately wrapped a small bandage around the finger. Once finished, she leaned over and whispered something in his ear.

"Heck yeah, I'm fit to continue!" The crisis averted, several hoots and hollers encouraged him on as he lifted the next cookie.

"Maggie, time's wastin'. I really need to run that update or the entire network's going to be trash." Greg tapped his foot with a scowl. "Plus, I hate cookies. And the holidays."

"And fidelity," I muttered low.

"You got something to say, Tipton?"

"Alright, alright, quit yapping." Maggie stepped in between us. "I need to prepare for this evening's special holiday edition of *Miss Maggie's Hour of Magic and Mischief*, anyway."

Watching her sagging shoulders as they made their way out of the hall, I wondered when her next opportunity to escape the confines of her book stacks would be.

I turned back to watch Orville work his way through the gigantic platter of cookies. With every bite, he offered his public commentary.

"Too tough."

"The caramel sticks to my teeth."

"Brown butter anything is a winner in my book."

"This supposed to be some joke?" He held out my misshapen attempt at an entry and received a few laughs in response.

When one last cookie remained, Orville dusted off his plaid shirt, and smoothed the napkin draped from his collar. Then he waved the cookie at the crowd and flashed a wide, streaky red grin.

The audience traded looks of concern.

"Hey, Orv, that notebook get yer gums, too? They're bleedin'!" A voice shouted out from the front.

"Huh?" Orville looked outward with vacant eyes. "Well, uh, maybe those dang toasted coconut concoctions must've cut 'em up." His words slurred together.

Then this town's biggest Scrooge began to sway from side-to-side in his seat. Before he said another word, a stream of blood oozed from his nose and dripped right onto the last cookie.

A few shrieks sounded around the Pavilion.

"I just need a minute..." Without another word, Orville darted from his seat and towards the restrooms.

Ken Marshall emerged from the crowd and rushed after him, a wad of napkins clutched in his fist. I fished my phone from my pocket, dialed those three trusty numbers, and followed Ken.

"9-1-1 what's your emergency?"

"I need an ambulance out at Coyne Pavilion."

"Oh dear," the operator on the other end sighed. "You didn't hear about the big pile-up out on the highway? A quarter-inch of ice is covering the bridge and all our vehicles are out there. Tons of injuries. I can try to pull one of them off, but it could be a while."

I poked my head into the men's restroom. "You gotta drive him to the hospital."

Ken nodded and quickly helped a pale, shaken Orville back out into the hallway.

"Stay here and keep everyone calm. I'll call you when I know more." Ken ushered Orville out a side door, so he didn't have to contend with concern from every direction.

"Let everyone know he's going to be okay," I asked Celeste when I re-entered the main room.

"Oh, thank goodness." Her hand fell to her heart and released a deep sigh. While she spoke my words into the microphone, I whispered a silent hope that it wasn't a lie. I'd never seen him look so small and helpless.

In my brief absence, the Baker's Choice Competition had taken on new importance. Suddenly, without Orville around to make his final judgment, the bakers were intoxicated with their newfound power. Whoever's entry they chose would be this year's de facto winner.

Some protected their ballots from wandering eyes by finding a quiet corner table to taste each treat individually and carefully mark their choices. Others formed small groups with other bakers tasting the same cookie together.

"This one *has* to be a joke." Amber's perfectly manicured hand held up a half-burnt, half-undercooked clump I recognized as my own entry and displayed it to the others.

"I'm sure it tastes better than it looks." Dina defended my offering like the loyal friend she was. She bit into it and chewed, smiling all the way through, refusing to give Amber the satisfaction of being right.

But my appetite had disappeared. When all the cookies had been eaten and all the ballots submitted, people started trickling out from the Pavilion back onto the icy streets of Clear Springs.

"Any cookies left for us?" Bill Jenkins and his sons lumbered over from the live nativity, where two sheep and one goat from their own farm were snoozing beside the manger.

"We've got a few volunteer plates back here." Celeste's eyes twinkled as she handed a loaded plate to the family. Without waiting another beat or bothering to wave goodbye to the crowd as they filed out the main door, the three men dug into their mountain of desserts.

A warm nudge against my thigh interrupted my train of thought. Two beady black eyes with a streak of menacing chaos flashing through them blinked up at me. Before I could react, the very awake sheep bolted, making its great escape to the opposite end of the pavilion.

"Sheep!" I screamed, chasing after the farm animal. "Sheep on the loose!"

But it was too late. The other sheep had already made its escape from its bed of hay, and the lone goat followed suit.

I nearly secured my arms around one sheep's midsection when my phone buzzed in my back pocket.

"Marn?" Ken's concerned voice cracked through the speaker.

"What's the update? Orville ready to come home?"

A pregnant pause took up space on the line. "Doc says it's more than a simple sickness."

I released the sheep.

"What do they think it is?"

"Don't panic, but he thinks Orville was exposed to a

toxin. They've ordered a bunch of tests but are going to keep him for now."

"Toxin? Like... poison?" I performed an immediate body scan. Orville fell sick while eating cookies. Cookies that I and the rest of this city chowed down on.

"Let's not jump to conclusions." Ken's overly rational nature kicked in. "You're not feeling sick, right? Nobody else fell sick?"

I checked to ensure I was still upright. Whatever got Orville hadn't taken me down yet. Or anyone else, for that matter. I scanned the near-empty pavilion whipped into a frenzy by non-human shenanigans.

But if nobody else was sick, that made Orville a target. And who in Clear Springs would want Orville dead?

"I'll be there in ten."

CHAPTER 2

"RELATION?"

The receptionist at Valley Green Hospital awaited my response with casual indifference. It was difficult to take him seriously with the reindeer antler headband and blinking red foam nose.

"Daughter... in-law." My back straightened with conviction. Confidence in delivery is the difference between a white lie and an obvious lie, right? At least that's the story I told myself.

"Fill out your name tag and check-in time. Room 239." He shoved a clipboard toward me and resumed a video of a cat chasing its own tail on his desktop screen.

I walked the long stretch to Orville's room. Light, upbeat instrumental holiday music filtered through hallway speakers, almost drowning out the sounds of beeping heart monitors and low chatter at the nurses' stations. For a hospital, the place felt eerily deserted. A few well-placed wreaths and stockings gave the environment some much-needed cheer.

The door to Orville's room was ajar, inviting me to enter. What greeted me once inside, though, rendered me momentarily breathless. There, unconscious in the bed, was Orville as I'd never seen him before. His larger-than-life personality was nowhere to be found, just a frail body alone attached to a smattering of machines.

Everyone deserves to have people looking out for them.

Orville had looked out for me more than a time or two, especially when I was just getting my bearings as a restaurateur after Stu's death. Figuring out who was responsible for this was the least I could do to repay him for being such a loyal customer. And, on his more generous days, maybe even a friend.

"Excuse me, may I help you? Only immediate family is supposed to be in here."

Myra Singh stood in the doorway in her hospital scrubs, arms folded across her chest and eyes daring me to lie to her face. She was every bit as intimidating as she'd been as a pint-sized Girl Scout in Troop 305.

Busted.

"Myra," I coughed in surprise. It's one thing to hear about people you grew up with going on to successful careers, doing amazing things like saving lives. It's another thing to be confronted with the reality of them. "So great to see you. Please... I can explain."

She narrowed her eyes at me and shifted into a more rigid stance. After a few beats, she cracked, doubling over in laughter.

"You should've seen your face," the nurse cackled, her thick brown ponytail swinging back and forth. "Like I was about to throw you in hospital jail. I'm just glad someone came to check up on the poor guy. It's good to see you, Marnie." My old acquaintance patted me on the back and moved to the patient's bedside. "Your secret's safe with me."

I slumped onto the hospital-issued couch.

"Is he going to..." I couldn't bring myself to finish the question.

"I know this looks scary, but we just have him sedated and are giving him blood and a coagulating agent." Myra's response was professional and confident. Was she faking it the same way I had five minutes earlier?

"So he's going to... make it?"

"The sedatives will wear off soon. We'll know more when we get the labs back."

After Myra was satisfied with the information on all the monitors, she jotted a few notes on her clipboard. Her ease navigating the situation helped me relax into the couch.

"Another man brought him in. Ken Marshall? Do you know if he's still around?"

"Said he received word that a lot of people were gathering at The Pumphouse and wanted to swing by to reassure everyone that Orville was stable. Hey, I hear you're running that place these days, huh?"

"Sure am." I checked my phone to see if any mayday calls had come in from Piper with the sudden influx of traffic. "I should probably call my staff to make sure they're surviving. Is it alright if I sit with him a bit?"

"Of course. I'm going to finish my rounds, but if you need anything, just hit the call button next to the bed."

Myra left the door slightly ajar as she departed. The

subdued sounds of trumpets from the "March of the Toy Soldiers" filtered in from the hall. I waited a few beats to see if Orville might stir before calling the restaurant.

"Hey, Marn." A dining room full of voices raised together singing "Let It Snow" made it difficult to hear my waitress-turned-acting-manager. "A warning of an incoming stampede would have been appreciated."

"Agreed, Piper. Sorry about that. I just heard about it myself." I grimaced. "I stopped by the hospital to check on Orville and only just found out everyone headed there after the Exchange."

"Well, don't worry about us. Allie, Damon, Luis and I got it under control. Although we're low on cocoa mix now, as the crowd has decided that's the drink of the hour." Her control of the situation didn't surprise me. The eighteen-year-old could run that place in her sleep. "Some licorice cookie won, by the way. They just tallied the votes here. People can't stop talking about it." I smiled to myself, thinking of Pru's last-minute entry that morning. My only regret was not getting to taste her unusual concoction myself.

"Did Ken make it there?"

"Yeah, everyone was beside themselves with worry until he showed up and announced Orville was finer than fine, and the whole thing was just a scare."

I stared at the frail recuperating body in bed and couldn't reconcile it with the image Ken had painted for everyone else. That was typical Ken, though. Keep everyone calm.

A few raised voices sounded from the hallway outside Orville's door. With a promise to check in later, I hung up with Piper and moved to close the door so as not to disturb the patient.

"That's cute, but I'm gonna need to speak to an actual doctor." I recognized Greg's voice before I saw him. My eyes peered through the crack into the hallway. He stood, one hand on his hip, talking down to Myra.

"Sir, we have a protocol for this kind of thing." Myra pushed back.

"But *I'm* Orville's next of kin. His *only* kin, for that matter."

"Rules are rules," Myrna shrugged. "The hospital will need you to submit a notarized affidavit recognizing you as next-of-kin to weigh in on medical decisions. It's standard practice. You are more than welcome to speak to the hospital's lawyers."

Greg stamped a foot into the ground and stared at her. "Yeah, you wanna talk about lawyers? You'll be hearing from mine!" With that, he stormed off down the hallway. The nurse rolled her eyes and went back about her rounds.

For a guy who didn't give a hoot about his uncle this morning, Greg was suddenly excessively concerned about his treatment. More specifically, Greg's input into said treatment. And the more I thought about it, the more suspicious this behavior seemed. Orville had a reputation for being a bit gruff, but the people of Clear Springs still loved him. In fact, his nephew was the only person I ever knew to express outward hostility toward the man.

A toxin.

Was Greg hostile enough to try to kill his uncle? Even I realized that was a big leap. I dropped my head into my hands. To accuse a man of attempted murder, I'd need way more to go on than a bad attitude and self-righteous nature. But it was the only puzzle piece I could see.

"Oh, dear!" A frail voice interrupted my thoughts. I lifted my head to watch Prudence Harrington burst through the door. "Orville? I didn't believe the nurses when they told me we admitted him. I just saw him at the cookie contest, and he was fine!"

"Pru." I gave a weak smile to the pharmacist. "He took a turn during the judging, so we're just awaiting some test results." The older woman's eyes drooped with concern. She was a little younger than Orville, but still well past retirement age. Though she was relatively new to Clear Springs, having only been the hospital's pharmacist since the beginning of the year, she was devoted to her job and community. "In happier news, I hear your cookie won the Baker's Choice Competition!"

"I can't worry about cookies right now." Pru waved me off and moved towards the room's computer. One part of my brain wanted to ask how common it was for pharmacists to review patient records, while the other part reassured me that Pru had way more experience in medicine than I ever would.

"See anything interesting?"

"Well, they've taken the right steps and ordered blood tests. Results haven't come back yet, and the lab might be slow with all the injuries from that highway pileup this morning."

I sat in silence while she clicked away on the keyboard.

"He have a history of bloody noses?"

Even though I interacted with Orville every day, I didn't know him *that* well. I shrugged.

"And when was his last checkup?" She leveled a stare in my direction.

"No clue, honestly."

"I see." Pru's lips settled into a disappointed line. She turned back to her screen and continued clicking around. "Well, this is odd."

"What are you seeing?"

The pharmacist sighed. "His chart lists different dosages for a few of the same medications. That might indicate his dosages have been recently switched around but, oh dear. This dosage of warfarin looks quite high. Perhaps it's *too* high."

I wanted to ask her to explain that all to me like I was five.

"Myra told me they found a few stray pills in Orville's breast pocket when he came in. She was hoping I could help her identify them. It took me three seconds to recognize it as extra strength Excedrin. But looking at his chart, that could create a dangerous interaction with the blood thinner."

"Dangerous interaction?" I felt like Charlie Brown listening to his teacher speak mumbo jumbo.

Pru shook her head and closed out of the screen. "Excessive bleeding, for one."

"So this all looks to be one giant mistake?"

"I'm no doctor, dear. But that's what I can interpret from his charts."

My stomach twisted with guilt. What if this was all some unfortunate accident? At least I hadn't spoken my theory about Greg out loud. Still, I couldn't shake the feeling that something was off with the guy. In all my years working at The Pumphouse, I'd never seen the uncle and nephew share a meal. Why, all of a sudden, was he so interested in his uncle? Greg hadn't even bothered to check in and see the man. He just argued with Myra then left.

The heart monitor continued its slow, steady beep. Orville hadn't moved an inch since I'd arrived. The man was a creature of habit. Waking up in a strange place, thrown out of his day-to-day routine, would not go over well.

I waved to Pru. "I think I'll swing by Orville's house and grab a few things to keep him comfortable. Looks like nobody else will do that."

"Hey, that's a great idea. While you're there, maybe look in his medicine cabinet and see if there aren't any other medications we didn't find in his report. That kind of info could be the key to this mystery." The pharmacist put a soft hand to his blanketed leg and gave him a gentle pat.

"Pru, I won't even know what I'm looking for. I know nothing about what drugs interact with others."

She checked her watch. "Y'know, my shift is ending. Plus, this place cheated me out of a real lunch, anyway. How about I join you? Two brains are always better than one."

Before we left, I asked Myra to keep an extra eye on him in case he woke up. Nobody deserves to wake up alone in a hospital bed. Not even grumpy old cookie monsters.

CHAPTER 3

I TURNED over the statue of a meditating frog.

A silver key, much smaller than your average house key, was taped to the bottom. Pru leaned over my shoulder for a closer look.

"Well, that certainly ain't it."

Leave it to Orville to contrive a complicated riddle for breaking into his own house. I freed the key from the adhesive then held it up to the lock on his front door. Definitely too small. But the actual hide-a-key couldn't be far off.

"There has to be something around here." My eyes searched every nook and cranny of his front porch, looking for the logical next step. "A-ha!"

Stashed behind a snow-covered wicker chair was a small rusty lockbox. I held the key up to the lock and gauged its size to be a perfect match. Without waiting, I shoved it in the lock and twisted, hoping to find our answer inside.

"It in there?" Pru called, still holding the frog statue in her hands.

I peered inside and frowned. There was no key, only a folded slip of paper with a few words scribbled on it in black ink.

Beneath the other frog.

The *other* frog? Since when did Orville have such a thing for frogs? And what was with the complicated scavenger hunt?

"Do you see another frog around here?"

Pru searched one side of the porch while I scanned the other. Just when I was about to give up and call it a loss, two globular eyes peaked up at me from the accumulated snow. Frog eyes. I dusted the powder away and pulled the shocked looking statue from its burial spot.

"I really hope that's it. I'm startin' to freeze out here." Pru crossed her arms and rubbed them with the opposite hands. "Plus, I gotta be gettin' home while there's still daylight."

Sure enough, taped to the bottom of the second figurine was a normal-looking house key. Only a paranoid person with memory problems would think to construct this. And Orville was definitely paranoid. But his memory was intact.

Wasn't it? Suddenly, the idea of him mixing up his medications didn't seem too far outside the realm of possibility.

My body relaxed when the lock clicked and the door slowly fell open. Pru stepped inside first and I followed. We both stopped dead in our tracks to process what greeted us.

"I have no words." Pru gulped, unable to peel her eyes from the floor-to-ceiling stacks of newspapers, file folders, piles of clothes, and heaven knows what else that took up ninety percent of the livable space.

"His wife passed a long time back." My chest and throat tightened thinking of him rotting away in here all alone, day in, day out. For as particular a person as Orville was, I'd always assumed his house would be spotless. But this looked closer to an episode of *Hoarders*.

"What a shame," Pru murmured, still overwhelmed by the sheer volume of stuff.

A faint jingle sounded from a distant room but grew nearer with each passing second. Moments later, a cylindrical mass of white and orange fur rounded the corner and waddled toward us.

"Who the *heck* are you?" I kneeled down to greet the pudgy corgi with some scratches behind the ears. A shiny blue name tag dangled from the collar. "Ralphie. Well, it's a pleasure to meet you, Ralphie. I hadn't the faintest clue Orville had a dog!"

The eager creature panted and searched my face with urgent eyes.

"Poor baby's probably starving! Orville hasn't been home all day!" Pru threw open a nearby closet in search of the kibble.

"You need to go out, boy?"

He panted a response but didn't move toward the door.

My partner in crime and I regrouped in the main foyer once the dog had settled. "You're the brains of this operation, so you hit the medicine cabinet and I'll grab some things from his room."

Pru nodded in agreement and we split.

I began through the open concept kitchen — though there was too much clutter for it to be "open" in any functional way — in search of his bedroom. But there, on the large island, was a collection of orange prescription bottles. Some still had their white caps off. At the far end of the island was a small basket containing another stash of similar containers.

My hands began grabbing the bottles closest to me. The ones out on the counter were varying levels of empty, while the ones in the basket were full, yet several labels were faded, and the dates stretched back more years than seemed healthy.

"So... the active set and the extra set?" I asked Ralphie who, fully satiated, had sprawled on the floor for a nap. The dog lifted his eyes at my question, but if he knew the answer, he wasn't forthcoming.

Next to the medications were more piles of papers. I flipped through the pages. Medical appointment reminders, invoices from doctors' offices, and Orville's chicken-scratched appointment reminders on a spiral-bound insurance calendar.

"Pru?" I called out to the brains. Clearly, Orville had grown accustomed to functioning within dysfunction. While I couldn't make heads or tails of the mess, maybe it would all mean something to her. "I think I got something in the kitchen!"

Think Marnie, think!

I pictured Orville at my six-top that he shared every morning with the group of retired farmers. Now that I thought about it, he frequently chased his orange juice with a handful of pills. I'd never really given it any notice. I supposed it happens. People get older, they develop health issues. Still, he never gave me the sense that he wasn't on top of things. He was a lot of things, but confused was never one of them.

Pru wandered into the room and her eyes widened at the orange mass on the counter. Without a word, she adjusted her glasses and began looking over the names and dosages.

"Something's not sitting right with me." I leaned against the butcher block countertop. "He's got that nephew... Greg? The guy appears out of nowhere and suddenly has all this concern? I don't trust him. Look how many meds Orville's on. Messing with his meds would take no effort at all."

Pru turned toward the refrigerator. "Some meds need to be kept cool, so..." She tugged the door open then stuck her head in.

"Anything?"

The pharmacist chuckled and shook her head. "Dang, Orville's a riot. By the looks of it, he's trying to grow his own penicillin. This is giving me flashbacks or my organic chemistry classes. I know drug costs are rising, but this at-home-lab is taking things a bit too far."

I left her to make heads or tails of whatever chaos was happening there and wandered towards the back of the main level, where I found an out-of-place, tidy bedroom oasis. In no time at all, I'd located the essentials of comfort. From his closet, I plucked the flannel shirt he wore at least twice a week, and from the armoire, a few pairs of thick socks so he didn't have to suffer in those awful itchy hospital grade ones that never stayed in place. A multi-colored crochet blanket splayed across his bed, clearly something he slept with. I took care to fold it into quarters.

With my final spin around the room, my eyes landed on a framed wedding photo that sat on his nightstand. His wife had passed nearly thirty years earlier, but nobody ever mentioned her, including him. The circumstances surrounding her untimely death were a mystery to me.

"I still think it's too much of the blood thinner," Pru announced as I returned with my armful of items. She'd bought a printed list of his medications from the hospital and handed it over, all marked up with her notes. "Then again, the pills he's been actively taking are a lower dose than what's in the pile of unopened bottles. It makes no sense!"

I inspected the paper while she slung her purse over her shoulder. "I hate to jump ship but I got a date with *Dancing With the Stars Holiday Spectacular*. That Igor does things to my soul." She wiggled her hips and shot me a wink.

"Drive safe, and thanks for your help today."

I ensured Ralphie had enough food and water in his bowl and put a reminder in my phone to come let him out in the morning. Then, after dropping my pile of Orville's belongings on my front seat, I secured the hide-a-key beneath the *second* frog statue, buried the ceramic amphibian back in his little igloo, then made my way back to the hospital.

This time, Rudolph the Receptionist waved me in without requiring me to sign in. A streak of gold light filtered out from room 239, along with voices deep in conversation. I pushed my back against the wall and positioned my ear to listen.

"Him being hooked up to all these machines ain't right."

Greg. Great. Just the run-in I needed to end my night. "Uncle Orv wouldn't want this."

"Sir, the lab is severely backed up. A little hospital like this isn't built to handle a mass influx of patients all at once. We'll have a better sense of options once we get the results." Myra's voice was soothing, but firm. Whatever scuffle they'd gotten into earlier, she'd smoothed over.

"If it came down to it, would one option be, you know, to put him out of his misery? I'm the next of kin and I get to make all medical decisions."

My legs nearly sprung into action at his suggestion. Somehow, Greg had out-Scrooged the biggest Scrooge of all. Pulling the plug?

"I think we're getting ahead of ourselves," Myra snipped.

"This conversation ain't over. Honey, we're out of here." Greg stormed out of the room, tugging a lanky blonde wearing a gaudy rock on her left hand behind him. They swept past me without so much as a glance.

The not-so-ex-wife.

"That money is non-negotiable, Greg. Understand?" She extricated her hand from his as they made their way towards the bank of elevators.

"Baby, trust that I'll make this right." He reached for her hand again. "We'll get it paid off and—"

"Oh, please." The wife ripped her hand away and disappeared into the waiting elevator. "I'll never make the mistake of trusting you again, you dog!"

Greg's head dropped into his hands as he followed her in like a poor, injured puppy.

Behind me, I heard Myra's footsteps, then a soft whoosh and click as she slipped into the next room.

Once the coast was clear, I released a deep breath I hadn't even realized I was holding, then slipped into Orville's room. He lay among all the softly beeping machines, unchanged since my last visit.

I needed a spot to sit and process the events of the day, and he needed company. I set Orville's things on the deep windowsill, then settled down on the stiff vinyl couch and pulled out my phone. Only one person could help me understand, Greg the Enigma Man.

"Well, isn't this a delightful surprise?" My mom's voice sang through the line. "How's my favorite daughter this evening?"

"It's a long story," I chuckled sadly into the receiver. "I'm calling because I actually need your help."

"Oooh! Are you doing another one of your investigations? What do you need? I got a guy who can run license plates. Need to break in somewhere? The tools for that are around here somewhere." Cyndi Tipton was always up for an adventure, no questions asked. Her loyalty was only trumped by her lunacy.

"Actually, I need you to tell me anything you can about Greg Johnson."

I listened to dead air long enough that I thought maybe the call had dropped.

"Mom?"

"That *dog*. I still haven't forgotten how he made me destitute and put me out on the streets last Christmas."

"Mom, you stayed with me. You were hardly out on the

streets," I reminded her. "Did he ever talk about money problems?"

"Darlin', we met at a casino. The man had a habit of overextending himself, borrowing a little from his guy, a little from that one, until he was in over his head and they were all at his door demanding repayment, plus interest."

A snippet of my conversation with Maggie came back to me full throttle. The librarian had mentioned how Greg was so hard up for cash, he was willing to do grunt work for her. And while Orville was no Daddy Warbucks, he had enough land to—

No.

I was trying to slow the steam train that was barreling through my brain when Orville stirred in his hospital bed.

"I gotta run, Mom, but this was helpful." I ended the call before she could ask questions and started spreading the crocheted blanket over my friend's fragile body.

"Hey Orv." I smiled down at him as he looked up with a slow, confused blink. "Look what I brought for you." I pulled the blanket up and tucked him in. A hint of a smile appeared on his face as he cuddled the blanket tighter. "Delilah." He whispered his wife's name, then drifted back to sleep.

"He's stable, but he's not out of the woods yet," Myra said from the doorway. Somehow, the nurse still looked as perky as she had hours earlier, while I was fighting off yawn after yawn. "You should get some rest. We'll know more tomorrow."

Without bothering to argue, I nodded my head and made the trek back to the elevators, back through reception, and across the parking lot to my car.

The trailer park was a ten-minute drive from Valley Green, though I couldn't tell you if I'd been driving for thirty seconds or a full hour when I pulled into my spot. Mustering my last bit of energy, I stepped into the night and stared up at home, sweet home.

Thick curls of smoke poured from the kitchen windows.

"What the..."

My nervous system jolted me back awake and pushed me through the front door, where the incessant beeping of my smoke detector sounded an alarm.

Elementary school training kicked in as I stopped, dropped, and...well, I didn't need to roll, but I did crawl until I spotted the source of the smoke. I made my way into the kitchen. My oven was set to five hundred degrees, baking something I hadn't put in it. I flipped the appliance off then threw open every window and door in the place.

My cat, T.C., bounded up the front stairs after another evening of prowling about the town and watched me contend with the chaos from her perch on the porch. A gentle *Mmmrow* told me she was glad I was okay. Or at least that she was glad I was there to feed her.

"Likewise, bud." I filled her food bowl and placed it on the step. If ever there was a time for stress eating, this was it.

When most of the smoke had cleared, I found a single piece of paper taped to oven window, a message scrawled on it:

"Leave it alone, or I'll finish the job."

I pulled open the oven door to find a batch of blackened slice and bake Christmas cookies.

CHAPTER 4

RALPHIE WADDLED over to greet me when I walked through the door just after six o'clock the following morning. He'd make the world's worst guard dog, but he sure was cute.

This time, I found the hide-a-key without the shenanigans of the day before, which was an impressive feat given how I'd been up all night airing out my trailer.

Plus, I wasn't really in the mood to sleep after someone tried to burn down my home. I let the dog out, refilled his food and water, then started the trek back to town.

Throughout the drive, moonlight reflected off the snowy farm fields as questions looped over and over in my brain. Greg was the only person who made any sense. If he'd seen me at the hospital the previous night, and he'd heard my reputation for getting mixed up in murder investigations, then maybe he'd take drastic measures to get me out of the way.

I hadn't come up with any other options when I pulled

into the guest lot at Valley Green and eased into the spot beside a familiar red pickup.

"Morning, Marnie." Ken Marshall tipped his hat to me as I stepped out of my car. "Fancy meeting you here."

"I'm just swinging by before I head to the restaurant. Hopefully, they have some results for us." Part of me wanted to tell him everything — from Greg to the medications to my trailer. But checking in on Orville seemed more important.

Rudolph rested his head in his palm at the reception desk, barely bothering to lift his hand and wave us in. The light in his foam nose blinked weakly. My waning holiday cheer could relate.

Myra stood at the nurses' station, her cheer defying the boundaries of human sleep deprivation. "Mornin'," she waved at us with a grin. "Perfect timing. He just stopped in."

"Doc, this is a pleasant surprise." Ken greeted Dr. Theodore Murphy with a handshake. "And now I'm reminded I need to schedule my physical."

"Ken, you're healthy as an ox. I'll give you that assessment for free." The doctor laughed.

"Hey." I waved awkwardly. After thirty-odd years, I still wasn't sure of the right way to start a conversation with the man who delivered me into this world. But I was grateful for his services. I turned to Orville, who rested soundly wrapped in the blanket crafted by his sweet Delilah. "Any update for us this morning?"

"In fact, we just got the labs—"

"You'd better have a real update." Greg stormed into the room, not even noticing me and Ken. The not-so-ex-wife wasn't with him this time, and after a quick evaluation, I determined he didn't look guilty of attempting to burn my trailer down. But then again, what was that kind of suspect supposed to look like? I didn't imagine he'd walk in with a gas can in one hand and a blowtorch in the other.

"As I was saying," Dr. Murphy continued, "the labs are all back."

"Is he going to be okay?" A twinge of genuine concern escaped from Greg. Fear clouded the rims of his eyes.

That was unexpected.

"Short answer, yes. He'll need some extra support, perhaps a caretaker." Doc Murphy peered over his glasses at Greg.

"Uncle Orv will never agree to that." Greg shook his head. "I've been trying to get him into an assisted living facility for years now. Have you seen that sty he calls home? He won't even let me send someone in to clean it. All I want to know is that he's taking his meds properly and eating right."

"I ensure Orville eats just fine, thank you very much," I interjected. "He has a permanent seat at the best restaurant in town."

Greg spun around. He looked surprised to see me and Ken. As recognition crossed his face, his gaze darkened. "Watch yourself, Tipton, don't cross the line."

"What, you mean like try to burn down someone's home? Attempting to murder your own uncle? That kinda crossing the line?"

"Excuse me?" He took a menacing step in my direction before Ken inserted himself between us.

"You and your wife were arguing over laying claim to Orville's money last night. Deny it all you want, but I heard you. I'm sure there's a security camera around here that recorded you saying it, too."

Dr. Murphy shook his head. "Actually, the hospital hasn't secured the funding for an upgraded security system. No cameras in the vicinity right now."

Greg's pasty face brightened to the red of Santa's coat. "Look. I asked the old man for a loan and got shot down. Is that a crime?" The veins in his neck pulsed. "But I just took a second job to pay my debt in a respectable, honest way."

I looked him up and down. "Second job doing what?"

His color deepened. "I'll be handing out food samples at Price Barn starting next week."

"So how do you explain last night, talking about wanting to pull the plug on Orville?" I crossed my arms, not backing down even a little bit.

Greg's eyes widened, and he twisted his head back and forth in disbelief. "I thought he was on the brink of death! I thought taking him off life support would be merciful or something."

"Umm," Dr. Murphy interrupted again. "To be clear, Orville was never on life support. Look, if you two don't mind, I'd love to give you the latest update and then maybe you can take this little whatever-it-is outside? I've got rounds to do and with yesterday's pile up, I've got patients waiting."

"Carry on, please," Ken encouraged the only other adult in the room, shaking his head at the two of us.

Dr. Murphy pulled in a deep breath. "The toxicology report showed elevated levels of Bromadiolone in his system."

"Bro-what?" Greg asked.

"Rat poison, essentially."

Our jaws simultaneously dropped.

"That's what led to the excessive bleeding. Orville actually had routine bloodwork done earlier in the week, so we were able to compare the changes, and it looks like he consumed a lot in a very brief amount of time. The toxin is interacting with the anticoagulants he's already on. What's more, his earlier bloodwork uncovered anemia and a vitamin K deficiency that exacerbated the bleeding."

I made a mental note to sneak in more iron and leafy greens into Orville's classic meat-and-potatoes diet. A little spinach never hurt anyone.

"Where on earth would he get *rat poison* from?" Ken howled.

"It's more complicated than just rat poison. You see, it would take some serious chemistry to formulate a high enough dosage to make him so sick so fast." Doc explained.

"Heck, anything could have happened in that house," I glared at Greg, who looked more confused than an attempted murderer should. Could he be telling the truth?

I pressed on. "The place was right out of a Hoarders episode, and Pru said it looked like he was trying to grow his own penicillin."

Dr. Murphy reached into the pocket of his white coat and withdrew a few strands of licorice. He chomped down on one and continued speaking, but I had stopped listening.

Instead, fireworks started exploding in my brain as it rearranged all the puzzle pieces.

Pru said...

My mind raced backwards to Pru's hunt through Orville's refrigerator.

"This is giving me flashbacks of my organic chemistry classes."

Licorice.

Chemistry.

Cookies.

Blood thinners.

Who would have a better knowledge of complex chemistry than a pharmacist? She had access to his medications, and she ran the pharmacy where he got his prescriptions filled. She certainly would know about interactions. And she'd claimed she was going home when she left Orville's yesterday, but what if she went to my trailer instead? What if I was actually closer than I realized...

It all added up. She had means and opportunity, even more than Greg did. But why? I couldn't even start to imagine her motive. There was only one way to find out.

"Hey Doc," I interrupted him. "I reviewed Orville's meds with Prudence Harrington yesterday. Why don't we bring her up here to talk us through what he was taking?"

I turned to Greg, whose face was shifting through various states of panic. "She's very good at explaining things clearly," I reassured him. His face twisted again, this time into confusion.

Five minutes later, Pru waltzed into Room 239 as "I Want a Hippopotamus for Christmas" played in the hallway.

"Good morning to you all."

Maybe I was seeing things, but Pru looked like her breezy attitude was manufactured. I needed to get this right. Now I had her here, how the heck did I get her to confess?

"Marnie thought you could shed some light on a comprehensive list of meds Orville is taking," Dr. Murphy began.

Pru's shoulders relaxed. "I'd be happy to."

A rustling sounded behind us, followed by a loud, extended groan.

"He's waking up!" Ken rushed to Orville's bedside.

My friend stared straight up at the ceiling for a moment before rubbing the sleep from his eyes. He fumbled for the bed controls, and Ken helped him sit up.

Orv's confused gaze bounced around from person to person, then landed on Pru standing at the end of his bed. His eyes widened.

"That's her!" His voice was raspy, but his words were clear. "Prudence. Harrington. That woman's been messin' with my 'scriptions!" He paused, looked around the room, and spotted the big whiteboard on the wall across from him. "Wait... I got a meeting with the hospital board today!" Orville peeled back the covers and tried to launch himself from the bed.

"Slow down there, Orv."

As Dr. Murphy rushed to prevent his patient from fleeing, Pru shoved past me and raced out the door. "I can't do this!" her frail voice screamed down the hallway.

I locked eyes with Greg. "Prudence Harrington tried to murder your uncle!"

Without waiting another beat, we fled the room together just in time to see Pru whip around the corner by the nurses' station.

"What now?" Greg panicked.

"Cut her off!" I pointed to the opposite hallway.

The thing about small towns is that they have small hospitals. And small hospitals make capturing a fleeing assailant a relatively straightforward task. I took off without waiting to see if Greg was on my heels.

Halfway down the hallway, a room attendant disappeared into a room, leaving a meal cart unattended. I grabbed the handle then ran full speed toward the corner that Pru was bound to be rounding any second.

At that moment, a rotund Santa Claus, who looked an awful lot like Bert Phelps, emerged from the bathroom. "Morning, Marnie!" He waved a white-gloved hand as I flew past him.

Just on time, Pru rounded the corner. At the same moment, the wheel of my meal cart hitched on something. The cart twisted wildly and toppled over sideways. Pru slipped on a gallon of spilled gravy and spun out right next to me. I snatched her forearm, then pinned her on a pile of potatoes, ensuring she couldn't flee again.

I heaved a sigh and waited for Greg to catch up.

"Cop's on the phone," he wheezed, holding up his device. "Sending someone." Wheeze. "Right away."

Glad one of us was fit enough to chase down a middle-aged murderer.

Doc Murphy raced around the corner, followed by Ken pushing Orville in a wheelchair. They all stared in wonder at the two of us covered in the remains of a hospital quality holiday feast.

"All I did was find a new supplier for generic drugs." Pru sobbed through the potato crust on her cheek. "I just wanted to lower costs for the patients. But Orville noticed the change and went on a crazy crusade to get me fired."

"So you tried to kill him?" Greg asked through gritted teeth.

"You don't understand," Pru continued, wiping a trail of cranberry jello from her chin. "I can't lose another job! My license is on probation. I barely got this one and no one else will hire an old lady." The pharmacist let out a long wail. "My only option was to neutralize him."

Fifteen minutes later, Sheriff Bryson Best strutted into a dank room in the hospital's basement where Rudolph the Receptionist-turned-security-guard had cuffed Prudence Harrington to a table. The officer let out a deep yawn and stretch, as if just emerging from the most restful night of sleep.

"Why don't you go on home and let the professionals handle this, Tipton?"

Typical. I do his job and he points me towards the door. But it's okay. I have a town to feed.

Three days later

"We're parking right now."

I set my phone on the counter and shouted, "Three minute warning!"

With the exception of Prudence Harrington, who was watching for Santa at the county jail, every baker from the competition was waiting at The Pumphouse to greet Orville on his release day from the hospital.

A round of applause erupted when he shuffled through the front door. Though his body was still recovering, it was nice to see the man wearing a smile, walking side-by-side with his only living family member. Greg helped him to a seat in the center of the dining room, then Orville raised his hands to quiet the audience.

"I think we're all aware that we must attend to some unfinished business," he began. "The Baker's Choice winner has been disqualified, for obvious reasons."

Sheriff Best had actually done a nice little bit of police work, and his techs had tested the remains of Pru's licorice snickerdoodle that they'd found in the trash. The judging cookie was loaded with rat poison. Thankfully, none of the treats she'd shared with the rest of the town were tainted. But everyone had thrown them away, anyway.

The old man felt around his coat pocket and withdrew a folded piece of paper. The dining room fell silent.

Orville relished in the crowd's anticipation, then finally croaked out, "Maggie McHugh's white chocolate peppermint cookies!"

Another burst of applause erupted from the room as chatter filled the air. Maggie stood up, both hands pressed against her cheeks in elated shock.

"But you hate peppermint!" Greg shook his head. "You never cease to surprise me."

"Nothing beats a holiday classic," Orville continued over the applause and the holiday soundtrack that Piper had turned on. He flashed Maggie a thumbs up and a grin. "And as for *you,* Marnie Tipton," he narrowed his eyes and waved me over.

"Am I in trouble?" I chuckled.

"I know you underperformed on purpose," he winked. "Your secret is safe with me, so long as you promise to bake me a *real* batch of snickerdoodles tomorrow."

About Ellie Ballard

There are only a few things Ellie Ballard will go to war for: The corner brownie, the middle lasagne, and Castle. All the rest is open for debate.

Ellie hails from a midwest town not so different from Clear Springs, feeds a cat not so different from TC, and would never be caught dead serving slice-and-bake cookies.

You can learn more and find Ellie's books at ellieballard.com/deadlytraditions

SANTA CLAUS IS NOT COMING TO TOWN

SAGE SO

It's three days before Christmas, and Santa is nowhere to be found. Can grinchy aspiring forensic sleuth Audrey Nott follow the clues to find the jolly old elf before the holiday falls to fragments?

CHAPTER 1

"Three more days till Christmas!" Micah jumped up and down. "Fa-la-la-la-la—-la-la-la-la!"

"Why are you so excited about Christmas?" I definitely was not this excited about the holidays when I was her age. Neighbors and Mom's friends would visit at all hours, dropping off cookies and cards one after another. The treats were the *only* good part. For some reason, they all felt the need to talk in a high-pitched, cheery voice instead of their regular voice, asking about school and sports and friends when all I wanted to do was hide in my room and read my book.

"Audrey!" Mom would scold after the first guest of the season. "No daughter of mine will be this impolite and ungracious! You may only be half Chinese, but this is totally unacceptable! How many times do I have to remind you about *haau*? Filial piety is our highest virtue! Why can't you be more like your big sister! If you want to stay in your room so much, go write *haau* a hundred times. In Chinese calligraphy!"

Ingrid, two years older, could do no wrong in Mom's eyes. So, I plastered a smile on my face and made small talk, trying not to grind my teeth or make awkward facial expressions. Meanwhile, Ingrid would put our guests at ease and knew just what to say, playing Christmas carols on the piano when requested.

And how could I forget the cheek pinching and hair ruffling? Total invasion of my personal bubble. My skin crawled at those memories.

"What was the question again?" Micah asked, looking up from her toy robot. Other kids carried plushies, not Micah.

"Why are you so excited about Christmas?"

"Presents of course!" My niece clapped her hands. "I wonder if Santa got my wish list. Mommy said I couldn't be greedy though, and she only let me put five things in my letter."

Knowing my sister, she'd have bought all five presents already and wrapped them in festive, classy paper with perfect bows. Mom would buy Micah another ten presents that weren't on the list. I, as usual, had gotten her books, which, as yet, hadn't been wrapped in the usual brown kraft paper secured with twine. Seven books this year for a seven-year-old.

"Have you been naughty or nice this year?" I asked.

Micah tilted her head. "Seventy percent nice and thirty percent naughty?" She frowned. "Oh no! I'll have to ask Santa what I can do to make up for it. Can you take me to Santa's Cabin? Pretty please?"

I sighed. What had I gotten myself into? Our small town, Happy Valley, hosted a big Happy Wonderland Festival each year that drew thousands of visitors. Mom was the chair of volunteers for the event. So, I had to make at least one appearance. Otherwise, she'd lose face among her friends if I didn't show appreciation in public. But now it looked like I'd have to be there at least twice this year. I was wracking my brain for an excuse as to why we didn't need to go right then (or ever) when my phone beeped.

It was a text from Mom. *Come to HWF NOW!*

HWF? I texted back.

Happy Wonderland Festiva! Of course. How could I forget?

Why? I'm babysitting Micah. Remember? I wished Mom would explain herself sometimes and not just make demands.

Santa's been kidnapped! Need your help to find him!

Kidnapped?

Wait! Did Mom just ask me for help instead of Ingrid for once?

CHAPTER 2

Clutching some paper in her hand, Mom ran over to us when Micah and I entered Santa's Cabin. The log cabin smelled of fresh pine, and the fire crackled in the fireplace. The whole room was decked out in blue and silver ornaments. I admitted, a ten-foot-tall Christmas tree full of fairy lights was quite magical. Maybe I should have a permanent Christmas tree in my cottage even though I never bothered to put up any holiday decorations.

"We need to find Santa pronto! Kids are coming in an hour for Photos with Santa, and he's the star in our Christmas Eve Parade. We can't have Christmas without Santa!"

"Santa's missing?" Micah looked up at Mom, eyes as big as saucers.

"Oh! Hi, sweetie." Mom patted Micah's head. "Yes, but I'm sure your Aunty Audrey will get him back as soon as possible. Why, with all those murder mystery books she's read since she was your age, she must know some tricks!"

Tricks? Forensic science, police procedures, and criminal profiling weren't tricks.

"Slow down, Mom. First of all, how do you know it's a kidnapping?"

Mom shoved the note in her hand out to me.

Great, now Mom's fingerprints were on the evidence. I took a pair of latex gloves out of my bag.

"You carry rubber gloves around?" Mom raised her eyebrow.

"You never know when they'll come in handy." Especially when you have to eat greasy food and there's no silverware. I took the note.

"If you want to find Santa, you must follow the trail," I read aloud. "That's it? How do you know it's not a prank? There is no demand for ransom or anything like that?"

"Maybe the kidnapper will tell you about that once you find the next clue!"

"But what trail is he even talking about?" I flipped the note over, but the back was blank. Was there another message written in invisible ink?

"Here!" Mom fished something out of her pocket. A key chain with three keys. A car key and two regular house keys.

"What are the keys for?"

"They were on top of the note on the rocking chair when I came into the cabin expecting to see Santa here getting ready."

"Have you called the police?"

"Nancy called her son, but he has to go to the next town to help with some big case they have over there. The other police officer ... What's his name again? He's really sick with the flu, and we definitely don't want him walking around spreading germs!"

The joys of living in a small town, with only two officers. But it presented me with the rare opportunity to play detective! "Where's Mrs. Nancy now?"

"She's going over to the backup Santa's house to see if he can step in for now. She can't let the Happy Wonderland Festival fail! She's up for re-election next year, and you better believe that vile man Leroy will hold it against her if our festival is ruined! He's been wanting to be mayor forever!"

"Backup Santa?" Micah quipped. I'd totally forgotten she was there.

I shot Mom a look, tipped my head towards Micah, took the keys from Mom, and turned towards the door.

"Where are you going?" Mom shouted after me.

"Look after Micah while I go find Santa!"

If there's anyone who could still make Micah believe in Santa—as per Ingrid's strict orders that no one, under any circumstances, ruin the magic for her daughter until Micah was twelve—it was Mom.

CHAPTER 3

At the parking lot outside of Santa's Cabin, I spotted a brown Volvo with peeling paint. Santa's, or rather, Mr. Brown's car. I went over and peeked inside. Nothing looked out of the ordinary. The leather seats were worn at the seams, but it was uncluttered. Unlike mine.

I selected the car key. My hand was shaking a little, and my heartbeat rose in anticipation.

"Hey, you!"

I jumped and dropped the keys. I turned around, ready to say I wasn't stealing the car. I breathed a sigh of relief when I saw who it was.

"Portia, you scared me to death!" I bent down to retrieve the keys.

"What are you doing? Did Mr. Brown forget his Santa hat again and ask you to fetch it for him? He's been getting a little forgetful lately." She looked down at my hands. "Why are you wearing latex gloves? They don't exactly keep you warm in this weather, you know."

"Mr. Brown is missing."

"What?" Portia's face turned pale. "What happened? He was totally fine yesterday!"

I briefed Portia and showed her the note. "Since you've been taking photos of Santa with various families these past few days, did you notice anything unusual?"

Portia furrowed her brows. "Not that I can think of. We've been so busy. Our schedule was full."

"When was the last time you saw Mr. Brown?" I took a notebook and pen out of my yellow bag.

"It must have been around 7:00 last night. Our last session was at 6:00. Then I helped clean up the cabin a little bit... "

I scribbled in the notebook.

"Audrey, what are you doing? Are you ... Are you taking my statement? I'm your best friend! Do you suspect I had something to do with his disappearance?"

"Of course not!" My cheeks burned. "But I do have to remain objective if I want to find him. I'm just taking notes so I don't forget anything."

"You don't forget anything." Portia murmured. "Do you believe me when I say I had nothing to do with this? I love Mr. Brown!"

"Even though everyone thinks he's a grumpy old man?"

"You just don't know him like I do. I've been doing Photos with Santa since high school. He could calm the most colicky baby!"

"Except me. He has scared me since Mom forced me to take pictures with him when I was little." I shuddered at the memory. First Mom made me put on a scratchy red sweater with a green corduroy skirt that was way too tight. Then she made Ingrid and I sit on this stranger's lap who said "ho ho ho" way too loudly. My skin prickled when his beard brushed my cheek.

"It's been over thirty years now. Don't you think it's time to get over it?"

"If only it was that easy." I unlocked the passenger door and opened the glove box. Car registration, the car manual, and a booklet of maps. I checked the rest of the car, including the trunk, for other clues.

Nothing.

"I'm going to go to his house to see if I can find the next clue there," I said to Portia and locked Mr. Brown's car.

Portia looked at her phone. "I have some time before Photos with Santa start. If the backup Santa gets here on time, that is. Let me go check with your mom. I want to go with you to make sure Mr. Brown is okay."

I nodded. As much as I liked being alone, I did appreciate having Portia as a friend. Her popularity had saved me from being bullied at school multiple times.

Portia returned a few minutes later. "We're going to start an hour later today to give Bernard some extra time. Let's go in separate cars in case I have to come back before we're done."

"Bernard? Bernard Barney?"

"Yep! He's the backup Santa."

"Interesting." I wrote something in my notebook.

"What is it?" Portia tried to steal a peek at my notes.

"I saw him and Mr. Brown arguing at the grocery store on

Monday night." I preferred to shop at the least busy time to avoid the crowd.

"What were they arguing about?"

"I wasn't sure. I saw Bernard pointing his finger at Mr. Brown, and his face was turning beet red. I was too far away to hear their exchange. The manager came out to have a word with them, and then they parted ways." I closed my eyes and rubbed my temples. "When Mr. Brown walked past me, he muttered something."

Now, what did he say? I visualized where I was in the store that night. Right by the fresh produce. Tomatoes. Cabbage. Lettuce. Peas. Peas!

"Two peas in a pod!" I opened my eyes and wrote it down before my thoughts vanished.

"Huh?"

"Mr. Brown said, 'Bernard and Leroy. Two peas in a pod,' while shaking his head."

"Leroy? The mayor wannabe?"

"Yes. They are best buddies."

"How do you know that?"

"My mom, of course." Mom and I couldn't be more different. She was the social butterfly and knew all the latest gossip in town. "Okay, let's go to Mr. Brown's house first. Then we'll talk to Bernard."

CHAPTER 4

Mr. Brown owned a brown bungalow. I used the same key to open the storm door and the wooden front door.

The interior walls and carpet were beige. The cabinets, the window frames, the curtains, and the couch were all different shades of brown.

"A record player!" Portia ran over to the turntable. "I haven't seen one in forever!" She touched the lid. Good thing I gave her a pair of gloves before we went in. She picked up the record jacket next to it. "'Roses are Red.' Bobby Vinton? Never heard of him."

"When my dad left, Mom played his song 'Mr. Lonely' non-stop for a month." That song still haunted me.

"Understandable. Her family was all overseas, and she had two young girls to take care of. Hadn't your parents just moved to town? She probably didn't have many friends either."

I hadn't thought of my mom that way. Portia was much better at this people stuff than I was. All I remembered growing up after Dad left was Mom yelling at Ingrid and me. "Study hard! Do chores! Practice piano! You don't want your dad to think you're lazy and stupid when he comes back, do you?"

And he still hadn't returned.

Portia played the record. The familiar melancholic sound of "Mr. Lonely" filled the house.

I looked around Mr. Brown's living room, taking everything in. There were a few photo frames–brown, of course–on the brown end table. They were pictures of the same person (they all had a cashew-shaped birthmark on their left cheek) as a boy, a teen, a young adult, and a grown man.

"Do you know who this is?" I pointed to the photos.

Portia came over and nodded. "That's Mr. Brown's nephew. His late brother's son. His name is Fred."

"I don't think I've seen him around."

"He lives in Florida. Mr. Brown loves him and wants him to visit more often now that Fred's parents have passed away. But Fred is always saying money's tight, even though Mr. Brown offers to pay for the tickets and all. I feel so sad for him."

"Maybe if he were less grouchy, Fred would want to visit more often."

"Audrey!"

"Just saying. Just because he's missing doesn't make him a saint."

I spotted some paper on the dining room table and made my way over there.

"Take a look at this." I held up the paper. "These seem to

be the blueprints of Mr. Brown's house. What are they doing here? Could they be the clue?"

"Maybe he's going to remodel?" Portia leaned in. "There are no messages on them though. So, they're probably not the clue?"

I took out my small blacklight. "Let's see if there's a message written in invisible ink. Let's go to the bathroom. It's darker there."

No secret message on the blueprints or the kidnapping note.

I put the blueprints back on the kitchen table and took some pictures of them and the note for future reference.

"Let's check the rest of the house," I said.

We checked the bathroom; the laundry room; the kitchen; Mr. Brown's bedroom with its brown duvet cover, brown sheets, brown pillowcase, and brown curtains; and a guest bedroom, also with brown bedding and curtains. We found no doorway to a basement or entry to an attic. Nothing out of the ordinary. Mr. Brown lived a simple life. He was neat and organized.

"What now?" Portia asked.

I looked around to see if we'd missed anything. The house looked much smaller from the inside than the outside. The all-brown decorations made it feel confining.

"Let's put down a list of likely suspects, and any known enemies." I sat on the couch and looked down at my notes. "Suspect #1: Bernard. We'll have to interview him to learn why he argued with Mr. Brown."

Portia sat down next to me. "He's wanted to be Santa for a few years now, but Mr. Brown isn't ready to retire yet.

Maybe he'd finally waited long enough and locked Mr. Brown up for a few days."

"But if he only intended to keep Mr. Brown for a few days, there's a chance Mr. Brown could identify him."

"Maybe he was extra careful or partnered with someone from out of town." Portia slapped her hand over her mouth. "Oh no, I hope… "

"What?"

"I hope he didn't kill Mr. Brown!"

I swallowed. "Let's not jump to any conclusions until the evidence tells us otherwise. As far as we know, he's just missing and we'll find him if we follow the trail. I'm going to check the drawers to see if the clue is hidden."

I opened the kitchen cabinets and was not surprised to see that Mr. Brown's dishes and cups were also brown.

Except one.

It was one of those personalized photo mugs. A picture of Mr. Brown dressed in Santa gear next to Mrs. Claus. Arms crossed, mouth turned down, and his head turned away from her. Mrs. Claus, on the other hand, leaned her head and upper body as close to Mr. Brown as possible, her forehead almost touching Mr. Brown's cheek. Her left hand crossed over her upper body and rested on Mr. Brown's left forearm. Her radiant smile and dimples were a stark contrast to his aloofness.

I took the mug out to show it to Portia. The back of the mug said, "Dear Nicholas: Everything's better with you. Love, Molly."

Portia wasn't surprised. "Molly's been in love with Mr.

Brown for the past five years now, since she was chosen as Mrs. Claus."

"Really? She seems to keep her distance from him in public." Maybe I wasn't as observant as I thought I was.

"He told her he wasn't interested. So, she relishes Photos with Santa. There, she can get close to him." Portia took the mug from me. "Look, she even drew a big heart and wrote XOXO on the bottom of the mug with a Sharpie. Mr. Brown probably could use some company, but he said she's too loud and too talkative. She's always trying to get him to open up and ask him a billion questions."

I turned my notebook to a fresh page. "Suspect #2: Molly Peach. Unrequited love." I looked up, my mouth gaping open. "My goodness!"

"What?"

CHAPTER 5

"She reminds me of Annie Wilkes in *Misery*! Her mousy hair, drab loose dresses, and all!"

"I thought you liked being objective." Portia shook her head. "Molly is a sweet lady. She'd never harm Mr. Brown."

"But her admiration could become an obsession." I scribbled some more in my notebook. "I'm going to look around to see if there are other gifts or letters from her."

I failed to find more gifts from Molly, but I did find a letter from Fred, the nephew.

I brought it over to read it with Portia. "Uncle Nicholas, how are you? I've tried calling you multiple times. I hope everything is okay. Times are hard. I've lost my job at the factory. After being a loyal employee for 29 years! Can you believe that? They said they don't need me anymore now that they have these machines. I hate to do this, but I wonder if I can ask you a favor. I've fallen behind on my mortgage. I've tried everything to no avail. Give me a call. Your beloved nephew, Fred." It ended with his phone number and was dated two weeks earlier.

"'Follow the money,' they say." I wrote "Suspect #3: Fred Brown" in my notebook. "Now, who should I interview first?"

Portia looked at her phone. "I'd better get back to Santa's Cabin to get ready for the photo sessions. Both Bernard and Molly will be there as the new Mr. and Mrs. Claus, but it's probably too chaotic to interview them now. Come back at 6:00, when the session is done. I'll make sure they don't leave early."

"Keep an eye on them. See if they act weird or let something slip about Mr. Brown. I'll give Fred a call." I took the mug back from Portia. "Something is bothering me though."

"What's that?"

"If Mr. Brown doesn't like Molly, why did he keep this mug?"

"That's for you to figure out. Maybe... " She paused. "Maybe that's the clue?"

The hair on the back of my neck stood up. "Portia, be careful around Molly. She could be a fake."

"Your imagination is running wild. Use it for your writing."

I already dreaded the next question she'd ask.

"How's Book One coming along?" Portia looked me straight in the eye, but I averted my gaze.

"I'm ... I'm still doing research."

Portia shook her head. "Just start. You took this week off work so you could write your first draft. Don't waste it!"

"You didn't tell anyone I'm writing a novel, right?" My heart quickened.

"Of course not. Your secret's safe with me." Portia crossed her heart. "But when you get famous, your mom will know."

"That's why I'm going to use a pen name."

"What's the pen name?"

"Don't know yet. Still deciding."

Portia sighed. "You think too much, Audrey. Just do it."

CHAPTER 6

While I psyched myself up to call Fred (why did phone calls give me so much anxiety?), I thought about the last key on the keyring. I used the third key to try all the other doors with a lock, but the back door and garage both had the same lock as the front door. There was no shed in the backyard. Did Mr. Brown own another property?

I searched the property records and only found this house under his name. Perhaps a rental property? I wrote a note to ask Portia later if Mr. Brown mentioned having a cabin up north. Or maybe he had a storage unit. Do storage units use regular keys? More research to do.

I stopped the music, sat down at the kitchen table with the notebook open, took a deep breath, and rehearsed in my head what to say to Fred before calling him. My palms were getting sweaty. I'd much rather text, but I would miss the non-verbal cues. I wanted to catch his reaction, using the element of surprise to my advantage.

I dialed Fred's number. My heart beat faster and faster as the phone rang.

"Hello?" I said when the call finally went through.

"Your call has been forwarded to the voicemail for Fred Brown. No one is available to take your call. At the tone, please record your message. When you're finished recording, you may hang up or press the pound key for more options."

I hung up without leaving a message.

What now? I could look up some storage units, call, and ask what type of key they used. If I were lucky, they might even let me know if Mr. Brown owned a unit. Or would that violate his privacy?

Something else was bugging me, but I couldn't put my finger on what it was. It'd come to me.

As I was about to dial the first self-storage company, after building up my courage for five minutes, a thought popped into my head.

If Fred had tried calling Mr. Brown multiple times, why didn't Mr. Brown call him back? Unless Mr. Brown used a landline. Then he wouldn't know there were missed calls. I looked around and spotted a wall phone by the kitchen. Beige, not brown! It blended in with the wall, and I hadn't noticed it before.

I went over to pick up the handset. No dial tone. So, Mr. Brown probably used a cell phone, and if so, he'd deliberately not returned Fred's call. Why? I wrote it down in the notebook.

Now where was Mr. Brown's cell phone?

I sighed. Being a cop would be handy. Then I could get a

warrant to trace his cell phone. Or ask his bank if any large sum of money had been withdrawn lately. Or track his credit cards. I could find out if he had a will.

I wrote down all these questions so I could share my thoughts with Drew when he was done with the big case in the next town. I still smiled every time I thought of him. Growing up, our classmates teased him about his name relentlessly, but he played it cool.

"Drew Nancy" because Mrs. Nancy loved Nancy Drew. He just happened to become a police officer after college.

Mrs. Nancy also had an interesting name. Her maiden name was Nancy Anderson, but when she married Drew's late father, she became Nancy Nancy. Our mayor. My boss.

Would I still have a job if Mrs. Nancy lost the election? Leroy was running for mayor again the next year, and never in a million years would I want to become his administrative assistant. Sorry, *Executive Assistant*, as Mrs. Nancy insisted. Titles were important according to her. I disagreed. It was the same job no matter how you glorified it. My pay didn't go up with the title change.

Staring at my cell phone, I smacked my forehead. How silly of me! I could ask my mom for Mr. Brown's phone number. I texted her and she responded within seconds.

My curiosity overcame my phone anxiety. I called Mr. Brown's number right then. As I waited for the call to be picked up, I heard a faint sound. I stood and took my phone away from my ear so I could hear better. Whatever sound I'd heard had stopped.

My call to Mr. Brown had ended on its own. I called

again, but this time it went straight to voicemail. How peculiar!

As I contemplated my next step, the doorbell rang.

Who could that be?

CHAPTER 7

I LOOKED out the peephole on the front door and saw the back of a man's balding head. He waved goodbye to the driver of the semi at the curb, and the truck drove off. He turned around and rang the doorbell again. Even though I'd never met this man before, I knew who it was.

Fred, Mr. Brown's nephew. He'd aged a few years since the latest photo, with more gray hair and more wrinkles, but there was no mistaking the cashew birthmark.

I opened the front door but kept the storm door locked. Could he be dangerous if he couldn't get what he was there for? He was at least a foot taller and 100 pounds heavier than me.

Fred did a double take. I waited for him to speak first. "Hello. Is my Uncle Nicholas home? I'm his nephew."

"No, he's not."

"Who are you? What are you doing in his house?"

What would be a convincing excuse? "I'm house sitting."

"House sitting? Where did he go? This is his busiest time

of year. Why would he go away?" At least he knew that much about his uncle.

Before I could answer, he said, "Look, let me in. Okay? It's cold out here." He was only wearing a blue hoodie with the text *Florida* in bright orange above a green alligator head. It had started snowing.

He rubbed his bare hands together and blew into them. "Besides… " He fished something out of his jeans pocket, and I stepped aside so I wasn't squarely in front of the door. "I have his house key. So, I'll get in one way or another."

I was tempted to run to the kitchen to grab a knife, but I held Mr. Brown's keys like a dagger in my hand instead and unlocked the storm door.

"I'm Fred."

"Audrey."

"You must be Audrey Nott!"

My eyes widened. "How did you know?"

"My uncle told me that, one day when it was very icy at the grocery store parking lot, you left your own cart at the entrance and helped him with his, loaded the grocery bags into his car, and returned the cart for him."

"Really?" I'd totally forgotten about it. It was years earlier.

"Yes. He said your mother was also good to him, making sure he was comfortable in Santa's Cabin every year. No wonder her daughter turned out wonderfully too."

I blushed. "So, are you visiting?" I didn't see any luggage except for a backpack.

His face darkened. "You could say that. Where did Uncle

Nicholas go anyway? I hope he's okay because I expected him to be here, playing Santa and all."

I decided to tell him the truth. Otherwise, I wouldn't be able to ask him questions without raising suspicion. "Let's take a seat." I directed him to the couch.

Elbows on his thighs, he clasped his hands and rested his chin on them as he listened.

He exhaled loudly once I'd finished. "So, that's why you're wearing latex gloves?"

"Yes, so I can look for the clue without leaving any fingerprints."

"Did you find anything?"

I shook my head. "Nothing seemed out of the ordinary." I'd skipped the parts about finding his letter to Mr. Brown and Molly's coffee mug. This wasn't exactly a lie since they might or might not be the real clue.

"Who would harm my uncle?"

"Do you know if he has any enemies?"

Fred shook his head. "He doesn't talk about himself much."

"How often do you talk to each other?"

"He used to call me maybe once a month, but I didn't hear from him the last couple of months. I tried calling a few times, but he didn't pick up or it went to voicemail. I got concerned. So, I wrote him a letter, but I still didn't hear back. So, here I am."

Gesturing to his backpack, I asked, "Where's your luggage?" Such a contrast to Micah when she had sleepovers at my house. She'd bring a full-size suitcase bursting at the seams, even though Ingrid lived only ten minutes away.

"I travel light."

"How did you get here?" If Fred was behind with his mortgage, how could he get money for flights?

Fred scratched his head. "What do you mean?"

"The semi that dropped you off ... It didn't look like a taxi."

He grimaced. "I hitchhiked."

I cocked my head. "You hitchhiked all the way from Florida to Minnesota?"

Fred sat up straight. "How did you know I'm from Florida?"

I had to come up with a reason without revealing too much. I pointed to his sweatshirt. "Just a guess."

He looked down and nodded. "Money is a bit tight, but I was concerned about Uncle Nicholas."

"You didn't happen to get all the drivers' contact info, did you?"

"No, why would you need that?" He squinted. "Are you a cop or something? Looking for witnesses? Checking my alibi?"

Being accused of playing cop twice in one day. I needed to learn to be more subtle.

I shook my head, "No, I'm not a cop. I'm just helping my mom find Mr. Brown."

"Besides, what would I gain from my uncle's disappearance?"

"Money? You said it yourself—"

"There's been no demand for ransom."

"Yet."

"Look, I'm a pretty simple person. I'm not smart enough to pull off something like that."

"And if your uncle dies?"

"What?"

"Wouldn't you be his heir since he has no other family?"

"No! He's already told me he's donating everything to charity. Something for children ... What's that hospital again? You can check with his lawyer."

"Maybe you're here to convince him to change his mind by, you know," I held his gaze, "kidnapping him until he does."

Fred jumped up and pointed to the door. "Get out of here or else!"

"Or else? Are you threatening me?" I stood up and braced myself.

"No! Just leave!" He tightened his fists. "Please."

I gathered my stuff from the kitchen table and left with the kidnapper's note, Fred's letter, and Mr. Brown's keys.

CHAPTER 8

THAT WENT WELL. I chewed my lip. I definitely needed to read up on the art of interrogation. Subtlety was not my specialty.

I drove home. I needed a quiet space to collect my thoughts before talking to Molly and Bernard. But first, I sealed Mr. Brown's note and Fred's letter in plastic zipper sandwich bags. Probably a little too late, but better late than never. I could finally take off my gloves.

My cat kept headbutting my hand while I sat at the kitchen table documenting my exchange with Fred.

"Nottson! Why do you think I need to feed you every time I'm in the kitchen?" I scratched behind his ear with my left hand. "And don't think I didn't catch Micah giving you some snacks earlier."

Micah spoiled Nottson. She couldn't have any pets because her parents were both allergic to cats and dogs. "I'm gonna adopt 1,000 cats when I grow up!" she'd said.

"You can start helping me with Nottson's litter boxes when you sleep over."

"We can train him to use the toilet!"

"I tried, but he's longer than he thinks. His bum kept hanging outside of the toilet. I almost stepped on his pee and poo when I went to the bathroom!"

Micah giggled. "Why did you call him Nottson anyway?"

"So, I can call him Naughty Notty?"

Micah threw her head back. Her laughter was one of the most beautiful sounds in the world, even if I favored silence. "Is it because your last name is Nott? So, he's the son of Nott?"

I nodded. "But it's also a play on words. Remember the book I got you, *The Adventures of Sherlock Holmes*?"

"Yes! So Nottson is like Watson!"

I patted her head. "A true and loyal friend."

Nottson gave up on food and lay on his back. I rubbed his belly with my left hand while drawing a table with five columns in my notebook labeled *A. Suspect, B. Motive, C. Means, D. Alibi, and E. Opportunity.*

I filled in Fred's details.

Suspect: Fred Brown, Mr. Brown's nephew from Florida

Motive: Money. But Fred said he's not in Mr. Brown's will. NEED TO CHECK.

Means: Much larger than Mr. Brown. Could easily overpower him. Mr. Brown trusts him.

Alibi: The drivers he got a ride from. No contact details. The semi had a lime green cab. NEED TO CHECK.

Opportunity: Without any solid witnesses, he could have gotten to Minnesota much earlier than when he showed up at Mr. Brown's house. It takes about twenty-six hours to drive from Florida to Minnesota, but it probably took him longer since he needed to find drivers. NEED TO CHECK: When did he actually leave Florida? Any witnesses? Ask for more details on the number of drivers, types of vehicles, and the route they traveled so a timeline can be constructed.

I grabbed a yellow highlighter from the junk drawer and highlighted my questions.

Satisfied, I closed the notebook and put it back in my bag. I saw that I'd missed a text. It was Mom. The message read, "???"

I rubbed the back of my neck. I hoped I could find Mr. Brown. Alive.

Working on it, I texted back.

I patted Nottson's long, soft hair. "Mr. Nottson, do I really want to solve the mystery or am I looking for Mom's approval?"

Portia didn't understand why, as a thirty-something, I still sought my mom's acceptance. She didn't realize the life-long impact a Chinese parent could have over their children. Only a 99 in your exam? Why not a 100? Got a distinction in an advanced piano exam when you were 14? Well, Wong's daughter did that when she was 13!

Nottson rubbed his face from nose to ear on my arm before sitting up. The sunlight behind him gave him a halo. With his towering Maine Coon stature, he was majestic. His jade eyes stared right into my soul.

He tapped my hand with his paw.

"What would I do without you, partner?" I caressed his giant kitty paw.

Since I still had some time before interviewing the other suspects at Santa's Cabin, I went to my library to find retired

FBI profiler John Douglas's books and Joe Navarro's body language books.

All the books had a bookmark in them, which meant I'd started reading them at one time or another but never finished them. I looked around the library, and I wondered how many books I'd actually read from cover to cover. I didn't even know how many books I owned.

Someday I'd scan all my books into an app so I could have my own library catalog. But who had time to do all that when they could read instead?

Or browse online about cold cases. Now *that* was a time suck.

CHAPTER 9

By the time I got to Santa's Cabin, Portia was finishing up with the last family session. Mom and Micah were nowhere in sight. Bernard had a beaming smile. Unless you were a long time Happy Valley resident, you wouldn't have known he was the backup Santa.

Molly's smile, on the other hand, didn't reach her eyes. There was a noticeable gap between her and Bernard.

I approached him first when they wrapped up. My guess was that Molly would stick around so she could find out more about Mr. Brown. Bernard was whistling "Jingle Bells."

"Bernard, could I ask you something?"

"Sure! What about?"

"I'm sure you know Mr. Brown is missing and I'm helping Mom find him."

"Playing cops now, are we? Are you sick of being the mayor's puppet?"

I bit my tongue. "I think it's to your benefit that your name be cleared."

"Is it now?" He snickered.

"You've wanted to be Santa for a long time. So, who gains the most when Mr. Brown is gone?"

"Listen, young lady... " His nostrils flared. "I may want to be Santa, but it doesn't mean I want him dead. I just want the decision as to who gets to be Santa to be fair. Not because *'it's always been this way, Bernard'*," he said in a mocking voice, mimicking Mrs. Nancy.

"So, where have you been since 6:00 last night?" I took out my pen and notebook.

"I was home. As always. Supper's at 6:00 on the dot with my lovely wife. What man doesn't want a hot meal at the end of a hard day?"

"And after that?"

"We watched a movie. Then we went to bed. I volunteered at the Humane Society all day today until our beloved mayor dropped by to talk to me." He rolled his eyes.

"What movie did you watch?"

"The Godfather."

"So, your wife is your only witness?"

"Isn't she enough?"

I almost said no. Bernard often praised his wife's obedience. I ignored his remark.

"Why were you and Mr. Brown arguing at the grocery store on Monday?"

"Monday ... Who told you that?" He glared.

"I saw you."

"Did you now?" He cracked his knuckles. "You know what? I don't have to answer any of your questions. We. Are. Done." He stormed off.

I wished I had the authority to make him answer me. I stopped writing mid-sentence, fetched my phone, and texted Mom. *Ask Bernard's wife what movie she watched last night. NOW!*

I'd have to interview her later (if he didn't ban me from going near his house), but I wanted to, at least, get her to answer before Bernard instructed her what to say. I hoped I wasn't too late.

CHAPTER 10

Molly was crying in Portia's arms when I turned around.

"Where is he? He must be so scared!" Molly said between sobs.

"Did you notice anything unusual in the last few weeks?" I asked Molly.

She shook her head.

"Do you know where he went after Photos with Santa yesterday?"

"Probably home." Molly paused. "No, wait! He said he had to go see Leroy!"

"He just told you out of the blue?" Portia asked. "I don't remember hearing him say that."

"You went to the bathroom. I asked him if I could drop off my homemade apple pie, but he said he wouldn't be home for a while because he had to see Leroy."

"Did he say why?" I added Leroy to the suspect list.

Molly shook her head. "I didn't even think they were

friendly. In fact, every time Leroy's name was mentioned, he'd clench his jaw and have this intense look in his eyes."

Trust Molly to observe all of Mr. Brown's behaviors. But could she be obsessed enough to kidnap him?

"Sorry I have to ask you this, Molly, but could you tell me where you were from 6:00 last night until Photos with Santa today?"

"I was home alone, eating my apple pie," Molly whispered.

"Did anyone call you or drop by? Mail delivery? A neighbor?" I asked.

Molly's shoulders slumped. "I was all alone."

"Oh, Molly!" Portia rubbed the woman's arm.

"Molly, do you know if Mr. Brown has a cabin, a rental house, or a storage unit somewhere?" Since Molly was a Mr. Brown-know-it-all, she might have some intel.

"Not that I know of. He's home most of the time. Why do you ask?"

I told her about the third key on his key ring.

"Oh, let me see. That might be my house key," Molly said.

"Your house key?" I was puzzled. I took out the key ring. Molly got out her own set of keys. Sure enough, it was a perfect match.

"I asked Nicholas if he could keep a spare key for me in case I locked myself out. I didn't want to use one of those fake rocks since everyone under the sun has one."

Mystery solved.

"Is there anything else you can think of that may help us find him?" Portia asked.

"I don't think so, but I'll let you know if I think of

anything. Anything at all." Molly's lips quivered and tears rolled down her face. "I just want him home safe and sound ... Even if he doesn't want anything to do with me."

"One more thing... " I watched Molly for her reaction. "We found the coffee mug you gave Mr. Brown?"

"The one with Mr. and Mrs. Santa on it?" Molly gave a slight smile.

"That's the one."

"He kept it?" Molly asked, eyes wide. She covered her mouth.

I nodded.

"Oh wow! I thought he'd have thrown it away for sure." Her eyes twinkled.

"Can you tell us more about it? Like when you gave it to him?" Perhaps the coffee mug was the clue after all.

"It was his birthday. May 4, this year. I used a picture of us from last Christmas since it was the only time we had pictures taken together. I made a cake. Black Forest, his favorite. He mentioned one time that his granny made the best Black Forest cake for his tenth birthday. She died in a car accident the next day. That poor soul. So, I experimented with all these different recipes until I perfected it." She clasped her hands to her chest. "Anyway, I went to his house, and he was surprised to see me. He was stunned when I wished him a happy birthday because he didn't think anyone knew! He'd mentioned it one time and I took note. You should've seen his face!" She chuckled. "I pushed past him and took the cake and present into the kitchen before he could stop me. I grabbed two plates and sliced up the cake for us. A chocolate cake on brown plates in a brown house!"

She basked in the memory. I waited for her to continue.

"I gave him the mug, and he just stared at it, speechless. I went to get a cup of water, but he stopped me. He told me to drink from the Santa mug instead if I was thirsty. Said he didn't want my lips touching his dishes." Her chin trembled.

"Oh, Molly." Portia gave her a tissue.

"I ran out of his house. I don't even know how I made it home." Molly dabbed her eyes and blew her nose. "So, I was shocked when you said you saw the mug. I haven't been back to his house since that day, and I was certain he'd have tossed it in the garbage."

"So, was it awkward having to play Mrs. Santa these past few days?"

"Of course, but I just pretended nothing had happened. I'm an actor after all." She sighed. Molly was active in our local community theater. "I couldn't stand the tension anymore. So, I thought I'd extend an olive branch and offer him the apple pie. If only ... If only I'd gone over to his house ... Maybe he'd still be here. What have I done?" Molly wailed.

"Molly, you don't know that. It's not your fault. Okay?" Portia said. "You're in no condition to drive. Why don't I drive you home? I can pick you up tomorrow before the photo session?"

Molly nodded.

I opened my mouth for one more question, but Portia shot me a look.

As they left, my phone beeped. It was a text from Mom.

CHAPTER 11

THE GODFATHER, she wrote. *Marlon Brando was so dreamy!*

I groaned. Mom had a thing for Old Hollywood. Hence our names. My sister was named after Ingrid Bergman, and I was named after Audrey Hepburn, her two favorite actresses.

The movie checked out. But who knew if Bernard's wife talked to Mom before or after Bernard got home? As much as I hated talking on the phone, I called Mom to ask. Too complicated to text.

"Did you find more clues?" Mom asked. "And what was all that about Lorraine?"

Lorraine. I'd forgotten her name, I remembered her as Of Bernard, similar to how the female characters were named in Margaret Atwood's *The Handmaid's Tale.*

"I'm still investigating. I've talked to a few people and have some leads. Tell me, Mom, when did you talk to Lorraine and was she suspicious?"

"I called her right after I got your text. I slipped that

question in. I was sure it was related to the kidnapping. So, I didn't want to alert her." She sniffed. "I may not read as many books as you do, but I'm not dumb."

I gripped the hem of my top. "I never said you were dumb."

She snorted. "Anyway, Lorraine and I kept chatting since we haven't socialized for a while. She hung up when Bernard got home, and I texted you right away."

Hopefully Bernard didn't text her beforehand. "So, she didn't seem to think that question was weird?"

"Didn't seem like it. You want to tell me what this is all about?"

I gave her a quick update. "I'm going to talk to Leroy next."

"Be careful of that nasty man! Maybe I should go with you."

"I can take care of myself, Mom. Besides, you have Micah. How is she?"

"She's fine. She has her nose in this big thick book. Just like someone else I know."

I tapped my foot. I definitely did not get my reading habit from Mom, who preferred movies and soap operas.

"Does she still believe in Santa?" I remembered Ingrid's order.

"Of course! Micah believes everything her *Popo* says!"

"Alright, I'd better go talk to Leroy before it's too late."

"Text me right after. I want to make sure you're home safe."

"I'm not a kid anymore, Mom."

"You'll always be a child in my eyes."

My Mini Cooper was the only car left in the parking lot beside Molly's and Mr. Brown's. Since mine was right next to the street lamp, even from far away, I could see that something was wrong.

My tires. Flat. Both the left front and rear tires. I looked around, making sure there was no one nearby, and ran to check the other side. Both flat. I checked the other two cars and their tires were fine. This was no accident. I looked back and scanned Santa's Cabin. No camera. I didn't want to alarm Mom, especially since she had Micah with her. So, I texted Portia.

She came within minutes. "We should call the police!"

"It could be a prank, and Drew is busy." If I'd called Drew, he'd want me to stop the investigation.

"You really should file a report."

"I will. Tomorrow. Just take me home." I yawned. "Wait, I need to talk to Leroy first."

"Can't that wait? You must be in shock."

"The first 48 hours within a person's disappearance are the most crucial! It's been more than twenty-four hours since Molly last saw Mr. Brown. We don't know exactly when he disappeared. Besides, we need more leads. We're hitting a dead end with our three suspects."

Portia shook her head. "I don't know why you don't become a cop or an FBI agent or something."

"You know I wouldn't pass the physical."

"You can train for it."

"I'm clumsy."

"Not that clumsy."

"Let's not talk about that right now. We need to talk to Leroy."

"You always avoid this question when I ask. What are you afraid of?"

"Nothing."

"I know you, Audrey. There's something you're not telling me. One day, hopefully you'll trust me enough to tell me."

"I do trust you."

Portia sighed. "Let's go talk to Leroy."

CHAPTER 12

Leroy slammed the door in our faces.

I kept ringing the doorbell, and he finally opened the door again but kept the chain on. He yelled through the gap, "If you don't stop, I'm going to tell everyone that the mayor's office is harassing me. Let's see what that'll do to her election campaign!"

"And let's see what the cops calling you a person of interest would do to your campaign," I said. "We know Mr. Brown was coming to see you last night."

"That's a lie! He was never here!"

I eyed his camera. "We'll see."

He slammed his door a second time.

Knowing Leroy, he probably didn't know how the camera worked. He wasn't someone you'd call tech savvy. His grandkids probably set it up for him. His wife got several packages every day from the gossip I heard from Mom. And the theft of packages had gone up in recent months.

Portia had stayed quiet the whole time. "I think we should go see Drew," she said as she started the car.

I stared down at my hands. She was right. Mr. Brown's safety was more important than my ego. Only the police could help now.

But I was so close! I sank into the passenger seat. Deflated like a balloon.

We decided to try Drew's house since he lived nearby. The lights were on. My heart dropped.

"What's up?" He let us in after we rang the bell.

I took out my notebook, and gave him a summary of the events.

"And you didn't call the cops when this happened?"

"I thought Mrs. Nancy did?"

"I didn't hear anything about this when I went to the station earlier. Wait!" He ran his fingers through his hair. "Mother did call me earlier, but she only asked if Chuck and I were busy. I told her Chuck was sick as a dog and I had to go to the next town. She didn't mention anything about Mr. Brown being missing."

Portia and I exchanged a look.

"Can you still go over there to have a word with Leroy?" I asked.

"Let me take a look at your notebook." He tilted his chin up.

I clutched it a little tighter before handing it over. Drew read in silence. Nodding often.

"This is really good work for someone without any police training." He handed the notebook back to me.

"You should check who punctured Audrey's tires too," Portia said.

"Alright. Let me take over from here." Drew yawned. "You go home and rest."

"Call me if you find anything out from Leroy?" I asked.

"We'll see. You know I can't reveal anything if it could impact the investigation," Drew said.

I nodded.

Portia drove me home.

"Are you sure you don't want me to spend the night? I can go home and grab some stuff," Portia offered when we arrived at my cottage.

"I'm sure. I promise I'll call if I need anything."

"You better. I'm here for you."

"Thank you." And I meant it.

CHAPTER 13

Even though Drew was taking over the case, I still wanted to complete my notes on Bernard, Molly, and Leroy.

Suspect #2: Bernard Barney – backup Santa

Motive: He's wanted to be Santa forever. Said it wasn't fair how Santa was chosen for the town festivities. Argued with Mr. Brown on Monday evening at the grocery store but won't say what it was about. Mr. Brown called Bernard and Leroy "peas in a pod" after the argument.

Means: Longtime Happy Valley resident with connections in town. Leroy's best friend.

Alibi: He was home since 6:00 the night Mr. Brown disappeared; his wife Lorraine was his sole witness. Said they had dinner and then watched a movie *(The Godfather)* together. Lorraine confirmed the movie. (NEED TO CHECK: Did Bernard coach her? Didn't sound like it, but don't make assumptions.) Home for the rest of the night. (NEED TO CHECK: Did he sneak out?) Volunteered at the Humane

Society the next day until Mrs. Nancy dropped by to ask him to be Santa for the day.

Opportunity: He could have told Lorraine to lie for him. He dominates her. Even if they had dinner and watched a movie together, he had the rest of the night. Maybe he drugged Lorraine so she'd be deep asleep. Maybe Lorraine would lie for her husband.

I read through my scribbles on Molly. My gut said Molly didn't do it since she seemed genuinely upset, but she did say she was an actor. Hello, *Misery*!

Suspect #3: Molly Peach – Mrs. Santa Claus

Motive: In love (obsessed?) with Mr. Brown

Means: Lured him into her house or drugged him with homemade baked goods? She is petite and would not be able to move him by herself.

Alibi: Home alone. No witnesses.

Opportunity: Told us Mr. Brown was going to see Leroy, but Leroy said it was a lie. Molly could be framing Leroy. Self-proclaimed good actor. Can she really be trusted?

Suspect #4: Leroy Jones – Mayor Wannabe

Motive: He could be teaming up with Bernard. If the Happy Wonderland Festival was a disaster, then Mrs. Nancy might lose the election and he'd have a chance.

Means: Powerful figure in town. Bernard's best friend. They could team up and cover for each other.

Alibi: Won't talk. (NEEK TO CHECK: Did Drew find out anything from the camera?)

Opportunity: Molly said Mr. Brown had a meeting with Leroy. If Molly was telling the truth, then Leroy's lying. He accused Molly of lying. (NEED TO CHECK: Drew to follow up?)

I put down my pen and stroked Nottson, who had settled onto my lap. He purred. If reincarnation really existed, I wanted to come back as a cat.

I raised my arms over my head to stretch. Nottson turned and gave me the stink eye.

I flipped through the profiling and body language books I'd put on the table earlier. Perhaps I could formulate some next steps or start a profile on who was most likely to kidnap Mr. Brown. Or I could read through the body language tips to see if any of the suspects had lied.

My phone beeped. It was a text from Drew.

I watched Leroy's video footage. Mr. Brown never dropped by. No camera at Santa's Cabin. We may be out of luck there. I called the tow truck for you, and they'll be in touch.

Was Molly lying? Maybe they were both telling the truth. Perhaps Mr. Brown was planning to go to Leroy's, but something happened on the way.

CHAPTER 14

I PUT Nottson on the floor. He scowled. I started pacing back and forth, going through everything to see if I'd missed something. Perhaps I was focusing too much on the details instead of looking at the big picture to see how all the dots were connected.

"*If you want to find Santa, you must follow the trail,*" the note said.

Mr. Brown's key ring was on top of it. Keys to his car, his house, and Molly's house. So, the next clue should either be at Mr. Brown's house or Molly's house since his car was spotless. I hurried over to the table and opened a blank page in my notebook before I lost my train of thought.

I drew the kidnapping note and keys at the top of the page, then added three arrows to show three possible pathways in the flowchart. The left arrow pointed to *Mr. Brown's Car* and I put a big X over it. The middle one pointed to *Mr. Brown's House,* and the right arrow pointed to *Molly's House.*

Under *Mr. Brown's House,* I listed the few things that could possibly be clues, things that stood out:

1. Fred's letter asking for money.

2. Molly's mug that was out of place.

3. Bobby Vinton's record playing "Mr. Lonely."

4. Blueprints of the house.

Under *Molly's House,* I drew a big question mark. I also linked Molly's mug from *Mr. Brown's House* to *Molly's House.*

I needed to go to her place! Then I remembered my flat tires. I weighed my options. I could walk the five miles in the cold, or I could run. Ha! Who was I kidding? Let's stick to walking. I could ride my bike. On ice? No thanks! Or I could call Portia or Drew.

Both Portia's and Drew's phone went to voicemail. I texted both of them, asking them to call me as soon as possible.

I could call Mom, but Micah would be sleeping by now. Ingrid was working nights at the hospital, and my brother-in-law, Jude, was on a business trip out of town. There was Mrs. Nancy, but she went to bed even earlier than Micah since she usually woke up at 4:00 to start her day with yoga. And no neighbors. My cottage was in the middle or nowhere, chosen specifically for that reason. I looked at my chart again.

Nottson jumped onto the table and dropped something on my notebook from his mouth. Not a dead mouse, I hoped. No, it was his toy hedgehog, Cactus. Usually Nottson had it hidden somewhere that I could never find. He would drag it out only when he wanted to do something with it.

Wait!

I looked back at the list of items under *Mr. Brown's House.* Both Fred's letter and Molly's mug were out of sight. Only the record and the blueprints were left out in the open.

I looked at the photos I'd taken of the blueprints. Two of them were blurry. (Note to self: Check pictures after taking them.) It was difficult to make out all of the measurements on a small phone screen. By enlarging the photo, I could only see part of the blueprints, and scrolling up and down was making me dizzy. Looking at it on my laptop was only a smidge better without a large monitor.

I needed to see the original again. There might be some clues I missed earlier. Maybe the numbers were ciphers?

Mr. Brown's house was just over a mile away. I could walk. I *would* walk.

CHAPTER 15

I put on my winter gear and cleats on my boots. The last thing I needed was to fall on the ice.

Even with the cleats, I almost slipped twice from ice hidden under a blanket of fresh snow. My glasses fogged from my balaclava. Blowing ice pellets hit the exposed portions of my face. My fingers were frozen even though my gloves had thick insulation.

Why was I living here again? I'd never liked the cold.

By the time I got to Mr. Brown's house, my throat was dry and my nose was dripping behind the balaclava. Luckily, Fred opened the door when I rang the bell. He squinted and cocked his head.

"It's Audrey!" I yelled, my voice muffled by my hat and the wind.

He cupped his left ear with his hand.

"AUDREY!" My voice cracked.

He looked down, eyes stopping at my crossbody bag. Recognition showed on his face. He must have remembered seeing it earlier. Not many grown women carried a giant cat face yellow bag. He opened the door.

"Audrey! What are you doing here?" Did he forget he'd ordered me out of the house earlier?

"I need to look at the blueprints."

"The blueprints?"

"The blueprints of the house that were on the table."

I took off my boots and hurried over to the kitchen. There they were. I stood and traced the perimeter of the house with my finger. Nothing seemed out of the ordinary. I took my notebook out and started writing down some of the numbers to see if I could crack the code. Fred sat down opposite me. When he was about to speak, I put my palm up to stop him. I couldn't be interrupted right then.

I looked up some common ciphers using numbers on my phone. (How did we live before the internet?) Nothing worked. Defeated, I collapsed onto a dining room chair and closed my eyes. I took some deep breaths. When I opened my eyes, Fred had gotten a glass of water and placed it in front of me.

I gulped it down. "Thank you." I hoped he hadn't tried to poison me, but I was too thirsty to give it much thought.

"No luck?"

I shook my head. I was so confident that the blueprints would give me the clue.

"Let me put on some music. Maybe that will help you relax. It helps me."

The haunting sound of "Mr. Lonely" filled the house for the second time today.

"Mr. Lonely?" Could that be a clue? Was Mr. Brown

telling us how he felt? The suspects. The hints. What did they have to do with loneliness?

"This doesn't make sense," I muttered.

A lightbulb went on in my head. I looked at the blue-prints again and studied the measurements of the exterior of the house. Then I added up the measurements of the interior of each room. They didn't add up. The exterior was ten feet longer than the interior on the back wall. Even with insula-tion, there shouldn't be that big a difference.

A hidden room! But where?

I stood up and looked at one short end of the house, and we were right there in the dining room and kitchen. There were two windows facing the yard on that wall.

It must be at the other end of the house. Mr. Brown's bedroom was on the south side at the end of the hallway, and the bathroom was on the north side. I ran to the bath-room first. The light was already on and there was no hidden doorway.

Fred followed me. "What are you doing?"

I pushed him aside so I could get through to Mr. Brown's bedroom. I wasn't ready to share my theory in case I was wrong. I'd already made enough of a fool of myself. I turned on the lights and stared at the bifold closet doors at the far end of the wall.

This must be it, the wardrobe with the secret passageway.

I opened the doors. The closet was full of clothes, mostly brown with some black and gray mixed in.

"Help me get all the clothes out!" I said.

Fred did as he was told without asking any questions.

Within minutes, the clothes were piled on the bed, and I saw a seam in the middle of the closet wall.

I ducked under the top shelf when I walked into the closet and pushed on both walls. The wall on the left side pushed forward.

"What the... " Fred whispered.

CHAPTER 16

I TURNED on the flashlight app on my phone before I took a small step forward. My heart was throbbing so loudly I swore I could hear it echoing in the room. I also heard another noise. It was faint, but there was no mistaking what it was. Snoring.

I motioned for Fred to follow me and tiptoed forward. I shone my flashlight around and paused when it illuminated an air mattress. Next to it was a small table on which sat some crackers and water. I saw a figure lying on the bed with his back to us. We approached him as gingerly as possible. I hoped his hands and feet weren't bound.

Fred kneeled and whispered, "Uncle Nicholas? It's Fred."

The man groaned. "Huh?"

He sounded half asleep, not in pain.

"Uncle Nicholas? It's Fred," he said a little louder.

The man rolled over. He put his hand over his face, shielding it from the flashlight.

"Sorry," I said and pointed the beam to my left instead.

"Fred?"

"Yes, Uncle Nicholas. It's me."

Mr. Brown pushed himself up onto his elbow.

"Fred, you're here."

"I am. But what are you doing sleeping in here? I didn't know there was a hidden room in this house. That's amazing!"

"And who else do we have here?" Mr. Brown asked, ignoring Fred's question.

"It's Audrey. Audrey Nott."

"Aha! I bet it was you who figured it out. Your mother always said you're one smart cookie."

"She did?"

"She sure did. She believes that if only you'll apply yourself, you'll achieve great things."

My heart sank. *Potential* was my middle name.

"Should we go back to the living room?" Fred asked.

My phone rang, and I jumped. It was Portia. "Are you okay, Audrey? I just saw your text now."

"I'm okay. I'm at Mr. Brown's house."

"How did you get there? Did you find something?"

"Yes. I found Mr. Brown."

"What? Is he okay?"

"Yes. Why don't you come over?" I eyed Mr. Brown. He owed us all an explanation. "Bring Drew too if he's up for it."

I'd let Mom know after I heard Mr. Brown's story, or she'd ply me with all kinds of questions I wouldn't be able to answer.

Portia and Drew arrived in less than ten minutes. We were sipping hot tea in the living room.

"Mr. Brown, you scared us!" Portia went to him and gave him a big hug.

"Are you here as a cop?" Mr. Brown asked Drew.

Drew shook his head. "No one has filed a police report yet. I'm just here as a concerned citizen."

"So, what happened, Uncle Nicholas?"

Mr. Brown inhaled, then exhaled loudly. "I was stupid."

"You were lonely." I corrected him. "Let me guess. You were listening to this record you haven't listened to in a long time. Then 'Mr. Lonely' came on, and your heart ached."

Mr. Brown rubbed his eyes. "I thought about my time in the wars and the friends I lost. Then I thought about my current situation. Everyone wants something from me. Like money."

Fred lowered his head.

"Bernard wanted me to retire because he didn't think it was fair that the mayor from thirty-three years ago promised me that I could be Santa for as long as I wanted. He argued there's no contract. I said handshakes were as good as it got. We live by our words," Mr. Brown said. "Leroy wanted me to sabotage the parade so he could blame it on Nancy. Nancy, of course, wanted me to do more activities and work longer hours to attract more tourists. So, that got me thinking ... If I went missing, would anyone even care?"

"My mom called me right away when she found the note," I said.

"But did your mother care about me going missing—or about Santa?" Mr. Brown looked me in the eye.

I opened my mouth, but no words came out.

"Molly was hysterical when she heard the news," Portia said.

"I told Molly she was wasting her time," Mr. Brown said. "What could she want with someone like me? I'm twenty years older than her.'"

"I think she really does enjoy your company and cares about you," Portia offered. "I was with her earlier, listening to her recite favorite memories of you."

Mr. Brown was lost in thought.

"So, what would you have done if Audrey hadn't found you?" Drew asked.

"I'm not sure. I didn't plan that far ahead. I was just going to wait and see."

"Fred cares about you too," I said. "He hitchhiked all the way here from Florida when you didn't call him back."

Fred mouthed a silent thank you when I caught his eye.

"I thought he just wanted money." Mr. Brown said.

"I'm sorry, Uncle Nicholas. I did ask you for money recently, but it's my fault that I have never told you how much I appreciate you. You were there for me after my parents died in that freak car accident when I turned eighteen." Fred rubbed his face. "I wouldn't be who I am today without you. I'm terrible at verbally expressing myself. All my ex-girlfriends told me that, but I thought they were just being petty."

Fred went over and gave Mr. Brown a bear hug.

My phone beeped. It was Mom. *Any updates? Have you eaten? I made dumplings, your favorite. Come for dinner tomorrow. Don't forget to drink some warm ginger tea before bed. It's cold tonight.*

Chinese families never showed verbal affection. But food? The ultimate Chinese love language.

I texted back. *We found Mr. Brown. He's safe.*

I hesitated, then added something I'd never written to her before. *I love you, Mom.*

<h1 style="text-align:center">CHAPTER 17</h1>

"I CAN'T WAIT for the parade today!" Micah jumped up and down. "Fa-la-la-la-la—-la-la-la-la!"

"Micah, are you ready to go?" I asked.

"Yes!" Micah said and then turned solemn. "Aunty Audrey, thank you."

"What for?"

"For finding the real Santa! Otherwise, *Popo*, Mommy, Daddy, you, and I wouldn't be able to go to the parade together! It's a miracle! I wish we could take Nottson with us."

"You can tell him all about it when we come back."

"Can I ask you a question?"

"Of course. You know I love your curiosity."

"How does Santa know whether I've been naughty or nice? Does he spy on us?"

I laughed.

❄

THE FIVE OF us waved to the people in the parade when they walked past.

Micah's enthusiasm was infectious. Ingrid and Jude stole a kiss when Mom wasn't watching. Mom beamed when people congratulated her on another successful festival.

Portia joined us. When Santa and Mrs. Claus came near us in the reindeer sleigh, Santa winked and pulled Mrs. Claus closer. Molly blushed.

"Ho! Ho! Ho!"

The marching band started playing "Santa Claus is Coming to Town."

Snow flurries danced around us. When the sun hit the fresh snow, the powder glittered like diamonds.

Magical.

About Sage So

Sage So dreamed of being a CSI until she almost failed biology, chemistry *and* biochemistry at college; and there was no way she would have passed the physical fitness test to become an FBI agent. But she gets to solve crimes (among other things) in her fictional world now! She lives in Minnesota in the US with her human and feline family members who may or may not make an appearance in her stories. Connect with her at https://sageso.com.

HAVE YOURSELF A SCARY LITTLE CHRISTMAS

GAYLE LEESON

Max, the Ghostly Fashionista, tells a story about how her dad's past came back to haunt him one Christmas Eve.

INTRODUCTION

Hello, darling! I'm sorry you can't see me; but as they say in all the romances, it's not you, it's me. In this case, it really is *me. I'm a ghost. My friend Amanda Tucker calls me the ghostly fashionista. We both adore clothes. In fact, she sews them right here in this delightful boutique, which used to be my living room.*

I don't want to go into too much detail about all that, though. I'd simply like to introduce myself and then get on with my story. You see, Amanda is usually the one who relays our adventures to you.

So, my name is Maxine Englebright, but I go by Max. I fell down that staircase out there in the hallway and broke my stupid neck in 1930. Be careful and hold to the railing if you go up or down those stairs. Trust me on that.

Amanda is one of a handful of people who is able to see and hear me. You might not think a ghost and a young living woman could be best friends, but we are. Anyway, sit back, relax, and let me tell you my spooky tale.

272

CHAPTER 1

DECORATING AT THE BOUTIQUE

AMANDA WAS fluttering around the lobby of the boutique in a green velvet A-line dress with a portrait collar. She and my great-niece, Zoe, resplendent in jeans torn at the knee and a white shaker-knit sweater, were hanging a garland over the mantel. Amanda's grandfather, Dave, a handsome man I often called a silver fox, and my nephew Dwight–Zoe's granddad who was so like my sister in looks and demeanor– were putting the pre-lit tree together in front of the main window. Jasmine, or Jazzy, Amanda's gray and white tabby, pounced on a beam of light created by the waning sun glinting off a strand of tinsel. I perched slightly above the desk and delighted in the scene before me.

"Watching the people I love decorating for Christmas really takes me back," I said.

"Tell us about some of your traditions, Aunt Max," Zoe said.

Clasping my hands together, I said, "Well, for one thing, we never decorated the tree until Christmas Eve."

"Christmas Eve?" Amanda turned to me, her brows drawn together in dismay. "That's terrible. You had hardly any time to enjoy it."

I laughed. "We enjoyed it well enough, darling. We had more fun spending the evenings leading up to our tree-trimming party making ornaments—paper chains, string snowflakes, popcorn garlands. Mother insisted on upholding her grandmother's tradition of telling ghost stories on Christmas Eve, so we did that as we worked—practicing up for the main event, I suppose."

"Ghost stories on Christmas Eve?" Dave shook his head. "That's a new one on me, and I thought I'd been around long enough to have heard of everything."

Amanda grinned at him. "See? I told you you're not as old as you think."

"I remember the ghost stories," Dwight said. "Mom kept it going with us kids. We had to do ours before Dad came home. He didn't think ghost stories had any place in Christmas celebrations."

"I kinda see his point," Zoe said. "Telling scary stories on Christmas doesn't make a lot of sense."

"Charles Dickens would beg to differ," I said.

"That's right." Amanda turned to take some red ribbon from a cardboard box. "The ghost story tradition is English, isn't it?"

"It is. Granny was born here, but she clung to her English heritage as if we were members of the royal family." I laughed. "Granny was a hoot. You would've loved her."

"Tell us one of your stories," Zoe said.

"Well, that's the thing, love," I said. "We didn't know

very many and didn't have a great deal of talent for making them up. So Daddy often told us stories from his childhood."

"Do you think Granddad ever stretched the truth?" Dwight chuckled. "I used to think he was king of the tall tales."

"As did I. Until one Christmas Eve."

CHAPTER 2

BACK IN TIME

"Dorothy! Maxine! You're eating more popcorn than you're putting on the string." Mother clucked her tongue. "We'll have the most pitiful-looking tree in the neighborhood if you two keep going at that rate."

"But you'll have the happiest girls," I said, winking at my younger sister.

Dot giggled. "We can't help that it's so good."

She and I were in our mid- to late-teens that year, but our exact ages escaped me upon telling this story. Suffice it to say that Dot and I were young, beautiful, and not lacking in mischief.

All of us brightened when Daddy came home—even Mother, who leaned more toward the serious side of life.

Daddy hugged Mother and kissed her cheek. "And what have my beauties been doing today?"

Shaking her head, Mother said, "This one has been trying to keep those two from eating all our Christmas tree decorations."

"Aw, let them have at it." He wedged himself between Dot and me on the burgundy sofa. "If they run out of decorations, they can eat the tree. There'll be more dinner for us if they're full." Putting an arm around each of us, he gave us a squeeze.

"Have you had a good day, Daddy?" I asked.

"Every day is a good day, sweetheart. I'm the most blessed man in the world."

"Tell us a story while Mother finishes dinner," Dot said.

"Shouldn't the two of you be helping with that?" he asked.

"We did our part. I peeled and diced potatoes while Dot pulled carrot duty." I held up my hands. "Look. I've worked my fingers to the bone."

"Me too." Dot held her hands out for his examination.

"They're spoiled," Mother called from the kitchen. "But keep them in there—I don't want them in here under my feet."

"You heard her." I snuggled against Daddy's shoulder and inhaled the faint scent of woodsmoke that lingered on his clothes. "Now you can tell us that story."

"Yes, Daddy. Tell about Freddy and the haunted house."

"I was saving that one for Christmas Eve," he said.

"You can tell it again, and it will be every bit as good," I said. "We never get tired of hearing that one."

He gave a low, growly-groan and then smiled. "All right then."

CHAPTER 3
DADDY'S STORY

FREDDY and I weren't the most well-behaved lads, but we weren't all that bad. I suppose you might say the two of us were simply left to our own devices more often than we should have been.

When we were around the ages you girls are now, he and I loved playing hide-and-seek in the woods near the haunted house on summer evenings. In fact, on this particular moonless night with the occasional flicker of heat lightning splitting the sky, and a whiff of rain on the breezes, we decided to use the haunted house as home base.

We flipped a penny to see who'd hide first, and Freddy won. That suited me fine. I went to the big maple tree, hid my eyes, and began counting. We were supposed to count to a hundred, but I never counted past twenty, and I knew good and well Freddy didn't either. He couldn't have, given how quickly he always yelled, "Ready or not, here I come!"

So, I counted my measly amount, yelled "ready or not," and moseyed on down toward the haunted house. My plan was to hide in the bushes and give Freddy a hearty scare when he approached the house.

You see, I'd heard the same stories everyone else had, but I thought it was all a lot of hooey. Just because what once had been a nice big house was now abandoned and dilapidated, and simply because it sat out in the middle of nowhere didn't make it haunted. To me, the house was sad. I could imagine a family gathered around the fire telling stories like we are now...laughter, music, life filling its rooms. I wondered what had really happened to the family who'd once occupied and loved the old house.

I know, I know—you want to hear a ghost story. So, here is the one that was told about the house.

Just after the Civil War ended—because, as you know, most good Southern ghost stories have their roots in the Civil War—two brothers came home to Virginia. One had fought for the North and the other for the South, but they both believed they were returning home to marry the lovely Blue-Eyed Bess. Now, mind you, Bess wasn't promised to either man; but they were both in love with her.

That fateful night, they met at Bess's home—what was currently known as the haunted house—by chance. Each man intended to declare his love for Bess and ask for her hand in marriage. How furious the two men were to see each other! Instead of being happy that his brother was alive, instead of embracing his brother in the spirit of forgiveness and a willingness to put an end to their years of strife, each soldier drew his sword. Instead of asking Bess if she even wanted either of them, they began to fight for her.

Bess cared for both brothers, and the last thing she

wanted was for either of them to shed a single drop of blood on her account. She ran down the front porch steps with her arms open wide, pleading for the brothers to put down their swords. But the men were focused on their hate rather than on their love.

Both expert swordsmen, neither could inflict a killing blow against the other. It wasn't until Blue-Eyed Bess crumpled to the ground that the men realized one of their swords had dealt a fatal blow.

Legend had it that on moonless nights, such as the one on which I planned to scare the hair off Freddy's head, you could hear Blue-Eyed Bess weeping. Some versions of the ghost story added that you could see Bess standing at the window or the brothers fighting on the lawn.

I knew the whole tale was a load of hooey. But I thought Freddy wasn't so sure. I hid behind a holly bush and debated the various techniques I could use to spring out at my unsuspecting friend.

Turns out, the joke was on me. Not ten minutes after I squatted down behind that holly bush, I heard two men commence fighting. I took off like Snyder's hound on a rabbit's trail and never looked back.

As soon as I got home, I felt like an idiot. Either Freddy had pranked me, or there simply happened to be two men walking in the woods having an argument near where I'd been hiding.

Shamefaced, I went around to Freddy's house the next morning. He wasn't there. He hadn't come home last night. Worse still? I never saw Freddy again.

CHAPTER 4

CHRISTMAS EVE

Well, I probably don't need to tell you how we two emotional teens wept for poor Blue-Eyed Bess and for Freddy. We had so many questions for which there were no answers: Which brother would Bess have chosen, if either? What if she'd already married someone else by the time they came back from the war? Was it the pair of phantom brothers Daddy had heard arguing? Had they stabbed Freddy with their swords? *Could* they stab Freddy? Or had Freddy seen the apparitions and died of fright? What if the men Daddy had heard arguing weren't ghosts at all but were bad men who'd kidnapped Freddy?

We guessed we'd never know what became of poor Freddy, but we were wrong. On that Christmas Eve, the very evening after Daddy had entertained us with Freddy's sad story, there was a knock on the door. Expecting carolers, all four of us went to answer it. But rather than carolers, it was a short, thin man who had his fedora pulled way down over his eyes and his coat turned up at the collar. Beside him stood a platinum blonde woman wearing a full-length white fur coat. She had the bluest eyes I'd ever seen.

When he saw Dot and me, the man tipped up the brim of his hat and said, "Hello, ladies. I'm an old friend of your daddy's. You can call me Freddy."

Dot gasped and looked at the woman. "Are you Blue-Eyed Bess?"

The woman grinned. "No, sugar. I'm Mavis. Who's Blue-Eyed Bess?"

"A ghost," Dot whispered.

Freddy threw back his head and laughed. "Been telling 'em about our childhood, eh?"

I turned my attention to Daddy, who looked like he was about to be sick. I didn't want Daddy to be upset. He had to know that whatever had happened to Freddy wasn't his fault.

"Where have you been all this time?" I asked Freddy. "What happened to you that night in the woods?"

"Maxine! Shh!" Mother's *shh* emerged as a hiss, but that poor woman never was able to rein me in.

"Are you all coming in or what?" I asked.

"Sassy. I like that." Freddy doffed his hat. "We'd be much obliged."

Dot and I moved aside, but Mother and Daddy seemed to have sprouted roots right there in the foyer.

I glanced at Mother as Freddy and Mavis handed me their coats. Although she was staring at me, she didn't appear to be angry. She was frightened. That was my first inkling that the story about Freddy's disappearance might not have occurred exactly as Daddy had told it. A lump formed in my throat as I took the coats and hung them in the hall closet.

"Freddy, I...I heard you'd moved up north," Daddy was saying when I returned to the living room.

Mavis and Freddy were sitting on the burgundy sofa, Dot perched on the piano bench, and Mother and Daddy had remained standing..

"Did you now?" Freddy leaned forward, rested his elbows on his knees, and steepled his fingers. "Beautiful family you've got here. You've done well for yourself."

"Thanks." Daddy's voice was flat. I found it odd that he didn't introduce any of us to Freddy. But I knew there had to be a good reason.

"Girls, go upstairs," Mother said.

Dot was watching me to see what I'd do. I left the living room, and she got up and trailed after me. Halfway up the stairs, I stopped but stamped my feet as if I was still climbing the staircase. Grinning, Dot followed suit.

I was such a bad influence.

We crouched on the stairs and listened. The adults were talking quietly, so we only caught a phrase here and there.

"...be a pal," Freddy was saying. "For old time's sake."

"I can't keep that thing here," Daddy said.

"You want me to..." Freddy's next words were unintelligible. Then his voice rose. "Listen, you *owe* me. I'm not asking you to keep it forever. Just 'til–"

"Until what?" Daddy asked. "Until the police come here and haul me away?"

Dot and I stared at each other open-mouthed.

"You think I'd let that happen? You think I'd set you up as a stool pigeon?"

I couldn't hear Daddy's response to Freddy's question, but I knew for sure I wouldn't stand by and let Daddy be taken to jail.

"You owe me," Freddy repeated.

"Forty-eight hours," Daddy said. "After that, you come back here and get it."

"It's a deal," Freddy said.

"I'll get your coats," Mother said.

Dot grabbed my arm.

I slipped off my shoes, and she followed suit. We crept on up the stairs.

In our room, Dot was wringing her hands. "What are we gonna do?"

"I don't know yet. We don't have all the facts."

A few minutes after Freddy and Mavis left, Daddy called us back downstairs. Our guilt over eavesdropping was likely written all over our faces. I would like to think I could feign innocence slightly better than my baby sister, who at the moment was being more dramatic than Clara Bow.

"Have your friends left already, Daddy?" she asked.

"You know very well they have," Mother said. "You and your sister were spying from the staircase."

"How did you know?" Dot huffed. "We pretended to go all the way up the stairs and everything."

I merely pinched the bridge of my nose and looked down at the floor. There was still much I needed to teach that child—mainly to keep her mouth shut when she was guilty.

"It doesn't matter," Daddy said.

Good old Daddy.

"I owe you girls an explanation," he continued.

"Talk while we trim the tree," Mother said. "It *is* Christmas Eve, after all."

Mother always had to be busy when she was nervous. Her being nervous made me nervous, but I was too intrigued by whatever Daddy was about to say to show it.

Picking up a popcorn garland, I said. "See, Mother? Dot and I didn't eat all of it. Go on, Daddy."

"As you guessed right away, that was Freddy from the story I've told you for as long as I can remember," he said.

"Yeah, but I'm awfully disappointed that the dame with him wasn't Blue-Eyed Bess," Dot said.

"Young woman, not dame." Mother rolled her eyes heavenward.

"Do you think we're in the midst of a Dickens' tale, being visited by the ghost of Christmas past or something?" I gave a little laugh.

"You'll never know if you don't hush and let your daddy speak." Mother snatched up a paper chain and wound it through the branches of the tree.

Daddy lit a pipe before telling us about Freddy. He seldom smoked, so I knew he was as uneasy as Mother—maybe more so.

I'll never forget the smell of the living room that evening. It was perfect. Pine, popcorn, cherry tobacco, and a hint of vanilla because Mother had been baking all afternoon. I almost didn't want Daddy to tell us the truth about Freddy or why he'd been here or what Daddy had agreed to keep for him for forty-eight hours. If he didn't tell us, maybe we could pretend it had never happened; and tonight could still be wonderful.

"I didn't lie." Daddy puffed on his pipe as he walked around the room. "I embellished. I *didn't* see Freddy again after that night of hide-and-seek, but I heard what had happened to him. The men I'd heard arguing were two flesh-and-blood brothers, not phantoms."

"Did they kidnap Freddy?" Dot asked.

Mother glared at her for interrupting, and she returned to tying ornaments on the tree.

"He wasn't kidnapped, but one of the men had seen Freddy around–knew Freddy's dad or some such. Anyway, he put Freddy to work that very night."

Dot opened her mouth to speak again, caught Mother's scowl, and wisely clamped her lips together.

"The men were criminals. I heard they used Freddy as their lookout at first; but he worked his way up through the ranks, I suppose. He did appear to be enjoying a measure of success."

"He looked like a rat caught in a maze to me." Mother hung a crocheted cross on the tree.

"Freddy came here tonight to ask me for help," Daddy said. "He's found himself in a bit of trouble."

"What kind of trouble?" Dot asked.

"Never you mind," Mother told her. "Your daddy agreed to help him just this once. He'll be back day after tomorrow, and I'd better not catch hide nor hair of either of you while he's here."

"Yes, ma'am." Dot looked at me, and I gave her a little shrug.

"Let's not dwell on unpleasantness." Daddy took the angel ornament from Mother's hand. "Play us some Christmas carols, won't you, love? The girls and I can finish the tree."

Mother went to the piano, and soon we were all singing and laughing and enjoying ourselves. We put Freddy and Mavis out of our minds. In fact, I didn't give either of them another thought until I saw the morning newspaper on December 26. Freddy and Mavis had been shot to death on Christmas Eve hours after leaving our home.

CHAPTER 5

THE SMOKING GUN

"DADDY, HAVE YOU SEEN THIS?"

He and I were alone in the kitchen, and the newspaper was lying between us. Mother and Dot were still sleeping.

I stared at the headline slackjawed while Daddy peered into the coffee mug between his hands.

Placing my hand on his arm, I said, "Talk to me. What was going on with Freddy?"

"Max." He shook his head.

"You know I'm the only one you can talk this out with. Mother and Dot would go all to pieces."

"You underestimate them." He sighed. "When he came here on Christmas Eve, Freddy gave me a gun wrapped in brown paper and bound with twine. It has his boss's fingerprints on it."

"I'm guessing the gun was used to commit a crime?"

"A murder," he said. "Of a policeman."

"Did the boss ask Freddy to get rid of the gun or something?"

"I suppose so, but Freddy wanted out of the organization and chose to use the gun to blackmail the boss into letting him go."

I groaned. "That wasn't terribly bright."

"No." He nodded toward the newspaper. "You see where that got him. Poor Freddy. He wanted an honest life with Mavis but didn't know how to go about getting it."

"Why come to you? The two of you had fallen out of touch."

"That's why. Freddy didn't think any of his boss's lackeys would think to look for him here."

"Did he ask you to hide him here?" I asked.

"No. He knew better. I'd never risk my family's lives for anyone."

I gave his arm a squeeze. "What did he hope to gain by leaving the gun here?"

"Well, naturally, the boss wants the gun back. Freddy figured that if he was caught but didn't have the gun with him, he and Mavis would be safe until he worked out a deal with the boss."

"But the boss wasn't negotiating."

"Obviously not." He looked at me. "I'm frightened. Not for me but for the rest of you. This gun I foolishly agreed to hide for Freddy cost him and Mavis their lives. Their killers could come for us next."

I stiffened. "You think they know he came here? To our house?"

"I don't know what they know. The newspaper said Freddy and Mavis were from Chicago and were believed to have been in town visiting family for the holidays." He sipped the coffee and grimaced. It had apparently grown cold. "I want you, Dot, and your mother to leave and—"

"No!" I quickly glanced around to make sure Mother or Dot wasn't coming down the stairs and had heard my outburst. Lowering my voice, I went on. "Send them away if you want to, but there's no way I'll leave you here alone at the mercy of some goons."

"I got myself into this predicament, Maxine. I'll get myself out of it."

"You did not get yourself into it. Freddy got you into it. Why did he keep saying you owed him anyway?"

"Because I left him in the woods that night and the criminals recruited him. Had I not left him, he wouldn't have gotten involved in—"

"Oh, please. Nobody's buying that. He stayed because he wanted to." I tipped his coffee cup onto the newspaper.

"Max!"

"Oops." Gathering up the coffee-soaked newspaper, I said, "Here's what we're going to do." I wadded the paper up and threw it into the garbage can. "Mother and Dot don't need to know what happened to Freddy and Mavis. If anyone should ever mention them or their deaths to us, we'll act as shocked as anyone would be to hear of their deaths. We have no newspaper this morning because of clumsy me, and we won't get a replacement."

Dad put his hand over his mouth. Looking back, I'm certain he was trying to hide a grin at my trying to control the situation. "Sweetheart, we can't simply pretend none of this ever happened."

"True, but we can't live in fear of something that might

never happen either. If you send Mother, Dot, and me away, it's going to look suspicious to anyone would might've been following Freddy."

"That's a good point."

"It's an *excellent* point." I brought him some fresh coffee, wiped off the table, and kissed the top of his head. "You're raising a genius, you know. I'm going to make breakfast now, and we're going to enjoy ourselves until someone gives us reason not to."

That reason came sooner than I was expecting.

WE WERE SITTING at the dining room table playing Parcheesi when there was a knock at the front door. Daddy and I exchanged glances.

"I'll get it," I said.

"Nope." He kept his tone light, but I could hear the vein of steel in it. "Your turn is coming next. I'll go."

I didn't want him to. What if he opened the door and got shot? "Aw, let's not answer it. We're having such fun."

He ignored me and went to the door. I clenched my fists beneath the table as Mother moved her game piece around the board.

"Mrs. Collins!" Dad exclaimed loudly. "What a nice surprise!"

As I deflated in relief, Mother said under her breath, "Ugh. Let's go and be sociable if we must. Maxine, it's your turn when we get back."

Mother didn't care for Mrs. Collins. She said the woman

was a busybody. I wasn't crazy about her either, but I was delighted she was the person at the door.

When Dot, Mother, and I joined Daddy and Mrs. Collins in the living room, there was a man with them. My eyes widened and flew to Daddy.

"Ladies, this is Mrs. Collins' son, James, who is home for the holidays," Daddy said.

Sizing up James, I asked, "Why have we never met you before, James? We've lived next to your mother for years."

James, a ham-fisted palooka with slicked back hair said, "It was only thanks to a Christmas bonus my new employer gave me that I was able to come visit Mom at last. Some of us aren't as fortunate as others."

"What others?" I asked.

"Maxine, don't be rude," Mother said.

"It's all right," James said. "It's simply that we couldn't help but stare at the visitors you had on Christmas Eve."

"They were ever so elegant," Mrs. Collins said. "Were they relatives?"

"No." Daddy smiled. "The man was someone I grew up with. I hadn't seen him for nearly three decades."

"They didn't stay long," James said.

The nosy apple didn't fall far from the tree.

"They did not," Daddy said. "It became obvious quickly that apart from reliving a few childhood memories, the two of us had little to talk about."

"That's often the case with old friends, isn't it?" Mother smiled. "You realize you don't know each other at all anymore. Would you like some coffee or tea?"

"I'd love a cup of coffee," Mrs. Collins said.

"Nothing for me, thanks." James looked around the room. "Nice place you've got here."

Daddy thanked him as Mother went to get Mrs. Collins' coffee. The clock's ticking seemed deafening as I wondered if Mrs. Collins had recognized our Christmas Eve visitors as the murder victims in this morning's newspaper. Should we have told Mother and Dot about their deaths? Was Mrs. Collins or her son going to ask about that next?

"Where do you live, James?" Dot asked.

"Up north."

"It must be hard not to get to come home and visit your mother often," she said. "I'd be heartsick if I had to go years without seeing my family."

"It is difficult," he said, "but I'm here now."

"What do you do up north?" I asked.

"I work in a factory."

Mother returned and handed Mrs. Collins a cup of coffee on a saucer that matched the cup. "Are you sure you won't have anything, James?"

"Positive. You know, it's odd an old friend coming to visit you out of the blue like that. Did he let you know ahead of time he planned to drop in?"

"No. I didn't even realize he knew where I lived," Daddy said.

"How about that." James shook his head.

I didn't see any resemblance between him and Mrs. Collins. Of course, for all I knew, he could be the spitting image of the late Mr. Collins.

Dot opened her mouth to speak, and I was terrified she

was about to entertain Mrs. Collins and her son with the haunted house story.

"Dot," I said quickly. "Why don't you play that new song you learned?"

"Oh, please do," Mrs. Collins said. "I'd love to hear it."

"Um...okay." Slightly frowning at me, Dot moved to the piano bench and began to play. She played with deliberation and nervous tension. It suited the mood in the room perfectly, as far as I was concerned.

James got up and moved closer to the fireplace.

"Are you cold?" I asked, going to stand beside him.

"No, dear. I suffer back pain from an old injury." He smiled down at me. "I'm unable to sit for too long at a time."

"I'm sorry to hear that. May I get you a pillow or something?"

"No, thank you. I'll be fine in a bit."

After Dot finished her song, Mrs. Collins requested her to play *Silent Night*.

"I'm afraid I don't know that one," Dot said. "But Mother does."

Mrs. Collins didn't have to twist Mother's arm, and it was at least half an hour before the playing of Christmas carols ended.

At that point, James said, "Mother, I feel we've imposed on these good people long enough.

Mother and Daddy made the requisite polite protestations, but we were all relieved when they were gone.

"What did you ask that man when you went to stand with him by the fireplace, Maxine?" Mother asked as we sat back down to our game of Parcheesi.

I told her and then picked up the dice. "I didn't like the looks of that guy. I felt like maybe he was snooping around where he had no business."

Mother clucked her tongue. "You're always suspicious of people."

"Better suspicious than naive." I rolled a four.

"Weren't Freddy and Mavis supposed to come back today?" Dot asked.

"They were," Daddy said. "I imagine something came up." He gave a hollow-sounding chuckle. "That's Freddy though. Always was one to flit from one thing to the next."

CHAPTER 6
ON THE SECOND DAY AFTER CHRISTMAS

I CAME DOWNSTAIRS the following morning to find both Mother and Daddy in the kitchen. Daddy had the week off from work, and I was glad of that. I didn't want him out of my sight until I felt confident that this Freddy business was behind us.

Wanting to speak with Daddy alone, I said, "Mother, why don't you go play us something, and I'll make breakfast."

She was a hard nut to crack, and she probably figured I was up to something. "I've already got biscuits in the oven, and I'd prefer not to wake your sister until they're done. If you'd prefer to speak with your father alone, the two of you may go to the living room."

"There's no need, Max," Daddy said. "She knows."

"How?" I asked.

"A double homicide in our town isn't so common that the newspaper wouldn't carry the story two days in a row," she said. "Especially when the killer or killers remain at large."

Huffing out a breath, I said, "Well, for goodness' sake, don't tell Dot."

"What did you want to talk with me about in particular?" Daddy asked.

"The gun." I sat at the table beside him. "What are you going to do?"

"I'm going to turn it in to the police," he said.

"You can't."

"Why can't he?" Mother asked. "We've been sitting here discussing it, and it's the most reasonable solution."

"No, it's not," I said. "Freddy ditched the thing here thinking his not having it with him would keep him and Mavis safe. But it didn't. If Daddy leaves here with that gun, he might end up like them." I looked from Mother to Daddy. "Don't you see? The shooter thought one of them was carrying the gun. Now they're dead, and their killer still doesn't have the gun. People know they were here. If you leave–" I broke off, unable to continue.

He covered my hand with his. "What do you suggest, sweetheart?"

"Call the police and ask them to come here."

Mother stood and went to the oven to check the biscuits. "I don't know. The police are trying to solve this case quickly in order to reassure the townspeople that there's not a madman on the loose. Some ambitious young officer wanting to make a name for himself could come here, make your father look guilty, and arrest him."

"Okay, then *I'll* take the gun to the police station."

Both parents bristled at my suggestion.

"It makes perfect sense," I said. "I can deliver the package, say I found it in the street or something, and –"

"Why are you afraid for me to leave the house with the gun but believe it's a fine idea for you to do so?" Daddy asked.

"I'm an innocent young lady, Daddy. Neither the murderer nor the police will think I'm up to anything." I batted my eyes.

"Innocent, my Aunt Fanny." Mother slipped on oven mitts and removed the pan of biscuits from the oven. "We'll discuss this after breakfast. I'm going upstairs to wake your sister."

When I heard Mother climbing the stairs, I told Daddy, "You know I'm right."

"Let me think on it."

OUR BREAKFAST WAS INTERRUPTED by a knock at the door.

"I'll get it." Mother's glare dared any of us to contradict her.

While Dot happily ate her biscuit and jam, Daddy and I locked gazes and strained our ears to hear what was happening at the front door. I, for one, couldn't hear a thing.

Mother returned momentarily, said the visitor was collecting for the widows and orphans fund, and asked Daddy for some money.

As he took out his wallet, I asked Mother, "Have you ever seen this person before?"

She rolled her eyes, "No, Maxine, but–"

Before she could finish her sentence, I was out of my chair and on my way to the foyer. There stood an old woman who was a head shorter than I was and at least twenty pounds lighter. I could see why Mother didn't find her threatening.

"Hi, there," I said. "Mother is getting you some money for the... what organization did you say you're with again?"

"The Abingdon Women's League," she said. "We're collecting for the widows and orphans fund."

"Interesting. I'd have thought you'd do that *before* Christmas rather than after."

Giving me a thin smile, she said, "We depleted the fund before the holidays making distributions to those in need. Now we have to build it back up."

Mother arrived and handed the woman a couple of bills. "Of course." She shot an angry glance in my direction before asking the woman if she'd like a cup of coffee to warm her before she went back out into the cold.

"No, thank you. I appreciate *your* hospitality and your donation."

She left, and Mother and I returned to the kitchen.

"Aren't you ashamed for giving that poor old lady the third degree?" she asked me.

"Absolutely not. I merely don't want our family to be snookered."

"I'm grateful we have you looking out for us," she said. "Heaven knows the adults in this family aren't as wise and worldly as you are."

"That's not—"

"Sit down and finish your breakfast." Her tone left no room for argument.

"Yes, ma'am." I sat down at the table and tore off a piece of the biscuit I'd been eating. I didn't want it now, but I put the bread into my mouth to keep Mother from accusing me of being wasteful or unappreciative.

Following breakfast, I went upstairs and took one of my favorite dresses from the wardrobe. I still had every intention of going to the police department, even though I wasn't sure Mother and Daddy would allow me to go. Maybe I could suggest taking Dot along.

It was as if she knew I was thinking about her because the little imp barged into my room and plopped onto my bed. "What's up with you?"

I shrugged. "What's up with *you*?"

"Come on. We don't hide things from each other, and you've been acting weird since yesterday morning."

"Have I?"

"Max, tell me. I know it has something to do with Freddy and Mavis. I overheard Mother and Daddy talking about them. They're dead, aren't they?"

I sat on the bed beside her and took her hand. "It's nothing to do with us."

"But it is. The person who killed them might come looking for us. That's what you're afraid of, isn't it? That's why the three of you tense up whenever you hear a noise outside?"

Running my free hand over her hair, I seriously considered lying to her. But she was right—we didn't hide things from each other, and we didn't lie to each other. As desperately as I wanted to protect my baby sister, I didn't want to lose her trust.

"Yes," I said at last. "It is." I told her everything I knew, up to and including my plan to have Daddy hand over the gun for me to take to the police station.

"I'll go with you," she said.

I nodded. "Two innocent young ladies walking down the street are more inconspicuous than one."

She grinned. "Or one innocent young lady and one know-it-all."

"All right, *Mother*. Go get dressed."

She was laughing when she left my room. I wondered if her laughter was hiding a fit of nerves. My insides certainly felt as if they were turning to jelly. I'd be so relieved when we got that gun out of our house.

GUMSHOES, SUGAR COOKIES, AND THINGS THAT GO BUMP IN THE NIGHT

I HEARD voices as I descended the stairs–Mother's, Daddy's, and a deep, unfamiliar baritone. I quickened my pace.

In the living room, I found my parents with a man of about forty years of age. He was wearing a brown suit beneath a tan overcoat. Had Mother not offered to take the man's coat? Or had he refused to take it off? Maybe he was hiding something.

"Maxine, this is Detective Sharp with the federal police," Daddy said.

"That's swell," I said. "What a fancy badge you must have! May I see it?"

"Not at the moment. I'm discussing serious business with your parents."

"Run on back upstairs." Daddy jerked his head slightly toward the doorway. "I'll be up in a little bit."

"All right." I hurried up the steps as Dot was emerging from her room.

"What's going on?" she asked.

"There's some gumshoe in the living room claiming to be a fed."

"Let's go to the top of the stairs and listen."

I caught her arm before she could dart past me. "No. Daddy said he'll be up here to talk to us in a few minutes."

"Daddy or the fed?"

"Daddy," I said.

"Do you think the guy really is a fed, or is he an imposter?"

"I don't know." I sat on the edge of her bed. "He wouldn't show me his badge."

"That's a sure sign he's a fake," she said.

"Either way, Daddy won't be fooled. I have confidence in him...and Mother, too, for that matter." If fact, I didn't have as much confidence in either of them as I pretended to have. I just prayed they'd be all right.

Looking back, I had to admit I was pretty full of myself in those days.

Once the detective left, Daddy found Dot and me still in her room.

"She knows everything," I told him. "She heard you and Mother talking, and I filled her in on the rest."

"That's good," Daddy said. "We should all be aware of what's going on."

"Was the man downstairs a real fed?" Dot asked, hopping off the bed. "Or was he a phony?"

"I'm not sure. Let's go to the kitchen and discuss it over cocoa."

Mother was already in the kitchen heating the milk in a saucepan. As she added cocoa powder and sugar, she asked

Dot if she'd like to stir. Dot, who was keen on perfecting her cooking skills, gave her an enthusiastic yes.

Even though I could make a passable breakfast, I never particularly cared for cooking; but I did enjoy cocoa and was appreciative of anyone willing to make me some.

"You said you weren't sure if the gumshoe was really who he claimed to be," I said. "Why not?"

"I feel that under the circumstances, we need to exercise an abundance of caution with anyone and everyone," Daddy said. "He told us he was retracing the actions of Freddy and Mavis on the night they were murdered and that he knew they'd been here."

"How did he know that if he wasn't following them or something in the first place?" Dot asked.

"Good point," I said. "Did he mention how he knew?"

"No, but I didn't ask either." He folded his hands. "Instead, I said yes, Freddy was an old friend that I hadn't seen since we were in school together. I explained that Freddy had moved away and we lost touch. He dropped by to introduce us to Mavis."

"Did he try to accuse you of anything, Daddy?" Dot asked.

"No. He asked if I knew where Freddy and Mavis were going after they left here, and I said I imagined they were headed to his mother's house."

"That *is* where he told us they were going," Mother said.

"The police officer said they never got there and asked if I'd seen the account of their deaths in the paper." He scratched his head. "I admitted that I had."

"The man acted as if he wanted to keep pushing but knew he didn't have a reason for doing so." Mother turned off the stove and poured the cocoa into four mugs. "He wanted to know if Freddy said anything unusual, did he talk about his work, did he mention any of his associates–that sort of thing. Your daddy said of course not, why would Freddy discuss any of that with him?"

"The only thing I did say was that Freddy talked about settling down and marrying Mavis," Daddy said. "And that was true."

"Did he show you his badge?" I asked.

"Briefly. It looked real though." He lowered his voice as if the detective might be outside with an ear to the wall. "We didn't mention the gun. We found it suspicious that he came to us without our even calling the police. Tomorrow morning, we'll go out–the entire family–for a walk. We'll drop the gun on the ground near the police station if we can do it without being seen."

"I have a better idea," Mother said. "Dot and I will make sugar cookies to take to the police station. While we're there, you can nonchalantly place the gun where it's sure to be found. We'll be rid of it, and if anyone is watching us, they'll know we've gone to the police. That should get us out of the soup all the way around."

"What an excellent idea, love." Daddy lifted his mug in a salute.

"Fancy a game of chess while those two are baking?" I asked.

"You're on."

We had a solid plan and could finally relax and enjoy

ourselves for the first time in two days. This nightmare was close to being over.

THAT NIGHT as I was on the precipice of sleep, I heard a light tap and then my door creaking open. Knowing before even hearing her voice that it was Dot, I whispered, "What's the matter?"

"I can't sleep."

I threw back the covers so she could get into bed with me. "Of course, you can't sleep. You're up wandering around the house."

"It's not that," she said, sliding in beside me. "I keep thinking I hear something downstairs."

"You're apprehensive about tomorrow, that's all. I am too. But–" I stopped speaking because I also heard something. Raising my index finger to my lips, I got out of bed and crept to the door.

Dot was right on my heels. We tiptoed down the hall to Mother and Daddy's room. I reached for the doorknob, but the door opened. Gasping, I jumped back, knocking into Dot. She righted herself as Daddy came out of the room.

"Have you two been downstairs?" he whispered.

I shook my head. "We heard something too."

"Go in there and stay with your mother. Close and lock the door. Don't open it until I say so."

"I'm going with you," I said.

"You are not. Now is not the time for your stubbornness."

"Then you stay with us." I threw my arms around him. "If somebody is here for that dumb gun, then let 'em have it."

He kissed the top of my head. "Stay with your mother and Dot. I'm counting on you to keep them safe."

He knew that would get me. I did as I was told. I went into the room, closed and locked the door, and walked toward the bed where Dot was clinging to Mother.

"Will Daddy be all right?" Dot asked in a small, sad voice.

"Of course, he will," Mother said.

I eased over to the window and looked outside. There in the light of the full moon, I saw the tiny old woman who'd been here collecting for widows and orphans. "Mother, look."

She extricated herself from Dot and came to the window. "What's she doing?"

"Keeping watch, I imagine. I'm going–"

Mother pointed her finger at me. "You'll stay here with your sister. I'll take care of that one."

As soon as Mother left, I asked Dot, "What do you think?"

"Get the ladder," she said.

Nodding, I sneaked into the hallway, opened the closet, and retrieved the rope ladder. By the time I'd returned to Mother and Daddy's room, Dot had opened the window. I secured the ladder to the windowsill and down I went.

The woman didn't see me, and she gave a shriek when I tackled her. Lucky for her, there was snow on the ground to cushion her fall. Since she was down, I sat her on to ensure she wasn't going anywhere.

Unlike me, Dot had the good sense to put on shoes before she climbed down the ladder.

"I'm going for the police," she called as she raced down the street.

The old lady started to scream again, so I shoved her face into the snow.

"You hush," I said. "And you're giving back that money my mother gave you for the widows and orphans."

"I am a widow." Her words were muffled, but I could understand her. "But you're gonna be an orphan when my son gets done with your parents."

I smashed her head more firmly into the ground and prayed Dot would return soon.

And then there she was–our little rescuer–and with her was that gumshoe and a bunch of other coppers.

"That didn't take long," I said.

"They were staking us out." She smiled like being surveilled was the greatest thing ever, and in that moment, I supposed it was.

A uniformed officer helped me stand and then put hand-cuffs on the old lady. Another one picked me up saying I'd get frostbite on my feet if I wasn't careful, and I fell in love with that handsome young man then and there. He and the officer with Dot–who'd been wrapped in a charcoal gray blanket– and the handcuffed old lady hung back until the other officers went inside and rescued our parents.

There wasn't a lot of "rescue" involved, however, because Mother had already brained the woman's son with her cast iron skillet. I doubted he'd remember anything about this night when he woke up.

And guess who he was? James Carter. Or, rather, the man we'd been introduced to as James Carter. He wasn't our neighbor's son at all. Poor Mrs. Carter had been forced to go along with the ruse because his real mom–the old lady I'd tackled in the yard–had taken Mrs. Carter's beloved cat William and had threatened to kill him if Mrs. Carter didn't cooperate.

My knight in shining uniform carried me into the house and deposited me on a chair by the fireplace. He took his gloves off to stoke the fire, and I spied a wedding ring. I was ever so heartbroken until I spotted another young officer on the other side of the room who was absolutely the elephant's eyebrows. Hope springs eternal, as they say.

BACK TO THE PRESENT

"Was William all right?" Zoe asked.

"How about the gun?" Amanda asked. "What happened to that?"

"William was fine and continued to poop in Mother's flower bed until he was almost twenty years old," I said. "He outlived me, as a matter of fact."

"And the gun?" Dave prompted.

"Oh, yeah. The boss went to jail for killing the other gangster and for ordering the murders of Freddy and Mavis."

"The other gangster?" Dwight frowned. "I thought you said the boss had killed a policeman."

"That's right. I misspoke."

My nephew was smirking at me, and I swatted at him. Never mind that I couldn't touch him.

"That's an amazing story," Zoe said.

"It is. And all that talk of cookies and cocoa made me

hungry." Amanda tried futilely to wipe the glitter off her hands. "I'm going to wash up and make us some cocoa."

"Real cocoa like my great-grandmother used to make?" Zoe asked.

"Yep."

As Zoe and Amanda left the room, Dwight said, "I'm surprised I never heard that story growing up, Aunt Max."

"Me too," I said.

Dave tried unsuccessfully to smother a chuckle. "Is it true?"

I grinned. "To the best of my recollection, absolutely."

IF YOU ENJOYED READING about Max and her friends, please check out Designs on Murder, the first book in the Ghostly Fashionista series, at https://books2read.com/u/bPgEl7. Please also visit my site at https://www.gayleleeson.com/ to check out my other books.

About Gayle Leeson

Gayle Leeson is the author of the Ghostly Fashionista Mystery Series, the Down South Cafe Mystery Series, and the upcoming Movie Memorabilia Mystery Series. As G. Leeson, she writes the portal fantasy Literatia series. Gayle lives in Virginia and loves Christmas. She's looking forward to pulling a reverse-Grinch on her son's apartment this year.

A PICKLE IN A PEAR TREE

ERIN SCOGGINS

A yacht decked out in tinsel. A romantic Christmas proposal. 'Tis the season for a holiday heist this bride-to-be won't soon forget.

A PICKLE IN A PEAR TREE

I FINISHED WRAPPING twinkle lights around the *High Tide*'s handrail and glanced across the yacht's lavishly appointed deck. Despite the warm, salty breeze that highlighted an unusually warm North Carolina December, it was the perfect setup for a Christmas engagement party.

The promise of three hours on a luxury yacht equipped with a high-end caterer, a full bar, and a gorgeous view of the sun setting over the coast was the ideal way to cap off Carolina Weddings' first year in business, and as "Deck the Halls" echoed from the sound system, I finally felt the holiday spirit start to flow through me.

Almost every surface on the two-hundred-foot ship boasted the kind of Christmas cheer only somebody with deep pockets could display. From the freshly cut pine boughs and sprigs of crimson-berried holly lining the four separate buffet tables to the hand-blown crystal goblets awaiting glasses of overpriced champagne, my client had spared no expense to ensure this party was a smash. Eliza Bullard, a

Flat Falls socialite, wanted everything to be flawless, and I had worked overtime to make each detail worthy of a spread in *Coastal Living* magazine.

The only thing that hadn't gone according to Eliza's twenty-seven-page plan was Santa. Apparently, the after-hours actor I hired from the mall to sit on the main deck and "ho ho ho" for photo opportunities had run off with the lady from the cinnamon bun kiosk and was spending the holidays in Aruba. Assuring me I had nothing to worry about, the agency sent over someone they called a "top-notch yuletide professional."

They were wrong.

Normally, I was a fan of the jolly old elf. He brought sparkly presents and gave me an excuse to eat my body weight in sprinkle-covered cookies on Christmas Eve. But when I spotted this version of Santa, with his crooked beard and scratchy velour suit that smelled like steamed broccoli, my flicker of holiday joy started to dim. Suddenly, three hours seemed like an eternity, and I searched through my handbag for a Tums while I counted exactly how many minutes I had left before this Christmas party was over and I could abandon ship.

When he caught me staring, Santa wiggled his bushy eyebrows and a flurry of snow—or at least the baby powder he'd used to whiten the wooly worms above his eyes— drifted to his pockmarked cheeks. He leaned back in his folding deck chair and kicked his feet up on the plywood cutout I had hand-painted in shades of gold and red to resemble the front of a sleigh. "Hey, Glory. Want to make it onto the nice list?"

Nausea rolled through me, and it had nothing to do with the rocking waves below. "No, thanks." I picked up one of the three-pronged oyster forks I had artfully arranged next to the seafood platter. "I'd rather stab myself with this."

"The night's still young." He pressed a hand to his belly and let out a low chuckle, and the chair's uncomfortable groan matched my own.

I debated launching the fork at him like a javelin, but coating the deck of the glamorous yacht with Saint Nick's arterial spray probably wouldn't earn me a five-star rating on Google. Since I was a relatively new wedding planner, I needed all the positive press I could get.

As the boat rocked against the pilings, I placed the fork gently back on the table and steadied myself with a hand on the railing. My aunt, Beverlee Wells-Bartholomew, sashayed across the ship, her flirty red dress with white faux fur collar making her look like one of Santa's helpers. She plucked a shrimp off the platter in front of me. "Mia still doesn't know what's happening. You did a good job setting up this surprise."

I glanced across the yacht's oversized deck toward the main salon, a two-story tower of reflective glass and chrome that practically twinkled beneath the Christmas lights. White tulle wound around the columns, frosted gingerbread surfers in tiny Santa hats topped wooden tables, and platters of imported lobsters rested on beds of crushed ice. It was all part of an elaborate surprise that Eliza Bullard had concocted to land her only son, Hampton, a suitable bride. I hoped Mia Whitlow, the unsuspecting guest of honor and

Hampton's girlfriend of just over a year, loved it as much as her future mother-in-law.

"Where's the pickle?" Beverlee asked, craning her neck to inspect the twelve-foot Fraser fir that had been draped with blush and sterling ornaments hand-picked by the groom-to-be's overly involved mother.

"Hush." I glanced around to make sure we were alone. Aside from Santa, who was studying my legs like he was making his own Christmas list, nobody seemed to be listening. "The pickle is supposed to be a secret."

Eliza wanted to pay homage to her family's German roots by hiding a sculpted glass pickle ornament amongst the Christmas tree branches. "It's our family's favorite tradition," she had said during our first meeting as she held out a hunk of glass that looked suspiciously like a seasick slug. "Whoever finds the pickle on Christmas morning gets a special present and has good luck throughout the next year." I hadn't ever heard of such a tradition, but I was always in favor of games that got me extra gifts.

She had the ornament handmade by a local artist, and it included a hinged opening that concealed a 3-carat diamond ring that Eliza had also selected. "Mia is going to be a Bullard," Eliza had said as she opened the pickle to show off the ring during our last meeting. She also directed me to find the largest, fluffiest tree within driving distance of Flat Falls so she could hide the ring amongst the branches before the guests arrived. "The tree should be grand enough to make a statement—just like Mia's ring."

The ring made a statement, all right. With its halo of

yellow diamonds surrounding a pear-shaped center stone, it was every bit as gaudy and over-the-top as Eliza herself.

I wasn't even sure why Eliza needed me to help her plan this party. She showed up at our first meeting several months ago wielding a binder stuffed with drawings of the boat and the ring, a full menu, and the names of every vendor she intended to use. Whenever I suggested changes, she referred me to the minute-by-minute timeline she had prepared and told me to stick to my lane.

As one of Flat Falls' only wedding and event planners, I could have argued that I was more than capable of creating the ambiance she desired but decided not to risk the much-needed paycheck. So I showed up dutifully to our meetings and spent today arranging snacks on silver trays and trying to placate the woman who was determined to spend the holiday season meddling in her only son's love life.

After Beverlee wandered off to check on the champagne, I stood back to ensure that the guests were appropriately awed as they boarded the boat. From the way their faces lit up with wonder as they took in the holiday decorations covering nearly every surface of the luxury yacht, I already considered the event a success.

Eliza stood near the front of the line to welcome people aboard, her strappy silver romper catching the lights from the trees flanking the gangway and making her look like a human disco ball. Hampton was at her side in a gauzy white button-up shirt that hung loose over fitted khaki pants. His floppy, sun-bleached hair and tan leather flip-flops were an ode to beach life, despite it being near the end of December.

After greeting a pack of young women boarding the boat

in short dresses and high heels, Mia joined Hampton. She leaned into him, her hands tucked into the pockets of the floral sundress that brushed against her ankles. Her long brown hair was pinned up in an elegant bun and embellished with a delicate crystal comb, and as he gave her a gentle kiss on the cheek, ideas for their wedding swirled around in my head. Although I'd only met her a few times, I could already tell that Mia would be a pleasure to work with. Unlike her future mother-in-law, I thought with an interior eye roll that didn't match the fake smile I had plastered across my face.

Her friends, though, I could do without. The tallest of the bunch, mainly because she wore heels that provided more height than the stepstool I kept in my kitchen, gave the boat a slow once-over. Her red-lacquered lips turned downward.

"Christmas trees on a boat," she said with a sneer. "How quaint."

I was tempted to offer her a quick exit by tossing her overboard, but since it was my job to keep the guests happy, I grabbed a glass from a passing tray and presented it to her with a flourish. "May I offer you some champagne?"

I tried not to snicker when, eyes narrowing, she grasped the delicate stem between well-manicured fingers and studied the frozen cranberries that floated in the glass. "Is that... fruit?"

"Yes, the berries keep the champagne nice and cold," I said. "And they look so festive, don't you think?"

She pushed the glass back into my hand and walked away without saying a word. So much for my grand gesture.

I was about to return the glass to the galley when Mia

approached. She tugged it from my fingers and took a sip. "Don't mind Jordan—she doesn't eat carbs."

I was willing to overlook Jordan's Bad-Tempered Barbie act, but only because I'd be grumpy without carbs, too. The loud clanging of a brass bell and a final boarding call from the captain signaled that the Christmas Cruise was officially underway. The deck hands threw their lines onto the dock and the *High Tide*'s motors rumbled to life. I gave Eliza a thumbs-up as we began the twenty-minute journey across the Intracoastal Waterway to a hidden cove where we would anchor for the rest of the evening, and I interpret her lack of a frown as whole-hearted approval.

The sun had completed its descent, and except when we crossed the wakes of the trawlers returning from a day on the Atlantic Ocean, the waves were low and steady.

The first hour passed in an uneventful blur, with guests chatting, humming along to Christmas carols, and filling their plates with tiny quiches and lobster meatballs. I watched the event from my post near the dessert bar, and Beverlee stationed herself on the side of the boat that housed the dance floor, where she had decided to watch the festivities from the arms of Hampton's college roommate, a redhead named Chad. She flashed me a toothy grin when she twirled him across the deck.

Beverlee liked to flirt with people almost as much as she liked to mother them, so it didn't surprise me that she had gravitated toward the younger crowd. But Chad, in his trendy bow tie and deck shoes, had no idea how to handle my vivacious aunt, and every time she whirled past me, I made a slitting motion across my neck to get her to stop. The last thing I needed was Eliza having a fit about the "hired help" mingling with her highbrow party guests, especially guests who were a third her age.

As if on cue, Eliza crossed the deck, tucking her chin-length frosted hair behind an ear and clinking on her champagne glass with a fork. The only person besides me who even noticed was Santa, and he turned a disinterested gaze back to his overflowing plate.

When clinking on her glass and stomping her foot didn't divert the guests' focus from the buffet line, she let out a loud screech that sounded like a wounded owl had been released on deck. More than a few people ducked and glanced up at the sky.

"May I have everybody's attention, please?" She placed her glass on the narrow rail and clapped her hands, barely acknowledging when an errant wave shook the boat, sending her champagne tumbling into the darkened waters below.

The crowd finally settled down, and Eliza cleared her throat. "I'm so happy you joined us this evening for our annual Christmas celebration. But tonight is even more special than usual, and I'd like my son, Hampton, to tell you why."

Hampton stepped forward, lurching slightly, either from the rolling waves or the one-too-many bottles of locally crafted beer he'd been indulging in with his buddies. After he greeted his mother with a kiss on the cheek, he swept his arm out to the crowd. His other hand clutched a beer bottle. "Thank y'all for coming tonight. As you are aware, it has been a long and busy year for our family, and I appreciate you sticking with us through the ups and downs."

Everyone knew the Bullards had been going through some tough times since Eliza's most recent husband croaked on the fifth green during a charity golf tournament at the Flat Falls Country Club. Nobody was surprised, of course. He had to be pushing ninety and smoked hand-rolled Cuban cigars as if it was his full-time job. But she handled his death like a champ, changing back to her maiden name and using her dead husband's fortune to buy a beach-front mansion and a new wardrobe so she could go on the prowl for her next victim.

Hampton pressed his fist to his chest and gestured to his mother with the bottle. "First, I want to thank my mom for hosting this wonderful party. It's great to see so many friendly faces. Let's give her a round of applause for doing such a fantastic job."

The crowd gave Eliza a polite acknowledgment, which she responded to as if receiving an Academy Award. She waved. She bowed. She beamed. And when she kept preening while everyone else on board had already stopped paying attention, Hampton continued his speech.

"We've had a lot of heartaches this year. But there have also been so many things to celebrate." He motioned for Mia to join him, and when she stepped toward him, he wrapped his arm around her waist. "I was lucky enough to find my true love."

Mia's friends let out a collective romantic sigh. The one holdout was Jordan, whose pursed lips and dramatic eye roll made it look like she had just been force-fed a bucket of lemons. When another girl elbowed her, she finally forced out a polite smile.

"I'm sure many of you know my father's family came from Germany," Hampton went on. "And to celebrate our heritage, we had a special tradition each Christmas." He motioned toward the Christmas tree. "When I was a child, Santa would hide a pickle ornament in the tree every Christmas morning. Whoever found it got a surprise gift and good luck for the whole next year."

Mia's friends inched forward, obviously ready to throw down the gauntlet *Girls Gone Wild*-style to find the ornament.

"Not the first time they've fought over a pickle, I'd wager," Beverlee whispered as she came up beside me.

I didn't have a chance to shush her, because Hampton seized Mia's hand and tugged her toward the tree. "Mia, I'd like you to have the honor of finding this year's pickle."

Beverlee's snicker was contagious, and I grabbed a napkin from the shrimp cocktail table to cover my mouth so nobody could see me giggling.

But Mia took it in stride. She gave Hampton a curious smile, then craned her neck to examine the tree. When she didn't immediately locate the ornament, Hampton encouraged her with a playful push. "You don't think it's going to be right up front, do you?"

Soon, the entire crowd was shouting directions at her.

"To the left, Mia," one man said.

"Check the top," Chad suggested.

"Why don't you come back here and sit in my lap, and I'll help you find it?" came Santa's booming voice.

But after fifteen minutes elapsed, Mia still hadn't found the ornament, and the guests got tired of watching a party game they weren't allowed to play. Even Eliza was growing impatient, and I could tell from the hawk-like focus in her gaze that she was less than a minute away from shoving her future daughter-in-law out of the way so she could produce the pickle herself.

When Mia finally discovered the green glass ornament hidden inside the branches, almost near the tree's trunk, a collective whoosh of relief reverberated through the crowd. She raised it in triumph. "I found it."

"What do you think your surprise is going to be?" Hampton asked, practically bouncing out of his flip-flops.

Mia shrugged and dangled it out in front of her as if she was holding a bomb. "I honestly have no idea."

"Why don't you open it and find out?" Hampton asked with a robust laugh, his cheeks pink and his eyes twinkling with excitement.

Mia gave him a tentative smile and flipped open the ornament's hinge. Hampton dropped to the deck in front of her. He misjudged the distance, though, so he ended up sprawled out on the deck with his face pressed to Mia's sandal instead of on his knee.

He righted himself, brushing his hand down the front of his shirt before turning back to Mia with his hair flopping over his cheek. "Sorry about that. Where were we?"

Eliza motioned for the photographer to start filming, then she edged past him so she would be in the frame as he captured the impending proposal.

Except there was no proposal.

Mia inspected the pickle and displayed it to the crowd, pasting a smile on her face. "It's a lovely ornament, Hampton. Thank you."

Hampton's eyes widened as he looked at his mother for support. She brushed past her son and marched up to Mia, yanking the pickle from her hand. "You just need to look a little harder, dear. There's a special gift in there..."

Eliza flipped the ornament over and shook it, then scrutinized it in front of her face when nothing came tumbling out.

"I put the ring here myself," she said, her lip trembling. She held out the pickle as an extension of her finger, pointing it at her son, who had awkwardly risen to his feet. "Your engagement ring is gone!"

Mia whipped her head back and forth between Hampton and Eliza. "My what?"

But Eliza dismissed her with the flick of a wrist and marched over to me, her pickle hand still extended. "What is the meaning of this?"

The crowd went quiet, and even Santa stopped shoving crab wontons into his mouth long enough to stare.

"I'm not sure what you mean, Mrs. Bullard." My voice came out steadier than it felt as my insides bounced around like they were being tossed about in hurricane-force waves. I motioned to the tree. "You handled the surprise yourself."

Her glare turned accusing. "But you were one of the few people who knew about it."

Which wasn't actually true. She had been bragging about the evening's plans to anyone who would listen. I even saw her flashing a photo of the ring to Hampton's old baseball coach over a plate of goat cheese crostini.

My fists clenched. Despite being taught the customer was always right, I couldn't allow the loss of a gaudy piece of jewelry to tarnish my already semi-rusted reputation as a wedding planner. It wasn't my fault crimes kept happening at my events.

Luckily, Beverlee was nearby, and she swooped in with a reassuring pat on Eliza's shoulder. "I'll bet it just took a tumble onto the deck. How about we all help you find it?" Beverlee said, her Southern accent even thicker than normal. She only pulled out the extended drawl when she was trying to get free guacamole at Fat Hectors or defuse an oncoming brawl.

Fortunately, it worked as well on crotchety, uptight social climbers as it did on drunk rednecks. Eliza agreed, and, within seconds, most of the guests were shining the lights from their cell phones into every nook and cranny on the *High Tide*.

As Beverlee edged closer to the buffet table, I wrapped my fingers around her wrist and pulled her toward me. "We have to find that ring," I whispered through a fake smile.

"Why? It's much more exciting this way. And I'm kind of enjoying watching Eliza Bullard pretend she's not about to throw up all over her expensive suede pumps. I mean, really. Who wears shoes like that on a boat?" Beverlee scoffed.

"We have to find it because the last wedding I planned ended up featuring a corpse." I shuddered. "I don't want to add suspected jewel thief to my list of business accomplishments."

Just then, Eliza stormed up to us, her cheeks as red as Santa's suit. "I have called the authorities," she said. "And I have also instructed the captain to return the boat to the Flat Falls marina."

I inhaled slowly through my nose. Beverlee had seen on television that it helped to ward off stress-induced headaches. "Eliza, there's no need to end your party early. I'm sure the ring just fell out of the pickle. Give us a minute, and we'll locate it for you."

"It didn't just fall out!" she snapped, her voice getting louder with each word. "It was stolen."

"Nobody hijacked your pickle, Eliza," I said, irritation rising in my chest.

She narrowed her gaze. "We'll let the authorities determine that. When they discover the ring was swiped on your watch, that will be the end of you and your little party business. And you'd better believe I'll be expecting a full refund."

She stomped away before I could react, but Beverlee had never refused an opportunity to confront a bully, so when she tucked her chin like she was heading into a roller derby, I clutched her arm. "We have more important things to worry about than Eliza's gloomy personality."

"Such as?"

The boat rocked as the captain started the engines and began the journey back to shore. "Well, for starters, we probably have less than twenty minutes to find that ring before we get back to the dock, and Hollis joins the party."

Hollis Goodnight, the Flat Falls police chief, had been a fixture in my life since I was a child, probably because he was half in love with Beverlee. But during my rebellious teenage years, I spent more than my fair share of time on the wrong side of his desk receiving lectures for everything from stealing bubble gum from the hardware store to getting caught making out with a loser under the bleachers during a high school football game.

Hollis had kept me on the straight and narrow, and I adored him, but I didn't want him anywhere near this Christmas party.

Beverlee unzipped her purse and rummaged through the contents, finally scooping out her cell phone with a triumphant wave. "I can call him to see if he can speed it up a bit."

"No!" I snatched the phone out of her hand. "We need to keep him off this boat."

"Why?" she asked, squinting her eyes as she studied me.

"Because every time I organize an event, Hollis has to swoop in and pick up the pieces. My business cards should read, 'Carolina Weddings, Your One-Stop Shop for Party Planning and Criminal Activities.'"

She considered that for a moment as if it was a viable business plan but finally patted my arm. "All those dead bodies weren't your fault, Glory."

Shivering, I recalled how many of my recent weddings had resulted in somebody kicking the bucket.

"We need to find that ring before he gets here, so yet another party foul doesn't go on my record." I pulled her toward the tree and crouched down, using my cell phone as a flashlight. "Help me look."

We searched the area around the tree for a few minutes, and then Beverlee stood, her hands at the base of her spine. "I'm going to need a massage after this. Maybe I should find that young fellow I was dancing with earlier."

"What if she was right?" I asked, choosing to ignore how she craned her neck to scan the boat for her new friend. I drug her away from the crowd toward the now-abandoned buffet table. "Maybe the ring was stolen after all."

She jerked her head around and took in the crowd. Some guests were still looking along the floor for the ring, while others had moved on to the upper deck to enjoy the breeze as the boat motored back toward the dock.

"Since we've been on the water this whole time, nobody has left the boat," I said. "It should be easy to make a list of suspicious people."

When Beverlee grabbed a napkin, I assumed it was because she needed somewhere to note our list of potential suspects. But instead, she piled it high with Christmas cookies and decapitated a gingerbread man with a satisfied smirk.

"Why did you eat his head first?"

"I always picture gingerbread people as the folks I don't like, and it gives me great satisfaction to eat their faces," she said, snapping another cookie at the neck and popping it into her mouth. "I do the same thing with chocolate Easter bunnies. So where should we start?"

I shook my head slightly to rid myself of the image of her as a cookie executioner. "My first thought is Santa." I tilted my chin toward the man sprawled out on the sleigh with a plate of food and a bottle of champagne with no glass in sight. Now and then, he'd throw up a peace sign when someone took a selfie with him.

Beverlee gasped. "You can't possibly think Santa had anything to do with this."

I glanced around, then leaned forward to whisper in her ear, "You know he's not the real Santa, right?"

"I know that, Glory," she responded with a huff. "That's Billy Mills from down at the tire store. He dresses up as Santa every Christmas for their holiday sales promotion. He stands out on the street, waving a plastic sign telling passersby if they buy three tires, they get the fourth one free. It's a great deal, and if you're really nice, he'll throw in an oil change."

While we were watching him, he looked up and matched Beverlee's stare with an eyebrow wiggle. He raised the champagne bottle with a flourish and downed a healthy swig.

Beverlee returned his toast with a finger wave.

"Please don't tell me you dated Santa," I said, pressing my fingers into my temples.

"It wasn't a date, Glory," she responded, brushing crumbs off her shirt. "But he bought me a hot dog once at the Founder's Day Parade and he splurged for relish." She let out a dramatic sigh and splayed her hand to her chest. "I just adore a man who goes the extra mile."

"Providing condiments isn't going the extra mile, Beverlee." I nudged her toward the deck chairs. "But you get to question the big spender because you already know him, and he gives me the creeps."

Beverlee didn't hesitate. Instead, she flounced across the deck, motioning to Billy to scoot over in his sleigh before dropping down on the seat next to him. I followed reluctantly behind her.

"Ho ho ho, ladies," he said. "Are you here to invite Santa down your chimney?"

"Gross," I muttered under my breath, earning a scowl from Beverlee.

Beverlee spun back around to face him. "I don't want you anywhere near my chimney, but I will tell you what I want for Christmas."

His eyes lit up. "You're finally taking me up on that set of whitewalls for your Volkswagen?"

She shook her head. "Glory and I are hoping you can help us figure out who took Mia's engagement ring, and since you've been lingering here all night, we figured you might have seen something."

He rested his plate on his thigh and ran his fingers along his beard, stretching out the white elastic cord that attached it to his head. "I'd like to help you, ladies, but I was sitting on my sleigh for most of the party, and I didn't have a good view of the tree."

I glanced over to the sleigh, and my stomach dropped. Billy was right: he had been angled away from the tree and probably hadn't even seen Eliza hide the ornament at all. "Did you notice anyone behaving strangely?" I asked.

He tilted his head and regarded me with a chuckle, his hand against his padded belly. "It's a Christmas party on a boat with a bunch of uppity people who think it's romantic to hide an engagement ring in a pickle and make the bride-to-be hunt for it like she's rummaging for psychedelic mushrooms." He motioned to the area surrounding the tree, where Mia and her friends were still on their hands and knees, searching for the missing ring. "The whole thing is strange."

I chewed the inside of my lip as I looked around, scouring the guests' faces for hints that one of them was a criminal.

My gaze landed on Chad, who was leaning against the railing apart from the crowd. Aside from his brief stint on the dance floor with Beverlee, he had mostly kept to himself.

"I will say, though," Billy continued, interrupting my thoughts. "Mia's friends all seemed jealous of the attention she was getting. Especially the lady in the slinky black dress…" He pointed to the group of young women.

"That's Jordan. What was she doing?" I prompted.

He shook his head to no doubt clear the full parade of inappropriate thoughts that were marching through it. "She had her arms crossed the whole time the boyfriend was up there making his grand gesture. And when it became obvious he was going to propose, she looked like she wanted to stab Mia with one of these fancy party picks."

He held out a silver olive pick from his plate, and I shook my head. Beverlee, however, accepted it and swiped one of his oysters. When she returned the pick to his outstretched palm, she gave him a saucy wink. "The zinc in oysters is good for a woman's va-va-voom."

I groaned and tugged her back across the deck before Santa could get handsy and test her theory. Not even four free tires were worth that. I steered her toward the group of Mia's friends, who had finally gotten off the deck and were milling around next to the chocolate fountain. I spotted Jordan and approached her. "Crazy night, isn't it?"

She dipped a strawberry under the chocolate stream, her expression bored. "This party is lame."

I took a moment to collect my composure, tempted to shove her face into the fountain. Unfortunately, doing so would result in the colossal waste of imported Belgian chocolate. "How's Mia holding up? This whole night must have been a shock to her."

Jordan nodded toward the bride-to-be. "She's right there. Ask her yourself."

"Oh, honey," Beverlee said. "That would be rude, and we don't want to upset her. So why don't you just tell us, girl-to-girl, what happened behind the scenes?"

Jordan raked her gaze over Beverlee, disdain dripping from her overly contoured cheekbones. "She'll be fine. She didn't need a ring that big—she wouldn't have appreciated it, anyway."

Beverlee turned to me with a knowing look before spinning back toward Jordan. "It sounds like you might be jealous."

That got Jordan's attention. "Jealous? Of what?"

"I saw the ring," I said. "And Hampton seems like a catch. He's handsome and charming…"

"And rich," Beverlee added.

"Maybe." Jordan wrinkled her nose with such force I was worried her makeup was going to crack. "But have you met his mother? You couldn't pay me to marry that man."

I couldn't disagree. I had no interest in seeing Eliza Bullard's perpetual scowl across the Thanksgiving table every year. It was hard enough to muster up a smile when she was cutting me a check for the deposit to plan this event.

Jordan glanced over her shoulder, then leaned in close so only Beverlee and I could hear her. "And she doesn't even like Mia. I wouldn't be surprised if Eliza herself was responsible for the missing ring. It would solve all her problems—she'd get a Christmas party full of drama and wouldn't have to watch Hampton propose to someone she didn't pick herself from the country club catalog."

Beverlee's eyes widened, and before she could blurt out anything, I said goodbye to Jordan and ushered my aunt to a dark corner beside the stairs leading to the yacht's galley.

"Did Eliza hide the ring before everyone else arrived?" Beverlee asked.

I shook my head. "Eliza and I arrived at the same time this afternoon, so she wasn't ever alone on the boat. You, the caterer, and Santa weren't far behind, and then Hampton and Mia and some of their friends boarded. The captain and several deck hands were also nearby."

Beverlee tapped a well-manicured fingernail on the railing as she considered the list of suspects. "Did you actually see Eliza put the ring into the ornament?"

"When the kids went inside the main salon, Eliza flashed the ring like she was a game show hostess and then insisted we all turn our backs when she was hiding it in the tree. She didn't want any of us to give its location away during the big reveal by accident."

"What if Jordan was right? What if Eliza never put the ring in the pickle in the first place?" Beverlee asked.

I considered that for a moment. I saw the ring, and I saw the pickle, but I wasn't watching when she put them together and hid them in the tree. "She's a piece of work, but would she really make this whole thing up?"

"Look at all the attention she's getting."

I glanced across the boat's deck to find Eliza dabbing her cheeks with a napkin while half a dozen party guests consoled her. She was certainly soaking up the sympathy.

"But wouldn't Hampton want to see the ring before he proposed to Mia?"

Hampton was huddled with his friends on a deck chair only a few feet away from his mother watching a basketball game on Chad's cell phone screen. "You've seen that boy," Beverlee said. "He's tucked so far in his mama's pocket it's a wonder he can brush his teeth on his own. If she told him she had handled it, I'll bet he wouldn't even question her."

I skimmed a gaze over the rest of the party guests, my heart thumping as I saw the lights of the Flat Falls marina coming into view. Hollis would be waiting on the dock, and I was running out of time to find the ring.

I walked over to Eliza. "Pardon my interruption, Mrs. Bullard, but I was wondering if I could have a word with you." She looked annoyed at the disruption that caused her minions to scatter, but I stepped forward anyway.

"What is it, Glory? Do you have any information about my missing ring?"

Beverlee, who had trailed me across the deck, peeked her head around my shoulder. "*Your* missing ring? I thought it was Mia's ring."

Eliza brushed her off with a wave, but not before a glare flashed across her face. "Of course it's Mia's ring. Don't be daft."

"We haven't found the ring yet, unfortunately," I said, wondering how to accuse someone who still owed me money of being a liar. But there was no way to go about it delicately, so I just plunged in. "Are you sure you put the ring in the pickle?"

"Yes, I'm sure." Her incredulous laugh was loud enough

to turn heads from across the deck. "What are you implying?"

"I was just curious. I never saw you hide it, and I was wondering if, in the evening's chaos, you forgot to put it into the ornament." *Or, you know, you're lying.*

Eliza didn't have a chance to respond, because the *High Tide* bounced against the dock and Chief Goodnight climbed aboard, grimacing when we made eye contact. "Good heavens, Glory," he said, straightening his duty belt. "Why doesn't it surprise me to discover that you're in the middle of this?"

"Merry Christmas, Hollis," I said, motioning to the buffet table on the far side of the deck. "Can I offer you a plate?" The least I could do if I was going to get blamed for losing an engagement ring was soften up local law enforcement with some brie and crackers.

Hollis shook his head, but all the irritation had left his features as he turned to speak with Eliza, who stood with her arms crossed tightly across her chest and her lips pursed. "Good evening, Mrs. Bullard. On the phone, you mentioned that a priceless piece of jewelry has gone missing. Can you tell me what happened?"

She jutted her chin toward me. "Ask her."

"All I know is that Eliza hid a ring in a pickle and the pickle in the Christmas tree," I said with a shrug.

He blinked slowly as he studied the tree. "Is that some sort of euphemism?"

Beverlee sidled up next to him and slipped her arm into his. "That's what I said. But it turns out there was a pickle ornament, and it appears to have eaten a fifteen-thousand-dollar ring."

He let out a low whistle. "How did you become aware of the value of the ring? Was Mrs. Bullard advertising that the… um… pickle contained such an expensive item?"

"She showed me a picture," Beverlee said with a shrug. "And I know my jewelry."

That was the truth. Beverlee had a string of ex-husbands and was on a first-name basis with every jeweler in the Carolinas. She had even flown out to New York City once on a whim when one of her exes said he'd buy her a tennis bracelet.

"But none of us saw her put the actual ring in the pickle," I said. "And I was just asking Mrs. Bullard if perhaps there could have been some sort of mix-up."

Eliza shoved past me and strode up to Hollis. "I'm not an idiot. I put the ring in the ornament just before I hid it in the lower branches of the tree."

"Who else was on board that could have seen you hide the ring, ma'am?" Hollis asked.

"Well, it was mostly just Hampton, Mia, a few of their closest friends, and the hired help at that point," she said, scowling at me. "The caterer was putting the finishing touches on the food tables, and the event planner and the tire guy were setting up."

Hollis lifted a brow, and I raised a finger toward Santa, who gave a jolly wave with a chicken wing from his perch on the plywood sleigh.

"I sent Hampton and Mia and their friends inside the cabin

to look over the menu while I slipped behind the tree. By the time I had found a suitable spot for the grand reveal, the guests started to arrive, and I got distracted playing the dutiful hostess for my boy's big surprise." Eliza's voice quivered. "I should have kept an eye on it, but I didn't think any of our guests would stoop so low as to steal such a sentimental piece of jewelry."

She seemed so sincere that I wondered if I was wrong and she actually had hidden the ring, but when she fixed her icy glare on me, all my sympathies vanished. I glanced at Hampton, who was now watching his mother with rapt attention.

"Did you see anyone take the ring from the tree?" I called out to him as I walked across the deck.

He shook his head. "There aren't any windows in the cabin that have a view of the Christmas tree, so I just sat on the sofa and watched the end of the basketball game until the party started."

"Were you with him?" I asked Chad, who was too busy ogling Beverlee to realize I was speaking to him. When he still didn't respond after a few seconds, I clapped my hands. He snapped his attention back to me and rose out of the chair. I wondered if Chad had taken the ring to keep his friend from proposing. After all, nothing ended the frat boy life faster than a wife.

"I'm sorry, what?" he replied, his cheeks brightening as red as Rudolph's nose. He would have been cute if he didn't look like a puppy who had just been caught having an accident on the rug.

Beverlee stepped forward until she was toe-to-toe with

him, her arms crossed in front of her chest. "Where were you before the party started, Brad?"

His hopeful expression turned into a dejected pout. "It's Chad."

"Of course it is." She straightened his bow tie and let her hand rest on his chest. "Now, where were you?"

She spun back to face me with a quick wink, and I realized she was toying with him. The strategic use of feminine wiles was one of Beverlee's areas of expertise, and that poor kid had no idea what hit him. If he wasn't careful, she'd know his high school locker combination and bank PIN before the night was over.

"Um... I was... um..." His face got even redder, and he stumbled over the words, unable to form a coherent thought.

Hampton tugged his friend roughly back toward the deck chair. "He was with me the whole time."

I turned to Jordan, who was leaning against the boat's railing, her frosty pink lips drawn in a thin line. "Were you with them, too?"

"No. Mia and I were in the bathroom. Parties make her nervous, and her stomach was hurting."

A flush spread across Mia's cheeks, so I nodded in sympathy. Parties gave me stomachaches, too. If I could just eat the food and hang out with the family dog, I was okay. When you added all the other people and the expectation that I could make small talk, I tended to get twitchy.

As Hollis continued interviewing the rest of the guests, I stepped away from the crowd. Something didn't add up. Except for the people Eliza had told, most of the party guests didn't even know there was a ring, so that marked them off the list. And Santa was too busy hitting on everybody to waste time treasure hunting.

Mia joined me at the edge of the crowd. "Quite a party, isn't it?" she said with a brittle laugh.

"I doubt anyone will forget it." Suddenly, I felt the need to escape. I'd thought this party would be an easy one, but it was evolving into just another disaster for my party planning portfolio. Maybe I needed to get away before I had a panic attack. "While everyone is occupied, I'm going to sneak off to the ladies' room. Can you point me in the right direction?"

"Step into the main cabin and it's the first door on your right."

I glanced over my shoulder and raised a finger. "Right there?" I asked, although I knew exactly where the bathroom was. I had stocked it with plum-scented lotion and ritzy monogrammed soap before the party began and admired the tinted one-way glass that allowed me to make faces at Eliza through the window without her seeing me in return.

When she nodded, I wrinkled my forehead. "That's where you were before the guests arrived?"

"I suppose so," she said with a shrug. "Why?"

My gaze bounced between the Christmas tree and the bathroom window. The *High Tide* had a standard layout, with the galley and bathroom being two of the first areas guests would encounter when they entered the main cabin. I hadn't thought about it before, but both rooms had clear views of the main deck, and the tinted windows would have prohibited Eliza from knowing she was being watched. "Because you would have had the perfect view of Hampton's mother hiding the ring."

Mia's smile disappeared, and she stuffed her hands in her pockets. "I'm not sure what you're insinuating, but I need to get back to my party." She started to walk away, but her shoe caught on an uneven deck board. Before I could reach out to steady her, she stumbled, slipping to her knees. When she reached her arms out to catch herself, the contents of her pockets tumbled out around her.

A crumpled-up tissue.

The wrapper from a piece of Christmas candy.

A three-carat diamond ring.

She gasped and closed a fist around it, peering over her shoulder to make sure it hadn't been spotted. But the guests were all watching Hollis as he made the rounds and not paying any attention to Mia.

"I do love a dress with pockets," I remarked, remembering her hands in her pockets earlier that evening, too.

Mia's panicked gaze darted between me and Eliza, who appeared to still be complaining about me to Chief Goodnight. "You can't tell her I have the ring."

"Why not? Do you think she's going to let any of us leave this boat until she finds it?" I asked. "I don't know about you, but I don't want to spend Christmas anywhere near Eliza Bullard. She's the worst kind of Grinch."

She grimaced and lowered her chin. "And now you understand why I came out here when everyone was occupied and took the ring out of the pickle."

Realization dawned on me slowly. "How did you know what she was hiding?"

"She has been showing a picture of the ring around town for weeks, and at least five people told me what she was planning. My hairdresser even offered to spot me the money to get out of Flat Falls. I knew it was going to happen; I just didn't know when."

"So when you saw her hiding something in the Christmas tree…"

"I knew this had to be it. Hampton mentioned the pickle tradition to me last week, but I didn't put everything together until I saw her with that ridiculous ornament."

Trying to summon my patient event planner face, I took a deep breath. "They put a lot of thought into this proposal. Why didn't you just let it happen?"

Mia let out a very unladylike snort that matched her dramatic eye roll.

I stifled a laugh. "Eliza would bring a whole new level of disaster to the term monster-in-law, wouldn't she? But what about Hampton? Do you love him?"

A dreamy smile replaced her frown. "I do."

"Do you want to marry him?" I asked quietly.

She nodded, then a single tear slipped down her cheek. "But now I've messed things up. I just wanted Eliza to back off. This is supposed to be our day." She scoffed. "And did you see the ring? I just want something simple and classic, and I don't want to lug around this gargantuan beast every day."

"I have an idea," I said, holding out my palm.

She regarded me for a moment, then dropped the ring into my outstretched hand.

"I'll get it back to Eliza eventually, but first I need to talk to Hampton."

I found Hampton seated in the main salon next to Santa-the-tire-guy, and I squared my shoulders and stuck out an accusing finger. "You're a mama's boy, and not in a good way."

"I beg your pardon." He looked to Santa for backup.

Santa shrugged. "You're on your own, man."

I leaned in close enough that I could smell Hampton's cedar aftershave. "Mia is a wonderful woman, and you almost blew it because you let your mother ruin your life. Do I need to remind you that you are a full-fledged adult? It's time to cut the apron strings, big fella." I made a scissoring motion with my fingers before sinking my knuckle into his chest.

I thought Hampton would argue, but he dropped his head into his hands instead. When he finally lifted his chin, he was nodding. "You're right. Mia deserves better than this."

"Three things are about to happen, Hampton. The first is that you are going to have a long talk with your mother about boundaries, and the second is that I'm going to return this ring to her." I opened my fist and showed him the ring.

"And the third?" he asked.

"The third is that you're going to go to the jewelry store first thing tomorrow, where you'll pick out your own engagement ring—preferably something your mother will hate."

"Understood," he replied as I turned to go.

I caught Santa's wink just before I whirled back around to face Hampton. "One more thing," I said, heat rising in my cheeks as I realized how close Mia was to a proposal based on a brined vegetable. That's just not something a bride would get over. "You'd better not propose to her with a pickle."

I left the salon and pretended to take in the view for a moment while I gathered up the nerve to complete my plan. When I was sure nobody was watching me, I dropped to my knees, sliding my hand along the teak deck boards until I felt the ring lodge firmly beneath an uneven piece of wood. And then I crammed it in with so much force I practically felt the metal bend.

"Everybody!" I yelled, waving my hand in the air. "I think I found something."

Within seconds, I was surrounded by a dozen curious guests and one police chief. "What is it, Glory?" Hollis asked.

"I can't tell for sure, but it looks like there's something shiny stuck between these boards."

Hollis directed his flashlight at the boat's deck, then withdrew a knife from his pocket and scraped it along the seam. "Hang on, I think I've got it."

When he pulled out the ring, the party guests gasped, then clapped. I plucked it from his fingertips and held it up to Eliza in triumph. But just before she grabbed it, I thrust it under the light and released a gasp of my own. "Oh no. It looks like a prong is bent. It wouldn't be safe to use it now."

Eliza eyed me with suspicion, but I just kept smiling and brandishing the ring in the air like the trophy it was. Only this time, it represented Mia's freedom. "It's a Christmas miracle."

I handed her the ring and watched as she searched the

crowd for her son. "Hampton," she called in a sing-song Southern voice. "I've got your ring if you want to come over here and talk to Mia."

Hampton joined us on the lower deck, giving me an acknowledging nod before taking his mother by the elbow and leading her away from the crowd. "Mom, we need to talk."

"Thank you," Mia mouthed from across the boat.

"You're welcome," I said when I got closer. "And I hope you and Hampton have a very merry Christmas."

"That was an exciting party," Beverlee said as she sauntered up with a plate of food. "And since I know you can't yell at your client for being a terrible person, I brought you the next best thing."

Beverlee had taken her fork to the frosting on a gingerbread woman, transforming the poor cookie's smile into a haphazard black scowl. "Looks just like her, doesn't it?"

I grinned and picked up the spicy treat, feeling more than a bit of Christmas joy when I bit the head off first.

For more Wedding Crashers shenanigans, visit https://www. erinscoggins.com or sign up for her newsletter at https://www.erin scoggins.com/news.

About Erin Scoggins

USA Today bestselling author Erin Scoggins writes lighthearted mysteries with a sprinkle of Southern charm. Although she started her career in marketing for a Fortune 500 company, she happily traded her MBA for a life creating fictional crime scenes and feisty small-town families. She lives in North Carolina with her husband, three kids, and an enormous lap dog named Murphy.

MRS CLAUS SAVES CHRISTMAS

WENDY H. JONES

The elves are on strike, there's been a murder in the North Pole, and to top it all, Rudolph's been arrested. With just three days to go, Christmas is on the brink of disaster. With the only option being to cancel Christmas, Santa doesn't know which way to turn next but the indomitable Mrs Claus steps in. Will millions of children wake up to empty stockings on Christmas day or will Mrs Claus solve the crime and save Christmas?

MRS CLAUS SAVES CHRISTMAS

"WHAT DO YOU MEAN, Rudolph's been arrested?" The speaker paused longer than was comfortable and added, her tone ominous, "Three days before Christmas?"

Nick could tell from his wife's crossed arms and the flash in her eyes that his already ghastly day was about to get a whole lot worse. Nicola Ariadne Karinna Claus may have been a vison in green and red, but she did not take disruptions to her schedule lightly. Especially not so close to Christmas and definitely not when it involved the incarceration of her beloved reindeer. No, this was not a good day.

IT HAD STARTED SO WELL. The nightshift handed over to the day shift with a sleepy wave as machines whirred at twice the usual speed, catapulting toys into the gift-wrapping department where they were expertly grabbed and stacked. The dayshift elves got to work, singing Christmas Carols and

Elvish songs, in a language only they could understand, as possibility and goodwill filled the air. The tunes echoed the rhythm of the clanking machines that churned out Christmas dreams as fast as they could turn. Demand for toys was the highest it had ever been, and everyone worked full pelt to fulfil last minute orders. No one whinged at the last-minute requests from anxious children, just worked harder to fulfil their wishes. Christmas was a serious business around these parts and not one child would find the bottom of their Christmas tree devoid of gifts come Christmas morning.

Freyja, the local postal worker, staggered in under the weight of sacks groaning with letters for Santa and dumped their contents on the pinewood floor. Chief elf, Oscar, grabbed a passing young lad by the collar.

"What's your name?"

The lad pulled himself up as high as an elf's stature would allow, stuck his chest out and said, "Bjorn, Sir. My mother is an Abba fan."

"I don't need your mother's musical tastes just your help," he said, his tone, never-the-less, kindly. Pointing in the direction of the letter mountain he gave orders to input all names and wishes into the computer.

Bjorn groaned but hurried over. "Aye' Aye, Chief. Not one child will go disappointed on my watch." He whipped a reindeer-handled knife out of the holder on his stout leather belt and set too with gusto, belting out a few Abba tunes of his own as he worked. Envelopes were chucked into a recycling bin on his left side as the pile of letters grew higher on his right. They'd be on the computer and in production in a twinkle of Santa's eye.

"Good lad. You'll do fine here." Oscar cuffed the lad lightly on the head and took his leave.

Nick, who was hunched over an Apple Mac computer, red of course, paused from his task of sending email replies to children worldwide, rubbed his back, and smiled. He stretched, stumbled to his feet, took in the look from Bert, his secretary, and said, "I'm off for a walk around the workshop. Cheer the troops on and all that. Need to keep the workers happy."

Bert, knowing his boss was off for a glass of apple cider and some shortbread, kept his council. Nick looked his age and then some. Each Christmas seemed to tell on him more and more. He watched as the man known the world over as Santa limped in the direction of the kitchen, rubbing his back.

It wasn't surprising Nick was feeling a bit battered. It had been 282 years since he took over from his father and it wouldn't be long before Nick Junior stepped into his own father's size twelve boots. He sighed longingly at the thought he'd soon be off to the Christmas Lodge Village for Retired Santas. Much as he loved his job it was year-round and gruelling; one for a much younger man. Also, all this Ho, Ho, Ho, and jolly was all very well but doing it twenty-four hours a day, seven days a week, 365 days a year, got harder with each passing year. Then, shaking himself, he let out a huge belly laugh and a booming Ho, Ho, Ho, looked around to see if anyone was watching, and took a side trip into the kitchen. He opened a tin festooned with a bright Christmas garland and liberated several pieces of shortbread. Nicola, knowing it was his favourite, had baked a fresh batch that morning and the buttery smell still hung in the air. He sat down in an ergonomic chair (none of this rocking chair malarkey that appeared in picture books) and stretched his feet out to the roaring fire. He chucked a few pinecones on to the flames. Sparks flew and the smell of pine joined that of the baking. He took a bite of the shortbread, and the flavour danced a samba on his tastebuds at the same speed crumbs spread across his coat. This was the life.

He was pulled from a dream of a holiday in Hawaii by the urgent sound of, "Santa. Santa, Sir. It's ur... ur... urjen. Grandad needs you. Sir. Sir. Santa." She tugged at his hand.

The insistent voice forced his weary eyelids apart. Benedicta, the six-year-old granddaughter of his Chief Elf, stared at him her face flushed, worry clouding her beautiful, green eyes.

He stood, picked the youngster up and said, "Whatever it is, child, Santa will sort it."

She relaxed into his ample chest and stuck her thumb in her mouth, her eyes brighter. All was now well in Benedicta's world. Santa would never let a child down.

Santa wasn't so sure about his own world. He had a feeling his day was about to deteriorate.

Entering the workshop, it soon became apparent that his world wasn't right at all. Eerie silence told him not one machine was producing anything that could be considered a toy. In fact, they weren't doing anything at all. Elves leaned against the machines or stood in a throng in front of him, each one sporting a determined look that matched every other in the room.

"Ho, Ho, Ho. What have we here?"

The looks turned mutinous, and several Elves took a step forward. Santa backed off. His usual tactic wasn't going to cut it. He scratched his head causing his hat to fall off. He popped Benedicta on the ground, picked up the offending garment, and stuffed it in his pocket. The child scurried to her grandfather who placed a reassuring hand on her head. Youngsters were encouraged to join in everything in Santa's Village, including the making of toys. Elf and Safety was taught young, and they were given tasks that would keep them safe whilst helping to bring toys to the children of the world. They adored it from the minute they could toddle and grew up knowing the importance of what they were born to do. They took the toy business seriously; sometimes too seriously if they thought Nick was slacking.

Until now that was. Nick pulled himself together, stood straighter and said, his tone stern, "What, in the name of all that's jolly, is going on here? I am sure each of you is aware of exactly how much time there is to Christmas - to the second?" His gaze swept the room. Some of his employees hung their head, others shuffled their feet, but most looked him square in the eye, their backs ramrod straight. No one uttered a sound.

"Now, now, ladies and gentlemen, something is obviously bothering you. Let's talk about it so we can all get back to work."

After a few moments of silence so thick it could be used to butter Swedish scones, Egbert, a self-appointed union manager, shoved a young elf called Jimmy forward. Self-appointed because they didn't actually have a union, but Egbert had watched a movie where the elves had one and decided this would be a jolly good idea.

Jimmy stumbled, caught his balance, and moved to the front. He took off his hat, held it in front of him and spoke. "We're not putting up with it." He turned and looked at Egbert, who nodded, so he continued, "He can't treat us like that."

Santa nodded and said, "I'm sure you are right, and I'll look into it. Who is treating you badly and what have they done?"

"We're not going back to work until you do," Egbert added, a bullish look in his eyes.

Nick groaned and scratched his head. *I'm getting far too old for this. Never in the North Pole's history has there been a strike.* He wondered briefly if his room at the home for Retired Santas was available yet.

"I'll be able to do something more quickly if you let me know what the bally problem is." He'd reached the end of his sleigh bell covered rope.

Egbert crossed his arms and spoke up. "Petter Brandysnap is what the problem is. We can't do anything right."

Another elf chipped in. "More of the toys are ending up in the reject bin than in the wrapping department."

"Our work's top notch and no one can say differently," another chipped in.

"I'm not—"

"Okay. Okay. I get the message. I'll speak to him so get back to work. Egbert, you're in charge of quality in the meantime." He watched the workforce as they stirred and hurried back to their posts, although disgruntled muttering could still be heard. Once he heard the reassuring whirr of machines he pulled his hat from his pocket, slapped it on his head and stomped off. This was serious stuff indeed. Actually, it was more than serious, this close to Christmas it was a disaster; stockings globally would go empty on Christmas morning. Brandysnap might be in charge of quality control but why on earth would he reject everything on the line? That was unprecedented. Even COVID didn't stop the wheels turning and Christmas for the last two years slid along as smoothly as brandy butter on a warm mince pie.

He'd no sooner left the workshop than the first flaw in his plan slammed into him like a runaway sledge. Where in the name of all that's Yule would he find Petter? Come to think of it, he hadn't seen him in a while. Oh, well, despite his quality control officer's size there weren't that many places he could hide. Other than the cottages where they all lived, North Pole Inc. real estate was concentrated into a few key areas, although they were usually awash in people who could spot a recalcitrant elf at a million paces. He asked a few workers who scurried past, arms loaded with presents, but they all denied seeing him for several hours. He stroked his beard, turned around and hurried back to the workshop to see if Brandysnap had returned to his post. Secretly he hoped not; there was only so much anxiety a man could take in one day and him manning the barricades of quality control was not going to help Christmas progress in a timely manner. The reassuring sound of the assembly lines told him Brandysnap was still missing in action. They didn't, however, give him any clue as to where the errant elf might be. On the off chance he went to the end of the assembly line anyway. Egbert was examining a toy train; even at a distance Nick could see it was exquisite, the design and painting of the highest quality. Some child would be lucky to have this in their stocking on Christmas morning. Just to be sure he walked up to the elf. "Can I see?"

Egbert handed it over without a word.

It was just as Nick had suspected; the toy was perfect. So, why would Petter be rejecting them. It was a puzzle indeed and Nick didn't like puzzles; they led to headaches.

He decided on the logical approach of taking it room by room and set off at a swift pace. Doors thudded against walls as he rammed them open and stormed into the rooms. His temper grew as they yielded nothing; each in turn was cosy, cheerful and infuriatingly empty. All staff were concentrated in the workshop, wrapping, and packing areas and there was no way Petter was hiding out there. He'd be lynched or at the very least dragged in his direction to answer to his crimes. Or alleged crimes he should say.

That left the cottages of which there were many. Nick pulled his hat more firmly on his head, took a deep breath and, heaving the outside door open, stepped out into an icy blast. He shivered and slapped his hands as he hastened towards the cottages, wishing he had a sleigh to speed things up even further.

The workers' whitewashed homes had a homely feel with each family choosing their own trimmings; blue, green, red, orange, yellow, purple, pink - each had an individual feel. Smoke curled from chimneys and reindeer were either tied up beside the house or roamed freely. Chickens, despite receiving regular grub, pecked at frozen ground hoping to pick up a few crumbs. Nick pulled a pack of food from his pocket, slit it open with his knife, and scattered it on the ground. Animals and fowl came running at the unexpected treat. Blixen pushed at his hand, begging for more. A huge, "Ho, Ho, Ho," disturbed the tranquil scene and his reindeer team moved in closer, nuzzling his pockets. As he stroked their velvety noses stress eased from his muscles. All was well in his world; or so he thought.

He was in for a big shock.

Petter Brandysnap's house had cheerful blue shutters and a yellow roof. The nautical theme, despite the sea being many miles away, gave it a jaunty feel. Smoke curled lazily from a blue chimney. Nick, ignoring the wildlife that milled about outside – reindeer, arctic fox, arctic hare – trotted briskly up the steps and used the reindeer antler knocker vigorously.

A portly woman, with a flour-smudged face, opened the door. "Why the blasted racket..." She wiped her hands on an apron decorated with a Christmas wreath and said, "Oh, It's yourself, Santa. What can I do for you? Come in. Come in."

She held the door wide, and Nick stepped inside. The tantalising smell of strudel tickled his nose. He swallowed against the drool that suddenly collected in his mouth and his stomach rumbled. The shortbread seemed like it was days ago. Before he could say hungry, he was seated at a table and a tankard of hot cocoa and a slice of apple strudel with steaming custard was set before him. Without even trying he found himself dunking his spoon in and taking the first ambrosial bite. It swirled around his tastebuds like an overactive whirlpool before sliding down his throat. He let out a moan before putting down his spoon and asking, "Is Petter around?"

"No." She gasped as her hand flew to her chest. "He's at work. Why...? What...?"

Nick's shoulders slumped and he shuffled in his seat. He hated awkward questions. The world was meant to love him and anything different left him somewhat nonplussed. He swallowed a couple of times and said, "I'm sure he's just busy somewhere."

Brandysnap's missus did not look convinced but thankfully she kept her council. Nick shoved down the rest of the strudel, barely tasting it, and stood up to leave.

"Tell Petter to let me know he's safe," were her parting words.

Nick jolly well hoped he was safe but was beginning to doubt it. He did wonder briefly why Mrs Brandysnap was not in the workshop. Every single North Pole resident was usually hard at it in the workshops at this time of year. Then, he shrugged his shoulders and thought she was likely on cake making duty that day. Cakes were as critical as toys when it came to the business of Christmas. Who could possibly do without a Kransekake or a Christmas cake come the big day? There would be weeping and wailing around the world if they failed to appear.

He left the house with nary a clue as to what he should do, or where he should go, next. All the other houses were locked up tighter than a seal's backside. Or were they? He wandered up to a few and tried the door. Yes, shut tight.

Then, one brightly painted green, wood door caught his eye. Was it ajar? He tripped as he hastened up the steps and went boots over hat, smacking the door as he did so. It flew open revealing a site never previously seen in the North Pole and one that should never be associated with Christmas. Brandysnap, hat lying beside him, lay drenched in blood his eyes wide open in a death stare.

Nick screamed and backed out of the door, doing a somersault down the stairs. He hauled himself up and bolted in the direction of a phone. Shaking, he pressed the buttons for the hospital. Three attempts later he was through to someone who knew what they were doing.

"Are you still with the patient?"

"N... N.... No."

"Did you check his pulse to see if he was really dead?"

Nick's voice grew stronger. "No, I bally well didn't. I ran as fast as I could."

"Stay calm, Sir, we need you to return to the scene and the paramedics will be with you shortly." There was a pause and then she added, "Check his pulse and see if he's breathing.

Returning was the last thing on Nick's mind but he trudged in the direction of Henrik's house, where Petter drew his last breath. This time he did not hasten. There was no doubt in his mind Brandysnap was as dead as any elf could be. Not that he'd tripped over many dead bodies, so his experience was limited, but he'd swear on Rudolph's life that Petter's life was at an end. What else could jolly well go wrong today?

It wasn't long before the paramedics tipped up and

pronounced Petter dead. Given the torn tunic and gaping hole in his stomach, it wasn't difficult to work out that he'd been stabbed.

"Yon lad's been murrrrdered."

"You what?" Nick wondered what language he was listening to. The paramedic was new, as was the accent.

"Murrrdered. He's been killed." He damped down his Scottish burr for the benefit of the obviously addled Santa. The Scot wondered how long it was until Nick retired.

"Murder?" Nick's already pale face turned fifty shades of white. "We don't murder each other in the North Pole.

"Well, someone never got the memo aboot that. He's definitely been murdered."

Nick staggered to a chair, grabbed the arm and thumped down into the chair's comforting embrace.

"Stand up right now, you're contaminating my crime scene." The speaker, a lanky streak with flowing blonde hair, was struggling into a jacket that looked to be for a much smaller specimen of manhood.

Leaping to his feet Nick said, Sergeant Balthazar. Thank goodness you're here."

"It's a good job I am with half the North Pole traipsing all over the place. Been selling tickets, have we?"

Santa, who ruled his kingdom with a benevolent air, leapt to his feet quaking in the presence of his sarcastic sergeant.

"Sorry." He pulled out his handkerchief and mopped his brow.

"You might be sorry but that won't wash in court when there's evidence that didn't ought to be anywhere near here."

"But it was me who found him. My DNA would already be here." Santa didn't know as much about crime scenes as he did Christmas, but he'd watched television.

"Everyone's an expert." Balthazar's chest grew larger giving him a self-aggrandised air. He pointed out the door. "Go and give a statement to my corporal."

Nick shuffled out, his head low. *How has it come to this at the most fabulous time of the year?*

Sven, the corporal, grilled him every which way until even he believed he was the perpetrator. Once it was finished, sweating, he asked, "Should I go and let his wife know of his demise."

"No, leave that to us. We don't want to miss evidence." Sven looked down his nose at the CEO of North Pole Inc a.k.a. Santa and added, "You're likely to make a right hash of it."

Nick was too shocked to pull the corporal up for his insubordination. Everyone was usually all jolly and nice in Santa's jurisdiction – not a one of them on the naughty list. He wasn't sure he could take any more surprises today. Christmas was turned every way but the right way.

"Should I tell the rest of the workforce?"

"What part of you'll make a proper mess of it are you not getting?"

Nick pulled his tattered wits about him. "That is quite enough of your rudeness. You will treat me, and everyone else in the North Pole, with respect."

"But I've—"

"Do I make myself clear?"

Sven tugged his cap down as his cheeks turned bright red. "Yes, Santa."

"Okay. Now, solve Brandysnap's murder and we'll say no more about it," said Nick, his voice kindly.

"Yes, Sir. Thank you, Sir." Sven turned towards the cottage door. He stomped his feet when he reached the mat and disappeared inside the cottage.

Nick turned in the direction of the workshop slapping his hands against his arms to generate some heat as he walked. What he wouldn't give for a tall glass of hot glogg with almonds and plump raisins at the bottom. The spices would restore his weary soul. How in the name of Odin had his day turned out to be like this he wondered as he stamped his feet against the heavy snow?

Goodness knows how but the news reached the workshop before Nick. The place was in an uproar with machines still turning but not an elf paying a blind bit of notice to them. Toys crashed to the floor with an almighty clatter, lying battered and broken where they fell. Nick pressed a button and a siren sounded three short blasts, the signal for pay attention. Voices silenced and Nick shouted above the machines, "Back to work. Now."

The chatter resumed but at least the elves were working. He sent six of the children scurrying around letting everyone know there would be a general meeting later. He grabbed three of his most gifted workers and set them too repairing the toys. By the time they had worked their magic the child who received the toy would not know the difference.

Next, he sought out his wife.

He found Nicola embroidering quilts for doll's cots - any

child receiving one of these on Christmas day would be lucky indeed. Her fingers flew across the fabric but stopped when she heard the news. "Poor Nora," she said as she cast her embroidery aside and pulled on her heavy outdoor cloak, the one embroidered with Holly and Lapland Rosebay. "I'll take her a tin of shortbread and a bowl of venison stew." The North Pole was no different to any other country when it came to supporting the mourning.

Despite the fact his wife needed to do this, Nick wasn't sure he was keen on the idea. His breath caught in his chest and threated to explode at the thought of how soon it was to Christmas. His wife downing tools wasn't factored in his business plan. He forced himself to take deep breaths and his heart steadied. How could his world have deteriorated so badly in just a few short hours? Then it hit him that his day was nothing compared to Nora Brandysnap who had lost her husband of 142 years. "Get a grip, Nick. All this will be solved, and every kid will have toys in his or her stocking come Christmas morning." The dog opened one eye and glared at him before going back to the serious business of napping.

Nick did the only thing he could do and returned to the workshops to make sure no child went without a toy.

A few hours and several thousand toys later Sergeant Balthazar stamped into the workshop all full of his own importance, Sven trailing several steps behind him. Sawdust rose in a cloud as the heavy-footed plods made their way in Nick's direction. "We need to speak to you, Mr Claus," said the sergeant.

Sawdust caught at Nick's throat causing a paroxysm of coughing. An elf rushed up with a glass of water. After several swallows, he wiped his lips and said, a tremble in his voice, "What have you got?"

Balthazar looked him straight in the eye. "In private."

Once ensconced in Santa's office, the heartbeat of North Pole inc., Balthazar sat in Santa's chair. Sven plopped himself down in the only other chair leaving Nick standing and at a disadvantage. He leaned nonchalantly against the desk in a bid to give the impression he was still in charge. He wasn't entirely sure he was fooling anyone.

After a few minutes of expectant silence, the sergeant, said, "We have a suspect in custody."

"Marvellous." Nick waited for the revelation, but none was forthcoming. "Are you planning on telling me?"

One side of Balthazar's mouth turned up and his eyelid twitched. He made Nick wait a few more seconds and then "Rudolph."

Nick's jaw dropped so far it almost hit his increasingly expanding stomach. He couldn't formulate a word. Eventually his mouth moved but not a squeak came out.

The police sergeant gave up all pretence of professionalism and grinned. "I can see you're impressed."

Santa pulled himself together enough to force some words out through suddenly dry lips. "Rudolph? My lead reindeer?" He didn't know why he was asking as there was only one Rudolph living in the North Pole.

"The very one."

The poor wee soul must be terrified, thought Nick. He'd never spent a night indoors in his life.

"He's the gentlest reindeer on the planet never mind the North Pole. He wouldn't hurt a tick if it was practicing terrorist manoeuvres on him." He stopped and grabbed his chest as a sudden pain clutched at it, but it had gone before he could pull the spray from his pocket. He sprayed a couple of shots under his tongue anyway, despite the fact he believed heartbreak, not angina, was his problem.

Balthazar stood and loomed over him wagging his finger in his face. "We have evidence. Irrefutable evidence. So, no trying to get the culprit off the hook. He'll hang for his crimes."

Good grief could this man get any cornier? I'd love to know what crime show he's been watching this week. Whitechapel was last week's favourite in the station, but they'd probably moved on to something else this week. The police force classed these as training videos, and they had nothing else to do.

Nick had had quite enough of this. He stopped lounging and got up close and personal in Balthazar's face. The sergeant took a couple of steps back. "What evidence? Show me."

"That's classified. I can't tell you." Balthazar's voice was a couple of octaves higher. Like all bullies he didn't like it when someone pushed back.

"Classified! You're Police North Pole not the bally FBI."

"I'll only tell his lawyer."

"Fine. Get out of my office and I'll ring one." He opened the door and ushered the officers through it, before slamming the door behind them.

He had no clue where to find a lawyer, so he went in search of the next best thing. His wife.

THIS LED to the exchange about Rudolph and his already miserable day deteriorating as far as it could go. The only thing that could conceivably get worse would be Rudolph, he of the lovely red nose, being hanged for his crimes. Not that Nick was sure the death penalty was a thing in the North Pole. He made a note to google it. Even the reindeer languishing in chokey would be a disaster. The other reindeer were adorable and worked like a charm together but none of them were capable of taking the lead.

"Who has arrested him and what for?"

Nick hesitated; He didn't want to say it out loud as it made it all so real. "Balthazar for the murder of Petter Brandysnap."

"Why am I not surprised. That fool couldn't find a peppernotter in a full biscuit tin far less solve a murder enquiry." She did a spot more glaring and tapped her foot. "Besides our gentle wee Rudolph wouldn't even know the meaning of murder. He's more likely to lick you to death."

Nick wiped his sweating palms on the side of his trousers. "But he's a sergeant, Dear."

"Only because there are precisely two officers in the police department and the other one is more incompetent than Balthazar." She tapped her foot. "The only reason either of them is in the job is because we have literally no crime here in the North Pole so it's the one job where they can do the least damage." She glared at her husband. "What are you going to do about it?"

"About Balthazar and Sven being in the police? His brows drew together as he pondered this knotty puzzle.

"Of course not. It's the best place for them. What are you going to do about Rudolph? He can't rot in jail this close to Christmas. He's got a job to do."

"There's nothing that can be done. They have evidence." Nick's voice shook and his shoulders slumped. He knew this was a battle he could not win. Not when his wife's dander was well and truly up. Plus, truth be told, he didn't know exactly what could be done about it.

"For heaven's sake, man, what evidence?" Nicola wondered why she had ever agreed to marry her husband it being pretty obvious he was hopeless in a crisis. Her heart softened when she thought about the last 301 years of marital bliss. She shook herself both mentally and physically.

"I'm not sure what the evidence is; Balthazar wouldn't tell me."

Nicola's gaze could shatter icebergs. "You've two choices. Cancel Christmas or leave it to me to sort out."

"Thank you, Dear, I knew I could rely on you." He gave a tentative smile in case he was saying the wrong thing.

Nicola performed an imperial swirl, her exquisite cloak fanning out like a peacock's tail, and swept out the door. Nick staggered to a chair, thumped into it, pulled out a handkerchief decorated with Christmas puddings and mopped his brow. "I'm getting too old for this," he informed a passing tabby cat who promptly sat down and gave its backside a good wash.

"Just about sums up my day," said Nick as he shut his

eyes for a snooze. Maybe everything would be all right when he woke up, hopefully this side of Christmas.

Nicola made a beeline for a cottage trimmed in Christmas green and red – the home of her best friend, Elsa. The freshly painted front door held a beautiful Christmas wreath and she knew Elsa would be inside making more of these; coveted throughout the world, they decorated doors from North to South Pole and from Scotland to Australia. Each employee of North Pole Inc. had their own speciality all of which were prized globally. Elsa rose as she entered, hurried to the stove and ladled steaming hot glogg over plump raisins in a tall Christmas glass. She plopped it down in front of Nicola along with a plate of serinakaker – buttery Christmas cookies.

Nicola couldn't avoid the temptation to have a bite or two and a couple of sips of glogg before sharing the reason for her visit. "Rudolph's been arrested." She took in the round O's of astonishment in her friend's eyes and continued, "For Brandysnap's murder."

"Rudolph? Those idiots in the police department couldn't solve a crime if it bit them on the nose."

"Precisely. Which is where we come in. We're going to solve this and save Christmas."

"What do you want me to do?"

Over glogg and cookies they strategized and came up with a plan of action. Elsa would spread the word amongst the women that there was a meeting before dinner. The men would grumble about eating cold cuts for their evening meal, but they'd have to thole it. Rudolph's freedom trumped warm bellies every time. Nicola went home to grab a tin of shortbread and took it to Balthazar's house knowing he'd be ensconced, full of his own importance, down at the jail guarding his prisoner.

Nicola often wondered why the delightful Ingrid married Balthazar. He must have a hidden side the rest of the world couldn't see as they seemed happy, and their nine children adored both of them. Ingrid put the baby down in his cot and welcomed Nicola with open arms. She fell on the shortbread like a polar bear in a famine.

"What a treat. Your shortbread is the best in the North Pole." She took a bite and mumbled through the crumbs. "wld lik coca."

Nicola translated this as would you like a glass of cocoa and agreed it would be good. It was on the table in a flash of a seal's tail.

By skilful use of gossip, she wheedled out the critical evidence in Rudolph's arrest. He'd been found in the vicinity of the cottage where Brandysnap was found with blood on one of his horns. This did, indeed, sound irrefutable but Nicola Ariadne Karinna Claus was not giving up that easily. She came from a long lineage of Nordic women, all of whom could fight their own or anyone else's corner and if she had anything to do with it, Rudolph would be out in time for New Zealand to usher in Christmas. Nothing would be cancelled, not on her watch.

Her next stop was the jail where Sven was lounging in a chair with his feet up on the desk, his jacket unbuttoned and fast asleep. He awoke and leapt up at her approach, scrabbling at his buttons in an impossible attempt to fasten his jacket. Her missed one and the effect, along with his rumpled hair and the drool on his cheek gave him the look of a badly made scarecrow.

"I want to see Rudolph." She hastened towards the cell without giving him a chance to answer.

He hurried after her saying, "Sergeant Balthazar gave orders that no one was to visit under any circumstances."

"The last I heard my husband was in charge around here, not your sergeant."

"But.... But.... But..."

"Fool. Don't you realise every prisoner is entitled to a visit from their lawyer."

He dashed in front of her in an effort to block the door. "You're not a lawyer."

She waved an imperious hand. "How do you know? Have you ever asked to see my University Degree Certificates?" She barrelled past him and reached the cell where a dejected Rudolph lay, both his eyes and nose dull. He could barely lift his head from the floor.

Her voice resounded throughout the police station, bouncing off the walls and echoing back to them. "Get this animal some lichen, willow and birch immediately. Also, some carrots and water."

Sven stood as if frozen to the spot.

"Now," she bellowed.

Sven leapt into the air and bolted off at a speed that would make her husband's reindeer jealous.

She turned back to Rudolph and spoke quietly to him,

reassuring the animal that all would be well. His eyes perked up a bit but his nose, his most important feature, remained dull. She didn't mind admitting she was worried.

The corporal returned with the food and with his sergeant trailing behind.

"Open this door," she demanded.

Only his—"

"I'm his lawyer." Her eyes dared him to challenge her.

In the face of such a fierce woman Balthazar took the path of least resistance and opened the cell door. He knew which side his parsnips were buttered and didn't fancy telling his wife he'd got the sack.

Nicola trotted in, bent, and stroked the reindeer's nose as he gazed at her with trusting eyes. Then she ran her hand across the 'blood' on his antler which was still suspiciously red. Bright red. Blood would be dark by now. Having raised seven children, she had seen her fair share of blood. She looked at her hand – pristine with not a single flake of red, bright dark, or otherwise. She bent down further and smelled the red area. Just as she suspected. Turning to the police officers she said, "How did you blithering idiots not work out that this is paint, not blood?" Her look could have blistered paint. "What do we pay you for?"

Balthazar wilted in the path of her anger. He tried a tremulous, "Why would we look for paint?"

"Because it's your job and because it's obvious."

The sergeant stuck his chest out, his lip taking a petulant turn, "Why would anyone paint his antler?"

Nicola shook her head. She couldn't believe this conversation was necessary. "To frame him."

"What a load of rubbish." Balthazar yanked her out of the cell and slammed it shut. Sven hurriedly locked it.

"You haven't heard the last of this." Nicola stomped out of the door and left the pair to it. She was determined they would be sacked and ex-communicated from North Pole Inc. There was dead weight and there was incompetence. The latter would not be tolerated.

THE HUBBUB from the meeting room could be heard from all corners of the North Pole. Every woman was there apart from Nora Brandysnap, for obvious reasons. Silence fell as Nicola swept in. She strode to the front, grabbed a microphone, and updated them on the situation with Rudolph. Murmurs echoed throughout the room.

"How can we help?" shouted one elf.

"Free Rudolph," shouted another and the refrain was picked up.

"Free Rudolph."

"Free Rudolph."

"Free Rudolph."

"Free Rudolph."

Nicola banged Santa's gavel several times and the noise died down. "Much as I love your enthusiasm, there's only time for action. I want you to get into groups, drink cocoa and chat. If anything at all comes up that could help, then let me or Elsa know." She gazed at them all. "Come straight to us no chatting to the other groups." She didn't want anyone slipping out and warning their husband, brother or friend.

For the next hour it was like the women's institute. Women quaffed cocoa and scoffed homemade biscuits and cakes as they chewed the fat in the way of gossip. It was reported that neither Odin, nor his wife Olivia, in whose house Brandysnap was discovered, could have done it. Several witnesses said they had not left the workshop all day. So that ruled out two of the most obvious suspects.

Kira, a beautiful elf, taller than the average, came up and asked if she could speak to Nicola.

"A few people have said they think Egbert is having an affair"

"Any scuttlebutt on who with?" Nicola's heart sang at the news. Not that she wanted any hanky panky in their midst, but it was a minor breakthrough. Or maybe even a major breakthrough. Although, on second thoughts, affairs didn't always lead to murder. Her elation sank faster than a deflated Christmas balloon.

"Word in the gata is..." Kira hesitated, unsure if she should be repeating it.

Nicola, sensing her distress said, her voice kind, "Christmas is at stake, so, this once, tell me what you know.

"With Petter's wife, Nora."

Multi-coloured fireworks lit up Nicola Claus's brain. "Good God in heaven, this changes everything."

Tears rolled down Kira's cheeks. "I didn't want to tittle tattle. What if it's wrong?"

"You did the right thing, my girl. Sit down, relax and chat with your friends." She handed her a beautifully embroidered handkerchief. "Here use this. You can keep it."

The young elf wandered off, her face looking slightly less weepy.

Nicola was just about to dismiss the girls when her husband dragged a couple of young boys in. They wriggled and cried as he clutched at their collars. The women stared as the boys' mothers leapt to their feet and stormed towards them.

"What have you been up to now?"

"Wait until I get you back home."

The boys' wails grew louder.

"Put them down dear," said Nicola in a gentle voice that held an inner core of steel.

Santa complied and the boys dropped to their feet. They looked like they would flee but their mothers prevented it.

"What's with all the commotion?" asked Nicola.

Nick pointed to something in the youngest boy's hand – a reindeer-handled knife. Anyone under the age of eighteen was forbidden to have a knife in the North Pole. At that age they were presented with their own and kept it for life. This was someone's knife – but whose?

"Where did you get this?" Nicola demanded, her voice firm. Not only was this a breach of elf and safety, but she had also more than a passing suspicion this knife was vital evidence. She also had a strong suspicion to whom the knife might belong.

The boys looked this way and that; as the silence length-ened one eventually blurted out, inside the magical pine tree.

Legend had it the tree was a place where objects and people disappeared and were never seen again. What these kids were doing there Nicola could only guess at. Most children gave it a wide berth.

"Hand it over." She held out her hand and the lad placed it carefully on her open palm. Holding it up to her eyes she inspected it, then pulled a magnifying glass from her pocket. As a seamstress she was never without one; you never knew when it might come in handy. Although, she never expected it to be used in a murder investigation. She turned to Nick and a smile lit her face as she took in his careworn face. She touched his cheek and said, "Could you get everyone into the workshop. Please?"

Nick smiled back, his worry lines fading, and disappeared from the room. A few minutes later a shrill siren sounded.

The workroom was packed, with bodies everywhere – no one was permitted to ignore that particular siren. Nicola asked a couple of elves to bring Egbert and Nora to the front and they soon stood before her.

"Your knives please."

Egbert and his paramour's eyes looked everywhere but at her. Nora took a few steps to the side but was stopped by a wall of bodies.

"Knives. Now." Nicola's voice invited no argument.

"Egbert opened the sheath in his belt and handed his knife over. Nora stood stock still staring at the floor. Nicola took a step forward and pulled the knife sheath open. Empty.

"What do you have to say for yourself?"

Nora looked up and looked her straight in the eye. "It was all his idea." She pointed at Egbert. "He wanted Petter's job, so he seduced me. He used my knife to kill my husband."

"I did no such thing. You killed him yourself for the life insurance money."

Balthazar and Sven materialised, slapped handcuffs on the pair of them and marched them off to jail to continue the discussion in custody.

WITH A SNAP of the reins and a jolly, "Take it away, Rudolph," the sleigh rose into the starry night and Rudolph pointed his once more red nose in the direction of New Zealand. All was well with the world. "Ho, Ho, Ho," echoed in the stillness of the night and the sleigh disappeared from sight. Just in the nick of time, Mrs Claus saved Christmas.

About Wendy H. Jones

Wendy H. Jones is the award-winning, best-selling author of the Detective Inspector Shona McKenzie Mysteries, Cass Claymore Investigates Mysteries, Fergus and Flora Mysteries, Bertie the Buffalo Picture Books and the Writing Matters series for writers. Her three loves are writing, reading and travel and she can frequently be found combing all three.

http://www.wendyhjones.com

A CHRISTMAS DINNER TO DIE FOR

SHEENA MACLEOD

Christmas is coming, and retired teacher Holly Barnes' to-do list is growing fatter than the poultry farmer's geese. But she couldn't be more excited, it's her favourite time of year. As well as helping to organise the Church Christmas Carol Concert, Holly is hosting a Christmas Day dinner using her mother's recipes, which are to die for.

When one of her guests is murdered, the sleepy Scottish village of Pine Meadows is thrown into chaos. With only three days to go before her friends arrive and another one of them may be murdered, Holly is compelled to turn sleuth and investigate. She discovers mysterious goings on in the night. Are foxes after the poultry, or is something more sinister going on?

Can Holly discover the identity of the killer in time, or is her festive meal destined to become a Christmas dinner to die for?

CHAPTER 1

ONCE THE LAST elf had left the stage in the church hall, Holly Barnes let out a deep sigh of relief and headed for the kitchen. A warming cup of coffee was in order. Why couldn't the church committee leave things as they were? Or rather, why couldn't Marjorie Thomas? The choir mistress, and local "know it all", had meddled and demanded her own way since taking over the running of the Christmas Carol Concert this year.

As a retired primary school teacher, Holly had suggested that villagers who didn't meet the required singing standard didn't have to be excluded. They could act as hummingbirds, standing at the side of the choir proper and humming along to the tunes. It's how she'd done it with her pupils, so no one felt left out. As far as Holly was concerned, there was no need for the hummingbirds to dress up as elves. But Marjorie Thomas had put her own stamp on Holly's idea - as per usual.

The carol concert was only three days away, on

Christmas Eve, and with so much still to buy and prepare for Christmas dinner, Holly had no time for such nonsense. She'd never been one to suffer fools and at fifty-eight would be unlikely to change her ways. Adults dressed up as elves, indeed. Next year, Marjorie Thomas would likely have the hummingbirds dressed as Christmas trees and dancing around the stage to the latest Christmas hits. Holly laughed out loud at the thought.

After filling her cup, she pulled on her red puffer coat and a scarf and took her coffee outside. She leant back against the window ledge and looked out across Pine Meadows to the village green where the vendors had set up for the Christmas market. The annual farmers' market would be starting soon, at one o'clock, and would run on into the early evening when there would be Christmas carols around flaming braziers, along with roasted chestnuts and warming drinks. Despite the chill in the air, a warm tingle flowed through Holly. Christmas was her favourite time of year.

Bringing her thoughts back to the present, she checked through the list in her head of things she had to buy at the market. Bert Bow's fruit and vegetable stall for parsnips and brussels sprouts. Oh, and cranberries. She couldn't forget them. Her mother's special cranberry sauce recipe was to die for. She already had the port bought in for it. Then, on to Stan Butcher's poultry stall for eggs and a turkey. Stan would save her a good-sized turkey, after all, he was coming to her for Christmas dinner along with his wife, Ivy. No doubt that would put a spoke in Marjorie Thomas's bubble, she always liked to play host. Well, this year it was Holly's turn, and she was set on making sure she gave her guests a meal to remember. She would cook them a dinner to die for.

Stan Butcher's van passed the church hall heading towards the market. Holly pushed away from the wall with her foot and followed the vehicle's trajectory as it made its way towards the village green. Strange, she thought. It wasn't like Stan to be running late. He should have been all set up by now. Most likely he'd been getting extra supplies to meet the Christmas demand. Ivy would have had them ready for him to pick up from their poultry farm. His brother, Simon, had left the rehearsal early to help him. Holly stretched forward to see if he was with Stan, but there was only a lone driver. She scrunched her eyes to better see who it was but couldn't make out the figure who was dressed in a white butcher's coat, blue striped apron and a beanie hat. It didn't really look like Stan or his brother, but from this distance it was hard to tell. Oh, well, likely she would catch up with Simon at the market.

Holly turned and made her way back into the kitchen. How things had changed since last Christmas. She felt a blush rise on her cheeks. Her friendship with Simon seemed to be blossoming into quite the romance. She would never have anticipated it. They'd both been widowed years before. But there was something very nice about spending Christmas with someone special in your life.

She raked through her bag for her shopping list. She didn't want to forget anything.

'So, this is where you are hiding,' her friend Lily Forrest said as she flapped in, already dressed in a long emerald-green coat and matching scarf. She held out a glittery reindeer antler headband that matched the one she wore on her own head. 'Here. Pop this on. It's time we were heading.'

Holly pulled a face at the thought but put the antlers on and held out her shopping list. 'I'm ready.'

As they made their way together to the village green, the chill in the air nipped at Holly's ears, and she pulled her scarf tighter around her. The market had already started to get busy and people bustled about, bundled up ready for the frosty evening to come and hurrying to get the best of the Christmas fare on display. The tinny sound of *Let It Snow* echoed from speakers set on a stall selling festive garlands, wreaths and mistletoe. A queue had formed outside Santa's grotto. Lily and Holly waved to Lily's husband, PC John Forrest, who stood near the front of the queue with their twin daughters. Excitement gleamed in the eyes of the six-year-olds as they waved back with matching mittens. Holly smiled at the memory of waiting to see Santa with her son. He lived on the other side of the country now and had a son of his own. They were coming to stay with her in the new year, and she looked forward to that. For the moment though, she needed to focus on getting the best buys at the market.

She decided to pick up cranberries first at Bert and Phyllis's fruit and vegetable stall, while Lily headed over to Stan's table. As she examined the fresh produce on display, Holly kept an eye out for Simon. Stan's van was parked beside his poultry stall, which was filled with all sorts of birds. Geese, ducks, chickens and turkeys were arranged beside trays of eggs.

As Holly placed her buys into her shopping bag a shrill

scream pierced the air. She raced over to the poultry stall, where Lily, the source of the scream, stood, her shaking hands gripping her throat, her wide eyes staring into the open back doors of the van at Stan's lifeless body. Theo, Stan's assistant, was bent into the back of the van, looking inside. He pulled his head from the van, his mouth a round O of shock and surprise. In his hand, he clutched a blood-covered rock.

CHAPTER 2

A CROWD quickly gathered around the poultry stall. Now that Theo had stepped away, Holly could see Stan's body lying face down on the van floor, he wore a dirt-encrusted, white T-shirt and the back of his head was caked in blood, before she was moved back by Lily's husband, PC Forrest, who closed the van doors. 'Everyone back,' he called. 'And no one leave. Stay here.'

After the police arrived from Dundee, and the area had been taped off, awaiting the forensics team, Holly and the others were ushered across to the local hotel. Those who had been making their way to the market had been turned back home. But at least forty people still milled around inside the lounge of the Flying Goose. The sound of *Oh, Christmas Time,* playing on the jukebox, was silenced when the landlord, Malcolm, switched it off and asked everyone to take a seat, be silent and wait to be interviewed by the police. Malcolm's wife, Cherry Ives, stood stock-still beside the glittering lights of the Christmas tree, a look of utter confusion on her pale face. Holly thought Cherry had looked washed out for a bit now and on reflection hadn't been her normal cheerful self for some time. Malcolm was a bit of a ladies' man, a renowned flirt. Cherry was well aware of Malcolm's affairs. How she put up with it, Holly didn't know. She would come back and speak to her friend later, once the police had left.

HOLLY HADN'T HAD to wait long before being called through to the back bar, which had been set up for the police interviews. Theo and then Lily, who had both discovered Stan's body had been taken in first. She was called in soon after them, having already confirmed her name and contact details to PC Forrest, who, as a local resident already knew everyone in Pine Meadows.

As she had sat waiting in the lounge of the Flying Goose, with nothing much to do but think, something had gnawed at Holly's thoughts. The more she had tried to shake the sight of Stan Butcher's lifeless body from her vision, the more the thought that had accompanied the brief sighting of him evaded her. She'd known it was something important, but her brain wouldn't register it. 'Perhaps, whatever it is will come back to me later, when I'm able to think clearer,' she told the Detective Sergeant who interviewed her and had arranged to speak to her again the following day as part of the police's door-to-door enquiries.

As she made her way back through the lounge of the Flying Goose to head home, Holly saw Simon but, as everyone had been instructed not to talk to each other until after they'd been interviewed, she didn't approach him. It was his brother who had died. She let out a deep breath. Poor Simon. He was being comforted by PC Forrest and another policeman, who now assisted him through to the back bar to be interviewed.

By the time she returned home to her cottage, Holly had started to shiver. Seeing the battered body of her friend had shocked her to the core. She piled logs high on the wood burner in the sitting room and lit the fire. As she sat in a chair beside the crackling fire, with a blanket wrapped around her shoulder, the thought she had struggled so hard to remember earlier suddenly struck home. When she'd seen Stan's body, he'd been wearing a dirty white T-shirt, yet she was certain that when he'd passed the church hall in his van, he'd been wearing a white butchers' coat and a blue striped apron. And a beanie hat. Something wasn't right.

CHAPTER 3

THE FOLLOWING MORNING, Holly sat on the sofa in her lounge and recounted to two detectives what she had observed. While likely this wouldn't have been news to them, the fact that she'd seen Stan's van arriving in the village not long before he was found, and that the driver had been wearing a white coat, striped butcher's apron and a beanie could be.

'So, what time was it you saw Stan Butcher's van passing?' one of the detectives asked.

Holly, who had heard the gossip that Stan had likely been murdered had already considered her answer. 'About fifteen minutes, twenty max before he was found. So, if Stan wasn't wearing them when I saw him, where are they?'

'That's for us to find out,' the detective said.

WHEN THE DETECTIVES LEFT, Holly couldn't settle. The image of Stan's battered body kept flashing through her mind, and she felt a need to keep busy. She made her way through to the kitchen, where she hummed along to the Christmas songs on the radio as she made a pot of tomato, basil and red pepper soup.

An hour later, and clutching a flask, she took herself off to see Stan's wife - to pass on her condolences and a bowl of hot soup to Ivy. It was only a ten-minute walk to the poultry farm along a minor road, sided by fields and tunnels of trees. Holly used the time to think about Stan's missing butcher's coat and apron. As she arrived at a clear section of road between the branch off to Bert Bow's and Stan Butcher's farms, she caught sight of a silver-coloured coin on the ground. When she picked it up, she realised that it wasn't a coin. Turning it around in the palm of her hand, she recognised it as a button from one of the elf costumes that Marjorie Thomas had made. Holly slipped the button into her coat pocket. Whoever had lost it might be looking for it.

She still hadn't managed to speak to Simon and was pleasantly surprised to see his car parked outside when she arrived at the back of the old farmhouse. Simon came out to meet her and showed her through to the kitchen where Ivy sat hunched in a chair beside the Aga. Simon apologised for not having called to see Holly but said he would drop a turkey off at her cottage as soon as he could manage. Holly thanked him and placed the flask of soup on the pine table beside an already iced Christmas cake and two plates of mincemeat pies.

Ivy looked up, a glazed look in her red-rimmed eyes. The police had told her that Theo had discovered her husband's body and that he'd had a rock in his hand. 'I can't believe anyone would harm Stan. But if it wasn't Theo, then who else could it be?' she said. 'I can't take it in.'

Holly listened as Simon recounted the events leading up to the discovery of the body. Simon had helped Stan and Theo set up the stall, then he left Theo tending to things when Stan had set off to return to the farm, while he went to speak with Bert Bow. Theo hadn't put some of the larger turkeys into the van, and Stan had gone back for them.

'How was Stan when he left here to go back to the market?' Holly asked.

'He seemed fine.' Ivy said. 'Well, apart from muttering about letting Theo go if he didn't buck up his ideas.'

Holly nodded. As a teenager, Theo had been a bit of a character who got into fights. 'Stan took him on when no one else in the village would employ him.'

'Stan wasn't keen on it at first,' Ivy said, 'but I wanted to give Theo a chance. We'd both known his father well before he died from that combine harvester accident all these years ago. And we got on with Theo's mother.'

A thought occurred to Holly. A few days earlier, Simon had told her about an issue that had arisen between Stan and Bert and Phyllis Bow who owned the neighbouring farm. She said to Lily, 'Simon told me the Bows have applied to expand their fruit and vegetable produce to include eggs and chickens.'

Ivy grimaced. 'Aye, and as you can imagine, Stan wasn't happy about that. He exchanged a few heated words with Bert Bow about it in the Flying Goose.'

Holly decided to check this out and made her way to the Flying Goose to see if Cherry had heard anything. She wanted to have a word with her anyway, to see how she was. The landlady or even her husband, Malcolm, might have overheard Stan and Bert's argument.

CHERRY WAS POLISHING glasses behind the bar when Holly arrived. The Flying Goose had just opened its doors and was still empty of customers. The smell of wax polish and burning logs masked the usual late morning smell of stale beer. Holly knew that she didn't have long to chat with Cherry before the lunchtime crowd started to arrive. Malcolm, who was stacking bottles of beer onto the shelves, nodded to acknowledge her arrival but continued with his task.

Cherry filled two cups from the Keurig coffee maker on the bar and brought them over to a table by the window where Holly had taken a seat.

When Malcolm went out the back for wood for the already blazing fire, Holly said. 'Are you two okay? You could cut the atmosphere in here with a knife.' Despite the warmth of the fire, there was a chill in the air. Holly wondered if she was the cause of Cherry's reluctance to talk. 'You are both still coming for Christmas dinner . . . aren't you?'

Cherry shook her head and then glanced over at the bar. 'Oh, it's not that. Of course, I am. I wouldn't miss one of your delicious dinners. It's just that...'

Holly touched Cherry's arm. 'Would you rather speak later?'

Cherry forced a smile. 'Malcolm's at it again. Isn't he?

Like always, I'll be the last to know if he is having another affair. But believe me, I'm going to find out. He's been well warned this time. He knows he's on his last chance, so he'll have been doubly keen to have covered his tracks.' She looked Holly in the eye. 'You would tell me, wouldn't you?'

Holly nodded. 'Of course. If I knew anything, I'd let you know. But what makes you think he's seeing someone?'

'He's been going AWOL. It's his usual pattern. At first, I let it go, and then I started to think about where he was going when he went out on his bicycle. Then Stan died, and I didn't want to say anything, and Malcolm stopped disappearing. But it's still playing on my mind. Likely it's just me being over watchful.'

Holly understood. She also understood that Cherry didn't want to discuss this any further. Malcolm had arrived back with an armful of logs and was stacking them into the basket.

'Did you hear Stan arguing in here with Bert Bow the night before he died?' Holly said.

Malcolm came over. Both he and Cherry had heard the argument. Stan had been furious that Bert Bow had applied for a licence to breed chickens and sell their eggs. Their farms bordered each other, and he accused Bert of trying to destroy his livelihood. It wasn't the first time they'd fallen out. The last time had been over a boundary dispute.

CHAPTER 4

AFTER LEAVING THE FLYING GOOSE, Holly joined the queue outside the local grocery shop. As the market had been closed off after Stan's body had been discovered, many of the villagers had been unable to buy a turkey or other poultry and much of the fresh fruit and vegetables they needed to make their Christmas dinner. Like the others in line, Holly hoped the local shop would have enough to go around. Most of the stock from the farmers' market had been redirected there. Given that Marjorie Thomas owned the shop, Holly didn't hold high hopes of nabbing the best of anything, even if Marjorie was coming to Holly's house for Christmas dinner.

At the head of the queue, Old Rosie held court. She spoke in a raised voice, and Holly picked up what she said. But, like most others, Holly disregarded much of what she heard as more of Rosie's ramblings. It was best not to heed her. Likely it was Stan's murder that had set her off again.

'I'm telling you,' Old Rosie said. 'All these strange goings on up at the poultry farm. I got a double yoker again. Something isn't right. The hens in the hen house have been squawking at night.'

Holly moved up the queue. It would soon be her turn to go into the shop. As she passed her, Old Rosie grabbed her arm. 'It's the foxes. At night. They are back. The hens are unsettled. I can hear them from my backyard. I saw people wandering about, you know. The other night, and many nights before that. People sneaking about with the foxes.'

Poor Rosie had never been right, but she'd been worse since her parents died. She'd looked after them both for years. First, her mother and then her father passed away. Her father had been a solicitor in Dundee, and her mother had been wheelchair-bound before her death. Rosie now lived alone in the large bungalow, with her ground bordering on to Stan's poultry farm on one side and onto Bert Bow's fruit and vegetable farm on the other. Although Rosie had been left well cared for financially, the bungalow had fallen into disrepair and needed a lot of work done to it. Rosie was always telling strange stories to anyone who would listen. The tales about the odd comings and goings on the poultry farm were just the latest of many episodes. Holly assumed she was lonely.

As she made to step into Marjorie's shop, the sight of Sam's assistant, Theo, being bundled into the back of a police car, stopped Holly in her tracks. 'What's going on,' she asked Theo's mother who wept as she watched her son leave.

'They're saying Theo murdered Stan. But it wasn't him. It couldn't have been.'

Holly was startled by the news. She took Theo's mother by the arm and led her into her house and sat her down.

'I know Theo had a reputation for getting into trouble but Stan and Ivy trusted him,' Theo's mother said between sobs. 'Theo hasn't been in any trouble lately. He's put those days behind him.'

CHAPTER 5

The next morning, after she'd finished wrapping her presents and placing them under the tree, Holly sat at her kitchen table with her friend Lily Forrest. They each clutched a mug of hot chocolate which they sipped deep in thought.

'So,' Holly said, 'What do you make of Theo being taken in for questioning? Do you think he murdered Stan?'

'Well, the police think so. They are certain they have their man. Why? Do you think he didn't do it?'

'You were there with Theo at the open doors of the van...'

'Aye, and it's a sight I'll never forget,' Lily said. 'It looks like Theo hit Stan on the back of the head with that rock. Then he bundled him into the back of the van and opened the doors as I approached so that I would be a witness to him finding the body. It's all so blurry now. I can't really be sure what happened.'

'Hmph,' Holly uttered and laid her empty mug down. 'Theo's mum said he'd never been out of her sight from the time Stan and Simon left until he opened the van doors. Her stall was right next to his. She said Theo had been busy serving customers until he went to unpack the van. It had been about fifteen minutes since the van had arrived back and there'd been no sign of Stan. If that's true, Theo wouldn't have had time to hit Stan and then put him in the back of the van. But. He *was* holding a bloodied rock.'

Lily lifted both mugs over to the sink and filled them with water. 'If Theo didn't kill Stan then who was it?' she asked after sitting down.

Holly wasn't sure what she thought, but something wasn't adding up. 'Well, for starters, where is Stan's apron, white coat and beanie? Have the police found them yet?' She reached into her pocket and pulled out the silver-coloured button she'd found. Something had dawned on her, adding to her confusion. 'And how did this get onto the road beside Old Rosie's bungalow and near to both the Butcher's and the Bow's farms?'

Lily peered at the button and screwed up her face as if totally confused. 'Anyone could have dropped that button. Are you saying it's connected? I can't see how.'

'What if I told you that it's a button from one of the elf costumes?'

'And?' Lily said.

'Think about it. We had the first dress rehearsal for the carol concert the morning Stan died. The costumes were only given out to the elves as they arrived in the hall for the rehearsal. So, no one could have lost a button before then.'

Lily tilted her head to one side. 'Except for Marjorie Thomas. She could have dropped the button. After all, she made the costumes.'

Frustrated by Lily's arguments, Holly sat forward. 'Okay, so who, other than Marjorie Thomas, had access to an elf costume before the dress rehearsal?'

'What?' Lily shook her head. 'I think you're looking for clues where there aren't any. We need to stick to what we know. It seems certain that Theo murdered Stan. How does finding a button change that?'

'That *and* the missing clothes. Humour me,' Holly said. 'Who was given an elf outfit that morning, and when did they leave the church hall?'

Lily nodded. 'Okay, if it helps. There are five elves. Cherry and Malcolm Ives from the Flying Goose. Neither of them can hold a tune, but they wanted to join in. Malcolm left not long after putting his costume on, but Cherry stayed until the end and left when we did.'

'And Old Rosie, Rosie Greene,' Holly added. 'But we passed her as we were leaving. She was heading through to the kitchen for a cup of tea with Marjorie Thomas and the minister.'

Lily held up a hand and tapped her fingers with the fore-finger of her other hand, counting the elves off. 'There was also Bert Bow. Phyllis is in the choir, but Bert is tone deaf. He was another of the hummingbirds dressed as an elf. They both left early to finish setting up their stall. That only leaves us with one more elf and he left the hall not long after he arrived.'

Holly froze. Her heart hammering. She licked her dry lips. 'Stan's brother, Simon.'

CHAPTER 6

STILL FEELING unsettled the next day, Holly paced her front room. She needed to speak to Simon to check where he went after he left the church hall and to find out if he'd seen or heard anything. She dreaded seeing a missing button on his outfit at the Christmas Carol Concert that evening. No, she had to speak to him before then to put her mind at ease, although she wouldn't say anything about any missing buttons. Before that though, she would go and see Marjorie Thomas. To find out exactly how many buttons she had left over after making the costumes. She didn't relish the thought, and it would have to wait until she did a bit more prepping for tomorrow's dinner.

As she turned towards the window, Holly was surprised to see Simon's car drawing up outside. She made her way along the hallway but stopped to check herself in the mirror. She raked her hands through her short hair. A visit to see Glenda at Happy Hair was in order. She would pop in today. As promised, Simon had brought her an extra-large turkey from the poultry farm. He handed the large parcel to her on the doorstep, saying that he didn't have time to stop for a chat as he was busy helping Ivy at the farm and that he had taken on the role of farm manager. When she waved Simon goodbye, Holly felt a surge of relief that he hadn't given her the opportunity to ask about his whereabouts when Stan had been murdered.

After preparing the turkey stuffing ready for the next day and popping it into the fridge, Holly set off to speak to Marjorie. She found her in the church hall, setting up for the carol concert. Holly had added a good splash of freshly squeezed orange juice into the sausage meat, onion, oats and herb stuffing mix. It had been her mother's recipe, and for years Marjorie had asked her how she made the tasty stuffing. Holly smiled at the thought of her asking again tomorrow what her secret was. Holly couldn't believe Christmas Eve had come around already. Despite Stan's death, Ivy had wanted the carol concert to go ahead tonight as planned. She said Stan would have wanted that.

Old Rosie was helping Marjorie place song sheets onto the chairs in the hall. Marjorie wore a long flowing velvet dress in bright shades of green and red. She looked up when Holly entered. 'Coooee! Holly. Have you come to help?' she said and waved. 'Rosie is about to go and stack the trolley up with the tea and coffee cups for later.'

Hmm, Holly thought, she hadn't anticipated that. She glanced at her watch. She had so much still to prepare for Christmas dinner. The Christmas cake and puddings were finished. She'd already set the table for tomorrow, in turquoise and white, using a Frozen theme, but it still needed some finishing touches, and there were all the vegetables to prepare. Still, she thought, she could spare some time, especially if it brought her some answers.

Holly ushered Marjorie aside. She hadn't planned what to say and realised that she had to ask about the button in a way that didn't arouse Marjorie's suspicions. After taking a deep breath she said, 'I don't suppose you have any of the buttons you used for the elf costumes going spare? I'm making something and they would be just perfect.'

Marjorie touched Holly's arm. 'Oh, there aren't any left. I used every one of them. I had thirty, which allowed six for each of the five costumes, with none to spare. I used four down the front of each jacket and sewed one onto the cuff of each sleeve.'

Before Holly could respond, Marjorie added, 'And, I don't think you can buy them now. I've had those buttons for years just waiting for the right moment to use them.' Marjorie gave a self-satisfied grin. 'They were perfect for the elf outfits, if I say so myself.'

Well, that was that Holly thought as she rolled her eyes and followed Old Rosie through to the kitchen, while Marjorie finished putting out the song sheets and setting up the hall.

Holly recalled speaking to Rosie outside Marjorie's shop. Something she'd said then had stuck in Holly's mind, but she'd dismissed it. Now, she had the chance to check out exactly what Old Rosie had seen and heard at Stan's poultry farm. She dreaded having to listen to more of Rosie's ramblings, but she seemed calmer than she had been when they'd last met, so Holly picked up some cups and asked, 'How are things with you, Rosie?'

'Why won't you listen? You're asking how I am, but don't listen to what I tell you. The policewoman who came to see me was the same. But I'll tell you again, some very strange things have been going on at the poultry farm.'

Rosie's comment caught Holly off guard. What she said was true, no one really listened to Rosie. Holly was listening now. 'Okay! Tell me more.'

Rosie lifted a milk jug down from a shelf and reached for another one. 'It's stopped now, but Stan knew all about the goings on. He told me he was going to have it out with them.'

Holly was definitely listening to Rosie now. She had her full attention. 'Have it out with whom?'

'Stan didn't say. He said he couldn't. But I saw them too. Sneaking about, disturbing the hens.'

'Do you have any idea who they were?'

Rosie shook her head. 'I don't, but Stan did. He said he was going to tell everyone about it at Christmas dinner at your house Holly unless it stopped.'

Sensing that what Rosie had said was important, Holly placed the cups she was carrying onto the trolley and turned her full attention to her. 'I'm sorry, Rosie. I'm not following. What was it that Stan knew?'

'I told you, I don't know.'

Curiouser and curiouser, Holly thought. She wondered if Rosie was indeed rambling but dismissed the thought. There was something important in what Rosie was telling her, and she was certain that it had led to Stan's murder. 'Did you tell the police about this?'

Rosie plonked down a milk jug and glared at her. 'Of course, I did. But they wouldn't listen to me either. Well, not after I mentioned the foxes.'

AFTER LEAVING THE CHURCH HALL, Holly popped into Happy Hair to see if Glenda could give her a cut and blow dry. Glenda was at the sink washing Phyllis Bow's long auburn locks. She waved Holly over. 'I'll be about half an hour if you want to wait. I'm ahead today because Ivy Butcher obviously couldn't make her appointment.'

Holly thanked Glenda for fitting her in. She took a seat and flipped through a magazine while keeping her ears alert. If there was anywhere better than Happy Hair to hear the village gossip, Holly had yet to find it. Lulled by the laughter and chat in the salon the locals opened up to Glenda, telling her all their news and giving their opinions on the latest happenings.

On returning home from the salon, Holly made straight for her small workroom and pulled a large notepad from her desk drawer. After her conversations with Rosie and then Glenda, a germ of an idea had formed in her mind but it still didn't make much sense to her. She wanted to get her thoughts about each of the elves down on paper to see if that helped.

Old Rosie – Lived near to where the button had been found. She didn't leave the rehearsal until after Stan's body was discovered. She reported seeing people on the poultry farm. Stan threat-

ened to let everyone know about this at Christmas dinner unless it stopped.

Stopped what? And. Who? Holly thought. And why at her Christmas meal? Was the murderer someone who was coming to her house on Christmas Day? Were they all in danger? She couldn't think how to find out who it could be, apart from asking Ivy if Stan had mentioned anything to her about it. She would phone Ivy and find out if she knew anything.

Bert and Phyllis Bow- Lived near where the button was found. Both left rehearsals early. Stan argued with Bert about the Bow's application to farm chickens. A previous disagreement about a boundary dispute. Bert wasn't at his fruit and vegetable stall when Stan's body was discovered, but Phyllis was.

Malcolm and Cherry Ives – Malcolm left the hall early. Didn't live near where the button was found.

Holly recalled seeing Cherry leaving the church hall behind her and Lily. When Stan's body was discovered, Malcolm and Cherry had both been in the Flying Goose. Cherry thought that Malcolm was cheating again. Who, if anyone, had he been seeing?

Simon – Could have lost the button near his brother's farm. He left rehearsal early to help Stan. Soon after Stan set off to return to the poultry farm, Simon left Theo alone at the poultry stall to go and talk to Bert Bow. As the oldest brother, Stan had inherited the farm from his parents. Simon returned here six months ago. He is now managing the farm for Ivy.

Holly paused. Had Simon resented Stan inheriting the family farm? It was through Ivy that Holly had met Simon. In the time she'd known him, she'd never seen any sign of friction between the brothers or heard any disagreements between them. And, Simon's cheerful, friendly manner had made Holly want to spend time with him. Simon had left the stall at the same time as Stan, to speak to Bert Bow. She hadn't seen Simon or Bert at Bert Bow's stall when she'd bought the cranberries, sprouts and parsnips, so they must have been together somewhere else at the market. Bert Bow's wife had served Holly. Phyllis was a modern, lively character, who was a lot of fun to be with and Holly remembered laughing with her just before she heard Lily scream.

She stood and paced the room. Was this the end of her friendship with Simon? Until Stan's death it looked like they were moving towards a long-term relationship. Now, understandably, Simon was too distracted and distressed by his brother's murder to spend time with her. Holly's life, once so busy while she worked, had in many ways become too mundane since retiring. She'd been enjoying the budding romance with the widower. Ah, well. Unlike her, Simon Butcher was now too busy for a relationship. It would be the last thing on his mind. Still, she'd have to face him at Christmas dinner tomorrow.

Holly sat down again at her desk. After reading through her notes, she drew up a list of things she needed to find out. When she had finished, she studied the list until her head ached. Then, like a bolt from the blue, something struck her full on.

First on her list now was a visit to see Cherry at the Flying Goose.

CHAPTER 7

Holly arrived at Lily's house with Cherry in tow. She'd called in on Lily first to ask if the three of them could meet there. PC Forrest, Lily's husband, wasn't due off shift for a few hours and Lily had put a Disney Christmas movie on the TV in the lounge for the twins to watch. Despite the women's questions, Holly had refused to tell them why she wanted to see them, only that she needed to speak to them both in private. Now, huddled together around Lily's kitchen table, the three of them sat deep in thought. Holly had told them what she believed had happened to Stan Butcher and had sworn them to secrecy until they checked some things out for her. If her thoughts were right, then between them they could prove it. And the clock was ticking. They had until the Christmas carol concert tonight to do so. And before then, they needed to tell PC Forrest everything.

While Cherry headed back to the Flying Goose with a list of things to do, Holly and Lily set off to speak to Ivy and to have a closer look around the area where Holly had found one of the elves' buttons.

ONCE THE APPLAUSE died for the performers who had sung, and hummed, their hearts out at the Christmas carol concert, Marjorie Thomas ushered the choir and humming-birds through to the large kitchen for celebratory drinks. PC Forrest led the way.

When everyone had settled, PC Forrest closed the door, and Holly called for attention. 'As you all know, Stan died a few days ago, and Theo has been accused of his murder. But someone in *this* room knows that Theo didn't murder Stan,' she said and glanced around.

A collective chatter broke out, and Holly called for order. 'Silence. Hear me out.'

She pointed to Bert Bow. 'Bert, you argued with Stan in the Flying Goose the night before he died. Cherry and Malcolm overheard you. Stan wasn't pleased that you and Phyllis had applied to include hens and eggs as part of your farm produce, as this would have impacted on his own profits.'

Bert stepped forward; his face filled with outrage. 'What? You think I murdered Stan Butcher over some daft argument . . .'

Holly held up a hand. 'Let me finish.'

'Simon, you left the poultry stall at the same time as Stan, to find Bert Bow so that you could talk to him about this. So, you and Bert were together at the market from then until Theo opened the van doors. Phyllis remained at your fruit and vegetable stall where she served me. So, we also know where she was.

'Rosie, you reported strange goings-on at night up at Stan's poultry farm. No one really listened to you, but you were right. Strange things were happening there.'

Rosie called, 'Aye, they were and for a good while too.'

Holly continued. 'Malcolm. You were behind these goings on. Weren't you? You were meeting your latest lover at Stan's farm.'

Malcolm looked around him. 'Now, wait a minute ...'

Holly held up the silver coloured-button that was now missing from the sleeve of Malcolm's elf outfit. When Malcolm saw the button his face paled, and he slumped forward, just as two policemen rushed in and each gripped one of his arms.

'I found the button you lost as you bundled Stan's dead body into the back of his van on the road beside his farm,' Holly said to Malcolm. 'Cherry checked for me and had already confirmed that a button was missing from one sleeve of your elf outfit. She also found Stan's apron and white coat hidden in the cellar of the Flying Goose along with your beanie hat, where you hid them after driving Stan's van back to the market with Stan lying dead in the back. It was you I saw passing the church hall. After parking the van, you removed the apron, white coat and beanie and slipped into the Flying Goose with them without anyone noticing. Fifteen minutes later, when Theo opened the van door, everyone assumed that Stan had been murdered there and that it was

Theo who did it. But Stan wasn't murdered at the market, was he?'

Malcolm tried to wriggle free from the policemen's grip. 'I didn't murder Stan. Dear God, it was an accident, and I haven't settled since. I know I should have got help for him, but I wasn't thinking straight. I could see he was already dead.'

As the policemen made to escort Malcolm Ives out, he called, 'Wait. I'll tell you what happened, but only if I do it here. They have to understand . . . it was an accident.'

The policemen stopped and nodded.

'I overheard Stan saying that he was going back to the poultry farm to pick up more turkeys, so I followed him on my bike. I hid my bike in the bushes and waited at the end of his road for him to make his way back to the market. When his van approached, I waved Stan down.

'When he stepped out of the van, I grabbed the front of his white coat and pleaded with him not to tell my wife what I'd been up to. Cherry would have thrown me out. After Rosie told Stan that someone had been coming on to his farm at night, he'd lain in wait and caught us. He threatened then to announce our affair when we were at Holly's for Christmas dinner unless we stopped seeing each other. I couldn't allow Stan to do that. I thought if I could talk to him, I could get him to see reason. But he wasn't having it. When he turned to leave, I tightened my grip. But, he shook free and fell backwards, striking his head on a rock. I panicked.

'After removing his outer clothes, I put them on and pulled Stan into the back of the van along with the rock he'd hit his head on. I only intended to ask him not to say anything. Stan Butcher may have had his disagreements with Bert Bow, but they were good friends. They grew up together. Stan wanted me to stop seeing Phyllis or he would tell Bert and everyone else about us.'

All hell broke loose as Bert Bow made to lunge at Malcolm but was held back by PC Forrest and Phyllis, who was furiously apologising to her husband. As the three policemen escorted Malcolm from the church hall, a stunned silence fell over the choir. Not even a hummingbird hummed as they tried to take in what had just transpired in front of them.

CHAPTER 8

At two o'clock on Christmas Day, Holly checked the parcels carefully placed under the glittering Christmas tree. A riot of blue paper tied with sparkly silver-coloured ribbons. One for each of her guests. Her lounge smelled as it only could on this one day of the year – the scent of pine mixed with the smell of burning logs, mingling with the delicious aroma coming from the turkey roasting in the oven. It was a smell Holly loved.

Simon arrived first, carrying a couple of bottles of Holly's favourite shiraz and a little gift that he wanted her to open before anyone else arrived. She reached into the small gift bag and opened the box inside to reveal an exquisite gold bracelet with a heart dangling from it. After hugging Simon, she poured out two glasses of Champagne and handed one to him. They clinked glasses and wished each other a Merry Christmas. Then, they rolled up their sleeves and finished cooking the perfect Christmas dinner together.

Later, as her guests sat around the table chatting

between courses, they took turns opening their presents from each other. Theo, who had been released immediately after Malcolm's confession and arrest, had a special thank you gift for Old Rosie who, as the hero of the hour, had a place laid for her at the table. Rosie's eyes glowed as she read the card from Theo, promising to spend every Saturday afternoon at her place working on and overseeing the repairs to her bungalow and arranging for tradesmen to do whatever was needed to bring her home back to its former glory.

Theo blushed at Rosie's delight and said to her, 'Honestly, I can't thank you enough for what you've done, Rosie. If it hadn't been for you noticing the strange comings and goings up at the farm, likely I wouldn't be sitting here now.'

Tears formed in Theo's mother's eyes and she swiped them away with her hand. 'And me too, Rosie. I'll come and help you get everything cleaned and ship-shape once the builders are finished, so don't you be worrying about that.'

As Holly pulled a spare Christmas cracker with Simon, he said, 'Remember to make a wish, Holly.'

Lily winked at Holly, leant in close and whispered. 'I think you should be careful what you wish for from now on. In more ways than one, you truly did put on a Christmas dinner to die for.'

About Sheena Macleod

Sheena Macleod is a published historical fiction author and a prize winning and published short story writer. She lives in a seaside town on the East Coast of Scotland. You can find her online at https://www.sheenas-books.co.uk

CHRISTMAS CARD AND FEATHERED

MOLLIE COX BRYAN

Welcome to Victoria Town, Va., where Victoriana meets murder…

Christmas is a busy time in the quaint Victoria Town, Va., with the residents preparing for shoppers and festivities. Irene Calhoun, owner of "Mourning Arts," is preparing to host a Christmas card-making party for the women of the town. Stumbling over a dead body in her back office was not in the plan.

Irene feels a sense of responsibility because the body was found in her shop and the police are getting nowhere. She rolls up her sleeves and pieces together a curious puzzle, its deadly pieces consisting of betrayal, drugs…and chickens.

CHRISTMAS CARD AND FEATHERED

Small jars of red, green, and gold buttons lined Irene Calhoun's kitchen counter. Warm

gingerbread cookies sat on the table, cooling off next to the still-wrapped Christmas-colored cardstock, glitter packs, and scrapbooking paper. She drew in the mouthwatering scent and nabbed one cookie, just for a taste.

Maybe, just maybe, she had everything she needed for the card-making party, a yearly get together before the mad rush of the season. This year, she was hosting—exciting, but not as exciting as the delicious spicy flavors popping in her mouth. A knock at the door interrupted her revelry.

"So early in the day?" She mumbled to herself. She opened the door to see Viv, her part-time employee and friend from Mourning Arts.

"Viv? What's going on?" Viv rarely visited Irene's home. Viv's jam-packed schedule included helping Irene at the store, her Aunt Libby with the Sweet Victoria B & B, and studying to be a private detective with her boyfriend, Stone.

No response. She just shivered, while snow flurries blew around her, a few landing on her red coat.

"Are you okay? Please come in out of the weather." Irene's intuition tingles spiked along the back of her neck. What was going on?

Viv stepped forward into Irene's home. "I ah—." "Viv? What? What's going on?"

"Stone—"

"Did he break up with you?"

She shook her head and words tumbled out, her blue eyes wide with emotion. "No. He was called out on a case this morning. I went with him. Carol Wheatley is missing. It's as if she vanished."

Carol was the new owner of one of Victoria Town's quaintest shops, "Queenie's Quill and Paperie," which had once housed The Queen's Cookies, until the owner sold it and moved back home to South Carolina.

"Perhaps she had to leave town fast." Irene pulled a deep purple velvet scarf from the coat rack. "A family emergency."

"No. I don't think so. Al, her fiance, would've said and he's the one who called the police. She was supposed to meet him and never showed. He ran to her place, and she was gone." Viv pulled her hat further over her ears.

"Signs of a struggle?" Irene wrapped the scarf around her neck.

"Nothing. It makes no sense" Viv's blue eyes lit with that I-can-solve-a puzzle spark Irene recognized too well. But, they were red and puffy eyes. She'd need to toughen up to become a PI.

Of course, this was different. She and Carol were friends.

"Not necessarily. Not if she just had to leave." Irene's arm slipped around Viv's shoulders. "Let's not jump to conclusions."

Viv nodded her head. "No signs of struggle could mean—"

"Shhh. Let's go to the shop. Busy day ahead. The police will figure this out." Irene wanted to calm down Viv, but she herself tried to ignore a creeping dark sensation.

If Carol knew her assailant, the police would more likely find him or her. But it's more heartbreaking when someone you recognized broke trust. Happened every day. Irene's hands clasped together. She experienced that more than most, perhaps.

Viv and Irene walked along the snowy cobblestone streets, lined with Victorian-themed shops. Victoria Town, Virginia, a haven for tourists who loved all things Victorian, was a snowy, surreal dream this morning. A townswoman was missing. The pink feather fans and lacey parasols taunted Irene as they walked by Fans & Feathers, though they both stopped to gawk. With a friend missing, frilly items assaulted the senses, as did the Christmas tree in the square, still lit from the night before, its star a shiny emblem.

"Did you go to Carol's apartment with Stone?" Irene asked. "Was anything off?"

"I visited her place before. I saw nothing off. Except for feathers." "Feathers? Like for crafting?" "I'm not sure. Just lovely soft-purple feathers scattered."

Irene shivered, even as Viv's warm arm encircled hers. "That's strange, isn't it? What was she
doing with those feathers?"

"Crafting?" She offered. "Kinky sex?"

Irene elbowed her, but couldn't help but laugh.

Viv was another transplant who had unexpectedly stayed in the small town. When she first

arrived, she was full of edges and darkness. But over the short time she'd lived here, those edges had softened. Irene loved to see more outsiders coming into the town, especially young people like Viv.

Victoria Town was Irene's home, now, though she hailed from the mountains and when she spoke of home, thought of home, it was Blackbird Hollow springing to mind. But she loved Victoria Town and her shop, Mourning Arts. The Victorians took their mourning seriously—and it suited her. Many

Victoriana collectors were into the lace and frill, others loved black crepe and mourning jewelry. The town offered something for all lovers of the Victorian.

Irene's little adopted town was living and breathing. People were just stirring now, and business owners were lifting shades, pulling back curtains, and switching on lights. December was Irene's favorite time to walk these streets. She loved all the traditions—the parades, the decorations, the carolers. The town logo, "Have a Merry Victorian Christmas." All of it. Of course, the word holidays reminded her of Blackbird Hollow. A pang of longing rose to the surface. But for now, this tableau of wintery charm, full of traditions and love, worked for her.

Admittedly, this year's Christmas card making party would be different —and that wouldn't surprise anybody who knew Irene was hosting. A few weeks before the fancy Christmas Tea, Victoria Town's huge yearly holiday event, a circle of its women gathered to make Christmas cards. The event began a few years ago and had become a tradition among longtime residents. Whereas the town's tea always took place at the Sweet Victoria B & B, the women took turns hosting the card marking party. It reminded Irene of the quilting bees her grandmother used to attend—women would gather once a week to work on a quilt together. If a neighbor was getting married, having a baby, or sick, the women of Blackbird Hollow pooled their resources and fashioned a quilt for them.

Of course, while quilting, the women shared plenty of food, drink, and Irene's favorite part, gossip. The women of Victoria Town were not so different from the women of Blackbird Hollow. Except they drank wine instead of moonshine. Which, of course, Irene would have available should anybody care to imbibe.

Viv and Irene stepped up to the shop, with its black fringed shades in the windows, in stark contrast to the other shops. But an authentic Victorian Town needed a mourning shop. It was a popular shop with tourists, which was no surprise to Irene. It was all about balance. Death and its trappings freaked some folks out, but Irene grew up in the heart of Appalachia, where they viewed death as a natural part of life.

Irene slipped a key into the front door. "Can we help the police?" She opened the door, and it swung with a creak she'd been meaning to fix.

"Not yet. I asked them. They may allow us to organize a search, but for now, the investigation is closer to home. They are just piecing things together." Viv walked behind the cash register and plucked at the keyboard to open it. Irene loved to watch her fingers on any computer. The young woman was a computer expert. Her hacking skills brought her trouble earlier in her life, but more recently she used them for good—to help the police and Stone, and he talked her into becoming a PI.

Irene was not a fan of computers. She didn't despise them. She just didn't want to live her life virtually, like so many people did.

"There." Viv struck a computer key. "We're open."

"Give me your bag and I'll take it into the office and plug in the kettle." Irene reached out her arm and took Viv's bag and coat. As she slipped off her coat, a deep mauve showed itself. "Oooo. A velvet morning jacket. How divine."

Viv grinned. "I think it's one you designed."

"Is it? All the better!" Irene had fallen in love with design and fabrics. She was a fledgling, but she had so much fun with it she didn't care. She grabbed the coat and bag and turned. What was that on the floor? She leaned closer. She blinked. "Viv?"

"Yeah?"

"What's that?" She pointed.

"Uh." Viv came from around the cash register. "A purple...feather?" Irene's tingling returned.

"Did you get one on you?"

"I could have. I guess." She brushed herself off and shrugged. "But wait, there's another one." She huddled next to Irene. "There's a trail."

They followed a path to the back room, where the office was located.

When Irene opened the door, she first noticed liquid on the floor. "What happened here?" She slipped on the light switch, her eyes traveling the length of the red-brown liquid, to a shoe and a leg and a person covered in purple feathers. The air rushed from Irene's lungs. She wanted to yell to Viv to call 9-1-1. But she couldn't get enough air. The floor wobbled. She reached for the doorjamb, leaned against it and tried to swallow more air. Sweat pricked on her face.

Poor Carol. Knees, don't fail me now. Air, don't leave me now. She attempted to catch herself, stopping from falling. But her body took over, and blackness overcame her.

Irene awoke to a fuzzy Viv on the floor, stroking her shoulder. "Irene? I've called the police and the ambulance." Irene struggled to sit. Why was she lying on the floor? What happened? "Well, now we know what happened to Carol." Viv's voice cracked. "Don't sit up yet."

"What? What happened to her?" Irene gasped.

"Murdered and stuck in your back room. That's what." Viv sounded almost official. Perhaps she was cut out for PI work. "I've not examined the body, but it looks like they shot her. There's a lot of blood."

Irene's stomach churned. What was wrong with her? She grew up in the mountains and killed and dressed chickens and hogs by the time she was twelve years old. A little blood never bothered her. She swallowed. Yet, the fresh memory of it on her floor sickened her. She swallowed again—she refused to get sick. That would not do.

The door swung open, and the paramedics swarmed on her like flies on honey. She tried to swat them away, but she dozed off. Dozed off? Yep, and then awoke fuzzy again and listened to Viv recount what happened to the police.

"Vivianne!" A loud woman's voice came screeching into the scene. "Oh my God, Viv! Are you okay?"

"I'm fine, Aunt Libby. Everything is under control here. You should go back to the B & B. I'll be home soon."

"I'm not going anywhere —Irene?" Libby came into her view.

"Ma'am, you can't be in here." A police officer escorted Viv's aunt Libby away.

A paramedic leaned over Irene. "We're taking you into the hospital for observation. You may

have a concussion. You took quite a fall. Hit your head."

"Is that necessary?" Irene tried to sit up and dizzied.

The paramedic frowned. "I'm afraid it is."

But she had a party to throw in two days. She had a business to run. "I'll take care of everything,"

Viv said, as if she'd read her mind. "But the shop—"

"Closed for the day," Viv said.

Irene's mind muddled. Of course, they have to close the shop. "The party–"

"In two days, you'll be doing jumping jacks by then." Viv smiled and patted her shoulder. When did young Viv become so comforting, so confident? Irene remembered when she first met

her. New in town, staying with her aunt, and fascinated with Mourning Arts. But the poor thing had run into several murder victims, which brought her to Stone, the local PI. Viv used to question herself constantly, rarely made eye contact, and shuffled along while walking. Now, she was rubbing

Irene's hand, looking her straight in the eye and soothing her. Hot tears pricked at her eyes. Viv had grown. It was an honor to witness it.

Her head itched, and she reached around to scratch it. When she brought her hand back, covered in blood. "What the–"

"Shhhh," Viv said. "You're bleeding. Just a few stitches and you'll be fine."

Viv blurred. Irene struggled to stay awake. The paramedics lifted her off the ground and whisked her away in an ambulance. *Well, there's a first time for everything.* She watched the lights on the poles go by through the window as snow spit.

Viv was right about Irene rallying in two days. She'd not be doing jumping jacks soon, though. But like her Grandmother Lilac used to say, "push through the pain and the next thing you know you'll

be fine." Of course, Irene's grandmother and the women of Blackbird Hollow held a prayer vigil for her last night. Irene considered herself a modern woman of science and sophistication, but she conceded the Universe simply couldn't explain everything with science. The power of prayer from a group of Appalachian women who loved you? You can't beat that.

Viv had been taking care of the shop alone. Irene was on her way to help, but the scent of chocolate beckoned. She ducked into "Cee Cee's House of Chocolate," which had the best hot chocolate Irene had ever had, and that included the chocolate she'd had in a sweet shop in Belgium.

"One Mexican hot chocolate, with extra pepper." Irene's mouth watered, even as she spoke.

"Sure thing, Irene. How are you feeling?" Cee Cee's dark brown eyes met Irene's with concern, even as her hands never missed a beat in preparing the chocolate.

"Better." She smiled. Her head was fine. She didn't have a concussion, just a few stitches.

A loud clanking noise erupted near her, and she clutched her chest, gasping. A child had dropped silverware against a plate. Irene's face heated. Every little odd noise set her on edge.

She looked around the cafe and spotted Al, Carol's boyfriend. And he wasn't alone. Viv didn't recognize his female companion. She must be from out of town. Had he been seeing someone else behind Carol's back? Could he be that crass? Two days after her death?

"Your cocoa," Cee Cee said. "To go?"

Irene wanted to stay and observe the situation, but Viv could use her help. "Yes, please." She watched as she poured the thick brew into a paper to-go cup and tried not to watch Carol's boyfriend as the woman across the table reached for his hand. Unbelievable! And stupid!

Of course, he was the top suspect. Everybody recognized that. But she didn't entertain it until now. A chill swept through her. A boyfriend killing his girlfriend happened every day. But why had he placed her body in Irene's store?

"Here you go." Cee Cee handed her the hot chocolate.

"Thanks." She reached for the warm drink, vowing to get her security camera fixed. If it had been working, they'd have seen and caught him already, instead of him snuggling up to a new girlfriend in public.

Her head throbbed. The audacity of Al! Carol's body was still in the morgue, not even buried yet, and he was already cavorting with another woman!

Irene walked by the shop and side-eyed the two of them as they drank their concoctions. They were so intent on one another that they didn't see her.

She heard a woman call out her name as she sprinted. She turned toward the voice. It was Sadie Hartwell, the owner of Fans & Feathers, and Aunt Libby's best friend.

"How are you, dear?" She touched Irene's shoulder.

"I'm fine." And already wishing people would stop asking, but no chance of that.

"It must have been such a shock. I was just telling Libby how I don't think I could function if I

ran into a dead body. I mean, you're tougher than me. But still. How dreadful for you." She fiddled with her scarf. "Are you sure you still want to host the party tonight? I could do it if you're not up to it."

"It's fine." Irene found that keeping her part of the conversation brief helped when talking with Sadie, who was a babbling brook of conversation. Right now, it was Carol's boyfriend on Irene's mind. She was certain the police would investigate him, but could it hurt to put a bug in the police's ear?

"If you need help for the party tonight, please let me know. Libby's bringing snowflake cookies, and I've got plenty of pumpkin bread. I was up with it pretty late last night. Viv mentioned strawberry shortcake Christmas cupcakes. They sounded delicious." She stopped in front of her shop. "We'll see you tonight, Irene. I'm here if you need me."

Sadie was a talker, but she had a heart of gold. "Thank you so much. I'll let you know if I need anything." Sometimes people just wanted to be needed. Irene understood that. "If people want to help, let them. It helps them more than you, sometimes. But that's a good thing," Granny Lilac's words rang in her head. And she was right. But Irene and Viv had it under control.

Fifteen of Victoria Town's women citizens answered yes to the invite. The shop was almost ready for it. The police finished with the forensics, and Mourning Arts was free of blood and feathers.

As she approached the door of Mourning Arts, a voice yelled out to her, "Irene Calhoun?" She turned to find a strange man crossing the street toward her.

"I'm so sorry to bother you. I'm Steven Jackson, with the Daily Virginian. If I could have a word with you, please."

The police warned Irene and Viv reporters might try to reach out. "I'm sorry, Mr. Jackson, I can't help you."

"I have a few questions about Carol Wheatly's being body found in your establishment. Any thoughts on that?"

Thoughts? Yes, the first one: she should've had that security camera fixed years ago. That way, they'd have captured the killer on film. So, her next thought, of course, was why her shop? Was it supposed to be clever because it was a mourning store? Or did the killer have a vendetta against her? She examined the man in front of her. "I have nothing to say to you." She opened the door and closed it behind her and locked it.

Irene longed to forget about the incident. She also wanted justice for Carol and blabbing to a reporter wouldn't help either. In fact, she and Viv had promised to the police they'd not utter a word about anything they saw that day to anybody, including friends and family. Fine with Irene, yes, indeed.

"Good morning," Viv said as Irene strolled across the floor of the shop. She placed her coat and handbag on a chair just outside the office. She had no reason to push herself to go inside the office. Not today.

"Good morning," Irene said.

"Are we ready for tonight? Anything I can do?" Viv asked.

"We'll fetch the stuff over here later. We'll set up the tables here." Irene gestured to space. "I

think this will fit fifteen crafty divas." She folded her arms.

"It's kind of weird to be having a party tonight," Viv said. "But Aunt Libby said it's for the best."

"I agree." Irene fluffed silky mourning dresses hanging on the sale rack. "Guess what I saw today?"

"What?" Viv reached under the counter for paper towels and glass cleaner, as was her usual. She walked over to the counter and began squirting and wiping. Viv liked it when the counters sparkled.

"Al was in Cee Cee's with a woman and they were very chummy." She continued to fluff. "That's interesting."

"Isn't he the top suspect?"

"Stone won't tell me."

"That stinks," Irene said. "You're his trainee."

"Apparently, the sharing stops during an open murder case, especially when you have a relationship with the victim." Viv squirted and wiped.

"Well, one can surmise... it's always the husband or boyfriend..." Viv spun to look at Irene. "Or girlfriend."

"Indeed," Viv said. "Anyway, I'm sure the police are looking at him."

The shop door swung open, as a small round woman bundled in scarves and a thick hat entered the shop with a box in her hand. She unraveled herself from the scarf. "Hello ladies, have a Merry Victorian Christmas!" Angie plopped the box down on the counter. Angie Antoni had moved to town last year and planned to open a Victorian bookstore, but word had it she'd not been able to secure funding.

"Thank you Angie!" Irene said. "What is it?" She opened the box to see a Christmas tray of brownies. Irene nearly swooned at the smell of rich chocolate cakes sprinkled with powdered sugar, which gave it a more festive look.

"Whatever you don't eat today, you can have for the party tonight. I have other stuff I'm bringing too. I love to bake!" Her eyes barely peeked out from the hat, pulled down over her forehead.

"It's so kind of you." Viv reached into the box and pulled out a piece. "I'll have this with my coffee. Yum!"

They watched as she moved behind the counter and drank from her coffee.

"I just wanted to say how sorry I am about everything. I can't imagine." Her voice was a near whisper.

"Thank you." Viv didn't want to talk about it and hoped

the tone she used communicated that. Angie took the hint. "Well, I have other deliveries to make. Tis' the season!"

Viv's phone rang. "It's Stone. I need to take it."

"Sure you do." Irene continued with Viv's cleaning, pulling a face at her in jest.

"Yes, I hung out with her." Viv's voice was serious. "Drugs? Not at all. I mean, she never mentioned it." Pause. "Whoa...that's weird. Cocaine?" She lowered her voice.

Irene dropped the paper towels, reaching over to pick them up, and the cleaner fell off the counter. "Cocaine?" She mouthed to Viv.

Viv nodded. "Hard to believe." Pause. "I don't know where she'd get it. Sorry. Wait. What about that guy from Culpeper?"

Culpeper was a sweet little town south of Victoria Town. It wasn't a hotbed of illegal drug activity. Well. Not that Irene knew, anyway.

Viv hung up the phone. "They found coke at Carol's place. And there were trace amounts in her screening. I just didn't know."

"Why would you? They only share with other druggies. She knew you didn't do that stuff. Of course, she didn't mention it to you," Irene said. "But it gives them another lead, doesn't it? Maybe she owed someone money."

"I'm sure that's what Stone was getting at." Viv bit into the brownie. Her eyes fluttered. "Mmmmmm. So good!"

"Why place her body here if she died of a drugs situation?" Irene asked. "It feels kind of personal to me." Just saying it slammed into her and gave it more power. She didn't like it. Her store! Why her store?

Viv waved her off. "I don't think you should worry about that. Killers don't have logical minds." She paused. "At least not the logic that makes sense to the rest of us."

Irene shuddered. It reminded her that you never really knew anyone. Who would've thought Carol was a cokehead?

When she first met Carol, it was the day of her shop's opening. She was conversing about paper that she was fond of with a customer. And the customer was enjoying it. She'd had trays of cookies and punch for the celebration, which Irene always approved of. Carol flitted around that day, bubbling, vivacious, and friendly. It impressed Irene. Perhaps her energy wasn't as natural as Irene imagined. Was it the cocaine?

The shop was quaint and fit right into the town. So did Carol. She had a lovely design sensibility and her store was always clean. Why didn't the killer put her body in her own shop?

Irene's questions led to more questions. She sent a silent prayer to the Universe that the police would find Carol's killer, as soon as possible.

Viv groaned as she slid a box of Christmas decorations out of the closet. "I can get started on these, since we're not getting much action."

Viv was a good kid. Irene caught herself: a 28-year-old was not a kid and wouldn't approve of being called that. Dark-haired and blue eyed, she was often dressed in black when she first arrived to town. These days, she dressed more colorfully. Was it Stone? Or was it Irene's influence?

Irene couldn't get two things out of her mind: Carol's

boyfriend and Culpeper? "Did you say Culpeper?" Irene asked.

Viv laughed. "Random. Yes. A while ago. There's a pretty big cocaine ring near Culpeper. And there's a man who deals there we've been trying to nab. He's slick, though."

"Does Stone think Carol knew him?"

"Yes, she did. He's her cousin."

Irene's heart raced. "What?"

Viv nodded, then dragged the stepladder over so she could hang the sparkling snowflakes from

the ceiling.

"She was such an amiable woman. I didn't realize she had drug dealers in her family. Or that she

did drugs."

Viv rolled her eyes. "Drug dealers are everywhere. You'd be surprised."

"So are cheating bastards." Irene handed her a snowflake, thinking of Al and his new girlfriend. Drug dealers. Cocaine. Cheating boyfriends. And murder. Irene was no spring chicken. She

experienced her share of all of that—but quite spread out in her life, not so compacted in such a brief period.

Viv stepped down from the stepladder and moved it over about three feet. Irene handed her another sparkling snowflake. She stepped back—the hanging snowflakes were a lovely touch.

A few hours later, she fetched lunch for her and Viv. On the way back from the diner, she spotted Al, Carol's boyfriend and his woman friend walking. The audacity! She grabbed her bag and reached in for her phone. She'd get proof of their affair by snapping photos. They hurried around the path. She followed, patches of ice on the sidewalks. Heels were no good for this, even boots.

They turned a corner and stood facing one another. Irene focused her phone and clicked. His arms opened, and she fell into them. They embraced for several seconds. Irene captured the whole thing.

She turned to head back to the store, else her food get cool, and she'd gotten plenty of proof. As she turned, she almost ran into Stone, a long, lean, and sharp detective. He stood observing above everybody, like a giraffe surveying the vista. "Hi Irene."

Did he see what she was doing? "Hello." She slipped her phone into her pocket. "It's a little cold for a walk." He plunged his hands into his coat pockets. "Agreed."

"You weren't just..." His square chin jutted out, pointing toward Al. "I was just walking." She coughed.

"And taking pictures. I saw that." He frowned.

"What? Is it illegal to take pictures? You're a PI, not a cop. You can't arrest me for taking pictures." Still, her face heated.

"I can have you arrested for impeding an investigation."

"I'm doing no such thing." She looked away from him. She didn't want to lie to him. He was one of the good ones.

"Just exactly what are you doing, then? I see Al is over there, where you're aiming your phone. Were you taking pictures of him?"

"Okay. Yes, I was. I planned to turn it over to the police. He's been hanging around with this woman all day. I saw them earlier. Very cozy. Carol's only been dead for two days."

He laughed. Laughed!

"What is your problem?" Irene couldn't believe it. He was laughing at her and she was trying to help the case.

"That woman he's so chummy with is his sister."

Irene almost hit him. "Well, you could've said."

He shrugged. "Would it have mattered?"

"I've got to go. I've got lunch for Viv and me."

He laughed as she walked away. He could be quite impertinent. But by the time she arrived at

Mourning Arts, Irene was laughing too. She supposed it was best to leave the sleuthing to the experts. Viv was helping a tall bald man at the mourning jewelry counter. "This jet is lovely. I think any

collector would be proud to have it." She held up the jet beads as they caught the light and gleamed. "I think I'll take the set," he said.

Viv packed it up and handled the register.

"Are you local?" Viv asked, stiff, Irene thought, not her usual self. Perhaps she was hungry. Viv needed to be fed at regular intervals..

"Not really. I wanted to shop early, before the rush." He took the package from Viv.

"Have a Merry Victorian Christmas." Viv waved.

Okay, something was off. Viv hated that expression, and didn't use it often. The man just ignored

her as he walked away.

Irene placed the "closed for lunch" sign in the window and locked up.

When she turned around, Viv was tapping away at her laptop. She picked up her phone.

"What are you doing?"

Viv held up a finger.

"Culpeper Mike just left the store," she said into the phone. Pause. "Yes, I'm sure. I'm looking at

a photo of him right now." Pause. "Yes, I know. But it's strange for him to be here, don't you think? Timing!" Pause. "Okay. He said he was here to Christmas shop. Christmas shop, Stone. Unbelievable! You all better get on him. I don't like the idea of him being anywhere near the shop or me."

Irene's heart skipped a beat. Who was Culpeper Mike? Was he the drug dealer Viv talked about earlier? In her shop? Could this day get any worse?

Someone knocked at the door. Couldn't they read?

It was Viv's aunt Libby and her best friend Sadie Hartwell. Irene felt as if she would explode. She needed more information from Viv. Was Culpepper Mike who she thought he was? Was he a suspect?

"Hello, dear," Libby said to Irene, as she let them in. "We just popped in to see if you needed any help."

"Thanks so much, but everything is under control," Irene said.

Viv eyes were on her computer screen and before she realized it aunt Libby was overlooking her shoulder, too. "What's he doing there?"

"Who?"

"The guy on the screen, dear." She pointed.

"Just looking him up for someone." Viv snapped it shut. "He's staying with us, you know." "What?" Viv and Irene said together.

Aunt Libby nodded. "Yes, he's been in the Prince Edward Suite for three days."

"How have I missed that?" Viv's eyes widened.

Aunt Libby shrugged. "You've been busy here, I suppose." She paused and smiled. "He's here

with his fiance. Today, they're hiking on the Appalachian trail."

"A hike? It's too cold for a hike. " Sadie piped up. "I can't tell you how many idiots have gone up

there in the winter and lost a digit or two from frostbite. My cousin Bill, for one. He was so stubborn. Wouldn't listen to anybody. Lost two toes."

"Sadie. Let's focus here." Aunt Libby pointed to her nose. "Why did you have him on your screen? Is there something I should know?"

Irene's thoughts raced. He was a known drug dealer. He was Carol's dealer and cousin, in fact. The woman who was murdered and left in her back room. And he'd been here when Carol was killed.

"He's bad news, aunt Libby," Viv said. "When is he leaving?"

"Tomorrow. What do you mean by bad news?" Her voice rose a decibel or two.

Irene needed to get into his room. No two ways about it. Did he have a gun? Did he have

purple-blue feathers in his room? Cocaine? She should have dialed the police. But an energy zoomed through her, compelling her to do it now, before Culpeper Mike could hide anything. "Ah, let's talk about that later, shall we?"

Viv looked confused.

"I need your help, come to think of it." Irene dug in her bag for her house keys. "You'd save us a lot of time if your brought the rest of the card-making supplies over." If she kept them busy enough, she'd have plenty of time to get into the B & B and check his room.

"Certainly. " Aunt Libby took the keys. "We're happy to help. And you!" She turned to face Viv. "You can tell me all about it later."

After they left, Irene explained her thoughts. "I need to get inside the room to find any evidence."

"We should tell Stone or the police," Viv said. Was she really the one having the common sense now? "That's breaking and entering."

"Not if you give me the key."

"And you're invading someone's privacy. I can't do that. Come on, Irene."

"He's a drug dealer who probably had a hand in killing Carol. I will not grant him the right of

privacy. I'm saving time. The police would have to get warrants. I'll go in, check it out. If I see anything suspicious, I'll tell them about it. Why waste their time? They already realize he's here. Besides, what if he has a gun? And it's at the B & B?"

Irene continued. "It will make me feel better. He was in my shop. Carol's body was found here. I feel so uneven and unempowered. At least I can do this for myself. For Carol."

Viv wilted. "Okay." She reached for the keys. "This is the one to his suite. Take linens from the closet with you in case they walk in on you. And hop to it. Those two little spry ladies will be back before you know it."

Confident, Irene grabbed her coat and took off down the street. The Sweet Victoria B & B was not over two minutes fast walking. She kept her gaze forward, to not meet anybody's eyes as a falter into a conversation.

Minutes later, towels in her hands, she slid the key into Culpeper Mike's room. Libby decorated the room in high Victorian style, soft blue and white, with a large canopy bed in the center. Blue lace curtain tie backs with satin ropes, allowing streams of sunlight to enter the room. She started with the drawers, slipped her fingers in socks and underwear, shirt pockets. Nothing.

She flew to the closet and performed the same task. No feathers. No small packets of white powder. A couple of books sat on the nightstand, she turned them over and shook them out. Nothing. She checked the sheets, pillowcases, and pulled out the luggage under the bed.

Irene opened it to find cash wrapped up in rubber bands. She didn't take the time chance to count it. But she estimated she held about $200,000 in her hands. Still, the suitcase was empty of white powder and feathers—and she checked every crack and crevice. She slipped the suitcase under the bed.

Other than the money, the place was clean. She was aware of people back in Blackbird Hollow who kept their money outside of banks. But, as he was a known dealer, the money was most likely dirty. But it wasn't enough for a search warrant.

She arranged fresh towels in a stack, placed them on the bed, and left the room. As she was leaving, she noticed that Mike and his girlfriend were coming up the front sidewalk. Her heart skipped a beat. Good that she was aware of the back door.

Irene turned to go, making her way through the kitchen, out the arboretum, and to the backyard.

She waited a minute to catch her breath, looked at her watch: she had about 4 minutes to get back to the shop.

One thing was for certain: if Culpeper Mike had killed Carol, no evidence in his room to suggested it. Except maybe the money. And if he was a pro, he'd have ditched any evidence. If he had a gun, it was probably in his car. And perhaps the feathers were as well. This was an exercise in folly. Still, she allowed herself some comfort in finding out Mike had no gun at the Sweet Victoria B & B. Now she could focus on the Christmas card party. Well, as much as she could.

Irene made it back to Mourning Arts just before Libby and Sadie, enough time to tell Viv what she did not find—and what she found.

"All that cash...he must be up to something." Viv leaned on the counter and crossed her arms. "I have a family like that. They don't keep their money in banks."

"But to travel with it like that?" Viv used. "Well, at least nobody spotted you."

"I slipped out the back."

The door flung open and Libby and Sadie walked in with their arms full.

Whether or not Culpeper Mike was up to no good, one thing was for certain, these ladies were

ready to party—and craft.

The shop closed, with card tables set up in a long group, bayberry and cinnamon candles lit and

sitting on the gleaming counters. Women trickled in with

baskets of goodies and bags of crafting materials. Viv, Libby, Sadie and Irene had piled card stock at each seat, along with glue, glue stick and trays of glitter packs, buttons, and stickers. Red, green, gold, and white splashes of color almost made Irene feel better about the holiday. Everybody was right. Moving ahead with the party would help her to keep her mind off things, things like finding Carol in her office. Though it was just beneath the surface of her skin, in the folds of her mind.

Irene shoved a nut cup into her mouth. It was so delicious. She decided more eating of delicious cookies could help as well. She reached for another.

"You've not gotten very far." Viv pointed at her red card.

"It's folded," Irene smoothed over the red cardstock. "I'm awaiting the muse."

"I saved this for you." Viv handed her a delicate black paper doily.

Irene's mood lifted. "Black paper lace. One of my favorite things. Thank you." She cut it into

something resembling a female figure, then fashioned tree branches to look as if they grew out of her. "That's nice, dear," Libby said, glancing at her creation for the side, trying to not look horrified. Libby finished cutting a paper angel for her cards and dipped it in light blue glitter.

"Angels again?" Sadie said. "You do angels every year. I remember the year you did lace angels.

They were so pretty...and the gingham...My aunt used to only do candles on her Christmas cards."

"To each or her own." Angie's card had two stickers on it; she moved at a decidedly slow pace as well, and drinking her second glass of Rose. Not that Irene was counting. But like any excellent hostess, she tried to monitor the alcohol consumption.

"In France, Christmas is not so commercial," Cee Cee glued a paper candle on the front of her card. "I can't remember ever getting a card when I was growing up. But perhaps we did and I just don't remember. We received a lot of food. And wine."

"I always said I must have a bit of France in me," Libby said and giggled.

Irene couldn't help but laugh, though the others pursed their lips and sipped their tea.

After they calmed, Libby asked Sadie about her cards. She already had a stack of them finished.

"You're on a roll."

"I plan out every year. A different farm animal each year." She bit into a cookie. "Last year it was

sheep."

"I remember!" Irene said. "And you sent me a black one. So thoughtful."

"This year, I'm doing chickens. Christmas chickens." She held up a card to show everybody.

Chickens wearing Santa hands. Chickens wearing boots and scarves.

"Very cute!" Libby exclaimed.

"I'm going to make red chickens, you know, the old rooster color." She reached for the red stock.

Cee Cee handed her a box of feathers.

Feathers: where did they come from?

Irene hadn't noticed, but she and Viv exchanged looks. They were craft feathers, not the kind of

feathers found on Carol's body. Still, a shiver traveled along Irene' s spine.

"Wonderful!" Sadie clapped her hands together. "I'm going to use these feathers." She picked

purple, black, and red feathers out of the containers.

"I've never seen a chicken quite that red." Cee Cee laughed.

"Oh, I have." Angie spoke up and poured herself another glass of wine.

"Angie! I heard you're taking over Carol's lease," Cee Cee said. "We're going to be neighbors."

Angie's face reddened. "That right." She looked around, as if in embarrassment. "I know it's soon after her death, but there were already others inquiring. I've been waiting so long for a place to open I'm hoping to buy it, eventually. Her family wants to get rid of it ASAP."

A long, awkward silence enfolded the ladies making cards. Scissors snapped and landed on the table. Cee Cee cleared her throat.

"Look at my purple chicken!" Sadie said with glee, breaking the awkwardness.

Has the conversation really turned to chickens again? Christmas chickens, or otherwise, Irene hoped to steer the conversation away. "You know, my favorite bird has always been the bluebird."

"I like them very much, too." Aunt Libby reached for her scissors. The group of women at the other end of the table giggled within their own circle.

"Oh, I could tell you stories about the beautiful bluebird houses my daddy used to make..." Sadie said. "They were always two toned. He'd painted the shutters and doors a complimentary color. Oh, my...Remember helping him paint those shutters."

"They look very fake purple." Angie pointed at the feathers. Her words slurring.

"How do you know? Since when are you an expert on chickens?" Libby said.

"I'm raising fancy chickens," she replied. "I know more than you think I do."

Sadie laughed. "Okay, you're the fancy chicken expert. I give up." She reached for another purple

feather.

"If you like purple feathers, my chickens have gorgeous purple feathers, edged in a deep purple.

It almost looks unreal." She lifted her glass to her mouth and sipped.

Viv and Irene locked eyes. Chicken feathers— scattered in Carol's apartment and near her body.

Nobody else knew anything about the feathers.

"Where could I get a chicken like that?" Irene asked.

"They are Purple Wyandottes and I'm the only local who's raising them." She sat her wobbly

glass on the table.

"How do you know?" Irene asked, trying to keep the conversation nonchalant, while chills were moving through her.

"Because there's a registry," she said, as if Irene should be aware of it.

Irene looked for Viv, but she was gone. She hoped she was calling the police. Why would Angie kill Carol and drag her body into Mourning Arts? How did she do it? Angie was the only person who had access to those feathers.

It clicked into place. Angie wanted to take over Carol's shop. It was already happening. She'd already said she planned to buy it, knowing that her family would want to get rid of it as fast as possible.

Was that cause for a murder? Irene suspected if one had the leaning toward murder, it wouldn't take much, but it seemed flimsy. There had to be something else. Was Irene looking into the bloodshot eyes of a killer?

She searched for Viv, but she was already gone, standing outside on her phone. No doubt she had it figured out and was calling Stone. This would be a party to remember.

Later, Irene found Viv in the storage room, sitting on a bin of black lace curtains, sniffling.

Irene's heart sank. Poor kid. So much had fallen on her shoulders while Irene was recuperating and investigating, and her friend Carol had died. "Are you okay?"

Viv raised her watery eyes. "Carol was a good person. Angie killed her for what? A store?"

Irene sat next to her on the bin, ignoring its slight buckling. "Evidently, they'd been fussing at each other for quite some time. Carol and Angie. They've known each other for years."

"I'll never understand people."

"Me neither. But you helped. That's the best we can do, be as helpful as possible. We can't control other people."

Viv stood. "So let me get this straight. They argued about the store. Angie had made what she considered a fair offer."

"Right. And Carol didn't want to sell. Though she gave her space for her books. We shouldn't talk about this now."

Viv ignored her. "So Angie shoots Carol. And calls her cousin to help her?"

Irene nodded. They'd already nabbed Culpepper Mike as an accessory. And they found white powder in his vehicle. Just as Irene suspected.

"Why all the feathers?"

"Drama, flair." Irene shrugged her shoulders.

"Why here?" Viv gestured to the shop.

"Because we're the only shop with no camera. Evidently, it was too cold to dispose of the body

outside." Irene stood and wrapped her arm around Viv. She was between weary and wound-up and needed to unwind. She was certain Viv needed the same thing.

They walked out into the front of the story, where aunt Libby and Sadie had finished cleaning up and were sitting at a card table drinking glasses of whisky. Jazzy Christmas music played on one of their phones.

"Smells like what I need." Irene reached for a glass and poured the caramel-colored whisky. "What a day."

Viv sat next to her.

"Justice has been served here tonight." Aunt Libby raised her glass. "It's not often one gets to witness it right in front of her own eyes. Thank you, both, for the part you played in it."

Irene didn't feel like she'd done much at all—passed out, investigated a bit to no avail, and threw a party where it all came together. "To Viv, who held it all together when I couldn't." She lifted her glass.

Viv beamed, reaching for a tin of cookies and opening it with a thwack. She reached in and drew out a white sugary snowball cookie and plopped it into her mouth. "If it wasn't for your search, the police wouldn't have known about the money."

Irene tucked a hair behind her ear. "That's good to know. Where did he get it?"

"It was Carol's," Viv replied. "Turns out he helped himself to her money right after he dumped her body here."

"Of course he did." Aunt Libby twirled her glass around, the ice crackling.

"How will we have Christmas?" Sadie said. "I mean, how will we manage to get in the spirit, and sell our wares, chat-up the tourists? I mean, I feel as if I'm living in a nightmare version of this town."

The women sat, circled around the table, jazzy jingle bells playing, each in her own thoughts.

"That's a good question, Sadie." Irene tapped her fingers on the table. "Let's focus on the swift justice in Carol's death. That's a blessing where we can begin to heal." She drew in air. "It won't be easy. She'll be missed. It's hard to make sense of all of this. But we must press on. In a few weeks, we'll be inundated with shoppers and tourists."

Viv stood, poured herself a whiskey, held up the glass. "To Carol. We'll miss you."

It was the perfect gesture to end the not-so perfect day. The women left the shop a little wobbly on their feet, arm and arm, down the snowy streets of Victoria Town, the moon blazing white gold in the sky.

IF YOU'D LIKE MORE of Viv and Irene, check out the Victoria Town Mysteries.

Click here to sign up for my newsletter for updates and fun!

About Mollie Cox Bryan

Mollie Cox Bryan writes cozy mysteries with edge. She's the author of several bestselling mystery series, also writing under the pen name Maggie Blackburn. Her books have been selected as finalists for an Agatha Award and a Daphne du Maurier Award and as a Top 10 Beach Reads by Woman's World. She has also been short-listed for the Virginia Library People's Choice Award. She's also penned a historical fiction: MEMORY OF LIGHT: AN AFTERMATH OF GETTYSBURG. She's the mother of two nearly perfect daughters, each pursuing careers in music. She lives in Crozet, Va.

A Little Christmas Villainy
Melicity Pope

When Holly Sharpe agrees to escape L.A. for a winter break at her English friend's family villa in Italy, she finds herself unraveling a series of mysterious events threatening to ruin Christmas. Will Christmas in Italy end up a *"Fatale Natale"*?

CHAPTER 1

"Just come!" my childhood best friend, Charlotte Hinley, urged me on our monthly-ish, bi-continental catch-up call. "Besides, a little Italian minibreak will give you some space to figure out what's next."

I *did* need to figure out what was next. California's "no fault" status meant that everyone split assets down the middle in a divorce, and Mike had opted to take his cut in cash. Not only was our house now on the market, but it was also looking like I would have to sell the businesses to pay him off. It was the absolute worst time for me to jump on a plane and leave L.A.

"I don't know, Char. I don't think I can right now. Besides, if I went to Europe, I'd be expected to swing through England to spend time with the grandparents, especially at Christmas."

"Never stopped you before."

"Hey!"

"Paris, Milan, Berlin... We just had to sit by Burney River waving at your plane as it passed us by all those times."

I started to protest, but she ignored me.

"I know, I know, Little Witherburne's hard to get to when you're on a tight schedule."

I rubbed the lines between my eyebrows. "I'm sorry I've been away so long."

"And now you can make up for it," she answered brightly. "To me, anyway."

"It's just that I've got a lot to square away with—"

"Didn't you tell me one of your *Love and Luxe* success story couples are getting married here?"

"Ugh. One of my high-maintenance success stories. Don't remind me. Besides, it was Venice."

She pivoted. "What about researching a new recipe for *Ginger Luxe*?"

While mentioning that gingerbread was more Polish than Italian, my stomach turned to lead. How must she view me now if she believed the only way to motivate me into visiting was in service of one of my businesses? Was that who I'd become?

Char exhaled into the phone and paused. "Will you do it for me, then, Holly? Ever since I got here, things have been strange. Something's going on, and I could really use the moral support..."

And that's how I found myself two days later in this picture-postcard, Italian hamlet of *Miele di Rosa* on Christmas Eve afternoon, choking down sips of limoncello at a rickety wooden table at *La Rosa Rosa*, the only restaurant for five miles. I blinked at Char through bleary, post-four-teen-hour-flight eyes. Maybe it was my hazy vision, but she totally hadn't aged in the ten years since I'd seen her in person. Her thick, straight black hair still hung to the middle of her back and framed a gorgeous face accentuated by dark eyes and lashes that wouldn't quit.

I could only imagine how my tangled, cinnamon-colored messy bun and puffy face, straight from the long-haul journey, compared to my shy but glamorous-looking friend.

"So, let me see if I've got this." I grabbed a napkin to take notes. "The villa – manor – whatever, and the vineyards belong to your great uncle, Ralph."

"Yes."

"And he has an Italian live-in butler."

"Carlo."

"Carlo," I repeated. "Right. And also in the household is Uncle Ralph's fiancée—"

"Much *younger* fiancée."

"Jackie."

Char nodded.

"And the guests for Christmas, besides us, are Ralph's brother, Bob, and Bob's daughter...?"

"Barbie. And Barbie was the one calling my dad night and day saying something's not right about Jackie and asking if any of us in England could come over and find out what's going on. Preferably before the wedding." Char took a swig of my limoncello and grimaced. "I was glad to do it, but honestly, I still don't feel any closer to an answer for her. Jackie's so lovely, and they seem really happy..."

"Despite the age difference," I finished for her. I'd matched a few May-December couples through my *Love and*

Luxe boutique, and it was typical for family members to jump to the same conclusions. "When's the wedding?"

"Boxing Day."

"Wow. Nothing like leaving it to the last minute."

Char threw her hands up in mock despair.

I finished my drink. "Maybe Barbie's overreacting?"

"*I* think so, but now she's got Uncle Bob all in a tizz, too." She sighed. "Thanks for agreeing to come, Hols. You've always been so good at reading people. I just want us all to have a happy Christmas, and I don't think we can until this is sorted."

I didn't know how great my powers of perception were going to be when all I wanted was my book and my bed, but I smiled. It really was good to be together again.

At that moment, several men dressed as shepherds came in and began serenading us with bagpipes, putting an end to any further conversation.

"It's tradition!" Char shouted at me over the table.

"It's nice!" I shouted back, stifling a yawn. I actually did like bagpipes, and these were fashioned differently than any I'd ever seen. Up until then, I'd only known them as a Scottish thing, so that was fun. *Every day's a school day.*

Char pushed her chair back and motioned to the door. "I should probably get you to dinner."

All across the medieval village square, little wooden stalls began to close up, ending last-minute shoppers' experiences of Miele de Rosa's Christmas Market for the day. As I set my carry-on down next to me, I breathed in the crisp December air and took in the scene. Villagers called out a chorus of "*Buon Natale!*" to one another while rushing home with their treasures. Strings of twinkling lights wove around every lamp post and criss-crossed above our heads, illuminating each market stall. But the giant fir tree decorated with hundreds of cool white bulbs would not be outshone. Towering over it all was the village church, its cream-colored stones reflecting the glow of the village square.

"Is there about to be a Christmas play?" I pointed to a group of people dressed like shepherds and wise men assembling next to the church.

"That's the living nativity they do here on Christmas Eve."

I zipped my coat all the way to my chin. "Isn't it a bit cold to stay outdoors at this time of year?"

"They might have space heaters, but yeah, it would definitely be too cold for you!" She nudged me as we walked, clearly having a dig at my lack of acclimation to the frigid air.

As if in response, my nose decided to start running.

"Come on. The market will be open for another week. You can still have a nosey before you go home." She grabbed my carry-on and it bump-bump-bumped along the cobbles.

"The cookies!" I called out for her stop so I could rescue my host-and-household gift.

"Please tell me you brought a big stash of gingerbread treats from *Ginger Luxe*."

After rescuing the pale pink box trimmed in gold—deciding it was much safer to hand carry—I responded with a lip curl and an exaggerated French accent that always amused us. *"Mmm, oui oui. But of course!"* It warmed me on the inside that I had a friend to share an almost thirty-year-old inside joke with. To us, it was still as funny as the summer we met when we were eleven and I was visiting my British grandparents for the school break.

Char deftly navigated the cobbled streets away from the market square as I dragged myself along beside her. Between the cold air and jet lag, my eyes started streaming. Oh, how I hoped there'd be a chance for a nap before dinner, though knowing myself, I probably wouldn't wake until morning. *Just don't think about the nine-hour time difference!*

A gray and white cat darted across the street, then scampered in our direction.

"Oh, hello, D'Artagnan!" Char cooed in greeting.

"You know him?" I leaned down to scratch the sleek fur behind his ears and was rewarded with a soft purr and a rub of his cheek along my jeans.

"He's one of the manor cats. He'll escort us back now."

Sure enough, D'Artagnan led the way, checking back every so often to make sure we were in tow.

"He's so cute! How many cats does your great-uncle have?"

"I don't know, but it feels like home." She smiled at D'Artagnan's fluffy little wiggle. "A whole bunch live on the grounds, but only a couple ever come inside."

A little spark of Christmas joy mini-exploded in my heart. My parents used to joke that I'd grow up to be a cat lady, and I had zero problem with that. But with Mike's allergies, my cat lady dreams had been dashed.

It was Char who ended up the cat lady. Back where she and my grandparents lived in Little Witherburne, she managed the village cat café, *The Cat's Meow*. It sounded like heaven. As we followed our four-legged Pied Piper, I started having visions of sneaking barnyard kitties into my room at night and filling the bed with all sorts of snuggly feline friends.

Before long, the cobbles gave way to a flagstone path lined with Cypress trees and my carry-on traded its bump-bump-bumping for a smoother roll along the ground. Quaint lamp posts lit our way toward a large, ornately decorated iron gate that creaked just as I imagined it would when Char pushed it open for us. D'Artagnan nimbly scooted through the bars and disappeared.

"We're here!" Char announced.

Here, was a steep hill flanked by more lamp posts and trees on either side of the path.

I gave her a sidelong glance as I huffed my way up. After several minutes, I managed to ask a short question between wheezes. "How much farther?"

"Not far," Char replied, slightly out of breath herself. "I would've had Uncle Ralph's butler, Carlo, pick us up from the gate, but he's got to get to the church. Besides, exercise is good for the jet lag."

I *hmphed* in her direction. But then I looked ahead as we made it to the top. And what to my wondering eyes did appear? The most stunning Renaissance villa standing at the end of a long gravel path. Roman columns shimmered in the flickering lamp light while at least a dozen arched windows gazed back at us.

"Wow!" was all I could manage as I stopped to take it all in.

"I know!"

I traded her the cookie box for my carry-on and whisked it over the gravel toward my much-better-than-expected home for the holidays. "And it's just your great-uncle, his fiancée and the butler in this massive place full time?"

"Mostly, but other family members come around from England on and off. My great-uncle Bob, whom you'll meet in a minute, has been spending more and more time here since he retired. Uncle Ralph jokes that he might as well move in, he's here so often."

"Sounds like he's wearing out his welcome," I said.

"Oh, no! It's all in good fun."

When we arrived at the villa's front entrance, D'Artagnan was waiting on the top step, licking one of his front paws. He meowed in greeting, zigzagging back and forth, his quivering tail aloft.

"Uncle Ralph's Jackie always puts a little something from dinner down for him in the kitchen," Char said as she opened the door. The cat became a furry gray streak as he flew inside.

"Hello!" Char called out.

"In here!" a woman responded amidst the clang of pots and running water.

Char told me to leave my bag by the door and beckoned me to follow her toward the noise. On the way down the hall, we passed a gorgeous reception room with Christmas stockings hung in a neat row on the mantelpiece. There was even one for me, although whoever made it spelled my name with an *i* instead of a *y*.

We entered a large farmhouse-style kitchen where an attractive woman I guessed to be around fifty was bustling between several workstations while a tall-dark-and-handsome, dressed in a medieval shepherd's costume was so busy pulling out chairs and bending to look under the large rustic table that he never noticed us.

Char introduced me to the woman—Jackie.

"Hello, loves!" She beamed at us and wiped an elegant hand on her apron before shaking mine in greeting. It was hard not to stare at the gigantic diamond on her left ring finger. "Welcome to *La Casetta*, Holly."

"*La Casetta*? Doesn't that mean, *The Little House*?" I laughed. "This place is anything but!"

Jackie laughed with me. "Oh, that would be Ralph. Loves his little jokes, our Ralph." She put a few bits of meat down on a plate for D'Artagnan. "All your friends keeping warm in the barn, hmm? Just means more for you, darling."

"Thank you for including me in the stocking hanging," I said to Jackie. No need to mention my name being misspelled, though I *did* wish she'd gotten it right.

"Oh, it's a pleasure! We're so happy to have you. The more the merrier and all that!"

"Wasn't Carlo supposed to be at the church by now?" Char asked in a lowered voice to Jackie, tilting her head toward the man in tights.

Jackie gave a dramatic eye roll and pulled a felt hat from the top of the refrigerator. "Oh, Carloooo!" she sang out, waving the hat in his direction.

Carlo ceased his frantic searching and heaved a great sigh of relief as he crossed the room to her. Lifting lids to investigate the dishes bubbling away on the stove, Char didn't notice Jackie wearing a cheeky expression as her gaze locked on Carlo's and as their hands, barely touching, lingered a fraction too long during the hat exchange.

But I did. And I know chemistry.

Suddenly aware of me, Jackie cleared her throat and went back to stirring.

Carlo turned his attention to me and took my hand. "Holly, like the beautiful Christmas plant."

"Holly Sharpe," I said, as he gazed dreamily at me. Did the kitchen just get *really* warm all of a sudden? Maybe I was wrong about the chemistry I thought I detected, and Carlo was just being... Italian.

"Holly *Sharpe*," he repeated and put his other hand on his heart. "Just so."

"Go on, now!" Jackie chided him. "The other bagpiping shepherds'll be waiting."

With an effusion of quick, Latin-esque phrases I didn't understand, Carlo raced off shouting finally, "*Arrivederci!*"

"Jackie, Holly brought us some of her luxury biscuits all the way from L.A." Char opened the lid to reveal dark golden gingerbread creations shaped as ornaments, snowmen, Santas, reindeer and candy canes, all decorated with delicate details of white icing. My bakers truly were artists. I would miss them when the business sold to pay Mike off.

"How stunning!" Jackie exclaimed. "They'll be perfect for tea before Mass."

I shot a look at Char. "Mass?"

"Christmas Eve Mass after dinner," she explained.

"*Eeet's tradeetion!*" Char and Jackie said in unison with put-on Italian accents and a giggle.

Jackie's smile faded as she shut the burners off. "But now

you're both here, I hope you can help me with something." She pulled a piece of paper out of her apron pocket and handed it to me. It was a note written in block letters.

LEAVE OR ELSE, JACKI. FINAL WARNING.

"Left the *e* off, you see. Didn't even have the decency…"

Just then voices could be heard coming toward the kitchen. Jackie snatched the note from me and returned it to her pocket with a brief shake of her head at us as a woman around her age entered with two men in their eighties.

They greeted me with big smiles, kisses on both cheeks, warm hugs and exclamations over my beauty and how exquisite my gift of luxury gingerbread cookies were. Then Bob and Ralph, transformed into mischievous little boys wrangling for a treat before dinner, broke a Santa cookie in half between them before gobbling him up.

"You'll spoil your appetite!" Jackie chided them.

Ralph embraced her from behind and peered over her shoulder. "Nothing could spoil my appetite for your cooking, *cara mia!*"

Bob snorted and exchanged glances with the middle-aged woman, who I assumed was his daughter.

"Barbs, would you mind putting out the plates?" Jackie asked her.

"Certainly, *Jacks*," Barbie replied overly sweetly, grabbing a stack of plates from under the kitchen island.

I raised my eyebrows meaningfully at Char. It was frostier between the two women than a pair of gingerbread snowmen. It had me wondering whether Barbie wrote Jackie's threatening note. And even more worrisome—what did "or else" mean?

CHAPTER 2

I RAISED my voice above the din of cutlery on plates as everyone was digging in. "So Jackie, how did you and Ralph meet?"

She was about to speak when Ralph cut in. "She picked me up in a bar, the cheeky minx!"

"Oh, Ralph." Jackie giggled, and then turned to me. "I was here on a solo holiday, having a drink at *La Rosa Rosa*—"

"When I opened the door and beheld the most beautiful woman in all the land. So I leaned over to Carlo, handed him my walking stick and told him not to wait up." Ralph winked at me as Jackie shook her head at him, her eyes sparkling. "Just the sight of her made me feel young again."

Bob shot a grimace over to Barbie, who rolled her eyes. Both were clearly unimpressed.

"Yes, yes, very romantic," Barbie said, sarcasm lacing her tone. She leaned over to Char and me. "What he won't tell you, though, is how he sold my grandparents' antique clock that was supposed to go to *me* so he could buy her that hunk of diamond on her finger.”

“Now, Barbie, you know I did no such thing!” Ralph protested.

“Then why is it missing?” She folded her arms and glared at him.

“Is it?” His smile faltered. “I’m sure I saw it just the other day.” He looked around him, confused.

“Maybe it was moved for cleaning or some such,” Bob suggested. “I’m sure it’s around here somewhere.”

I did *not* want to get in the middle of a domestic dispute, especially on Christmas Eve. “So, what time is Mass again?”

Jackie smiled gratefully. “It’s at seven.”

I glanced at the clock above her head. “Then we only have about five minutes to leave.”

“Oh, no!” Jackie cried. “I wanted to bring your darling biscuits out for dessert.”

“Later, later.” Ralph shooed everyone from the table.

The next few minutes were a whirlwind of coats, hats, scarves and shoes as we all bustled around to leave the house. Finally, we made our way out into the bracing midwinter air. But then Barbie said something about wanting to change her scarf to match her handbag, and we waited another minute for her to reappear before we set off.

“Wait, where’s Ralph?” Bob asked.

“Oh, he said he didn’t want to slow us down,” Jackie answered. “Said we were all to go and he’d catch us up.”

“And you’re going to just leave him to walk all alone?” Barbie said. She muttered, “Typical,” and shook her head.

"*I'll* walk with him," she announced, then turned back toward the house.

Jackie stopped her. "To be honest, I think he might be planning some sort of Christmas surprise." She directed her attention to Char and me. "He has a certain way about him when he wants to get rid of me for some scheme of his."

"That's very sweet," I smiled, stomping my feet against the cold.

"It is," Char agreed. "But are we sure he's going to be okay walking alone in the dark? Barbie might have a point."

"Thank you!" Barbie smirked at Jackie.

"I don't believe he's actually coming, *Barbara*." Jackie hurled back at her and then moved on ahead of the group.

"That woman!" Barbie panted as we hurried along down the hill. To me, she offered, "I'm sorry. This must... be so... uncomfortable... for you..."

"Let's just not be late," Bob said.

When we arrived in the village, the bagpiping shepherds were in full swing, and it was even more crowded than when the markets were open. The church bells rang what I assumed was a last call to come inside.

I scanned the square. "Maybe Jackie's already inside saving seats?"

"Probably," Char said, leaning in close. "Though I doubt those two would want to sit next to her. I'm so glad you're here, Hols. I'd really struggle with all the tension if I was on my own."

I squeezed her arm. I must've gotten my second wind because I didn't feel as tired as I had earlier. Maybe it was the drama or the chilly night that had my blood pumping. As we filed into the church like cattle, I whispered, "The shepherds sound really good."

"Oh, that Carlo!" Barbie grimaced. "Easy on the eyes, but not so easy on the ears. He's spent the last week practicing and practicing, but always just sounded like he was strangling cats, bless him."

She and Bob shared a slightly-too-loud laugh.

"Sounds fine now." Char shrugged.

My gaze traveled around the vaulted room, and I was agape at the stunning frescos of Bible stories adorning the ceiling. The living nativity had moved inside to stand behind the altar, creating a touching element of pageantry. After tearing my attention from the ornate splendor of the church, I inspected the crowd. No sign of Jackie.

"Shall we just find our own seats?" I asked everyone.

"I see some space in the fourth row," Bob said, leading the way up the aisle.

The music began shortly thereafter, and a hush fell across the congregation. Though not Catholic, I'd always felt a sense of awe in a Catholic church. My nose tingled, and I started welling up. I told myself it was just travel fatigue, but I think I knew that this moment of stillness had made way for my undealt-with grief to surface. The life I'd known was about to be gone forever. I looked up at the ceiling again and willed my tears back into their ducts. Nevertheless, they spilled down my temples. Char put a comforting arm around my shoulders as the congregation sang *Silent Night* in Italian.

When the singing finished and we all sat, I turned around and saw Jackie several rows back. Though I tried to get her attention to join us, she didn't notice me. How did we manage to miss her when we came in?

"*Cara mio!*" Jackie called out as she unlocked the door to let us into the house. "It's Mary and the three wise men!" Over her shoulder, she said to us, "Don't want to interrupt his surprise."

I gave her an obligatory smile. The burning eyes were back with a vengeance, and even though part of my bedtime ritual was to read at least a few pages of fiction before the lights went out, I probably couldn't manage a sentence. It was a shame, too, because I had almost finished the first book in M.C. Beaton's *Poor Relation* series on the plane and only had another chapter or so to go.

"If you don't mind, I'm going to head off to bed," I said to the group. "Enjoy the cookies... I mean biscuits. And merry Christmas!"

They all wished me a good night and *happy* Christmas.

"I'll say good night to Uncle Ralph and then walk up with you," Char said.

I had just taken my shoes off when a horrible shriek came from the kitchen area. D'Artagnan tore out of there, tail high and puffy, before scampering up the stairs.

Bob, Barbie, Char and I raced toward the screaming. Maybe D'Artagnan had made a massive mess in the kitchen? But gravy paw prints and overturned milk bottles was not the sight that met us. Instead, it was Char's Uncle Ralph slumped over in his chair, head resting on the table. A garland of shiny silver tinsel was draped around his neck and shoulders. Before him lay an open box of gingerbread cookies. *My* gingerbread cookies.

Jackie clutched a Christmas stocking to her chest. "I found this on his head!" she cried, nodding to the stocking.

Barbie shoved her way over to him. She put two fingers on his neck while we held our breath. "He's alive," she announced with relief. We all exhaled as one, watching her pat his cheek and shout his name.

But he didn't come to.

"We should get him to a hospital," I said.

Barbie lifted her chin indignantly. "I'm perfectly capable of looking after him." And then she muttered something about foreign doctors.

"Barbie's a nurse," Char told me.

"What's that powder around the corners of his mouth?" I asked. "And his—" I was about to ask about the residue on his fingers when Barbie cut me off.

"Why don't you tell us? It obviously came from the icing sugar on *your* biscuits!"

"It most certainly did not!" I shot back. "My cookies are glazed, see?" I held up what was left of a piece of reindeer. A paw print in the thick icing of a round ornament-shaped cookie told me D'Artagnan had been there. I pointed at it. "Besides, the cat seems to have had his fill and he looked fine."

"I had a piece earlier," Bob offered.

"Well, *somebody* did something," Barbie choked out, her bottom lip trembling. "Luckily his pulse is strong and his breathing is regular."

Carlo came in at that moment. *"Dio mio!"*

"Oh, Carlo!" Jackie let out a sob.

Carlo ran to her and pulled her into his arms. "Is he dead?" I was close enough to hear him whisper into her hair.

Barbie must've heard, too, as she snapped, "No, he's not! But you'd both like that, wouldn't you?"

Ralph snorted as he took a deep breath.

Jackie and Carlo broke apart.

Barbie gasped. "Ralph? Ralph, can you hear me?"

He groaned and started snoring.

Bob sniffed at him and chuckled, wrinkling his nose. "Smells like the old chap needs to sleep it off." He took one of Ralph's arms in a futile effort to lift him up. Carlo jumped in on the other side, and together they hoisted him out of his chair, half carrying, half dragging him out of the room.

Barbie followed with admonitions for the men to be careful with him, leaving Char and me with Jackie, who still held the stocking. I only realized that Char had been squeezing my hand when she let go.

"Whose stocking is that, Jackie?" I gestured for her to give it to me.

She gripped the stocking tightly to her chest before showing us the front of it. "Mine," she whispered. "It's mine."

"I knew it!" came Barbie's triumphant voice from the kitchen door. "I'd say a call to the *carabinieri* is in order."

"Oh, Barbie," Char protested. "Surely that's not necessary. We don't have all the facts."

"I have all the facts I need. It was either Jackie... or *you*." She pointed at me.

I let out a deep sigh. Barbie was really getting on my nerves. "Why don't we wait for Ralph to wake up? Surely he'll tell us what happened." And then it hit me. If this *was* foul play, the guilty party might want to make certain Ralph *didn't* wake up. "But maybe someone should stay with him through the night to be on the safe side."

"I'll do it," Char volunteered.

"No, *I'll* do it," Barbie insisted. "After all, I'm the one with medical training."

"Why don't you both do it?" I suggested. "Unless Char's trying to poison him, too."

Barbie rolled her eyes. "Fine."

"I have medical training," Jackie said. "And he's *my* fiancé. I should be with him."

Barbie sneered. "But I'm the one who *completed* medical training. Besides, *we're* family. Come on, Charlotte."

Ouch.

Char gazed back at me helplessly as Barbie took her arm.

"I'll sit with you," I said to Jackie. I felt bad for her.

And that's how I found myself at the dining table, ringing in the wee hours of Christmas morning with my best friend's great uncle's fiancée.

Jackie was attractive for her age. Sure, she had that shiny Botoxed forehead, and her bosom had had a bit of "assistance." But I was from L.A. and had seen much more garish work. It was no wonder Carlo was attracted to her. Even though he was at least twenty years her junior, I'd ordinarily be rooting for them if it wasn't for the fact that she was already engaged.

There was obviously a lot going on beneath the surface, and my curiosity was piqued.

"So, Barbie's... something," I offered to break the silence.

"She's always been like that," Jackie replied. "Negative, jealous. She's one of those unhappy people who hate to see other people happy."

"Always? How long have you known each other?"

"Oh, yonks! We met at nursing college, actually."

My eyebrows shot up. "Really?"

"Only I never finished since my dad took ill. I had to come home to care for him. After he passed... I never did go back."

"I'm sorry to hear that."

She nodded her thanks.

"It's quite a coincidence that you're here, about to marry Barbie's uncle. What're the chances?"

Jackie shifted uncomfortably. "Oh, he's not her uncle."

"Sorry. I thought Char said—"

"Of course, everyone *thinks* Ralph's her uncle on account of the fact that he wasn't married to Barbie's mum." Jackie paused for effect. "Bob was."

I wrinkled my brow. "Bob was, what?"

"Married to Barbie's mum."

"Oh," I said. And then I got her meaning. "Ooooh. Does Bob know?"

Jackie shrugged. "I don't know, and frankly, I don't care. But I do care about how Barbie's obsession with Ralph's 'last will and testament' has been affecting him. She denies it, but she's been trying to talk him out of marrying me. Said our age difference was 'tacky.' And now this... incident." Her focus settled off into the distance. "You know, she's probably the one who put my Christmas stocking on his head. To make it look like I wanted to hurt him!"

"Golly," was all I managed for a moment.

If someone *had* wanted to hurt Ralph, I could understand how Barbie might be first in line. If he'd refused to acknowledge her as his biological daughter, all that hurt and rejection could be a powerful motive. And what about that bit about going back into the house to change her purse to match her shoes? Or so she *said*. If Barbie had found Ralph passed out when she came in, she could've easily put Jackie's stocking on his head. Jackie struck me as a smart lady. She wouldn't implicate herself like that. Each thought branched out to two more.

"Would you like a cup of tea, Jackie?" If I was about to pump her for some more info, she might as well have a hot beverage in hand.

She shot up out of her chair. "Oh, where are my manners? Why don't I make us both a cuppa?"

I followed her across the room to the kitchen area where she directed me to the pantry to choose the tea I wanted. But when I went inside and flicked on the light, there were several boxes of teabags knocked over, some to the ground. And they weren't the only things on the floor. Lying on its side among an assortment of chamomile, peppermint and Earl Grey was a mortar and pestle. White powder coated the edges of the marble bowl and spilled onto the terracotta tiles. Was this the same white powder Ralph had on his mouth when we found him?

I bent down for an inspection. Someone must've meant

to hide the mortar and pestle on the tea shelf, but either missed the ledge or knocked it off in their haste. It was a wonder the bowl hadn't broken.

I was about to call Jackie in to confirm my suspicion, but stopped myself. What if she wasn't being entirely truthful? So far, I only had her word for everything. And the way she and Carlo were obviously carrying on, maybe Barbie was right to be concerned.

"Finding it all okay in there, love?" Jackie called.

"Yes!" I scooped up the nearest teabag and led my way out of the pantry with it, closing the door behind me. I handed the packet to her. "Here you go. Sorry, I was having a hard time choosing."

She glanced down at the wrapper and nodded sagely. "*Smooth and Steady*, eh?" She put a hand on my shoulder. "Don't you worry. If this doesn't do the job, we've got a big bottle of castor oil here. Ralph simply swears by it."

So not the visual I wanted. And not only did Jackie now think I was constipated, I could only imagine what kind of effect this *Smooth and Steady* tea was going to have on my bowels that were moving-along-just-fine-thank-you.

I really wanted to talk to Char.

"I'm going to check on Ralph," Jackie said abruptly.

"I'll join you." I was more than happy to leave that steeping cup of *Smooth and Steady* right where it was.

"By the way, thanks again for my Christmas stocking. That was a really lovely gesture," I said as we headed for the stairs.

"Oh, you're welcome, love. But I can't take all the credit. I mean, it *was* my idea to get them, but Barbie was actually the one who embroidered your name on it."

And spelled it wrong.

"Jackie, that threatening note you received, didn't you say the person misspelled your name?"

"Yes, left the *e* off. Why do you ask?"

"Well, because my stocking—"

As we approached the top landing, a commotion interrupted me. It sounded like Barbie was crying, and Bob and Char were trying to calm her down. We hurried the rest of the way up to see what had happened.

"No, I will *not* be quiet! Who would do this to me?" Barbie wailed.

"Is everything okay up here?" Jackie asked.

Barbie pushed past Bob to confront her face to face. "Was it you? Did you leave this disgusting note for me? You have some nerve, madam!" She shoved Jackie. Hard.

Jackie fell back against me. Had I not been holding onto the banister, and had Carlo not grabbed Jackie's hand, she and I would both have taken a tumble down the stairs.

Char gasped audibly and grabbed Barbie's arm. "Stop it, Barbara! You stop it right now!"

We all turned toward her for a moment of stunned silence. She was not one to raise her voice. Barbie must've exhausted even Char's saintlike patience, which was saying something.

Barbie dropped the note on the floor and collapsed into a nearby chair with her head in her hands.

Jackie sounded shaky as she told us she needed to check on Ralph. She and Carlo slipped into Ralph's room, leaving the rest of us out on the landing. I picked up the note—written in the same block letters as Jackie's.

I KNOW WHAT YOU'VE TAKEN, BARBI, AND I WANT IT ALL BACK. OR ELSE.

I read it aloud and then voiced what everyone wasn't saying. "What does this mean? What have you taken?"

"Nothing!" she sobbed. "I don't know what it means. Ask that witch, Jackie."

"It's utter tosh," Bob said. "Of course nothing's missing. And even if something was, our Barbie's no thief."

Barbie looked up at him through her tears. "I'm certain the little antique clock has gone, and the gilt picture frame from my room has disappeared now, too."

"There, there," he said, patting her shoulder. "I'm sure it'll turn up eventually."

Why wasn't Bob more concerned about the missing items? And why did it seem he was trying to hush Barbie up about it?

I leaned over to Char. "How's Ralph doing?"

"He's still sleeping."

"Shouldn't someone call a doctor?" I knew Barbie was a nurse and everything, but if he couldn't be awakened…

Just then, Ralph appeared in his doorway, clad in a silk paisley robe over silk pajamas. "The reports of my demise are grossly exaggerated. Or something to that effect."

"Oh, thank God!" Char cried and went to hug the old man. "How're you feeling? We were so worried."

He appeared delighted to be fawned over.

"What happened? What was the last thing you remember?" Bob asked.

Ralph paused in thought for a moment. "I was eating those lovely gingerbread biscuits. The next thing I knew, I was tucked up in bed."

Every gaze fixed on me.

"I... I don't know what to tell you. I had one on the plane over, and I was fine."

"Could it maybe be a blood sugar thing?" Char asked Barbie.

"He doesn't have a blood sugar thing," she responded with thinly veiled contempt before turning toward Ralph. "I know you probably don't want to hear it, but I'm sure someone tried to poison you."

CHAPTER 3

Everyone gasped.

"No!" Jackie cried. "Who would do such a thing?"

"Certainly nobody here!" Bob protested.

"Now, now, I'm fine. Absolutely fine." Ralph waved off their concern. "Why don't you all get some rest? I'm sure things will look better in the morning. After all, it's Christmas!"

At his pronouncement, everyone reluctantly agreed and began to shuffle to their bedrooms.

I wasn't so ready to let it rest, though. "Sorry, but what about the threatening note Barbie received? Surely we should be paying attention to that. And the other note? I don't think that will look better in the morning."

"What notes?" Ralph responded.

"Oh, it's nothing really, darling." Jackie put an arm around Ralph's waist and made to turn him back to the bedroom door. "Probably just a Christmas prank. Nothing that can't wait until morning," she added, clearly for my benefit.

The bad feeling that had been steadily growing in my chest was now in full bloom. What the heck was going on here?

"Yes, I'm tired now," Barbie said. "But I'm locking my door. *Someone* around here can't be trusted." She turned on her heel and strode down the hall.

"*Bene, my* door is unlocked, in case *signorinas* feel the fright before morning." Carlo addressed Jackie, Char and me in turn, then grabbed each of our hands and planted a kiss, one by one, much to Ralph's obvious chagrin.

I turned my face to Char to hide my incredulous expression. Though it was nice to be referred to as a *signorina* rather than a *signora,* it all felt so cliché. "Okay, thanks," I said over my shoulder in Carlo's direction "Night!"

Linking my arm with Char's, I pulled her down the hall, around a corner and into my room. When I flicked the light on, D'Artagnan looked up and blinked at me from the bed. He burrowed his nose back under his tail, resuming his roly-poly shape, then went back to sleep. Char and I found our own spots on the mattress, making sure not to disturb the gray and white fluff ball in the center of the crocheted cover.

"What is going on around here?" Char said in a low, quavering voice. "It's not the Christmas I wanted. I'm so sorry to drag you all the way over here for this. It's a nightmare."

"And we're going to get to the bottom of it!" I dug around in my backpack and produced two wrapped candy canes. One was the traditional red and white peppermint, and the other was brown and orange and tasted like root beer. I thought the root beer ones were gross, but Char lit up.

"You remembered!" she cried, reaching for it. D'Artagnan made an annoyed kitty noise, and she whispered, "Sorry!" to him before biting into her candy.

I broke off a little piece of mine and popped it into my mouth. The peppermint vapors tingled my nose, and I marveled at how awake I felt. Well, it *was* only 4:00 p.m. to my body. I must've pushed past the exhaustion. That, or the adrenaline was taking over. "Okay, this is what we know—"

"Should I be writing this down?" Char asked.

"Ah, maybe." I handed her a little notebook and a turquoise sparkly gel pen from my bag. "Okay, in no particular order, here's what we know. Jackie received a threatening note from someone who didn't spell her name properly. I *thought* maybe she'd written it to herself because the stocking she made for me had my name spelled incorrectly, too."

"But why would she—"

"Hang on. I *thought* it might've been her, but when I thanked her, she said Barbie was the one who embroidered my stocking. So, I was convinced *Barbie* wrote the note to Jackie."

"But then Barbie got a note, too."

"Right!" I said. "And maybe she wrote it herself to throw suspicion away from her, but she was really upset."

"Yeah, it's doubtful she was faking it. Though she's always been pretty dramatic." Char jotted that down in the notebook.

"How does Barbie spell her name? With an *i* or an *ie*?

"Definitely *ie*," Char confirmed.

"Then her name was spelled wrong, too."

"So, we're hunting for someone with bad spelling?"

"Maybe." I sucked on the end of my candy cane while rubbing the spot between D'Artagnan's ears. "And what about the missing antiques?"

"Oh, *that*!" Char bounced up, earning the side-eye from D'Artagnan. "When I was with Barbie and Uncle Bob in Uncle Ralph's room, Barbie was just beside herself about it. *She* said when she visited in the spring, Uncle Ralph told her she could have anything she wanted from the house, so she'd made a long inventory list. Now several of the items just aren't there. She said Jackie must've done something."

"Did you know Barbie and Jackie knew each other in nursing school?"

"No! But that makes sense now."

"What does?"

"Well, during her rantings, Barbie also said she wished she'd never run into her in London last summer. Next thing she knew, Jackie had moved to Italy, was living with Uncle Ralph and things started disappearing," Char said.

"Maybe when they ran into each other, Barbie told Jackie about her rich uncle-slash-father, Ralph, and put the idea in Jackie's head to do some gold digging?"

"Wait. What do you mean, 'uncle-slash-father'?"

"Jackie told me that Ralph is Barbie's father."

"No. Uncle Bob is her father."

"Bob may have raised her, but according to Jackie, Ralph is her birth father."

Char gasped. "Does Uncle Bob know?"

"Jackie said she didn't know. But how could he not, especially if everyone around him does?"

"Poor Uncle Bob," Char said with a twinge of sadness.

I bit my bottom lip. "Something's been bugging me about how Bob dismisses Barbie every time she mentions noticing another antique's gone."

"Hmm. That *is* strange. Uncle Bob would know all the pieces Uncle Ralph has."

"Really? Why?"

"Well," Char began. "Uncle Bob was the one who got Uncle Ralph into antiques in the first place. He has his own shop in the Midlands, and I think Uncle Ralph gave him the money to get started."

"You should write that down, too."

She dutifully put pen to paper again. "I wish Adrian was here."

Adrian was Char's new boyfriend, who happened to be a cop.

"No way!" I protested. "Nancy and Trixie ride again, wrapping up the case in time for dinner," I said to remind her about how we used to play Trixie Belden and Nancy Drew when we were little, solving all the neighborhood mysteries. "Now that we know Ralph is fine, the real police would only get in the way."

"I just can't believe Uncle Ralph is really Barbie's father. Do you think that's why he said she could have whatever she wanted? To make up for not raising her?"

"Maybe," I said. "People do a lot because of guilt."

Char shook her head and wrote some more.

"There's something else I haven't had a chance to tell you."

She sat up straighter, pen at the ready.

"When I was downstairs with Jackie, we went into the kitchen for a cup of tea. She told me to choose a flavor from the pantry, but when I went in, I found someone had knocked the tea boxes over. And on the floor was a mortar and pestle with some bits of white powder."

Char stared at me, pen still poised.

"You know, like the white powder that was around Ralph's mouth?"

Realization dawned for her. "Oh! Do you know what the white powder was?"

"No," I sighed. "Jackie was waiting for me, and I didn't want to mention it in case..."

"In case she had something to do with it." Char finished for me. "But if she did, surely she wouldn't have sent you in there to find the evidence."

"Unless she wanted to look innocent. Or she hadn't realized everything had fallen over."

"Good point." Char made more entries in the notebook.

"Now that everyone's in bed, we should go down and have a look."

I hopped up. D'Artagnan yawned and stretched, then walked around in a circle before settling back in position.

Char and I crept along the hall and were about to head down the stairs when Ralph startled us on his way up, holding a mug.

"All right, Uncle Ralph?" Char said nervously.

"Oh, fine, fine," he said. "Came down to get a cup of

Smooth and Steady tea, and there it was, waiting for me—a little cold, but nothing a turn in the microwave couldn't fix. Jackie takes such good care of me."

"Are you sure you should be drinking that?" I cautioned. "After what happened?"

"And what happened, my dear? Just an old man with too much Christmas cheer. Now, did you ladies need something?"

Carlo, dressed only in boxers, appeared in his doorway. He flexed his abs. "Have the *signorinas* received the fright in the night?"

I pursed my lips to stifle a smile. "No, *grazie,* Carlo. Just getting a cup of tea."

"*Bene.* If you need, my room is here, anytime."

Ralph considered Carlo as if he'd just smelled something stinky.

"Okay. Thank you," I said to Carlo in a serious tone that I hoped masked my amusement.

"Night, Uncle Ralph," Char said, giving the old man a kiss on the cheek. "I'm glad you're okay."

"You're a good girl, Charlotte." He smiled at her. "Don't stay up too late, now."

Char and I made our way downstairs, the soft glow of the elegant table lamps down on the entry table below guiding our path.

When we got to the kitchen, the first thing I noticed was the absence of the tea I'd left earlier. Maybe that was the cold tea Ralph had found and assumed was his. I made a beeline for the pantry door, flung it open, then flicked the light on. To my dismay, the tea boxes were all in their proper order, and the mortar and pestle were clean and back on a shelf next to the microwave. Did the person who left it come back to cover his or her tracks? Or had someone stumbled upon the mess and just cleaned it up?

I let out a deep breath. "Well, that was a dead end."

"Cup of tea since we're down?" Char offered.

"Might as well."

This time I chose a festive cinnamon apple blend that, when I lifted the bag to my nose, enveloped me in a comforting Christmas hug. While Char boiled the kettle, I sat at the table and poured over the notes of what we knew so far. Char had written the names of everyone in the house, but there wasn't much about Ralph's man, Carlo.

"So, that Carlo... What's his deal? He definitely lives up to the stereotype." I grinned as Char brought our mugs to the table. Mine was deep blue with a logo of a bubbling test tube and the words *Her Majesty's Pharma Consortium* stamped on the side in gold. "Huh," I said, lifting the mug to my lips. "*Her Majesty's Pharma Consortium.* Sounds fancy."

"Must be Uncle Ralph's. He was a scientist. Made his money in pharmaceuticals before going into antiques with Uncle Bob."

"What kind of pharmaceuticals?"

"Not sure. Experimental. Cancer? Tumors?" Char shrugged. "Whatever it was, my grandfather said his brother made a whole lot of money and then ran off to the continent. Only he didn't say, *ran,* if you know what I mean."

I did.

Char continued. "Granddad said Uncle Ralph was a lucky so-and-so who left just before his company went under. Said he was terribly good at not being the last one holding the bag." She propped her head up and yawned widely. "Anyway, it was all a long time ago, and I'm quite ready for *Bedfordshire* if you don't mind."

"No, of course not." I smiled at her. "Sorry for keeping you up. I should probably try to sleep now, too."

We put our mugs in the dishwasher, then headed up to our rooms.

Sliding into bed, I hit a nice warm patch next to D'Artagnan, who had burrowed under the covers and was snoring softly. All set to read before turning the lights out, I reached for my *Poor Relation* book. But the minute I found my place, a thought struck me. What if what was going on here at La Casetta was just like the story? What if Char's relatives had been descending on her uncle every few months to grab an item or two they thought wouldn't be missed so they could sell them to stay afloat back in England? Bob was in the antiques business, after all. But why would he take pieces earmarked for Barbie's inheritance? I'd only been around a day, but that didn't feel like Bob's style.

D'Artagnan crept up to nestle against my ribs, his little pink nose poking out from under the covers. I turned over to run a hand along the length of his fluffy side as the unanswered questions surfaced. The remnant of a howling wind found its way through a crack between the window and the sill, rustling the curtains. My bedside lamp flickered. It all would've been deliciously atmospheric if I hadn't been so preoccupied with the feeling I was on the cusp of some sort of discovery.

Turning back to my phone, I searched for Her Majesty's

Pharma Consortium. I found several articles about a lawsuit from the 1990s and a photo of a much younger Ralph. The caption surprised me though.

Another Day in Court for Robert Hinley.

That wasn't Ralph in the photo. It was Bob. If Ralph took his money and ran, leaving Bob to clean up, Bob would definitely have reason to hold a grudge. Two reasons, actually, considering the whole question of Barbie's paternity.

"Golly," I whispered. What had I gotten myself into this Christmas? Ralph seemed like a nice old man, but maybe he was really awful. Bob acted like he was relaxed and always trying to keep everyone calm, but maybe he was a seething volcano ready to erupt. Where did Jackie fit in? And Carlo? Was Jackie as lovely and warm and devoted to Ralph as she made out to be? But then there was definitely something smoldering between Carlo and her. Wasn't there? And if so, why did she stay? Why didn't she and Carlo just run off and be together?

Then there were the threatening notes Jackie and Barbie had received. Both of them had their names spelled incorrectly, as did I on my Christmas stocking. I knew Barbie was the one who embroidered my stocking and spelled my name wrong. Was she the one who wrote the notes, too? But why? Speaking of Barbie and Jackie, was it mere coincidence that Jackie was here after running into her old classmate in London earlier this year? And what about what happened to Ralph tonight? Did he *really* drink himself unconscious? He had powder on his face. Were there more nefarious forces at work trying to implicate me by using my cookies as a vehicle to put him out? *Rude!*

I noticed my foot had started jiggling in slight frustration. I felt so close to answers, but not close enough.

As I stared up at the wooden beams on the ceiling, my lids grew heavy. The grandfather clock in the hall chimed twice, and D'Artagnan stretched out a paw until it rested on my cheek. I sighed. I had to admit to myself there wasn't much more I could discover until morning, and at times like these, it was best to let my brain take over while I slept.

CHAPTER 4

Four hours later, I became aware of a weight on my chest. I opened my eyes to find D'Artagnan staring down at me, his whiskers tickling my cheek as he sniffed around my nose. When he discerned I was awake, he jumped down and pawed the door. A vibrating tail signaled to me that this was probably his breakfast time. But it was a *crunch, crunch, crunch* sound that drove me to the window first.

I pulled the curtain aside ever so slightly. Someone was making tracks in the freshly fallen snow toward an outbuilding, holding a box. The dark, cobalt blue of the pre-dawn winter morning made it hard to get a proper view, but it was definitely a man. He didn't have the limp of someone who needed a cane, so it wasn't Ralph. And he didn't have a youthful swagger, so it wasn't Carlo. That left Bob.

What was Bob doing up this early? And what was in the box?

The house was still dark as I followed D'Artagnan down the hall, but voices coming from Carlo's room stopped me in my tracks. I positioned my ear near the door and heard another British man I didn't recognize say, "I expect this has gone far enough, don't you? Someone might actually get hurt."

"Nonsense! It's the only way to... them out."

Rush them out? Flush them out? I couldn't hear the word, but it sort of sounded like Ralph. Who was the other man? It couldn't be Bob if Bob was outside. Or was he?

I bit the corner of my lip as I leaned in more closely. No, I was certain I'd seen Bob through the window. So, who was in this room with Ralph then?

"What was that?" the other man said as the wooden floor creaked beneath me. I gingerly stepped backward, then hurried to the kitchen.

Someone had tidied up, and my elegant Ginger Luxe box peeked out from the recycling. Luckily, it was on top and easy to rescue. If they hadn't planned on keeping it, it was only fair to take it back and reuse it myself. As I lifted the pink and gold cookie carrier, another bit of shiny cardboard caught my eye. It was a box for prescription sleeping pills with Ralph's name on it. I immediately had a picture in my mind of the mortar and pestle, and my intuition said this was the white powder around Ralph's mouth. Someone *had* to have laced my cookies with crushed up sleeping tablets to knock him out.

Or worse.

I fished the little box out of the recycling bin and shoved it into my bathrobe pocket just as I heard someone come up behind me. I wheeled around.

Barbie.

I blurted, "Sorry. D'Artagnan was hungry, but I didn't know what to give him."

"What have you got there?" she asked, nodding to my bathrobe pocket.

"Nothing?" I answered, but it came out more like a question.

"Then you won't mind showing me."

Barbie was smiling, but there was something menacing there, too. I pulled the empty prescription box out and held it up.

"I knew it was you all along," Barbie said slowly, her voice dripping with venom.

"What are you talking about? I just found this in the recycling."

"You tried to poison him!" Barbie cried. "Was Charlotte behind this? Was she too weak to do away with him, so she invited her henchwoman over for Christmas to do it? What did he promise her, hmm? How much is he leaving her!?"

If I wasn't so shocked, I would've laughed at being referred to as a *henchwoman*.

Barbie's voice was shrill and thankfully brought several pairs of feet pounding down the stairs before she became really unhinged.

Jackie was first on the scene as D'Artagnan bolted out of the kitchen. "What's happening?"

She was followed by the rest of the household, save for Bob who rushed in through the side door brushing a bit of snow out of his thin hair. So it *was* Bob I'd seen from my bedroom window.

He hurried to Barbie's side. "I heard yelling. What's going on?"

"That's what we'd like to know," Ralph answered.

"It was her!" Barbie wailed in Ralph's direction, pointing a bony finger at me. "She tried to poison you last night. No doubt she and Charlotte cooked it all up together."

"Me?" Char gasped.

Barbie tore the pill packet out of my hand. "See? When I came downstairs, I caught her trying to hide *evidence*!"

"You have officially lost it, Barbie," Jackie said, staring at the woman in disbelief.

"Now, wait a moment!" Bob shot back at Jackie as he put a protective arm around Barbie's shoulders. "There's no need for that. I know we had an agreement, but I draw the line at bullying my Barbie."

Every head swiveled toward Bob.

"Agreement?" Ralph asked, glancing sideways at Carlo. "What agreement could you have with my fiancée, Bob?"

Bob was a deer caught in the headlights. Jackie's eyes were wide as saucers. Nobody said a word, allowing the tension to build until neither Bob nor Jackie seemed to be able to stand it anymore.

His shoulders drooped as he caved. "All right!"

"Bob, no!" Jackie said.

Like a tennis match, all heads turned to Jackie.

"Does this have anything to do with the box you were carrying to a back building earlier?" I asked Bob.

"What box?" Barbie sniffed.

I remembered the plot of the *Poor Relation* book I'd been reading and took a chance. "Char told me Bob has been visiting more and more often. My guess is he's been helping himself to a few items each time he comes, assuming nobody would miss them."

"Well, that's just not true!" Barbie shot back. "I was here twice in autumn, and he hadn't been since summer. My grandparents' clock disappeared in between my visits."

"Maybe he had help." I turned to Jackie. "From you?"

"What... what do you mean?" Jackie stammered.

"It would only be fair since you and your family lost so much when your father became ill..." *Here goes nothing.* I softened my voice. "He did die from taking Ralph's experimental drug, didn't he?" Jackie's breath caught as I turned to Bob. "And you were left to face the music when Ralph took off with the company money and moved to Italy. A few pilfered pieces here and there would hardly make up for it, but at least it was something."

Jackie appeared resigned as her lip trembled. "I had to leave school, give up my dreams. I thought it was a sign when I ran into Barbie in London and she bragged about coming to Miele di Rosa to visit her rich, single old uncle, Ralph Hinley."

"Uncle!" Bob scoffed.

"How could you?" Barbie howled at Bob. "You were stealing from *me!*"

"I did it *for* you, love!" Bob objected. "He left me with nothing but a pittance to buy a failing little shop, and then was here promising you the world. Your mum passed, and I didn't want to lose you, too. I wanted to have something to give you. Yes, I sold the pieces, but I saved the money for you."

Barbie brightened at that last statement.

What a piece of work.

"You told me the money was being held up because you couldn't find a buyer!" Jackie shouted.

"Oh, you haven't done too badly for yourself, love," Bob countered. "Living *la dolce vita* over here…"

Char appeared completely flabbergasted as she watched her bickering relatives, and I offered what I hoped was an apologetic smile.

Ralph sighed heavily. "I had a feeling you had something to do with this, Jackie."

"So you were just pretending not to notice the missing items, Uncle Ralph?" Char asked.

"I was. And I didn't want to believe it of Jackie, but I had to be sure." He addressed her then. "So, it was all a lie."

"Not all of it." Jackie's tears flowed freely, but she turned away from Ralph to face his butler. "I truly do care for you, Carlo, and I'm sorry I'm not who you thought I was."

"Oh, you're not the only one, Jackie." I turned to Carlo, too. "I have to say, the Italian act was very entertaining, but who are you *really*?"

He put a hand to his heart. "But *signorina*, I swear to you—"

"Come on," I interrupted. "I just heard you and Ralph talking upstairs. I know you're not Italian."

He froze for an instant, then shrugged at Ralph.

"Fine," Ralph began. "When I began to notice items missing earlier this year, I hired a private detective to pose as my butler. Ladies and gentlemen, I present to you…"

"Charles Phillips." Carlo, or *Charles*, introduced himself with a crisp English accent.

"That explains the caricature performance," I muttered.

Charles gave the impression of genuine hurt.

Jackie glowered at him. "So, you pretended to fall for me in order to... to what? Trap me?"

"Let's not forget, *you* were essentially stepping out on *me,* old girl," Ralph reminded her.

"Guess the wedding's off, then," Barbie announced with an air of triumph.

"Yes, it is. You win!" Jackie said through gritted teeth, ripping the ring off and tossing it. It landed on the floor several feet away and Barbie scrambled to retrieve it.

I was having flashbacks of a very public confrontation between the families of one of my *Love and Luxe* couples and did not want to go down that road again. I rubbed my forehead. "Okay, then who drugged Ralph? Was it you, Jackie? You weren't at the church when we arrived. Or was it Carlo, I mean, Charles? Barbie said your bagpiping was dreadful all week, but the shepherds at the church sounded great. You clearly weren't there." I turned to Barbie and Bob. "Or maybe it was one of you. Barbie, you went back into the house to change your purse—"

"Handbag."

"Fine. Your *handbag.* And you made a big deal telling us all about your medical background. Or what about Bob? You worked at the pharma consortium, too."

"I was just a shareholder. I don't have a medical background!" Bob answered.

"And he was with us the whole time," Char added.

"Ah, right. So?" I prompted, looking at the rest of them.

"Much as I hate to admit it," Jackie spoke up through her tears. "I was with Carlo. Charles. Whoever he is. He was promising next Christmas we'd be... in Mallorca!" Jackie dissolved into quiet sobbing.

"Well, it wasn't me!" Barbie cried.

Charles looked intently at Ralph.

"Oh, all right!" Ralph said at last. "I did it. I drugged myself."

As if on cue, a clock struck the half hour. Its somber notes punctuated the shock registered on every face.

I waited for the chimes to finish. "So, you cleaned up the mortar and pestle when you reheated my tea," I said to Ralph. "Putting Jackie's stocking on your head was... an interesting touch."

He inclined his head to me. "Charles was to gauge Jackie's reaction while I was *indisposed.*"

Jackie looked up from her crying and scowled at him.

"And the notes?" I continued. "I assumed it might've been Barbie because everyone's names were spelled with an *i* at the end, including my stocking, which Jackie said was due to Barbie's embroidery. But now I'm not so sure it *was* Barbie."

"Of course it wasn't me!" Barbie erupted. "I got a terrible note, too!"

"You could've just been misdirecting everyone, though," Char answered gently.

"Me, again." Ralph raised his voice above Barbie's splutterings. "With Charles' help, of course."

Char turned to him. "But why, Uncle Ralph?"

"To scare the guilty person into an admission," I told her.

"Why not just ask?" Char said.

"Where's the sport in that?" Ralph smiled at her. "I'm an eccentric old man with an enormous fortune. This really is the most fun I've had in years."

"But Carlo knew!" Jackie said in an almost whisper, turning to Charles. "You knew months ago I had agreed to help Bob. Why didn't you say something then?"

Charles grinned sheepishly. "Maybe I'm an eccentric *young* man and was having too much fun myself."

I wrinkled my nose at him in disgust.

"I wondered," Ralph said quietly, narrowing his eyes at Charles.

A little *mew* was the only reply. I glanced down and noticed D'Artagnan had crept back in and was gazing up at Jackie.

"D'Artagnan'll need feeding, and then I'll go pack my things." Jackie sniffed quietly.

"Oh, no you don't!" Barbie shouted. "The police will be dealing with you. I knew you were stealing from me, but I could never prove it. Until now, that is."

"Oh, Barbie, that's honestly not necessary," Char said. "Uncle Bob said he kept the money for you, and, well, hasn't Jackie been through enough?"

"It definitely sounds like it," I chimed in. "And, Jackie, maybe you should take D'Artagnan with you."

Jackie turned a hopeful face to Ralph.

"Yes, take the cat. What do I care? Happy Christmas." He threw up his hands. "Well, I'm not a monster."

Methought the man didst protest too much, but I wasn't

about to say so. Jackie wouldn't be the only one packing her bags this morning. Now that the truth was out, I had no interest in spending one more minute at La Casetta. Hopefully, Char felt the same way.

I motioned to her with my head to follow me upstairs. As we ascended the steps, I whispered, "Sorry about all this."

"*You're* sorry? Oh, Hols, I'm so mortified. What a terrible Christmas!"

We went to Char's room and sat on the bed.

"Strange as this may sound, it was actually kind of fun," I told her.

She grinned and shook her head at me. "Trixie and Nancy, back in action?"

"Always!" I laughed. "Listen, our holiday is not over. The Four Seasons in Florence owes me one. What do you think? Christmas at a luxury spa? Sounds pretty magical to me!"

Char threw her arms around my neck. My heart brimmed over with gooey Christmas joy for a moment, then she pulled away. "But if you *really* wanted to make Christmas magical..."

"Yeeeesss?" I responded, feigning suspicion.

"Please say that when everything's sorted in L.A., you'll come back and live in Little Witherburne. You know, a fresh start?"

She had such a shimmer of hope in her eyes, how could I refuse? But I shook my head.

Her face started to fall.

"Char," I began, doing my best to appear stern at first. "Whether it's sleep deprivation or the high from mystery solving..." I heaved a deep sigh for effect, giving her my most magnanimous expression, complete with a royal circling of my hand. "I'm inclined to grant you a Christmas miracle."

Char grabbed my hand as we shared a little squeal of excitement.

And as we snuck out the front door to the waiting taxi, I felt lighter than I had in many months. I mean, bagpiping shepherds and European market stalls were nice and everything, but Christmas at the spa with my best friend?

That was a tradition I could get behind!

About Melicity Pope

Melicity Pope is the cozy pen name for Melissa Williams-Pope and the embodiment of one of her many heart-dreams. When not writing and president-ing the UK/EU chapter of Sisters in Crime, she cycles through her variety of passions such as acting, singing and traveling the world fostering adorable furry friends, while using her positive psychology and ministry background to coach other women to experience their own dream-come-true lives and businesses. She's a whimsical American, married to a down-to-earth Kiwi, currently based in a small Victorian castle-mansion in Scotland.

Come visit her at: www.melicitypope.com

MISTLETOE AND MURDER

DIANNE ASCROFT

Marge Kirkwood gets more than she bargained for under the mistletoe at the Fenwater Association Christmas party: a bothersome blast from the past, and a murder to investigate. A nostalgic festive mystery set in small-town Canada in 1983.

CHAPTER 1

"WHAT THE DEVIL?" Marge Kirkwood almost gagged on the scent of Aqua Velva aftershave as strong arms trapped her in a vicelike bear hug.

Sometimes she wished she didn't have such a keen sense of smell. She thrust her arms outward, trying to free herself from the unexpected contact as she looked up to identify her assailant. Wet lips clamped onto hers before she could pull away.

"Merry Christmas, sweetheart!"

Marge barely resisted the urge to wipe her lips. "Just because it's Christmas doesn't mean you can grab me like that, Mike. What do you think you're doing?"

Mike Wilson pointed toward the ceiling and Marge groaned inwardly as she looked up. Another blasted sprig of mistletoe. She thought she knew where all of them were. She had checked the bar and lounge carefully when she arrived and had been ducking quickly through doorways to avoid unwanted gropes. But she hadn't spotted this one hanging from the chandelier in the middle of the main hotel foyer.

"What are you doing here?" Marge spat out.

Mike gave her the confident smirk that she remembered too well. "Don't look so surprised. Or pretend you're not glad to see me. I'm still a member of the Fenwater Association."

Marge raised her eyebrows. "But you closed your dad's hardware shop."

"Just ended the lease on the building. I didn't sell my stock. I'm gonna rent a place on St Andrew's Street. I couldn't get a better location than the main street. You should partner with me. We could work closely together." Mike gave her a suggestive wink.

Marge couldn't help thinking of the Aqua Velva slogan 'there's something about an Aqua Velva man'. Well, there was nothing appealing about this one.

"Not a chance, mister." Marge managed to choke out the words, keeping her tone level.

She knew she should at least be polite since this was the local business association's annual Christmas party, but Mike Wilson was the one person she had been happiest to leave behind after high school. All through their school years he never got the hint that she wasn't interested in him even when she started dating Ted Kirkwood in their last year of school.

"We haven't had a chance to catch up since you moved back to Fenwater. Let's get together for a drink," Mike said.

Marge fought to keep her expression neutral as she scanned the foyer for an excuse to escape. Ignoring Mike's invitation, she exclaimed, "Oh, there's Lois. I was looking for her."

Before Mike could reply, Marge made a beeline for her friend Lois Stone. After a quick hello to Lois's escort, Bruce Murray, Marge drew Lois aside. "Am I glad to see you!"

Lois raised her eyebrows. "What's got you so rattled? You're usually in your element at a party."

"Mike Wilson's driving me nuts. He's had a crush on me since high school and won't stop pestering me tonight."

"Is that the guy you were kissing under the mistletoe just now?"

"I wasn't kissing him! He grabbed me. I didn't even see that blasted bit of mistletoe there."

Lois grinned mischievously. "Isn't it the season for memorable moments under the mistletoe?"

"For you and Bruce, yeah. But not for me and Mike, no way."

Lois grinned. "You might have other options. Mike's not your only admirer tonight."

Oh, maybe this evening will get better, Marge thought. She pulled her shoulders back and stuck out her ample bust. Flipping her dyed-blonde hair out of her eyes, she batted her eyelashes coquettishly. "What can I say? I'm a flame that draws those moths." She narrowed her eyes at Lois. "So, who's interested?"

Lois kept her expression neutral. "Your ex."

"What!"

A laugh burst from Lois. "Yeah, when you two were in that clinch under the mistletoe, across the room I saw Ted glaring at Mike."

Marge scrunched up her face. "Yeah, Ted can't stand Mike 'cause he never got the message to scram once Ted and I started dating. But we've been split up for years. He shouldn't care now."

"I know Ted was a jerk when you were married and you were glad to split up with him, but he certainly looked jealous just now."

Marge really didn't want to think about her ex-husband possibly still having feelings for her. She shuddered. "Let's not even go there. Looks like I better tag along with you and Bruce tonight for protection." She grinned at Bruce. "As long as I'm not cramping your style."

Bruce gave Marge one of his easy smiles. "Not at all. I'll have Lois all to myself after the party."

Lois nudged her. "Actually, you'll be an asset. You know everyone so you can introduce me."

Bruce squeezed Lois's hand where it rested on his arm. "Absolutely."

Marge shifted position to stand beside Lois. From their vantage point near the entrance, Marge surveyed the festively decorated foyer. Hawick Hotel certainly had gone to a lot of effort. Strings of silver and green tinsel were entwined and draped over the pictures hanging on the walls. The shiny decorations complemented the deep green floral-patterned wallpaper. Holly garlands bedecked with red ribbons hung from the mahogany reception desk and even the clock behind the desk was ringed with a festive wreath. A huge Christmas tree stood in the corner beside the desk. The other end of the desk was transformed into a mini-bar with glasses of rum and eggnog, and hot whiskeys set out in neat rows.

Local businesspeople milled around the foyer, mingling and chatting. Marge spotted antique stall owner Dave Stewart in his red tartan kilt serving drinks at the mini-bar while chatting with Dean Walker, a fellow market trader.

As Marge noted how Dave's brightly patterned garment added to the festive mood, the market trader glanced across the room and met her gaze. She raised her hand in greeting and Dave smiled. He turned to speak to Dean then left the other man at the mini-bar and headed toward Marge and her companions.

As he approached, Marge said, "This is a change from helping at civic events. You're fixing something stronger than tea and coffee tonight. We'll have to find out what kind of bartender you are."

Dave laughed. "Oh, I'm not mixing the drinks, just serving. The hotel staff are whipping up the rum and eggnogs, and hot whiskies. And both of them are good."

Marge chuckled. "And how would you know that?"

Dave turned an innocent gaze on her. "Someone has to be responsible for quality control."

Marge raised one eyebrow, skeptically. "Not that you would volunteer, of course."

Her expression quickly deteriorated into a frown as Mike appeared and stepped between Marge and Dave. Marge edged closer to Lois on her other side. *Why couldn't this guy go and bother someone else tonight?*

"Howdy, everyone!" Mike said jovially. He narrowed his

eyes at Dave and raised his nearly empty glass. "Hey, shouldn't you be at the bar? I'm almost ready for another."

"Never fear. Several Fenwater Association committee members are manning the mini-bar. You won't go without."

Mike grinned broadly and put his arm around Marge's shoulders. "That's what I like to hear. Great party, isn't it? And even better since I ran into my old buddy Marge."

Marge squirmed under Mike's embrace, trying to subtly shake him free, but his grip was firm.

"Making new friends, I see," a woman said sarcastically behind them.

Marge craned her neck to look over her shoulder. A tall, broad-shouldered woman standing behind her glared at Mike. Marge had heard Helen Young and Mike had split up recently. From the looks of it, they weren't on good terms.

Mike squeezed Marge's shoulder. "Nah, me and Marge go way back."

"We knew each other in high school. But not that well," Marge ground out.

Marge took a deep breath and tried to appear unconcerned as Helen turned her hostile gaze on her. She did not want to get in the middle of anyone's romantic troubles, nor did she want Helen to get the wrong idea about her and Mike. *Why couldn't Mike just clear off?*

"Well, I hope you enjoy rekindling your *friendship*," Helen snapped.

The woman turned and stomped away, pushing roughly through the crowd toward the mini-bar. Marge sighed, watching Helen's retreating figure. She didn't know the woman well, but she didn't want to make an enemy needlessly.

Marge's gaze was drawn away from Helen by a smaller woman in a cream knit top and black velvet skirt who stopped where Helen had just stood, a glass of eggnog cupped in both hands. The woman caught Marge's gaze and rolled her eyes, shaking her head slowly.

Marge raised her eyebrows in response and huffed out a breath to conceal her annoyance. Why did Sue Howard have to overhear the conversation? She wasn't afraid to give people something to talk about, but only if there was a grain of truth to it.

"Hi, Sue! Are you enjoying the party?"

"Yeah, it's even better than last year."

Marge pointed to the other woman's top. "Nice! Definitely your colour."

Smiling, Sue indicated Marge's red cocktail-length chiffon dress. "Thanks. Gorgeous dress."

Marge nodded her thanks then peered more closely at Sue's top. She motioned to a spot just above the waist. "You spill something?"

Sue glanced down and her face coloured. She vigorously brushed at the smudge of beige powder clinging to her top. "I'm such a klutz! I must have dropped foundation powder on it. I never even noticed it before I left the house."

Marge squinted at the top. "You got it. I can't see it now."

"Good, but I'd better go and sponge it. See you later!"

"Do you want me to hold your glass 'till you come back?"

Without answering, Sue gave a quick wave and disappeared.

Marge turned back to the group and tapped Lois's arm. "I'll have to introduce you to Sue later. Her fruit and vegetable stand in the market always has the freshest produce."

On her opposite side, Mike peered over his shoulder at the people surrounding the mini-bar. "Anyone see where Helen went? I don't want to run into her at the bar."

Dave stretched to look at the mini-bar. "She's not there."

Mike turned back to the group. "Good. Time for a refill. Anyone want anything?"

When no one spoke, Mike said, "Drinks for one then. Back in a minute."

As soon as Mike left, Marge whispered to Lois, "I hope not. I've had enough of him tonight. But I won't let him ruin my evening." She spoke to the group. "Okay, where's the food? I'm starving."

"They're setting out the buffet at seven o'clock. But there's potato chips and cookies," Dave said.

"Okay, I could devour some peanut cookies."

"Sorry, the choice is gingerbread, sugar cookies and shortbread," Dave replied.

"That'll do. Where are they?"

Dave motioned toward the lounge doorway. "Inside on the bar."

Marge scrunched up her eyebrows. "Funny, but I could have sworn I smelled cookies out here. Well, why don't Lois and I grab some nibbles for everyone?"

After a murmur of agreement from the group, Marge slipped her hand under Lois's elbow and nudged her toward the lounge, skirting the mistletoe hanging from the chandelier in the centre of the room. She wasn't taking any chances this time. From the corner of her eye, she saw a flash of movement as someone barrelled across the room. She turned her head to see who was in such a rush and immediately wished she hadn't. Of course, Mike was trying to catch up with her. It figured.

Still moving, Mike's gaze met hers and he held up his drink. "Have you tried the eggnog? Don't know what they've put in it but this glass is better than the last one."

"Not yet. We'll get some in a minute," Marge replied, edging toward the lounge.

If only she could make a run for it, but that was too obviously rude. With a couple of long strides, Mike caught up with the women. "Really, you've got to try some. Why don't I get you a glass?"

"Like I said, we'll get some soon."

As Marge spoke, she noticed that Mike was taking short, shallow breaths. She knew she could still turn heads but even she didn't have such a drastic effect on men. Good grief, he must be really out of shape. She would admit they weren't getting any younger, but a middle-aged man should be able to hurry across a room without being ready to collapse.

Mike wheezed, "Are you sure? I'd be glad to—"

"Thanks, but I'm starved." Marge turned back in the direction of the lounge. "I need some sustenance before I get into the eggnog."

Ignoring her comment, Mike continued, his voice hoarse. "So good. Spice or something . . ."

Marge turned back to look at Mike. He was staring vacantly into his glass, swaying slightly.

She rested her hand on Mike's forearm. "You okay? Maybe you should ease up on the eggnog." Not receiving a response, she spoke louder, gently shaking him. "Mike! Are you alright?"

Mike looked at her then bent over, wheezing heavily. Marge slid her arm under his to support him, looking around for somewhere he could sit down. Suddenly Mike slumped to the ground, pulling Marge down on top of him and knocking the breath out of her. She quickly collected herself, pulling her arm out from under Mike and rising to her knees, heedless of the rip she heard in the chiffon fabric of her dress.

Marge peered into Mike's unconscious face then shouted, "Somebody find Doc McKinlay!"

She was aware of a flash of red as Dave Stewart knelt beside her.

"What happened to him?"

"He wasn't making much sense and just collapsed."

Marge gladly let Dave take over. He had first aid training and always knew what to do in a crisis. She crawled backwards to give him room, and Lois helped her to her feet. As she rose, her gaze fell on the damp patch under the mistletoe where Mike's drink was seeping into the thick red and gold carpet.

CHAPTER 2

Marge flipped her hair back from her face, shivering in the stiff breeze. "I still can't believe Mike died. I mean, he bugged me and I tried to give him the slip at the party, but it's awful that he died." It had been two days since the party, and she hadn't wrapped her head around it yet.

"I know, and in such a tragic way," Lois agreed.

Marge picked up her pace, eager to reach the end of the block so she could get out of the cold. Several buildings ahead sat the square brick building they were heading for. Ontario Provincial Police officers used the local station as a base when patrolling the area.

Marge pulled the lapels of her red wool coat tighter around her neck. "At least the station is so small it'll be warm inside."

Lois thrust her hands deeply into the pockets of her dusty rose wool coat. "I wish we didn't have to go back to the police station. Not after our run-in with Constable Riley last fall."

"Try not to think about the fall fair. This is only a few routine questions because Mike's death was unexpected. They must be talking to everyone who was at the party. We'll be out of there in no time."

"I sure hope so."

Marge bent her head against the breeze and plowed on.

"I can't believe the nerve of that broad!"

Marge looked up to see her ex-husband stomping toward them.

Ted stopped in front of the two women and glared at Marge. "She's not much older than our kids. The nerve of her!"

"Who?" Marge asked.

"That cop."

"Who, PJ?"

"Constable Ross. She doesn't like you calling her by her first name," Lois reminded her friend.

Marge gave a quick nod of acknowledgement then spoke to Ted. "So, you've been interviewed about Mike's death?"

"It was more like an inquisition."

Marge snorted, quirking up one side of her mouth. "Sure it was."

"I'm telling you, she wanted me to account for where I was the whole time I was at the hotel. And she asked why I had a grudge against Mike."

"Why would your history with Mike matter?"

"I don't know but she was acting like I was responsible for his death."

Marge shook her head. "That's ridiculous. Mike had a bad allergic reaction and they couldn't get him to the hospital in time." She regarded her ex-husband as he stared into the distance, his jaw clenched. "I'm sure Constable Ross isn't accusing you of anything. Lois and I are headed to the station now. I'll clear this up and call you later."

She'd mostly avoided her ex-husband after his recent move back to Fenwater, but she wasn't going to let her children's father be accused of murdering anyone.

Ted shrugged. "Well, I hope you have more luck with that broad than I did. Like I said, she's got it in for me."

Marge glared at Ted. "Don't go around badmouthing Constable Ross. That's not gonna do any good. I've known her since she was a kid and she's always fair. I'll get to the bottom of this."

Ted muttered, "I hope that'll be before I'm sitting in a jail cell."

Marge stifled her grunt of frustration. Ted had always tended to overreact. Hopefully his fears were unfounded this time. "Well, the kids will be home for Christmas in a couple weeks, and I don't intend to tell them their dad's been accused of murder so I'll get to the bottom of it alright."

After a quick goodbye, Marge strode even faster up the street. She heard Lois puffing beside her as she struggled to keep up. When they reached the police station, she turned to look at Lois. Noticing her friend's tense stance, she gave her a big grin. "We didn't get arrested the last time we were here so stop worrying. This isn't even about us."

Marge opened the door and stepped into the small utilitarian front office. Sitting at the battered wooden desk in the centre of the room, Constable Riley didn't look up. The two chairs that usually sat in front of his desk were missing.

Instead, four straight-backed chairs were lined up under the front window.

Marge, with Lois trailing reluctantly behind her, strode to the police officer's desk. "Afternoon, Constable. I thought Constable Ross was interviewing people about Mike's death."

The officer glanced up at her then motioned to the chairs under the window. "She is. Please take a seat, ladies, and she'll call each of you shortly."

Marge stared at the officer for a moment, surprised by his brusque manner. He couldn't have forgotten them in the couple of months since the fall fair. She gave Lois a puzzled look as they took their seats.

Marge rubbed her hands together, enjoying the heat in the room. "Better day in here than out there," she said to the officer.

When she got no response, she looked at Lois again and shrugged. Why was Constable Riley so uptight today? He was the new kid on the block last fall but he should be settling in now. Investigating unexpected deaths must be routine in police work. For this case, the officers just had to talk to the people who were at the party then they should be able to easily wrap up their enquiry.

A sandy-haired female officer opened the door of the back office and Dave Stewart stepped out. He greeted the women as he walked past them. "Nice to see you, ladies. I'd love to stop to chat but I left another trader watching my stall."

From the doorway to the back office, Constable Ross said, "Who's next, ladies?"

"Me." Marge turned to Lois and winked as she whispered, "I'll go first. Soften her up for you."

Marge chuckled at the look of alarm on her friend's face. She stood up and followed Constable Ross into the back office. The officer motioned to a chair in front of her desk and Marge sat down.

"I have a few questions about the party on Saturday night and Mike Wilson's death," Constable Ross said.

"Okay but I hope they won't be as strange as the ones you've been asking already."

The officer frowned at Marge. "The questions we're asking are pertinent to the enquiry."

"Then why ask people whether they had a grudge against Mike for an accidental death enquiry?"

Constable Ross silently regarded Marge.

"Isn't that going a bit too far?" Marge persisted. "You were born sensible and I don't think you've changed. So why are you going off on wild goose chases?"

Constable Ross narrowed her eyes. "This is a suspicious death enquiry."

"What? He had an allergic reaction. There must have been something at the hotel that he didn't know he was allergic to."

Constable Ross was shaking her head. "I got the preliminary autopsy report back this morning. They found a small fragment of peanut in his stomach contents."

"Peanuts! Even back in high school Mike was severely allergic to them. He wouldn't have eaten any ever. So how did he get it?"

"That's what we're trying to establish. So now I need you to tell me everything you can remember about the party."

Marge felt like she was in a daze as she recounted what happened at the party. Afterwards she returned to the outer office and motioned for Lois to go speak to Constable Ross, barely managing to give her friend a reassuring smile. She flopped onto a hardbacked chair.

The front door opening disturbed her revery. A well-dressed man walked in and sat down beside her.

"Hi, Marge. I guess I'm second in line?"

"No, you're next, Gary, I'm just waiting for my friend."

Judging by his smart, dark suit, Marge figured that Gary Hunter was on his way to work. Marge's eyebrows drew into a frown as she regarded the Hawick Hotel manager. Were his kitchen staff responsible for Mike's allergic reaction?

Marge sighed. "Mike's death is just terrible, and at the party of all places."

"Yes, it is. Our staff are very upset about it. They put so much work into the party and then a tragedy like that happens."

"Were you serving any food or drinks with peanuts in them?"

Gary shook his head. "Nope. I don't think we've ever made any drinks with peanuts. We didn't even start serving the buffet before the party ended, but none of the food had peanuts in it anyway."

"What about the snacks before the buffet?"

Gary narrowed his eyes at Marge. "Why all the questions about the food?"

"I've just heard that Mike died because of his peanut allergy."

Gary's eyes widened. "Oh, no! That's such a shame." He paused for a moment, staring at the floor. "I don't know how that happened but it definitely wasn't caused by the hotel. Like I said, all that we served before he died were snacks – potato chips and cookies. Definitely no peanuts in any of it."

Where did he get it then? Marge wondered.

Marge was jolted from her thoughts as Constable Ross called Gary Hunter into the back office. Lois re-joined Marge, looking more relaxed than she had before the interview.

Making an effort to paste a smile on her face, Marge said teasingly, "You aren't under arrest then?"

Lois chuckled, but glanced around her nervously. "No, but I was beginning to wonder if she suspected me of something with the questions she asked."

Marge patted and smoothed her hair. "Let's get out of here and I'll fill you in on what's happening. Fancy a drink?"

"Sure. The Honey Pot?"

"Not the diner today. I need something stronger than coffee."

CHAPTER 3

Marge finished recounting her conversation with Constable Ross to Lois. She leaned back in the padded chair and sipped her whiskey, relishing the heat from the crackling fire in the small Rumford fireplace near their table. Dave Stewart was right. The Hawick Hotel made good hot whiskies. The traditional hotel was also a very comfortable place to unwind after her shock at what she'd learned at the police station.

She idly glanced toward the lounge doorway. Gary Hunter poked his head in, leaning his hand against the wide architrave as he surveyed the room. He smiled and nodded a greeting to the two women.

"Looks like the manager is back from his interview. I hope the hotel didn't make a mistake that caused Mike's death," Lois said.

"Yeah, and I hope the police don't get the wrong man. I'm gonna make sure they don't try to pin it on Ted. What a Christmas present that would be for the kids. He's pulled some stunts in his time but that would beat all, and it wouldn't even be his doing."

"Do you think someone slipped Mike the peanuts?"

"They must have. He would never have deliberately eaten them."

"Who would want to hurt him?"

"I guess that's what we need to figure out. My first thought is Helen, his ex-girlfriend. You saw the looks she was giving me, not to mention her snide comments. I don't know her well but we've seen she's the jealous type. I heard she moved to Fenwater about four years ago – before I came back from Toronto." Marge paused. "Helen often meets clients here. If we're lucky she'll stop by today."

"What does she do?" Lois asked.

"Interior designer. I heard she met Mike when he hired her to redecorate his house."

Lois frowned. "Are the police sure the hotel didn't accidentally serve something with peanuts in it at the party?"

Marge inclined her head toward the bar where the hotel manager was now talking to the barman. "I was chatting with Gary while you were in with Constable Ross and he's certain they didn't serve anything with peanuts in it."

As Marge watched the hotel manager, a tall woman in a tweed wool coat, trimmed with a fake fur collar, stepped into the lounge. She scanned the tables at the back of the room, hesitating briefly when she noticed Marge and Lois seated beside the fireplace. Without acknowledging them, the woman headed to a table on the opposite side of the room beside the window.

"Will you excuse me for a few minutes? I think I better speak to Helen on my own," Marge said.

Lois waved her away. "Go ahead. I'm fine here."

Marge rose and made her way to Helen before she had time to sit down. "I'm glad I caught you, Helen. I'd like to offer my condolences on your loss."

Helen regarded her coldly. "You know Mike and I weren't together when he died."

"Yes, but you had been going out until recently. I also wanted to clear the air between us. I think you got the wrong impression at the party."

"That you and Mike were hitting it off? I don't think so. You looked pretty cozy to me."

Marge shook her head slowly and took a deep breath, trying to keep her temper under control. "Sometimes looks can be deceiving. Mike was the one who was trying to get friendly. But I've known him since high school and I've never been interested in him. I was trying to get that through to him without making a scene."

The look Helen gave her dripped disbelief.

"I'm sure it wasn't easy seeing him looking at another woman when you hadn't split up that long ago, but for what it's worth, I didn't reciprocate his interest," Marge continued.

Helen gave a harsh laugh. "It doesn't matter. It just reminded me how he never could resist women."

"It sounds like he didn't treat you very well."

"Yeah, well, he put everything he had into wooing me when we first dated, but after a while his interest broadened, shall we say. Eventually I'd had enough of it."

"So you left him."

"Before I could dump him, he dumped me."

"Oh, that must have really stung," Marge said.

Helen narrowed her eyes. "True, but not enough to want him dead."

"You've heard that his death might be suspicious then?"

"Yeah, I've just come from the police station. But, like I said, his philandering annoyed me, and I guess I flew off the handle when I saw him with you at the party, but I wouldn't have tried to kill him. It just irked me to be reminded of what a low life he was. But, there's other fish in the sea, and I've got my business. I didn't need him."

Marge nodded. "You're probably one of the people who was closest to him lately though. So, if you didn't want to kill him, do you have any idea who else might?"

Helen pursed her lips as she gazed past Marge's shoulder toward the door. "My best guess would be Dean Walker."

"The shoe repair guy in the market?"

"Yeah, he loaned Mike money to upgrade shelving and other stuff for the shop he was opening, and I know Mike was avoiding him. He wouldn't set up a repayment schedule."

"But why would Dean want to kill Mike if he still owed him money?"

Helen shrugged. "I don't know. Maybe he just got fed up with the run around he was getting and snapped." Helen glanced toward the door again then turned to Marge. "Will you excuse me? There's my client."

Marge held out her hand. "Thanks for talking to me. I hope we've sorted things out and don't have any hard feelings."

Helen shook her hand. "None at all. Now I must go."

Helen went to meet her client as Marge returned to her table and sat down.

"How did it go?" Lois asked.

"Well, we've cleared the air." Marge quickly recapped the conversation for Lois.

"So, what do you make of it?"

"I don't know. I can't see why Dean Walker would kill Mike without getting the money he was owed. With an informal loan there may not be any paperwork to claim the money back from Mike's estate. And Helen says she's over Mike, but her feathers were certainly ruffled on Saturday night. I don't think we can completely discount her yet, but we also need to pay Dean a visit at the market tomorrow morning."

CHAPTER 4

MARGE CRINGED THEN MENTALLY SHOOK herself as she heard Perry Como singing over the loudspeaker about turkey and mistletoe making the season bright. Of course, she would be surrounded by all things Christmas in the market. It was the season to sell things after all. She scanned the overhead support beams for any sign of dangling greenery as she walked with Lois down the first aisle of the building. She wouldn't get caught out by mistletoe today.

Lois wore a huge grin. "The traders have their stalls decorated so beautifully. I love it!"

"I've no objection as long as they keep their mistletoe to themselves," Marge said.

Lois nudged her. "Don't be such a spoilsport. You never know, you might meet someone interesting under the mistletoe."

Marge narrowed her eyes at her friend. "Banish that thought. Just keep that stuff for you and your sweetheart. I'm giving it a wide berth." She stopped at a stall and turned to Lois, indicating wooden bins filled with an array of vegetables, including loose potatoes, carrots, Brussels sprouts and wax beans. "Aren't these amazing vegetables? You have to meet Sue. This is her stall."

Lois's eyes widened when she spotted a box of large ripe tomatoes. "Where does she get tomatoes like that at this time of year?"

The stallholder approached them, smiling. "I've got a heated greenhouse in my backyard so I grow all kinds of vegetables year round."

"Sue, have you met my friend Lois? She moved here last summer," Marge said.

Sue extended her hand to Lois, and the two women exchanged greetings.

Marge chuckled. "I bet Lois will be your best customer now. She loves fresh vegetables almost as much as apple and cinnamon muffins. And after the harvest next fall, she'll probably be around to stock up on apples for her baking."

Sue smiled. "Great. It's always good to have a new customer."

"While I'm here, can I get half a dozen tomatoes?" Lois asked.

"Sure." Sue picked out several juicy tomatoes and put them in a paper bag.

"Terrible about Mike, isn't it?" Marge said as she watched the stallholder.

Nodding, Sue took the money Lois handed her. "Must be awful to have an allergy like that."

"And even worse when someone used it to kill him," Marge replied.

"Yeah," Sue said.

Marge frowned. "Who would do such a thing?"

Sue quirked up the corner of her mouth and shook her head. "No idea. I hope they catch the guy."

Marge nodded agreement, then nudged Lois. "We better get on with our errands."

The two women walked on to the next aisle. Lois slowed as they passed a stall selling handknit garments. "Isn't that sweater gorgeous!"

Marge grinned. "And it just happens to be burgundy — your favourite colour." Marge inclined her head to indicate a stall on the opposite side of the aisle where a middle-aged man was tapping on the sole of a shoe with a small hammer. "There's Dean Walker's stall. We can come back here after we talk to him."

Marge crossed the aisle and stopped in front of the shoe repairman. "Working hard, Dean?"

Behind the counter, the man finished securing the sole of the shoe then looked up. "Yeah, flat out. With Christmas coming, everyone is rushing to get shoes repaired for parties."

Marge opened the flap on her large pink purse and pulled out a black velvet shoe bag. She pulled the drawstrings open and slid a pair of bright red sandals with three-inch stiletto heels onto the wooden counter.

"Can I add to your work? I need these reheeled for the museum staff party next week."

Dean lifted one of the shoes and studied the heel. "Yeah, that's no problem. I should have them ready in a couple of days."

"Great. Thanks. Speaking of parties, wasn't what happened Saturday night awful?"

Dean raised his eyebrows and huffed out a breath. "Yeah, it sure was."

"Did you talk to Mike during the evening?"

"Just to say hi. I hadn't been there too long when he collapsed. I was chatting with Dave Stewart at the mini-bar then I filled in for him for a few minutes so he could take a break. Then the party was over."

"So, you didn't spend any time with Mike?" Marge asked.

"No."

"Mike was talking to us then went to get a drink when you were on the bar. You didn't talk to him then?"

"No, it got busy on the bar so I didn't have time to talk to anyone. I didn't even notice him."

"You guys knew each other pretty well though," Marge said.

Dean shrugged. "Yeah, I guess. Everyone who has a business in town knows one another."

Marge frowned. "I thought you guys were buddies. Someone told me you helped him financially to set up his new shop."

"I did, but that was just helping a fellow businessman."

"That was good of you. It's a shame you probably won't get back what you lent him."

"Yeah, but there's no sense crying over spilled milk. I can't do anything about it."

"No, I guess not."

"But it's not the end of the world. I'm doing okay."

"I'm glad to hear it. Thanks again for fixing those shoes for me."

Marge and Lois said goodbye to the shoe repairman and walked down the aisle, stopping to have a quick look at the handknit garments stall.

Lois lifted the burgundy sweater then set it down and picked up a rose one. "Oh, I like them both. How can I decide? I better have a think about it."

As the two women walked back to the entrance of the building, Marge slowed and looked down the aisle nearest to the front doors then back at Lois. "Your tomatoes looked really good. I think I'll get a couple. Back in a sec."

Marge left Lois and headed to the vegetable stall. "Back again, Sue. I couldn't pass up the tomatoes. Would you give me three?"

Sue stooped to reach under the counter, which was set behind the bins of produce. A soft thud as she pulled out a small paper bag drew Marge's attention to the wooden floor behind the counter. A small bag of roasted mixed nuts had fallen from the shelf.

Sue lifted the bag of nuts, folded the top closed and set it under the counter again. "Thankfully, it didn't spill or I'd have nothing to snack on."

"I'm sure you need something to munch on when you're here all day," Marge said.

"Yeah. Otherwise, I'd be off to the bakery stall in the next aisle. Too many cakes won't help my weight."

"I'm waiting until after the Christmas festivities before I worry about mine," Marge said, laughing.

Sue put the tomatoes in a bag and took the coins Marge

handed her. "It's a shame the Fenwater Association party took such an awful turn. Have you got any other parties coming up?"

"The museum's staff party next week. I just left my shoes with Dean Walker to get them reheeled."

"The party should be fun. Mmm, I guess Dean will be staying here now."

"Where was he going?" Marge asked.

"He was supposed to get space in Mike's new shop but I heard last week that Mike had changed his mind. Told Dean there wasn't room. He definitely won't be going anywhere now with Mike gone."

Marge tried to hide her surprise. "That's too bad for him."

Marge took her bag of tomatoes from Sue and went to meet Lois. As the two women stepped out of the market building, she turned to her friend. "I just heard something interesting."

"What?" Lois asked.

"Let's go across the road and grab a coffee and I'll tell you."

Marge strode toward the traffic lights and Lois half-skipped to catch up with her.

CHAPTER 5

MARGE CAST AN EXASPERATED LOOK at the sprig of mistletoe hanging inside the door of the Honey Pot diner. She was fed up with seeing them everywhere she turned. If Mike hadn't caught her under the mistletoe and kindled Ted's jealousy, she wouldn't be investigating his death.

She sighed loudly. *My bad luck, but I can't turn the clock back. Looks like I'll have to see this through.*

Marge took another breath and made an effort to smile as she met Lois's gaze across the table in the window booth. She cupped one hand around her steaming mug of coffee, waving her other hand to indicate the plates of muffins set in front of them. "I'm not thinking about healthy eating until well past Christmas. After gingerbread muffins are off the menu."

Lois took an appreciative sip of her coffee, murmuring agreement. "Uh huh, ginger and cinnamon together. Wonderful. Now tell me what Sue said that was so interesting."

"Well, before we went to see Dean, I found it hard to believe that he had any reason to kill Mike. After all, Helen said Mike had borrowed money from him."

Lois nodded. "I know. He wouldn't get his money back if he killed Mike."

"Exactly. So, I'd pretty much ruled Dean out. His business is doing well and it looks like he could survive losing the money. But then Sue mentioned just now that Mike reneged on renting space in his new shop to Dean. I bet that made him mad."

Lois shrugged. "It must have been annoying but he still has his stall in the market. And, like you said, his business is thriving."

"Yes, but Mike's new shop was right on the main street. More people would see Dean's shoe repair there than where he is in the back aisle of the market. He lost a great opportunity. That might have been enough to make him angry."

"But angry enough to kill Mike?"

Marge cocked her head, considering the possibility. "Maybe. Or at least angry enough to want to make him ill. Maybe he didn't realize how severe Mike's peanut allergy was."

Lois nodded thoughtfully. "That could be."

"I know it doesn't all add up but I think he has to be considered."

"And what about Helen? You didn't sound like you completely believed her about being over Mike."

"I don't, no matter what she says. Not after her attitude Saturday night."

"So, there's Helen and Dean. Anyone else?" Lois asked.

Marge flipped her hair back from her face. "I've tried to avoid Mike since I moved back to Fenwater so I don't know much about his life now. He always had an eye for the ladies. I'll have to ask around and find out who else he's dated recently, and whether he's made any enemies for any reason."

"Like jealous husbands?"

"Possibly. That's a good point."

Marge glanced across the room to where the waitress was stacking clean glasses onto a shelf, her back turned to the room. "Josie!"

The waitress spun around and picked up the coffee pot. Slipping out from behind the counter, she headed over to the window booth. "You ladies need a refill?"

"Great, thanks, Josie." Marge watched the waitress refill their cups. "I didn't see you at the Fenwater Association party on Saturday. Thought you would have represented the Honey Pot."

"We didn't close until six. By the time I got changed and headed over, with what happened to Mike and all, the party had shut down."

"Mike's death was a terrible shock."

Josie nodded agreement.

"I don't think I've ever seen him in here," Marge said.

Josie set the glass coffee pot on the table. "He didn't sit in often. Usually stopped by for takeout coffees."

"On his own?"

"Used to be him and his dad on their way to the shop. Then just him after his dad retired."

"What have you heard about him? Did he have many girlfriends? Or any enemies?"

Josie put her hand on her hip. "Now, you know I don't go in for gossip, Marge."

"I know that. I'm only asking 'cause the police were grilling Ted about how he and Mike got along. They might not have liked each other, but Ted had nothing to do with Mike's death. I want to make sure the police have the whole picture."

Shaking her head, Josie looked at Marge. "I can't believe Ted would have done anything to hurt him. I don't know much about Mike though. He dated Helen Young recently, but I don't think they were still together when he died." Josie tapped her lips. "Mmm, who else did he date? Oh yeah, I heard he dated a couple of women from out of town and used to drive down to Guelph to see them."

"Whoever killed him must have been at the party, so it has to be someone local," Marge said. "A businessman he got on the wrong side of?"

"I never heard of him having any big feuds with anyone. Nothing anyone would want to kill him over."

Across the table Marge heard Lois humming softly. She stopped speaking and looked at her friend, becoming aware of the Christmas background music in the diner.

Lois started under the scrutiny and blushed. "Oh sorry, I love that Rudolph song. I didn't mean to hum out loud."

Josie laughed, ignoring Marge's mock scowl. "Everyone's getting into the holiday mood. Have you heard about the Christmas bake sale? The market is letting our church set up a table to sell cookies to raise money for charity. Would you two like to donate cookies to the sale?"

"Sure, I can bake a couple dozen. Just let me know what kind you want," Lois said.

Marge winked at Lois. "My talents lie elsewhere but I'll buy the ingredients if my good friend here will bake my batch."

Lois nodded. "Sure."

Marge laughed. "Make mine peanut cookies. I've had a hankering for them since the party. I could have sworn I smelled them Saturday night."

Lois shook her head. "I can't see how. We weren't even near the snacks and Dave said they didn't have peanut cookies."

Marge shrugged. "I know but I still think I smelled peanuts. So make mine peanut cookies."

Josie lifted the coffee pot from the table. "Thanks, ladies. We need all the cookies we can get for the charity sale." She started to move away but turned back again. "You're going to the Christmas Lights hayride tomorrow night, aren't you?"

"Hayride? Isn't that for kids? Our youth group had them when I was a teenager," Lois said.

Marge shook her head emphatically. "Nope, not around here. Townsfolk of all ages come. The market stays open late and they serve hot apple cider and gingerbread cookies after the hayride."

Lois laughed. "Let me guess, Dave Stewart organizes that."

Josie nodded. "Of course. Who else? The evening is lots of fun."

Marge winked. "And you'll have an excuse to cuddle up to your honey on the wagon. Come on, we should go."

Marge laughed when she saw the blush creeping up Lois's cheeks. Lois and Bruce were so cute together.

"Okay, I'll phone Bruce tonight and invite him," Lois said.

"Great. I'll see you two there tomorrow then." Josie crossed the room and set the coffee pot back on the burner then spun around. "Oh!"

Marge and Lois turned to look at Josie, waiting expectantly.

"I just remembered. I think Mike went out with Sue Howard four or five years ago. They dated for a few months."

"I never knew that. Was it a bad breakup?" Marge asked.

Josie quirked up one side of her mouth. "I never heard anything like that. I think it just ended."

"Thanks, Josie." Marge turned to Lois. "Interesting. Sue didn't sound like she knew Mike any better than any of the other businesspeople in town."

"Is that Sue at the vegetable stall?" Lois asked.

"Yup. We'll have to catch her when her guard is down and chat with her some more. Hopefully she'll be at the hayride. I'd like to know more about her relationship with Mike."

CHAPTER 6

Lois snuggled against Bruce, her hand nestled under his elbow. "There's such a great atmosphere here tonight."

Marge chuckled, watching her friend's wide-eyed expression. "I told you everyone comes. Wait 'till you see the houses lit up. Our townsfolk go all out."

Lois's expression changed to dismay. "Oh, dear. My little electric candle wreaths in the windows probably won't measure up to the town's expectations."

Bruce squeezed her hand. "I can help you put up lights along your porch and roof if you want to."

Lois smiled. "Thanks. I might take you up on that. Marge sure is lucky with just a couple windows in her condo to decorate."

Marge laughed. "That's about all I can manage. And I do it without even the tiniest sprig of mistletoe."

"Marge, where's your Christmas spirit?" Bruce chided.

She gave him a mock glare. "I have it. I just focus on the important aspects of the holiday."

Lois smirked. "Like gingerbread muffins, hot whiskeys, and parties?"

The perfectly coiffed blonde patted her hair. "Nothing wrong with that."

Marge swivelled so that she stood beside Lois, and scanned the crowd milling around outside the wooden market building. Children darted in and out among the adults, yelling and chasing each other, but stopped to stare when six flatbed wagons pulled by pairs of muscular draft horses stopped on the road in front of the building.

"How will they ever fit everyone on those wagons?" Lois asked.

"Some people like to walk the route. It's only a few blocks. There'll be enough seats for everyone who wants to ride," Bruce replied.

Marge hoped Sue would be here tonight. She needed to ask her a few questions.

Bruce bowed and swept his hand toward the wagons. "Our carriage awaits, ladies."

Despite Bruce's encouragement, Marge didn't budge. She thought quickly to find an excuse for stalling. "Let the crowd thin a bit then we'll pick a wagon."

Marge scanned the crowd until she spotted a short woman wearing jeans and a turquoise ski jacket with a pink hat and matching gloves. "Oh, there's Sue. It looks like she's on her own. Let's join her," she said quickly.

Without waiting for her friends to reply, Marge barrelled toward the woman. "Hi, Sue! Won't this be fun?" She motioned toward one of the wagons that was nearly empty. "I like the look of those big grey guys. Let's take that one."

Marge urged Sue toward the wagon, not giving her a chance to refuse. Behind her, she heard the footsteps of Lois and Bruce crunching on the snow and knew they were following her. When they reached the open-sided wagon, Marge asked Bruce to help the women climb aboard. He offered his hand and steadied Sue as she mounted the movable wooden steps set beside it.

Before Marge could follow her, Helen appeared from the opposite side of the wagon and started up the steps. "Sue, I'm glad I spotted you! I've got some ideas for your bedroom revamp."

Lumbering up the steps in Helen's wake, Marge damped down a huff of annoyance as she watched Helen settle beside Sue on the near side of the double row of hay bales. She plumped down next to Helen, taking a deep breath to calm down. Lois and Bruce climbed on and took seats on hay bales facing the opposite side of the wagon with their backs to the women.

When all the seats were filled, the driver flicked the reins and called to the horses. Making a sharp creaking sound, the wagon jerked forward. After several steps the horses settled into a smooth stride.

Marge leaned forward to speak to Helen and Sue, focusing her gaze on Sue. "I haven't done this in years – not since before I moved to Toronto. When were you last on a Christmas Lights hayride?"

Sue shrugged. "I come along some years."

Marge glanced at Helen. Although she wanted to talk to Sue, she couldn't ignore Helen sitting between them.

Helen glanced away then back at the other two women. "Mike and I came last year," she said softly.

Marge heard the sadness in her voice. No matter how much Helen protested that she no longer cared about Mike after the couple's breakup, it was obvious that wasn't true. Marge felt sympathy for the woman, but she couldn't help wondering what was the balance between sadness and anger in Helen's feelings for her ex-boyfriend.

Out of the corner of her eye, Marge noticed that Dean Walker was sitting next to Lois and Bruce. Dean's wife sat primly beside her husband.

Marge twisted her upper body and leaned across to speak to Lois. "You two comfy over there?"

Lois leaned against Bruce as he slipped his arm around her shoulder. "Yes, thanks."

Marge turned her attention to the shoe repairman. "Oh, hi, Dean. You having a night off from the holiday season repair rush?"

"Yeah, my wife loves the hayride, but don't worry. Your shoes will be ready for your party." Dean reached for his wife's hand and held it loosely in both of his as he turned to smile at her.

Before Marge could try to regain Dean's attention, the wagon jolted as the horses made a sharp right turn onto a residential street. Marge gripped the edge of the bale she was seated on and rolled with the motion of the vehicle. Behind her, she heard Lois's exclamations of awe and knew her friend had spotted the decorations on the houses they were now passing

"Oh, look at that house. All blue lights. It's so beautiful with the snow on the lawn!" Lois said.

"Didn't I tell you?"

Despite her comment, Marge was also impressed. Driving to work each day, she didn't pay much attention to her surroundings. This was the first time she had noticed the Christmas decorations in the neighbourhood. The bright, twinkling lights on the houses really were pretty. A house several doors further on caught her eye. It was decorated completely in red and white lights that flashed in ever-changing patterns. She loved it.

Marge turned her attention back to Dean, leaning closer to speak to him privately. "It's a shame Mike didn't have space for you in his new shop."

As Dean turned to look at her, she watched carefully for his reaction to her comment but he didn't seem perturbed by it.

Dean gave her a nonchalant shrug. "It didn't matter really. And it's just as well I never made any arrangements with him since there won't be a shop now. I'm glad that was my second choice."

Marge was aware of Dean's wife turning to look at her. The other woman didn't say anything but her eyes narrowed. Marge would have to keep this conversation short so the woman didn't get the wrong idea.

"What do you mean?" Marge asked.

"I had another offer. Canada Hardware has space to set up shop with them. I'm moving there after Christmas."

Marge's eyes widened but she pasted a big smile on her face. "Oh, that's great."

She wasn't sure which she was most surprised about: that Dean's motive for murder had just evaporated or that the shoe repairman would soon be working at the same premises as her ex-husband. Since she was trying to avoid Ted as much as possible, maybe she should find a new shoe repairman. She sighed. It seemed she was at a dead end with Dean. Time to learn more about Sue and maybe Helen.

Marge listened to Lois exclaim over another outstandingly illuminated house they passed and murmured agreement then turned back to her side of the wagon. She leaned toward Helen to join the women's conversation.

"I'm having a man-free Christmas," Helen said.

Sue laughed. "Tending my greenhouse plants keeps me busy. I don't have time for men."

"Make that three of us. I'm firmly single too." Marge took a deep breath. It was time to see if she could ruffle a few feathers to learn a bit more about her companions. "I guess dating Mike has put you both on your guard."

In the ensuing silence, Helen and Sue looked at each other. Marge waited.

"You dated Mike?" Helen asked Sue.

"Yeah, several years ago. Just for a few months."

Helen clasped her mittened hands together on her lap. "Not that it matters to me, but I didn't know."

"It was before you moved to Fenwater. I'd pretty much forgotten about it." Sue's gaze slid away from Helen.

"Mike was a hard guy to forget easily," Marge observed.

Sue rested her hands on the edge of the bale and leaned forward to look directly at Marge. The pitch of her voice rose.

"Like I said, it was ages ago. Both of us moved on with no hard feelings."

"Just like Mike and me," Helen said quickly.

The conversation turned from the women's plans for Christmas to other topics, but there were awkward pauses and Marge often had to ask questions to keep it going. She watched each of the women closely, trying to gauge what thoughts and emotions might be churning inside them.

Beside Sue, two teenage boys were wrestling over a chocolate bar held by the one nearest to her. Leaning forward on the bale to avoid their elbows, Sue gave the boys a sharp look then turned back to the other women.

The boys were still for a moment, then the boy furthest from Sue made a lunge for the candy. He missed it but shoved his friend hard against Sue's hunched form. Marge gasped as Sue tumbled forward and fell from the wagon. She hit the ground with a thump.

Without hesitation, Marge slid off the hay bale and slithered to the edge of the wagon bed, letting her legs dangle over the side. Helen leaned forward as if she planned to follow her.

"It's okay. I'll go. We'll catch up with you," Marge called to Helen.

CHAPTER 7

Marge leaned backwards, letting her heavier top half anchor her as she slid awkwardly from the wagon. She held her breath and hoped her feet would land first. The breath she was holding whooshed out when she felt the ground beneath her boots. As she hurried toward Sue, she saw an event marshal heading in the same direction. Sue was struggling to her feet as the pair reached her.

Marge offered her arm for support. "You okay?"

Sue's voice was shaky. "I think so."

"You're lucky you didn't break anything," the marshal said. "We better get you checked at the hospital."

Marge turned at the sound of the familiar voice. "Ted!"

In her rush to get to Sue, Marge hadn't looked at the marshal until he spoke. Her ex-husband nodded a greeting then turned his attention back to Sue.

"I'll call one of the guys to come and pick you up." Ted raised his walkie-talkie to his mouth.

Sue shook her head. "No, I don't need to go to hospital. Just my foot's a bit sore. It'll be okay if I walk on it."

Marge glanced around them for somewhere Sue could rest. Pointing at a fence on a nearby property, she said, "Let's get her over there."

Marge and Ted each gripped one of Sue's arms and helped her hobble to the fence. Sue huffed out a breath and sank against it.

"Let me take a look at your leg," Ted said.

"Okay."

Ted ran his hand down the lower half of Sue's leg and gently flexed her foot. "Does that hurt? Are you sore anywhere else?"

"No, like I said, just my foot. It'll be fine in a few minutes."

Ted straightened up and Sue pushed off from the fence. She gingerly limped back and forth, testing her foot as the trio watched the rest of the wagons pass them. After several minutes, the last wagon had disappeared into the darkness and the sound of harnesses jingling grew fainter.

"When you ladies are ready, we can cut across a couple of blocks to catch up with your wagon. Or I can get someone to pick you up and take you back to the market. Your choice," Ted said.

Sue stopped pacing. "Maybe a ride to the market. I don't know how I'd climb onto the wagon again."

"That sounds best." Marge doubted that she would be able to jump onto a moving wagon either. Without the steps, she would be like a whale hauling herself onto the beach.

Waiting for their ride would also give her time alone with Sue. She still had questions for her.

Ted pressed the button on his walkie-talkie to speak to the event organizers then turned to the women. "Dave Stewart will be over in a few minutes." He addressed Sue, "By the way, we've got the mortars and pestles you were looking for in the store now. Want me to put a set aside for you?"

"Ah, no. Th-that's okay," Sue stuttered. "I got one."

"No problem. Well, I should get back to my duties. Are you ladies okay here until Dave picks you up?"

"Yeah, we'll walk a bit until he arrives," Sue said.

After Ted said goodbye and strode off, Marge and Sue slowly made their way toward St Andrew's Street two blocks away.

"Why do you need a mortar and pestle?" Marge asked.

"For baking."

Marge chuckled. "You're more talented than me. I can't bake to save my life. What are you baking?"

"Cookies for Christmas gifts."

"Sounds good. I've been hankering for peanut cookies this week for some reason."

Sue winced as she took a step. "Oh, I made some of those."

"Do you crush the peanuts?"

Sue gave Marge an uneasy look then glanced away. "Uh huh, I don't like them crunchy."

"Lois uses peanut butter. Less hassle she says."

Sue shrugged. "Yeah, I guess."

Marge noticed that the lights ahead on the main street

were little more than a block away. She needed to take advantage of the time she had left alone with Sue.

"So, you and Mike used to date, eh?" Marge said.

"Yeah, like I said, it was ages ago."

"I think Helen was surprised to hear that."

"It shouldn't matter to her. I'd never have gone out with him again."

"Why not?" Marge asked.

"He was such a Casanova."

Marge nodded. "Yeah, he always did go after what he wanted."

"You can say that again," Sue muttered, a hard edge creeping into her voice.

Marge had to strain to hear her comment. "What?"

Sue waved her hand dismissively. "Ah, nothing important."

Marge looked at Sue. The other woman's fingers were curled tensely and her jaw was tight. Sue's foot must be more painful than she let on. Maybe she should ease up on her. It sounded like Sue and Mike were ancient history. What reason would she have to kill him now?

Marge sighed. It looked like she could cross Sue off her suspect list. So that only left Helen unless she could find anyone else who had a grudge against Mike. When the wagons returned to the market, she would ask Helen a few more questions.

Marge changed the topic. "Have you got much more baking to do for Christmas?"

"Nah, I've got most of it done."

"You must have started early."

"No, only last week."

"After you got your mortar and pestle."

There was a short silence. "Uh, yeah."

As the women walked, Marge thought about the previous Saturday evening, picturing Sue in her cream top. It was right after she talked to Sue that she could have sworn she smelled peanut cookies. Marge had to stifle a gasp as a sudden realization hit her. Was that powder on Sue's top really makeup foundation? Could it have been powdered peanuts? Sue had the mortar and pestle by then. And she skittered away after Marge mentioned the powder on her clothes, supposedly to clean her top. She would have passed the mini-bar on the way to the ladies' restroom. Did she add peanuts to a drink then? But it didn't make sense. Why would she do it?

Marge turned to Sue and found the other woman staring back intently. Marge quickly broke eye contact with her, trying to hide the disturbing thoughts that were going through her head.

Smoothing her red ski jacket with both hands, she tried to sound upbeat. "Good thing it's not too cold tonight since I've only got my short jacket. I hope our ride gets here soon. We don't want to walk right to the other end of St Andrews Street."

"I need a break." Sue stopped walking abruptly. "Why were you looking at me like that?"

"Like what?"

"Like you were shocked."

"No, I wasn't. What gave you that idea?"

Sue leaned toward Marge, her leather barrel purse

gripped tightly in one hand. "Why all the questions about Mike?"

Marge laughed, nervously. "Just curious."

Marge didn't expect the blow and staggered backwards onto the snow-covered lawn beside them, clutching her pounding head. Sue dropped her purse then jumped on her, punching wildly. Marge automatically raised her arms to block the blows.

"Why did you have to ask so many questions!" Sue screamed.

Stopping a blow aimed at her head, Marge caught Sue's arm and held it tightly. Sue's crazed, determined look scared her.

Marge ground out, "They know we're together. If you do anything to me, everyone will know it was you."

Panting, Sue tried to twist away from her. "I'll tell them you slipped on the ice. Hit your head."

Sue struggled, trying to free her arm from Marge's grip, but Marge used her larger size and weight to tip Sue from her. She flipped the pair of them to put herself on top of the smaller woman, hoping she wouldn't succumb to her dizziness and could restrain Sue until their ride arrived.

Marge held on grimly and was relieved when she heard a car's engine. The vehicle was moving slowly along the street toward them. Silently, she urged Dave to quickly spot them and come to her aid. As if the driver had heard her thoughts, the car increased its speed. It stopped at the curb. Car doors clicked open then two police officers were beside them, pulling the women apart.

Constable Riley tugged Marge's arm. "Break it up, ladies."

Marge let go of Sue and stood up, her vision blurry as she watched the other officer help Sue to her feet. "I'm glad to see you, PJ, uh . . . Constable Ross. I think Sue murdered Mike. I might have been next."

Constable Ross tightened her grip on Sue's arm.

"She's lying," Sue screamed.

"You know I'm not."

"Let's go to the station, ladies. Constable Riley, will you ride in the back with Sue?"

Constable Ross steered Sue toward the police cruiser. Sue gave Marge a hate-filled glare over her shoulder.

Her head fuzzy, Marge tried to make sense of what she had discovered. "Why, Sue? Revenge? Jealousy? Did you still want him?"

Sue spit out her reply. "No, I didn't want that jerk. But I had no hope of competing with him."

Marge frowned. "What?"

"We'll finish this at the station, ladies. Marge, you ride up front with me," Constable Ross said.

Marge made an effort to smile even though her head ached. "Sure thing. Will you let Dave Stewart know we got a better offer and won't need a ride now?"

CHAPTER 8

"Sorry I couldn't meet you earlier but I couldn't skip band practice. Our pipe band has lots of engagements coming up for the holiday season," Lois said.

Marge took a sip of her hot whiskey and leaned back in her chair. "It's me who should apologize for just disappearing on you like that last night."

Lois waved her hand dismissively. "Don't give it another thought. Dave Stewart told us where you were and you've explained what happened. It's lucky the police patrol spotted you 'cause Dave got delayed going to pick you up."

Marge glanced around the room, noticing several of Lois's bandmates standing near the short mahogany bar at the front of the Hawick Hotel lounge. "It was lucky alright. Did you manage to enjoy the rest of the tour without me?"

Lois smiled. "Bruce and I had a good time. But I missed you and you missed the hot apple cider."

"But you missed all the excitement. Things happened pretty fast."

Concern wrinkled Lois's brow as she looked at her friend. "I'm really sorry I wasn't there with you. When you went to help Sue, I never imagined that you would be alone with a killer."

Marge shook her head. "Neither did I. Even though I was asking questions, I didn't actually think it was Sue. Boy, was I glad PJ spotted us."

"You said Sue killed Mike over his shop?"

"Yeah, after we got to the police station she got really upset. I didn't have to be in the back room with them to hear her. That shop is a guaranteed money-earner on the main street. When it became vacant, Sue and Mike both wanted to rent the premises. Sue does well in the market but she would do even better on St Andrew's Street where people could park outside and nip in. She was really angry that Mike offered to pay a higher rent than she could afford. I guess it didn't help that he was such an idiot to her when they dated too."

"Well, now neither of them will get that shop. Her business will go down the drain and who knows how long she'll spend in jail." Lois frowned. "She seemed nice. I would never have guessed she could kill someone. How did she get Mike to eat the peanuts?"

"Earlier in the evening, she got a glass of eggnog from the bar. No one paid any attention to her sitting at one of the tables at the back of the lounge. When no one was looking, she added powdered peanuts from a small container she had ready in her purse. Then she just had to carry the drink around until she found Mike."

"And you realized that the powder on her top was

peanuts because the smell made you think of peanut cookies.”

“Exactly. After I talked to her, instead of going to the restroom like she said she was, she headed to the bar and intercepted Mike when he went to get a refill. After she gave him the drink with the peanuts in it, she made an excuse and left him. No one saw her give Mike the drink or remembered seeing them together. Of course, she never mentioned to the police that she even spoke to Mike at the party.”

“So, if you hadn’t figured out that she had peanut powder on her top, it might have taken the police ages before they considered her. You were so clever!”

Marge huffed out a breath. “And scared. To be honest, I wish I hadn’t confronted her on my own. I don’t know what she had in her purse but I still have a headache from the clout she gave me. No concussion, thankfully. I prefer it when we do our snooping as a duo.”

“There’s definitely safety in numbers,” Lois agreed.

A cough beside the table drew the attention of both women.

“Snooping? I thought you ladies were giving up on that? Look at all the scrapes you’ve landed in when you poked around in police matters.” Bruce gave the two women a reproving look as he pulled out a chair and sat down beside Lois, wrapping his arm around her shoulder.

Marge finished her whiskey, reached for the brown leather handles on her large pink bag and stood up. “I think I’ll leave you two to discuss that. I’m heading home to have an early night.” She winked. “Make the most of the season, you two. There’s mistletoe everywhere in this place.”

After a quick round of goodbyes, Marge left Lois and Bruce and crossed the lounge. She waved and called good-night to several people standing near the bar but didn't stop to talk. Her fire-red Skylark Buick was parked out front and it was only a short drive home. She would be able to kick off her shoes and fall onto her sofa in no time.

At the doorway, she came face to face with Ted entering the lounge. Before she could react, he clasped her shoulders and leaned in to kiss her. She pulled away from the kiss, glaring.

Ted pointed to the doorframe above. "Mistletoe."

Oh, blast, Marge thought. *I forgot all about that one.* "Don't you go getting any ideas. I divorced you for good reason."

Ted held his hands up in a placating manner. "I know. I'm not trying to rekindle us. That's a thank you for figuring out who killed Mike so I won't spend Christmas in the slammer."

"Well, uh, you're welcome. I couldn't let you ruin the kids' Christmas." She fixed him with a hard stare. "So don't get into any other trouble in the next week or so."

Ted gave a mock salute. "No, ma'am."

Marge left Ted and crossed the foyer, giving the mistletoe hanging from the chandelier a wide berth. She moved with her usual confident flounce, but she felt the tiredness seeping in. She had had more than enough mistletoe and murder this Christmas.

ABOUT DIANNE ASCROFT

Dianne Ascroft writes the Century Cottage Cozy Mysteries, set in rural Canada, as well as The Yankee Years, an historical fiction series set in WWII Northern Ireland. She loves creating places that beckon readers to step in and stay a while, and characters that readers will adore as they delve into the mystery at the heart of the story. An ex-pat Canadian, Dianne lives on a small farm in Northern Ireland with her husband and an assortment of strong-willed animals. Writing stories set in her homeland Canada is a nostalgic journey for her and she enjoys every minute of it.

Visit her website: https://www.dianneascroft.com

Signup for her newsletter: https://landing.mailerlite. com/webforms/landing/y1k5c3

YOU'VE MADE IT TO THE END!

We hope you've enjoyed our collection of twelve Christmas cozies. If so, please feel free to tell a friend or leave a review!

Thank you for reading, and Merry Christmas!

-The Authors of Deadly Traditions